Mad Denny would always swear that the ghosts of the dead-and-gone Dimbos woke him from unconsciousness that night. A more clinical person might remark it was simply the pain on his arms and rib cage, for indeed, after hanging with hands tied overhead to a meat hook for longer than a few minutes, the pain becomes intense. A more rational person would simply say it was a night to settle scores, and so of course he had come out of his blessed sleep. But Denny, made so aware of the *ma* of this old accursed land by his several brushes with death, saw shadows and heard whisperings on that night, and for him, they always would be real. . . .

CRAZYHEAD

John Klawitter

IVY BOOKS • NEW YORK

To my best fans:
my wife, Lynnie
and our three boys
Jason Walter
Christian Robert
and Matthew Michael
who gave unselfishly
who know what it is to dream
and helped keep this dream alive.

Ivy Books
Published by Ballantine Books
Copyright © 1990 by John Klawitter

Library of Congress Catalog Card Number: 90-92927

ISBN 0-8041-0531-6

Manufactured in the United States of America

First Edition: July 1990

PROLOGUE

HIS NAME WAS HALLER, DENNIS HALLER. U.S. ARMY. SPE-
cialist Fifth Class. We all called him "Mad Denny." That's
not his real name, but it's close enough that he'll smile when
he reads this, somewhere in another part of the world.

I met him in the early '60s, and thought he wouldn't last
six months in the army, much less in a war zone. He was
wild, emotional, impulsive, irrational. He carried the curse
of his youth like a silk scarf around his shoulders, and he had
a big mouth that always seemed to blow off at the wrong
time. I was young myself then, though three or four years
older than he, and having my own troubles "coping with the
military" . . . and so we soon became fast friends.

In spite of all my apprehensions, he did stick it out to
"fulfill his military obligation," which was the nice way of
saying he didn't go AWOL and did eventually receive his
honorable discharge. In fact, once we got overseas, he thrived
in the chaos and madness that was Saigon at that time. He
outlasted me—I came back in '65, and he was still over there
several years later.

The things that happened in his life that I am about to
relate to you took place in 1967, and though I'd had hints and
snatches in letters over an eighteen-month period, he nar-
rated it to me cover-to-cover during a weekend in San Francisco.

When "all the fun began," as he put it with that wry,
distant smile of his, he was only twenty-one and had already

been in Nam almost four years. He always claimed he shouldn't have been there in the first place, that he'd been forced into the armed services on trumped-up charges. He would talk about that a lot in the old days. I remember his intense blue-gray eyes as he ran a nervous hand through his tousled hair, his boyish tone of protest as he launched into a semilurid story about how he was accused of raping the local minister's daughter and given a choice by his small-town police chief—the army or jail.

This is important to note from the first, if you are to try to understand Mad Denny; you can't just dismiss him as a war lover, even though he got quite good at it. If anything, he was a survivor who no longer had a place he could call home. And in that sense, he was like those of us who did come back . . . or perhaps better off, because he recognized and accepted where he stood.

He had a romantic streak a mile wide, but that wasn't uncommon, we all did back then. We got it from Jack Kennedy, who inspired us to fight for freedom's frontiers in brushfire wars around the world. And I suppose some of it came from our noble, decayed book and film heroes . . . Lancelot and Arthur, Gene Autry, Roy Rogers, and Hopalong Cassidy, Renfrew of the Mounties, Horatio Hornblower, Conan, Rudford Riley (Daredevil of the Air), Lucky Terrell (Spitfire Pilot), Pappy Boyington (*Baa Baa Black Sheep*), Errol Flynn, John Carter of Mars, Richard Halliburton.

Looking back, I now realize that Denny didn't really dream adventures, he lived them. I think he must have visualized himself as some sort of tainted Terry and the Pirates type of guy, particularly after he met his Dragon Lady.

"What?!" you say, "but we're talking about Vietnam here, the Vietnam of maimed GIs coughing out their lives for nothing, and napalm-fried little kids, I saw all that on my TV."

Yes, I suppose so . . . but you may not have seen and felt and tasted and smelled it *all*. There may have been one or two things that never found their way into your tube experience, into the compressed and factual thirty-second combat "exposés" that became your Nam reality.

And realize something else: I only call them adventures in retrospect. While it's going down, the hot *pho*—noodle soup—of real life is filled with peppery grits of self-doubt, pasty clots of fear, and slippery noodles of the unknown.

True, the Southern Cross was there, hanging globes of light on crisp nights after the monsoons. And the rain forests were there, too, the green jungles where the air is thick and tepid, and the ancient ruins and ceremonial places, the miles of deserted white beaches, the lithe, beautiful women, and Saigon, the decaying pearl of the Orient . . . but who had the time or inclination to appreciate those things? By '67, the war was beginning to sour on many levels, and it had become very difficult for the military people and for those reporting their every weakness and defeat to concentrate on anything but each other and the body count.

The official military line, of course, was that everything was going great (a posture they maintained to the very end, when the bamboo curtain came crashing down), while it was fashionable among the press to aid and abet the enemy by showing just how the same everything was going to shit. Denny didn't have illusions either way about the things he saw. In spite of his top secret security clearance, he disagreed openly with the ignorance, the bungling, the lies and pomposity, the waste. No one listened to "good old Mad Denny spilling his guts," or he would have been busted more than he was, which was a lot. . . . Nobody took him seriously, and, bottom line, no one cared. The Americans mostly had their own fish to fry . . . earning that next golden stripe or silver bar, building personal fortunes, finding the booze and drugs to survive the craziness and the violence for a few more weeks or months until they could go home, keeping their boots shiny and their brains from oozing out of their skulls, the rats off their feet, the bottlenose beetles away from their lips, the damp from rotting the skin off their balls, the sun from cooking their craniums, making a name for themselves by "exposing" this or that facet of the war effort, seeing who could fuck the most virgins, hold the most beers, smoke the most dope, shoot the most water buffalo. And after all, Denny didn't have any answers . . . just embarrassing questions.

And, like I said, he was no angel; calling him a "tainted Terry and the Pirates" is putting it mildly. From the first day he hailed a cream-and-blue *Xe* taxi and headed downtown, he was out to get even with the world, to get what was his back, to make his own bundle.

Still, the social order feeding off the war effort in and around Saigon was complex, and he didn't particularly stand out at the trough of corruption. To put it more bluntly, you'd have to look a long time around that sophisticated ex-French city to find an American who was lily white, believe me. Everyone from the lowliest private on through the military ranks right up to the top, and the civilian contractors, AID personnel, and Peace Corps as well, all dabbled in the black market. Take Westmoreland out and get him drunk and I'll bet he'll admit to trading his Uncle Sams for P's (or to getting someone to do it for him) at the "going rate" over at Johnny's Bookstore or some other fine Tu Do Street establishment of financial exchange. Imagine these guys, big, klutzy sergeants or plump and pimply lieutenants fumbling through Camus or de Sade or Samuel Johnson while nervously eyeing each other and waiting for Johnny to return from the back room with their piasters. But before you get sanctimonious or skeptical, put yourself in their place—in a situation where *everybody's* looking the other way, would you trade your hard-earned at the official rate of 87 piasters to the buck when you could get 200 P from a humble cigarette lady on any block in the city or maybe even 240 from Johnny?

But Mad Denny . . . well, he went at it with a vengeance. . . . By 1967 he had already acquired a small fortune, somewhere around twenty or thirty thousand dollars, through his petty dealings, which had gradually drifted from booze and cigarettes into hash for the guys at his unit. He kept his money and the stuff locked in the Top Secret Code Word files over at the White Shack, until it looked like he was going to get caught. And then he moved too quickly and got in a little over his head. . . .

We all know the despicable end results of the heroin business, and what a social evil it has been to our country. However, Denny told me that in Southeast Asia, where the chief national product of areas the size of whole New England states is the fruit of the poppy, the dope business has a certain respectability. Not that he was without conscience for the part he played for a small time in that cruel business, but I want to point out that there are other points of view. Shake your mind and then consider the following: Scratch an old cat, and the least you're going to get is fleas. What am I talking about? Well, there are respected, respectable people in other parts of the world who consider it a crude form of justice—or at the least, a natural reaction—that a few thousand pounds of white dust were indiscriminately dumped on the country that sowed more bombs on a tiny corner of Southeast Asia than had been detonated in all of World War II, to say nothing of the napalm, or the defoliants that still ravage the earth there today, or the various types of live ordnance that lie in wait for the unwary foot or wheel or plowshare. It is not my place to pass judgment, but only to bring to your attention that there are lesser and greater evils, as we shall see.

We are about to deal with greater evils. If this story had come out at the time it took place (and it nearly did), it would have sent a shudder through the U.S. war effort. It might have changed history, and certainly would have ended in the trial and execution of at least a score of American and South Vietnamese citizens. But when these facts first came to light to a limited few, those suspected of the greatest crimes were themselves dead or missing, and, of course, the struggle against Communism in Southeast Asia had to go on at all cost, so the story was suppressed. Yet at the heart of it is an unspeakable evil, a wrong so vicious that the word that did leak out over there was whispered and muttered in the ranks, and generally considered to be nothing more than a rumor. Surrounded by death and mutilation in a losing and unpopular war half a world away from your own homeland, there are still horrors too vile to be contemplated as true.

The image of that pale lifeless body
and what they did to it
would haunt him always.
Years later he would wake,
a light, cold sweat covering his limbs,
having remembered yet again.
It had to be a dream,
anything so simple, so horrible. . . .
Cold light from a naked bulb
shines on still, waxy flesh.
Some GI, nameless to him and his associates,
spread-eagled on the stainless steel slab.
The war has already done its worst here—
why the faint feeling, Mad Denny?
You've seen everything in your few short years.
Your mind's at peace, you owe nobody,
feel no guilt, no pain.
So why does your heart skip and stutter
like it's pumping stones?
And why do your eyes stare,
your silent lips crying No No No. . . .

CHAPTER ONE

HE STOOD ON THE CRACKED AND OFF-KILTER CEMENT SIDE-walk thinking murder, the clean-cut boy who looked like he should be studying broadcast communication at Iowa State. He was watching two sign artists working across busy Hai Ba Trung Street on a ten-foot-high platform, painting bold letters in dragon red and gold: TUYET LAN BAR. *Tuyet Lan.* Snow White. The milky white skin of the Vietnamese girls of legend, pride of the race, prized by generation after generation of northern barbarians who swept down on the delta lands to carry them off to their silk-swathed love nests . . . a common enough name.

Mad Denny had at first been amused to see the legend commercialized. In Nam you could have Snow White Cook-ies and no one would blink an eye, and Snow White Delta-Fried Chicken and Snow White buffalo burgers swimming in *nuoc mam* fish sauce, Vietnam's vile smelling answer to catsup. But then the girl floated into view, and his breath caught, his mood thickened, and his fists clenched until the nails bit into the palms of his hands.

She was wearing a silk *ao dai*, the traditional slit skirt dress with long white trousers underneath, light and graceful gowns really, that make all Vietnamese women seem to drift along in a separate reality, silk trains trailing behind. The *ao dai* was a simple one of pastel green, where he would have expected a woman in her position, *ba* in charge of an uptown whiskey bar, to wrap herself in heavy brocades and thick

9

rouge. Yet this was no angel, although her hair was up in a plain bun and she wore no makeup that he could see. She screamed from the brass ornamented doorway, craning her neck up at the painters, hurrying them because the afternoon's rain was coming and they had to cover the wet paint before it all was bungled. They never did anything right, she felt like she was in Bay-ONNE. . . . Her sharp imperative cut like a knife into Denny's mind. Dimbo Charley had lived in Bayonne. It was Tuy—it was her! Improbable that she should still be alive—impossible that he should uncover her like this—yet, in a land known for its tough tiger ladies, nobody had a voice like that. The light lime *ao dai* replaced the sexy evening gowns she had worn as a bar girl, and her simple hair style made her look years older, but he knew her. She had said it the way Charley said it: "Everybody fucks up in Bayonne, New Jersey, Den-Den. Even the syndicate's got the stupids there—that's how dumb they are!" And Charley had laughed the rich Italian baritone that said he knew a lot more about such things than he could ever say, the laugh Mad Denny had come to rely on spilling out through strong even white teeth. But Charley had died, and Larkey, another buddy from the old Dimbo Patrol, had moved in on Tuy. She was just too sweet, like the potato chips you couldn't stop eating, young and fresh in a moldering Asiatic city where they turned rotten by the time they were seventeen or eighteen. At least that was how she had looked to them. And then Larkey too was dead, shot to rag dolls in a stinking dark Gia Dinh back alley ambush. And foolish Beale, trying to blow himself away in a fit of guilt and self-pity. And Tuy, the teenage seductress, the bar girl's bar girl, the whore who'd become rich off of GI pay stubs and passion, had simply disappeared. Gone but not forgotten. Safe until now.

A low angry curse sounded in his throat. He shoved a frail peanut boy, pesky with his two-piaster newspaper rolls of shelled nuts, out of his way and started across the busy street. The little kid, cute as a starving-waif poster photo, looked at his scattered goods and yelled, "Fucker—dirty pig American fucker, you number ten ugly!" Denny never looked back.

Mad Denny, né Denny Haller, was a loose-muscled, lean kid from Wisconsin, weeks away from his twenty-first birthday. He wore a blue and red striped rugby shirt with a white collar, white shorts, and a pair of fairly clean tennis shoes. Scrubbed. Close-cropped hair. Light blue eyes and a quick, challenging smile. He looked like the kind of young man concerned parents prayed their daughter would have the good sense to bring home rather than one of those long-haired radicals, because the year was 1967 and ugly change was everywhere, with the new generation lighting out to utopian experiments like the hog farm and Haight-Ashbury to see if sex still worked, lighting up to Mary Jane and dropping acid to find new realities while violent youthful amateurs trashed the streets of urban American in the name of civil rights and justice for all, and the sweet cream of the hippie movement began to curdle and take on a rancid smell.

He strode across the street, oblivious to the traffic; a pedicab swerved to avoid him, the heavy legged peddler and fat passenger's high-sung oaths riding the air. A blue and white Renault taxi had to switch lanes abruptly, bleeping away like a distraught beetle. Then he was on the other side, rushing up to her.

Trouble came easily to him. Four years before, a final misunderstanding with his hometown authorities caused him to enlist. It was that or go before the judge on charges of rape and whatever else they could drum up. She was low-IQ—a few points above moron, the senior class whore and the local Baptist minister's daughter—and he'd been discovered under circumstances less than clear. She'd had just enough intelligence to save herself by hanging him, or maybe they had gotten together to keep her mouth shut, the mayor, the police chief, and the minister, the pillars in that small town he'd called home.

He'd resented everything—loss of his clean little life; the two-year program he'd started at the local college; his old ways, Saturday nights at the A&W root beer stand, the inner circle gathered to chew over last night's high school game, brag about their latest sex exploits and to eye covertly the stable of local beauties while posing as cool and untouchable.

Once established in his new career, the focal point for his anger became the army. His indiscretions were spontaneous and undiscerning. "Flares up awful quick," his first squad leader said in Basic. Denny, frustrated at having to march in time with an arrhythmic Polack, popped the poor fish in the nose, spraying blood over the dusty uniforms of three kids in front and behind them. "Intractable," his conscientious first lieutenant wrote thoughtfully in his file after Denny went AWOL the second time. "Belligerent son of a bitch," the CO added, as Denny slipped from bad to worse, belting a fat corporal who'd showed the bad sense to cut a chow line in front of him. In those early days it was common to be startled by his clear war cry, "Fuck the *AAAARRRRMMMMYYYY*!" drifting from some near or distant barracks or parade grounds. You may think black thoughts against Mother Military, but you just don't say those things out loud, because they've got you dead-ass cold for any number of years. "Stupid," his classmates said, for the most part shying away. "Borderline," the med psyche officer had warned in heavy maroon block letters.

They called him Mad Denny because he was crazy. Abso-fucking-lutely loony. He knew it, too. But there was nothing he could do: throw shit on a wall and it sticks. On the other hand, he didn't care what they called him. Why should he, he was mad.

The army's interest stemmed from his ability to grasp language, or he would have been out. Vietnam was heating up, and the kid had a talent. He also scored high in linguistic ability and in something called crypto-analysis, though he didn't know it and had no idea what that meant at the time. "Worth some effort," they all agreed. He was granted dozens of KP tours, weekends of burn bag detail, countless butt patrols. He had and lost Private First Class three times before it stuck, finally got Specialist Fourth Class months after his fellows only to lose it over the quality of Mess Sergeant "Ma" Baker's apple pie, which he insisted resembled sugar-crumbled cow turds. And he saw at last the wisdom of more carefully selected outbursts; but by then the name had stuck.

He let drop the paper bag containing the two cartons of Winstons he'd brought from the black market ladies, the *ba*s of commerce who huckstered GI cigarettes from their knock-up street trays along with their everyday wares of candy, gum, and vile French smokes. He flexed his fingers. He thought he was going to kill Tuy. But he didn't even get close. He was too eager, and as he made the sidewalk his foot struck the curb and he stumbled sideways, upsetting an iced-Coke serving tray with pineapple cubes stuck on bamboo splinters. The cheap tray clattered on the already stained city cement, juice and ice sprayed everywhere, and the vendor howled at him. Off balance and half-crazed, he rushed up to her and swung. But he'd lost his edge—if he'd ever had one. Somebody caught his arm, a burly foot came out of nowhere and caught him in the crotch, a fist hammered the side of his head, and he went down, puking and with lights flashing in front of his eyes.

They rolled him over and he saw, looking up through a haze of pain, that it was the wrong girl. She had a thin scar that ran through her right eyebrow, a scar too deep for makeup to hide. Tuy had been perfect, with the round innocent face of an adolescent cherub. He felt for a moment of shock and self-doubt . . . and then she recognized him, he was almost sure of it. Her tulip mouth formed an *o*. She looked like she was going to say something. A brief flicker of indecision, and then she spoke to the men holding him. "A crazy American. I pay you for this, to protect me?" She turned into the dark doorway, speaking over her shoulder in rapid-fire Vietnamese. "See that he is gone."

The two men moved in on Mad Denny. One was heavy-set, probably Chinese or Thai, and the other was a big mulatto. He got up quickly as he could, feeling everything in slow motion. They came forward, pinching him toward a darker space between the bar and the Diplomat Tailors next door, into a narrow crack he figured probably led to a deserted back alleyway and considerably more pain. He gave ground, backing away, hunched over in his agony. "Wait. . . . She just said I should go. She didn't mean kill me. We're just old friends." He saw the two men eye one another uncertainly as he spoke in fluent Zip. It was enough, a second distraction. He lashed out with a high leg kick. It was off center and a little weak in his present condition, but it took the goons by surprise, knocking one back far enough so Denny could slip out into the pedestrian flow on the sidewalk and try for his getaway. He ran on, hobbling in his pain, with their footsteps loud in his ears. Where were the Americans, his fuckin' compadres when he needed them? The MPs, those lousy assholes who were all over him every time he spit funny, or even a rotten White Mouse? No, no Saigon police either. He turned a corner right into the arms of his second assailant, who had made use of a shortcut. They half dragged him back into the waiting alley. The last thing Mad Denny remembered was lying on a pile of foul-smelling garbage, his ribs and kidneys a raw aching wound from the pounding, looking up at the two men. The one he had kicked had dusted off his hands and grinned down at him. He took a familiar package from his accomplice and tossed it on Denny's lap. "Here's your cigarettes, little thief," he said with a tone of bemused scorn. "Don't come back.'

1-2

"May your goddamn Jesus-nuts shear off!" Mad Denny howled up at the flapping metal insect hovering two hundred feet over his head, "and may you fall to your death like a stone!" He stood naked in the center of the Thirty-third Radio Research Unit's compound, waving his towel, soap dish, and toothbrush up at the offending Huey. *"Fig puckers!"*

The chopper charlies couldn't hear him, of course; from overhead, the Thirty-third looked like a child's plastic army set, the little gray barracks arranged in neat rows, their mossy old roof tiles gleaming under the slow falling rain. If they could see him at all, he would be a little plastic GI Joe out of uniform, arms raised in the predawn gray mist that hugged the ground.

"Uck-in-fay ar-mayyyyy!" Mad Denny screamed at the sky.

"Jesus Christ, Denny," a sleepy voice complained from a nearby open-slat barracks. "Night shift just got off. . . ."

"How do you know it's me?"

"Does a dink have tiny balls?"

A second voice, more irate, sounded from another barracks, further down the line, "Goddamn it, Haller—*shut the fuck up!*"

Denny turned his wrath on this new intrusion. "Come on out here and I'll tear your dick off. Then you'll be dickless, just like you sound! . . ."

He chuckled at the uncertain mutters from inside that followed, the guys talking it over. At almost twenty-one he was the old-timer in the enlisted barracks, going on his fourth year in-country and infected with unpredictability. Nobody really wanted to tangle with him. Good thing, too, he thought as he limped on to the showers, feeling the week-old bruises that were deepening from maroon and purple to black on his chest and flat stomach. It would be another few days before he could go back to his downtown gung fu lessons—for all the good they'd done him, he thought ruefully. He made a

snap decision not to go anymore. Life was too short. Next
time he'd tote a gun.

The chopper boys really bothered him. Hot-shit college
grads dancing lazily over the hills and deltas, kings of the
war, and then home to the heavily air-conditioned cinder-
block barracks that had sprung up all over Tan-Son-Nhut
Airbase. The Thirty-third RRU was stationed in an old
French compound, relic of another war, a well-groomed
place of gray teak-slat barracks with only the screens to keep
the elements and the insects out, and high lazy fans overhead
to blow the heavy air around.

The eastern half of the Thirty-third's compound was taken
up by four neat rows of enlisted barracks surrounding the tin-
roofed open-air john and showers. A compact parade grounds
of carefully raked gravel separated these rustic old buildings
from a more casual group of structures which included the
commanding officer's headquarters, the noncom's barracks,
the mess hall, and a tin-roofed open-air assembly hall that
doubled as a movie house. The compound area was surrounded by rotting eight-foot-high wooden fences that
showed generations of slipshod repair topped by sagging
rusty barbed wire. In a way, the occupants were lucky, because most of the new troops pouring in-country lived in Tent
City. On the other hand, the Thirty-third wasn't a country
club condo either. . . .

If the chopper pilots had only known what discomfort they
caused their neighbors every morning they would have been
delighted, for they scorned the members of the Thirty-third
as desk pushers, not a real part of the war. Each day as they
rose through the uncertain gray mists to meet a gambler's
fate with sniper bullets and rocket fire, the Thirty-third's
morning shift could be seen sauntering on by in neat fatigues
down the edge of the pad, walking slowly and weaponless
between the whirlybird perimeter and the edge of the runway.

Anyone curious enough to follow them would have gone
about a half mile along the runway strip, past rows of parked

C-47 Dragonships and needle-nosed F-101s and gray, pup-pylike Piper Cub spotters, to where the straggling line turned and disappeared into a small, whitewashed cinder-block building with a little false front porch stuck on it.

Had such a follower gotten that far, he would have con-firmed his earlier notion that they were lowly desk-fliers, supply clerks or the like, and wandered off to gaze on more enlightening subjects like the cleavage of the half-Chinese broad down at the chopper-boys' Officers' Club. However, they would have quit too soon, for a more thoughtful inspec-tion would have revealed the little white cinder-block house had no identifying signs or markers whatsoever in a world where everything was labeled, ranked, stenciled, or tat-tooed; and the building's small, well-mown perimeter was surrounded by a ten-foot-high cyclone fence with barbed wire at its tip that on occasion hummed slightly in the thick air.

Within the fenced area behind the square building was a tall, potbelly burner with a huge propane tank to one side, the kind of oven one might use to dispose of a good deal of paperwork or other articles rather quickly. But even that wasn't the kind of thing to arouse notice. The military churned out a lot of forms; there had to be some method for disposing of waste, and a big blazer like that was just another example of army overkill.

However, had the idle interested gone so far as to actually approach the entrance, rounding the side of the false-face front porch, he would have gotten no farther, for hidden from the street by the two-walled facade, a stout and surly young guard armed with an automatic weapon would stop him, de-manding relatively exotic identification.

Here common GI dog tags had no coin, and a California driver's license was as useless as Confederate money. The errant wanderer would have been turned away to pursue his own life, with a little cold feeling in the pit of his stomach and the knowledge that there were things in every war one was better off knowing nothing about. His entrance photograph would be filed under INERT somewhere, never to be activated unless he was foolish enough to come back.

Mad Denny burbled under the unsteady flow of lukewarm water from the showerhead,

> "She had a pair of legs
> Just like two whiskey kegs
> And when they knocked together
> MMMMM-boy! what a sound. . . ."

"Hey, Denny, you sound like a lovesick cow! . . . You got any stuff for me today?"

The words floated over from the stall next to Denny. He ignored them.

> "She's got a pair of hips
> Just like two battleships. . . ."

He paused, searching for the next words to the chanty. "What kind of stuff?" The water went icy on him without warning and he hopped up and down, scrubbing frantically to get the soap off.

Animal poked his head out of his own stall. "Uhh, you know, Denny—Laoie wowie or something like it." Animal stepped from his stall, slapping the water off his stumpy red body.

Denny eyed the area to make sure they were alone. "What makes you so sure I got anything?"

"Oh, fuck—come *on*, Den. If a guy needs anything, you got it, ya know? Old Crow, fuck books, dope, Oreo cookies . . . *any*thing. Look, I'll come to your locker, bring you the dough, be there in ten minutes."

"No, thanks."

"Well, God*damn* . . ." Animal brindled. "Ain't my money good enough?"

"Sure, Animal, sure . . . you bring me twenty dollars,

bring it back here while I'm shaving, and maybe your barracks boy or a laundry kid or one of the girls in mess will drop you off a pack later today.''

Animal looked like he was thinking it over. ''I don't like it. Sounds iffy.''

Denny shrugged and turned away. He didn't trust Animal, who worked for the CO, Captain Anderson. ''It don't bother me. I don't know nothing about anything anyway.''

Animal ground his teeth. ''What do you think, I got a fuckin' tape recorder up my ass?''

Denny grinned. ''It could be the latest rage, in certain circles. You ever think of becoming an inventor?''

''Okay, okay. Your way.''

Denny began whistling a sadly out-of-tune version of ''Whistle While You Work'' as he spread white lather from a Foamy can on his face. He looked up to see Animal standing uncertainly in the open doorway. ''What, you still here? Look, it-face-shay, I know and you know and everybody in the Thirty-third knows you and Asshole Anderson would love to catch me sitting on a hundred-kilo dung heap of grass. Well, it isn't ever going to happen!''

''You better watch it, calling the captain that!''

''How can you be so dumb?''

''What do you mean, dumb?!'' Animal flared back at him.

''Look at your face,'' Denny cackled merrily, gesturing to a mirror, ''it's red like somebody stuck a toilet plunger on it!'' He shook his head, and took a more serious tone. ''I mean dumb, like you guys lose me and you'll be buying off the street down in Cho Lon! By the way, I happen to know Asshole himself takes a snort, time to time. . . .''

''Bullshit!'' Animal snorted. ''And things might be a lot cheaper if we did do it ourselves!''

''Sure . . . it's that easy. You ever try? No, of course you didn't—don't speak their language, do you? I can see the whole thing now, *Animal's Last Day on the Planet:* You are incredibly lucky . . . you waltz past the spooks and the MPs and the QCs and the White Mice, only to have some Chinaman who will probably turn out to be your own contact blow your head off for that miserable twenty bucks—it's called short-term profit in the business world. By the way, that's more than you're worth. . . ."

Mad Denny struck up his awful whistling and stroked his face with a safety razor, carefully avoiding the occasional acne pimple he still got. He didn't turn around again. He was sure Animal would be right back with the money.

1-3

"Quinine and salt tablets," the rail-thin corporal drawled endlessly, "quinine and salt tablets." Passing with his food tray, Mad Denny took a few, then looked at the blank eyes starting across the room. He waved a hand directly in front of Corporal Stringer's bony face and got no reaction. "Quinine and salt tablets," the corporal said again.

"Hey everybody. Look at this." Denny rapped the man on the skull. "Hey. Anybody at home in there?"

The corporal's eyes widened, then slid over to focus on Denny as he came back to reality from some drug-coated dream. "Spec-five Haller, you gonna get killed some day. I might do it myself."

Snake's eyes, Denny thought to himself, be careful. But he grinned at Harv, the spec-four in line behind him, and continued the baiting. "Look, Finegold, it talks! My God, straight from the pharaoh's tomb—speak to me, oh mighty Tutankhamen!"

Harv Finegold, who worked for Denny, tried hard not to laugh. "Come on, Denny—he can't help what he looks like."

"Finegold, you'd defend a sex fiend–rapist–murderer . . . two thirds of which, incidentally, you see before you. You, Harv, are entirely too altruistic, the only flaw in an otherwise glorious persona. What you don't know is this piece of putrified dog guano has been helping himself to the local help again." Denny took a fistful of Stringer's starched shirt and pills went flying halfway across the mess hall. "Sweet Hoa in barracks seven, wasn't it? Wasn't it!"

"You can't prove nothin'. . . ."

"Yeah. Well if that little sixteen-year-old has a kid with shit-colored hair and an IQ under a hundred, we'll see who goes home in a body bag!"

"You're tiltin' windmills, man—you gonna protect the whole decadent race?!" His lip curled; he despised the linguists, who fell in love with the rotten fish-sauce lovers, hated them more because the whole unit was hung up on actually trying to figure out what the little fuckers were saying, rather than just winning the war.

"De-ca-dent! That's a big word for you, Stringer—didn't know you klanners had a dictionary! Where do you keep it, right next to your big hungry dick?"

Stringer's eyes flashed hatred, but he knew better than to make a move. He looked around for help, but the ten or twelve enlisted men in the room seemed to have their noses in their trays. Denny pushed him back against the wall. "Get this simple lesson: there's two economies around here—us rich invader-gangster slobs and the dirt-poor locals unfortunate enough to have to work for us. So pay for it or fuck your soggy pillow." Denny shoved harder, and the lean man fell halfway through the screen behind him.

Harv cleared his throat. "Ahh, Dennis—*trung ta phai di*!" He had spotted Captain Anderson with Toady on the gravel path to the mess hall. The Dimbos saw Toady as another of the CO's flunkies; they scorned him as a thin-lipped Bible clutcher and one of Stringer's few friends. Even without the captain he meant trouble for them. Denny, recognizing the emergency, did the only thing he could think of and pushed the corporal the rest of the way through the screen. The slats cracked and Stringer landed with a heavy thud on the muddy ground outside. By the time the captain entered, Denny and Harv were seated across the room at a table with Weird Elliott, the ordnance sergeant whose major duty at the Thirty-third was maintenance of the small-arms room. Elliott looked up from his almost empty tray with a whimsical grin. "Hey, I got enough trouble—would you two guys mind sitting in the next province, maybe over in Cambodia somewhere?" He laughed a big hearty guffaw at his own joke and spread some vanilla ice cream on a piece of pie with a butter knife.

Harv mimicked a panic that he more than half felt. "Elliott, cover for us, please!"

Denny sat down and calmly picked at his reconstituted scrambled eggs and fried chicken. Since the Thirty-third worked three shifts, mess always served breakfast and dinner in the morning, so the graveyard shift wouldn't feel cheated. Everyone simply picked around in the glorious mélange of bad food to find the edible stuff, and no one paid any attention to combinations of foods that would have raised eyebrows and turned stomachs anywhere else in the world. So while Stringer howled and ran around the outside of the building, bumping into Captain Anderson at the front screen door, Denny ate his eggs and chicken, and Harv started in on a steaming mound of shit-on-a-shingle topped with seven or eight strips of fried bacon and a piece of watermelon on the side. Denny eyed the sergeant across the table from him. "Elliott, I need a little blaster. Personal weapon."

"You're gonna need more than that. . . ." Elliott let out another merry chuckle, nodding his head toward the door.

"I'm talking about something else, Weird. Serious business. I want a hideout heater."

"*Heater, yet!* You seen too many old gangster black-and-whites on back-home TV!" Again the huge chuckle at his own words. No one could ever figure out what Weird was laughing about, but he had such a great friendly laugh you didn't really care. "Anyway, you got that huge .45 that was Larkspun's."

"Too big, man. I want a little pistola. Leg holster, maybe."

Elliott thought for a moment. "One of the pilots is selling a .38 snub-nose. Police special."

Denny sighed and spoke as if to a child. "Nooo, Elliott. Something not registered." With tens of thousands of marines moving through Saigon on their way to the bush or back stateside, there was a sizeable float of weapons nobody could account for. "Two hundred bucks. Just for a little pea shooter . . ."

Elliott nodded and returned hastily to his soggy apple pie. Denny looked up to see Captain Anderson bearing down on him, wiping mud specks from his uniform. "Haller, you've gone too far this time!"

"Oh sure, Captain, hang a man before you know the facts."

The captain folded his arms, a sardonic frown on his brow. His balding head gleamed from the bare overhead bulbs. The cooks looked up from their serving line. Mad Denny could always be counted on for a little drama. "And the facts are? . . ."

"There are two incidents which I would like to report. The first was the rape last week of Sweet Hoa out behind the movie shack by this redneck bastard who's too cheap and lazy to walk a couple of blocks to Hundred-P Alley—"

"He's just got her word on that!" Stringer flared.

"Nobody was takin' photographs!" Denny roared back.

Toady, who was standing next to the captain, clucked reproachfully at Denny. "So all you've got is the word of a foreign national against one of our own."

"The word of a *human being*—who was fucked by a *pig*!"

Stringer was a picture of rage. The cords on his neck stood out, and he balled his fists. "Sure—it's always the other guy, never you!"

The captain held up his hands for silence and turned to Toady, who was the personnel clerk. "Who is this 'Sweet Hoa,' and where is she?"

Toady shrugged. "God only knows, sir. Hasn't been here for a week. Anyway, we got four Hoas."

"You know her, you lying sack!"

"Toady is right, Captain," Stringer cut in, his reedy voice rising until it nearly cracked. He never took his eyes from Denny for a moment as he spoke. "There was four of 'em in camp at one time, which is why we had a Fat Hoa and a Sweet Hoa and a Short Hoa and a Gum-Tooth Hoa—and I can get statements from honorable men right in this company that they've had every one of them! Not just one guy either, sir!"

"You bastard—she was just a kid!"

"Sure Denny, the last virgin south of the DMZ," Toady mocked.

"All right!" the captain shouted over all of them. "I don't want to know about every indiscriminate balling that goes on in Nam! What happened here, Haller? Did you attack Corporal Stringer?"

Denny saw the subtle little flash of victory pass between Stringer and Toady. The Hoa case was lost. Harv put a restraining hand on Denny, who was trembling and had turned a grim pasty white color. "Captain, I came in with Spec-five Haller. When we entered, the corporal didn't seem to be feeling well. He was staggering around and trying to pick up the quinine he'd dropped all over. We tried to help him and he fell out the screen over there."

"You lingies all hang together, don't you? If you expect me to believe any of my men were on drugs—particularly while on duty—that is an accusation you will have to substantiate with more than hearsay. And if you are wrong—"

Denny suddenly took Stringer's shoulders and spun him halfway around like a puppet. "Look at his eyes—all pinpointy pupils. Of course he's on something. Nobody looks that way, not even a cretin. . . ."

"Oh, now you're a *medic*, Haller," Toady butted in. "You

really have been around a long time—you seem to know everything about everything."

Denny smiled at the CO. "Captain, I *do* know that's a tiny little ball of opium wax our sweaty rapist here's got tucked under his lip. . . . Here, if you'd just like to check it for yourself—"

They all looked at Stringer, but he had turned away and was frantically trying to swallow something through a dry throat. He started to cough, and Denny handed him the water glass from his tray. After he gulped it down, Denny said calmly, "You know, that can *kill* you. I'd say you got about a half hour." The skinny man rushed out, blubbering he had to change his uniform.

Captain Anderson sighed, feeling like the sane man in an asylum. He looked around the room. "Did anyone else here see what happened?" His problems were very real. He had only a limited security clearance and no access to the White Shack. While he was CO of the Thirty-third, most of his men—the linguistics, cryptographers, the computer specialists, and even the directional finder pilots—reported to NSA people, some of whom were civilians. "In charge of law and order without a gun," he bitterly described himself in long letters to his wife. All he wanted was a serious outfit in the bush somewhere with a bunch of straight guys kept busy rooting up snaky VC infrastructures. That was the way to move upward and onward in this man's army . . . what he got instead was *this*. He gave the room a second stare, a disgusted look on his face. The cooks stirred the aluminum food pans silently, and the rest of the men looked down at their plates. "I thought not. You're not going to get anywhere protecting this half-living legend. He's not going to be here among us much longer. One of three things is going to happen: I will get him transferred to the boonies where he will get his ass shot up, which would be the most pleasant of the three. Or two, one of his precious gook pals that he seems to prefer over his own buddies is going to stick a knife in him. Or three, somebody around here is going to blast his brainless head off before the gooks get to it.'' He turned back to Denny. ''Have you anything more to say?''

Denny, who had sat down and begun eating during the captain's last words, now looked up as he chewed thoughtfully. ''The eggs aren't really as good as they have been. . . .'' He shrugged and grinned at good old Harv as the captain stormed out of the mess hall, slamming the double screen doors behind him. ''Mmmmm, he's not going to dine today. I guess he takes my word for it.''

Harv breathed a sigh of relief. ''Can Stringer really die?''

''Naw . . . least I don't think so.''

''How the heck did you figure he was sucking that stuff, anyway?''

''Like I said, you can tell by the eyes.'' There was a long pause and a look passed between the two linguists. Elliott had finished his ersatz meal and was wandering away out of earshot. A faint wry smile flickered over Denny's face. ''And I sold it to him a couple days ago. . . .''

1-4

The air-conditioning was shockingly cold, so cold he had put on a cotton turtleneck sweater under his fatigues. He leaned his chair back against the block wall, half-asleep in the bright fluorescents, and dreamed of how he was going to off Tuy. Typewriters and a teletype clattered away unnoticed, and from another room came the hum and whine of a computer bank. At first he had simply been content to blow her away, fantasizing about the little pistola Weird was supposedly getting him bucking in his hand and Tuy gasping in shocked surprise as the tiny red marks spread on the swirling patterns of her heavy silk bar girl's gown, just retribution for what she had done. As the days went by he added detail; he had to fight his way past her guards, chopping and spinning as the Korean gung fu artists from the Fighting Tigers had taught him. And lately she was wearing the simple flattering *ao dai*, the way he had seen her last. No longer did he simply pull the trigger, that would be too quick, too easy for her. They talked about it, with her begging and swearing her innocence. Toward the end she would get down on her knees, promising him anything, all the erotic pleasures she knew so well. But she was guilty, of course, and the daydream always ended the same, with him blasting away. The gun, however, had changed. Now it was Larky's huge smoking army .45 automatic punching fist sized holes in her, and that was justice, too, for there were times in the restless moments of his real sleep when Larky seemed to speak to him from the grave, crying revenge, revenge, revenge!

"Denny! Oh, Dennnnyyy!" Harv's voice cut through the soft mush of his fantasy. "We got the latest transcripts off the recorder. . . . Do you have even the mildest interest?"

"Uhhh, yeah—sure." Denny started up and his chair slipped backward with a little crash. The guys chuckled a bit, and Harv helped him to his feet. He yawned and looked around at his section: Harv, who of course did what he could to take care of him; Brownstone, the black intellectual who had joined the army to learn how to be a tough mother just like his Muslim brothers—only to find his eyes peeping through wire-rimmed glasses at a textbook on the Vietnamese language: And Doober Hayes, a funny little kid with asthma problems.

"Who sniggered?" Denny grumbled, looking them over. Everybody raised their hands, grinning madly. "Well, it's all right then—it must have been *spontaneous*." He was proud of this new bunch of lingies, to him they were the focal point of the Thirty-third, the only guys who could make sense out of any of the stuff they gathered before it was sent stateside. They all knew code-busting, too, a necessary tool because their intercepts were VC or DRV origin. "Okay, Dimbos—buffalo burgers tonight, and you buy. Bring me back a half—my much-abused body couldn't take more than that. And I want everybody out of here by nine, got that?"

There was a chorus of Yes, sirs! and they left with a clatter for the local burger stand, a packing crate lean-to nearby on the base where the locals served greasy buffalo meat on french buns and sticky-sweet orange pop. The shift wasn't supposed to be over until midnight, but with the rainy season begun there were fewer intercepts, and Denny couldn't see his guys sitting around doing nothing when they could be whoring it up downtown for an hour or two before curfew. They were the latest members of the Dimbo Patrol, the first group of lingies Mad Denny had been with in Nam. "Only the names have been changed to protect the innocent," he muttered as he picked up his olive green Ridgeway cap and wandered toward the door. "Or to identify the living . . ." whispered through his mind as a grim unbidden afterthought.

Outside, the air clung to his skin like Saran Wrap, and he stopped in the street to slip off his turtleneck. Several officers stared as he stripped to the waist, but the war had started to go strange and they were new to it. "Evening, sirs!" Denny said, passing off a snappy salute with one hand and his head still in the sweater. They returned the salute, bit their lips, and passed on.

Denny put his fatigue shirt back on, threw the white turtleneck over one shoulder, and sauntered along, singing a soul-felt imitation of Harry Belafonte that would have made any black man within hearing cringe.

When he came to the edge of the Tan-Son-Nhut runway, he turned right and walked a short distance. It was one of their more loosely held secrets: the Thirty-third Radio Research Unit had its own aircraft pad, a wide concrete stretch shared with the red-and-white Air America planes operated by the CIA. The Thirty-third had two planes, lumbering old Otters stuffed with radio directional finding gear. A single glance told him that neither of the RDF birds had returned yet.

Denny turned it over in his mind. The afternoon rains had ended in a light warm drizzle that would probably continue all night. There was some visibility yet, with the low bellies of the dark gray clouds hanging a few hundred feet off the rain-slick runway. They could have landed at some outlying airfield, though there had to be special instructions or an emergency for them to do so. NSA didn't like the idea of that highly specialized gear sitting on some tiny runway at night with the VC sappers scrabbling around thick as fleas.

The sirens went up then, and he got a crawly feeling as he crossed behind an Air America Beechcraft Bonanza and headed for the main runway. Suddenly the world seemed to be headed for the landing strip. Three red fire engines howled away from a nearby hangar, and he heard the flop of a medevac helicopter lifting off. He hitched a ride on the back of a scooter driven by a zip air force officer with no better reason than his own curiosity to be there. MPs waved them back, but Denny yelled he had a clearance and urged the driver on. By the time they got to the strip, one of the trucks had laid down a sheet of foam. The medevac chopper, a square-shaped AH-43 Huskie with contra-rotating blades, hovered twenty feet off the ground on the other side of the runway, blowing big holes in the foam and whipping it up into the air.

Denny stood as close as he could get to the runway, squinting up into the gloom. When the planes broke under the clouds they were close enough to make out the markings on the wings. It was Otters One and Two. One had a huge hole in its wing; Denny could see air through it and wondered how it could fly like that. As it lumbered over, he saw that it wasn't going to land, just circling to look the situation over. Otter Two seemed okay, hovering protectively behind and a hundred feet up and to the right of One. As One went by directly overhead Denny saw that one of its landing wheels was missing, the rigid landing structure on the same wing side as the hole taken off as cleanly as if it had never been there. A murmur went up from the crowd watching below as they realized the landing would be a belly whopper.

Otter One finally swung around in a big circle tight of the line of trees at the end of the runway and began its descent. Denny edged down the field, away from the crowd a bit, thinking there might be some risk from the incendiary self-destruct mechanisms planted in the intercept equipment. The plane looked like it moved in a trance as it gingerly floated down, going impossibly slow, hanging five feet over the foam-coated runway until it stalled and hit on its one wheel and belly. Then it skidded fast like it was on grease, turning with nightmare precision to aim itself directly at the spot where Mad Denny stood. He spun around and ran without a moment's hesitation, flinging himself in a shallow depression surrounded by rotted sandbags left over from one of the local coups. The wing with the hole in it dug in the edge of the runway close to him and the Otter flipped over neatly like a metal pancake and disintegrated in a ragged, flaming blossom.

"Jesus," Denny muttered as he peeked timorously over the sandy burlap in front of his eyes, "bet I could get that .38 for nothing now. . . ."

CHAPTER TWO

2-1

THE SAIGON COWBOYS EACH HAD WOODEN BATS MADE from lengths of two by four, bats short enough to be tucked in their pants and concealed under loose shirts. The home-made clubs had to be smooth to avoid splinters when carried next to the skin, and represented weeks of careful whittling and sanding. And so they were disappointed on their first outing with their new toys when Kim their leader cracked the old man over the head and he stayed down. No one else even got to take a swing. The old man was out, no doubt about it, sprawled on the deserted street in the glaring noonday sun with a trickle of red blood flowing from his ear. They quickly dragged him into an alley and took what little they could find. The leader gave the frail, limp body a savage kick when he saw the smallness of their prize, and then the cowboys divided up the 160 piasters they'd gained and swiftly dis-banded. Ironically, they missed two items that could have given them riches beyond anything they had imagined; the one a ring in a hand-sewn pouch under the old man's arm, and the other a piece of knowledge he carried with him.

Phong, a plump White Mouse cop, found him a few hours later wandering in the Zoo Park. The old man was delirious and babbling. Since he was an out-of-towner and a rural on top of that, he probably saw the policeman as an authority figure. Still, with the sense of caution that comes from cen-turies of dealing with city tax collectors, the old man spoke in parables. He told of the ancient times, of a poor man of

31

authority who helped an old man who actually turned out to be a god, indeed the turtle god. Because the poor man of authority helped the turtle god and his offspring, he was richly rewarded. Phong was not the brightest of men, nor well educated, but he knew enough to realize he was in over his head. His choices were simple—turn him in to the chief down at headquarters, or hand him over to the people who paid him four times his regular salary.

The old man's head was bandaged and he was brought to a somewhat out-of-the-way table at the back of the Tuyet Lan bar. He sat erect, having collected himself, and looked neither frightened nor out of place. He refused American whiskey, so one of the girls brought him a pot of tea and some sliced lemons.

There were over a dozen GIs in the place, half in uniform and half in civvies, but none of these gave any notice; they were after other game, and the old fellow was just a spot of local color, if they thought of him at all. However, his presence was a ghost from the past for the girls, for each could remember a stern grandfather or great-uncle who carried himself as this one did, the ruling head of the family.

He had seen many years. His sagging face was incredibly wrinkled like a prune's skin and trimmed with a wispy white mustache and goatee. One eye, his right, was almost entirely glazed over with a translucent, milky white film. He had seen war and misery and famine and flood, man's endless cycle as promised by the orange-robed priests. He was frail; he could not have weighed a hundred pounds. And the formal country dress he wore, the silk jacket and pantaloons, bespoke of this as a formal visit, some form of negotiation. Of course, that was the old way, a way of life scorned by the sophisticates of Saigon, who moved in the rhythms of the French, and lately to the beat of the Americans.

"I don't want to see him!" Tuy stormed. "Why should I? What is this old man to me?" Tuy had no desire to see anyone from the countryside. This one came from a life she wanted very much to forget. She had arrived in Saigon as a very young girl in the late '50s, riding in the back of a truck packed with refugees, pigs, chickens, and even a cow. She came from the outlying province of Vinh Long. Her father had been a village chief, very outspoken against the terrorists. He had been singled out as an example. Early one morning Tuy came home from an overnight stay with her cousins to find her father and mother, brothers and sisters scattered in dark bloody pools, their bodies twisted, arms outflung, the ugly deep gashes in their throats crying out for mercy, or vengeance, or just to be covered up. In accordance with the VC way, no living thing was left in the house, and their scruffy pet dog (so cute as a pup her father had refused to have him butchered) and her big yellow cat also had their throats cut. Goldfish lay limp in a drying patch of water where they had been scattered from their glass bowl. No one in the village would even look at her, knowing she was already dead. She *had* almost given up, shivering helplessly on the porch waiting for night and the knife that would come for her slim young neck. When afternoon was well along and she saw the truck moving through their village, she had moved as if in a trance, out of some primitive urge for survival. She had not known where the driver was going. An old man from the back of the lorry with its rusty dented fenders silently held his hand down for her. No one asked her questions, and she did not look back.

Phong stood in the center of the small room at the rear of the bar while she stormed around him like a wildcat. He nervously fingered the white patrolman's hat in his hands while her guards eyed him with amused indifference. "B-b-but lady, I just thought—"

"No you didn't—you didn't think! Why, Phong, *why*? Why did you bring him here?" She reached on the table for a long leather shoehorn braided into a short whip, which she impatiently slapped against her hand.

The fat White Mouse, who had been catching her verbal

abuse for a half hour, was sweating freely, the moisture forming damp crescents under his arms. Everything had seemed so simple when he found the old fellow. He realized she was tapping her foot, waiting for an answer. He gave it, not realizing it was the same one for the fifth time. "I—well, I didn't know what else to do with him; it isn't exactly a government case—and he did talk of giving a golden treasure to the right people."

She eyed him carefully, finally shook her head and turned to the carved lacquer on the wall. God of wisdom, give me a break! Risk, the thing she hated above all, and here was Phong, one of the handful of officials she owned, plunging her into the unknown again. Phong was safe; she was fairly sure of him. He had made a small mistake a few years ago; the disappearance of a few miserable sticks of furniture that had been held as evidence in a case of theft long since dismissed . . . in itself a petty thing, but someone working for Tuy had been able to trace it to the chubby little man. Saigon police officers had a bad lot. Theirs was tough, dirty, often dangerous work. They made tiny salaries and suffered a lot of abuse, both from the Americans and the denizens of the city. Once they had a little on Phong, they simply fed him enough to hang himself, and then took his soul. Oddly enough, he seemed genuinely grateful.

"The difficulty with you, Phong, is that you care too much." She frowned at him, and he crumbled.

"B-b-but wh-what—he's j-j-just an old man!"

"Never mind. It's one reason I trust you . . . a little bit. But here your softness leads to nuisance."

She kicked a perfumed pillow, which went sailing past his ear. Her two guards, the French mulatto and a thick-limbed Chinese, sat with crossed arms and eyed Phong with stealthy, heavy-lidded amusement. "B-b-b-b!" the mulatto said to his companion.

"Enough!" Tuy barked at him. "I can't think with you two bickering at each other like a bunch of kids!"

The black Frenchman sighed and looked down at his feet. Tuy pointed an imperious finger at them. "You may wait at the entrance."

"But you may need—"

She waved them away with a flick of her hand. "You'll hear me yelling. I do scream rather well—as you both have remarked behind my back. . . ." The two exchanged looks as if each believed the other had told, and left the room. She turned to Phong with an air of resignation. "All right, my dear private police protector and troublemaker, bring your old man in."

He would not give his name, insisting on just being called "old one." He was the head of a rural Catholic family from the reclaimed swamplands north of the city, where they had lived since the '50s, having migrated from farmlands near Hanoi after the fall of the French. If he was surprised at the transition from the heavy scarlet and gold decor of the bar to her more businesslike back room, he didn't show it. Nor did he bow to beg for favors, or look down on her in any of the hundred ways that come so easily to the middle class Vietnamese. She found herself giving him a slight curtsy, memories of her childhood too strong to do anything less. "How may I help you . . . venerable one?"

He acknowledged her gesture with a slight nod. "Madame, I have come to bargain for the last seed."

"I do not understand."

"When I was a young man, my grandfather watched over almost a hundred. But the seasons have been harsh, all of them. My sons and his sons are gone. Just one great grandson remains, now sixteen years of age. I would have him in Thailand before the last harsh wind cuts down the last seed."

"That is impossible! No man draft age can get a passport!"

"Nothing is impossible. . . ." He held her attention with ancient rheumy eyes that seemed to have seen everything the world had ever known.

"You said bargain. . . ."

The old man nodded and with trembling fingers took the ring from the pouch under his arm. A large red gemstone gleamed in the light from her paper lanterns. Tuy could see Phong go bug-eyed at her side. "Phong, you may wait with the guards." Once he had gone, she eyed the old man more carefully. "Is it genuine?"

"Ruby," he said simply. "A gift from a Frenchman for getting *his* family out fifteen years ago. It never lies."

"Never lies . . ." She eyed it skeptically, but with respect, too, for she knew old jewelry could have other lives rubbed off on it. "What does that foolishness mean?"

"I do not know. It's what the Larouses told me. The ring never lies."

The ring in his old wrinkled hands had to be worth a small fortune. Tuy couldn't take her eyes off the stone, which was bigger than her bright red thumbnail. "It is beautiful, but what you ask is very difficult. It would take many American dollars."

"This is just a token of faith." He amazed her by taking one of her hands and slipping the ring on her finger. It went on smoothly, third finger left hand, a flaming drop of blood on the finger Westerners used for the marriage band. Her breath caught, she had a momentary stab of fear, and then was lost in the beauty of the stone. The old man continued, "I have another thing to bargain. It is worth many hundred times over the price of this ruby. But for you to win it, I must see the last seed sown in Thailand."

She shook her head in wonder. "And what might *that* golden treasure be?"

The old man gazed back at her with a confidence that would not be shaken, "A battered truck filled with another type of seed . . . the fruit of the poppy flower."

2-2

Captain Edgar Munson got his first command in Nam because he was totally right for the job: looked good in uniform; graduated from the Point, middle of his class; special interest, infantry and tactics; played football, pulling right guard; married a two-star's daughter. War was promotion time, and Edgar put in for Nam, eager to try out on the wily Cong some of the things he'd learned.

Edgar himself didn't realize it, but he deeply resented his career in the army. He had always loved knives, not as weapons, but as tools for carving things. And ever since he had been a little boy, he had a passion for biology, for taxidermy, for cutting creatures up to see what made them tick. Other kids played doctor with a makeshift stethoscope and perhaps got the little girl next door naked so they could do an examination. Edgar did all that, and then went on to operate on Old Fudge, the venerable and much-loved family pet. He managed to knock Old Fudge out by tying a Baggie with some airplane glue over his head. Using his model building X-Acto knives, he opened the old cocker spaniel up to see just what made him tick. He didn't do too badly, and was able to examine a majority of Old Fudge's internal organs and even to do a fairly decent job sewing the long jagged incision in his tummy back up. There was even a chance Fudge might have lived through the experience, had he made it back out of the anesthesia . . . but the young would-be surgeon failed to consider that once he was under, it might be a good idea to take the Baggie off his head and give him a little fresh air.

His father had been overseas at the time; after suffering his mother's fury, Edgar got to bury the dog under the willow tree out in the backyard. This he did in an angry black mood. His mother, who got to be both parents through much of his growing-up period, was on his death list. He sometimes could hear her shrill nagging voice in his sleep, or when she wasn't even around, and he imagined a thousand tortures for her. He should have put the Baggie over her head! He carefully marked the spot where he put Old Fudge to rest, and a year later dug him up and mounted the bones on a special board he had prepared. Everyone in the neighborhood complimented him on the neat way he wired the skeleton, and even his mother praised him, until he attached the little plaque which identified his project as Canidae family, species cocker spaniel (Old Fudge).

He always had a way with knives, whether it was carving up a piece of wood or a family pet, and probably would have made an excellent surgeon. But when he went away to pre-med, against his family's wishes, the good grades had not come. His father swooped down like a hawk, and pressured until Edgar could bear it no longer and agreed to a transfer to West Point.

At the Academy, his grades were still average, but the army didn't make a big deal out of it, after all, some of their greatest generals, men like Grant and Ike, had practically bombed out in the classroom scene.

For all that, in spite of his credentials and gung-ho attitude, and much of a lifetime spent dealing with army ways, he somehow wasn't meant to command. The basic problem was, men died when Munson took the field . . . his own men. He was well aware it wasn't really his fault, it was just one of those awful things that happens to a person, a really bad run of the dice.

Whatever the reasons, his men seemed to wear away like flesh rubbed on stone. They caught lucky mortar shots while snuggled deep in their bunkers, stepped on mines that shouldn't have been there, set off one-in-a-million chance tripwire grenades, caught stray sniper fire. After four months, his company was wiped out to a man, and it hadn't been in any major action.

MACV couldn't see any reason for it and certainly wasn't

blaming him; but being superstitious, they gave him another company in another province. The first week in his new post eight grunts bought the farm. True, there was a fragging incident and a suicide, but that company hadn't lost eight men the entire month before. An unofficial inquiry revealed three had been shot by a friendly sentry while on patrol. The frag took a second lieutenant who had an attitude problem anyway (no witnesses, no clues). The other three were ambushed as their patrol exited a village they had just torched. Ambushed and wounded and then shot in the back of the head and hung one night like raw meat on the rolls of barbed wire outside LZ Dorthy Kay. It wasn't his fault, as far as they could figure, but they quietly pulled Munson back to Saigon while they tried to figure out what to do with him.

Those were black days. Edgar had always put his career first, before everything. The day was never long enough to spit-shine his career. There was always another tactics or history book to read, another contact to make over at the Officers' Club, time to be with his men, time to plan and dream and scheme for the future when he would wear two stars just like Trudy's old man. But now, thanks to his string of bad luck, he was relieved of his command and there was nothing to do.

There was no dishonor, no reprimand, no official stripping of his duties. He simply hung out in limbo, stunned with the painful realization they'd never give him another infantry unit. It was unfair, and he had nothing left to live for.

Officially on leave, he had to get away from the base. He rented a room at the Caravelle and spent the long days waiting for a call, moping around with a dozen cassette tapes constantly twanging in his ear, mostly Elvis and Country-Western Gold, and reading World War II novels. The weeks dragged on, no word came, and his spirits sagged. He tried writing, but he'd never been one to explain his feelings to anyone, particularly his wife, and the experiment ended on the floor in crumpled balls of light blue scrap. He took it seriously, even had a frustrating little fit where he tried to break the ballpoint pen. It was plastic and resisted valiantly; he finally was able to bend it into a U-shape and slam it in the waste can. He took to drinking more than had been his custom.

There were times when he had to get out of the room, to go anywhere to get some air—he felt he was physically choking, just as fate had strangled his career. He walked the half-lit downtown streets in the hours after sunset, past the darkened shops and garish bars, past the sidewalk cafés and milk bars, on down Tu Do Street to the riverbank where lovers walked and young ladies whispered, offering love for sale.

Despondent and lonely, and more than a little drunk, he finally took one of the girls to a hotel. He was smart enough to rent another place, a tiny room in a sleazy crackerbox side-streeting Nguyen Hue, the "Street of Flowers." The fat bored Chinaman at the desk took his wadded two-hundred-P note, not even bothering to look up, much less have him sign in . . . and that was a lucky break, because that was the low night in his life, the night he found out he couldn't get it up any more.

She was pretty in a cheap sort of way. Her young face was too heavily made up, but she had shiny straight black hair, huge luminous eyes, and thick sweet lips. She slipped easily out of her brocade silk dress, and he saw she wore a lacy PX bra and no panties.

She said her name was Hoa. She kissed him lightly on the cheek—he had turned his lips away at the last minute—and then they held one another and drifted toward the bed. They tried and tried and tried for hours. The girl, who'd seen everything in her short time, did everything she'd seen to help. She caressed him, kissed him, fondled him, undressed him, held him. They took a bath together, perfumed water and candles. They tried it on the floor, standing, sitting in a chair, against the wall. She tried teasing, she was all over him like a lithe young cat. She licked him, sucked him, her darting tongue and sharp little teeth found him everywhere . . . to no avail.

They lay naked, he frustrated and shamed, she feeling guilty that she hadn't finished her job but couldn't return his money, side by side on the dingy sheets in the little bedroom. Edgar listened to the electric sputter of the defective old fan slowly turning above them. He watched a dirty curtain flutter in the open window. He held his feelings close and tried to ignore her.

The girl kept apologizing in her stumbling Pidgin English. "Sir, you no like, I do more, all my fault, but I do more, whatever please you, all my fault. . . ."

If she would only stop yammering her foolish apologies, if he had only never given in to this ridiculous shack-up in the first place, if she would only shut her thick stupid lips! Thoughts spun in his brain like angry hornets and she wouldn't keep quiet, going on and on with her stupid rotten lying excuses. . . .

Hoa wasn't going to give up. She knelt over him again, her lush black hair spilling forward to hide his loins. "I need money, GI—I no can give *My Kim* back, but what you want I do, I go long time, all my fault, I do more, I do over, all my fault. . . ."

As he watched the top of her head struggling fruitlessly with his impotency, a thick heavy feeling seeped into Edgar Munson's bones, a denseness that came without his actually being aware of it. Weeks would pass before he would be able to sort everything out and realize it had glided in on the tepid air, risen from the vile home of all the rotting smells of Southeast Asia, drifting in through the open window like evil spirits from all the graves of all the injustices done in that unhealthy climate, in that land not fit for civilized man. But at that moment, lying on the bed with the slight brown-nippled girl he'd never seen before hovering over him, his dazed mind clung to one clear significant thought—She had got at least that right, it *was* her fault! This decadent little dink cunt in fact represented the Vietnamese people, and the people represented the land, and the land, this evil land, had selected him for an enormous injustice. And in so doing, had ruined his life. His feelings were insidious and totally over-whelming. He didn't realize he was angry until he hit her. And he didn't stop hitting her until she was dead.

2-3

You see the acts of meanness, both large and small, in areas suffering military occupation around the world . . . the little cruelties to urchins and beggars, the misunderstandings with merchants, the harsh words for the street girls, the care-less slaps at frightened old men and women. What is there about being on their own in a foreign country that makes soldiers act so badly? They are all the same, whether they are Russians in Poland or Afghanistan, or Cubans in Angola, or GIs in Korea or Vietnam. Is it that they are just kids or young men ignorant of other people's customs and unaccus-tomed to power? Or do they really unconsciously in some subtle and yet controlling way sense their own superiority . . . and feeling it, act accordingly? Are the barriers of lan-guage and custom so great that we forget we all are human?

Whatever the reasons, Edgar Munson ran like the devil was after him through the streets of Saigon back to his hotel room. He threw up in the bathtub, taking off his clothes as he did so. Then he turned on the tub shower, and made a mess of things by trying to wash his clothes before his choked up half-digested food was rinsed down the drain. He couldn't think; he had to sober up. He grabbed a bar of soap and got in the tub, standing on his clothes. That went well enough, and the spray of hot water seemed to bring some clarity back to the situation, but when he went to get out of the tub he slipped and cracked his head on the tile bathroom floor. Thoroughly panicked, he looked dizzily at the room spinning around above him, and then crawled into the next room to make a long distance call to his father-in-law.

General Garnstalt was called in off the ninth hole at Merryweather to take the black receiver, which was handed to him by a polite black man wearing a white vest with brown vertical stripes. It took him five minutes just to calm his distraught son-in-law down, and another five to get the pieces of his rather disjointed tale. The general was a good listener, when his daughter's well-being was at stake, and he let Edgar rattle on until he'd heard the whole sorry thing a second time.

Then he reminisced a bit, letting his hearty take-charge voice roll out across the continent and even further across the wide Pacific to where it sought out and comforted Edgar Munson. He told a story he'd never told any man since it happened—a story all the men involved had been sworn to secrecy about, on pain of death. It was Korea, in the last frustrating days after Truman had cut MacArthur off at the knees and the troops knew they weren't going anywhere. Garnstalt had been a major then, with a staff job in intelligence. One bleak night in March the men picked up a gook agent, a young girl carrying maps with GI gun emplacements and trenches all marked out. She had been shot in the arm, a flesh wound. And she was pretty.

He heard about it when a captain called him to report the men were frustrated and pretty sick about some of the losses they'd been suffering, and were treating the captive a little more roughly than the Geneva Conventions permitted. By the time he got there, she was in a daze. They had her naked, spread-eagled on the floor, and tied firmly to several heavy wooden desks. Somebody had punched her, and a thin dribble of bloody spittle leaked from the ruined corner of her mouth, but they hadn't broken her spirit. The minute she saw him, a steady spatter of foul abuse ran off her tongue. She didn't speak very good American, but she cursed good enough to get to him. She was glad for the broken lives and the blown-out guts and the torn eyes and shattered bones of the hated GIs—of his buddies, his charges, his men.

He came closer, examining the woman. Upon his question, the captain admitted some of the men had raped her—in fact, by the time he got there, they all had. Her head was back, her eyes were glazed, but they bored into Garnstalt as she spoke. She had been responsible for the shelling last week, and the one before that, and the one before that. American devils had been blown to bits, and she was glad.

He asked the captain if he wanted her. The man thinned his lips and shook his head no. The then-major ordered this to be treated as a security matter and dismissed him. As the man strode out of the room, slamming the door behind him, Garnstalt looked around at the rage that burned in the eyes of the twenty-odd men left in the interrogation room. The gook bitch yammered away about how delighted she was that all those good American boys had been separated from their privates and would get shipped home in boxes if they could find all the pieces. The men were all watching him now. He sighed and sat heavily in a chair near the woman. He slowly took off his boots, lining them up in a neat row next to the chair. Then he began to take off his pants.

He'd never thought Edgar was a terribly bright boy, and when the thin terror-stricken voice on the other end of the line went on and on, Garnstalt was forced to tell more of the story than he'd originally intended. Somewhere in the fifties during that long night that had followed, the gook bitch spy had given up the ghost. Whether it was from rough handling or too much banging, no one would or could ever say. But that was war.

And that was his point to Edgar. He spoke a little while longer, firmly and clearly, giving orders. He made sure the kid cleaned himself up, got a new batch of civvies on, and went out to hang around the Officers' Club bar for the rest of the night where he would be seen, just in case. . . . After he hung up, he stared at the phone for a full thirty seconds before realizing the other members of his foursome were hanging around, politely out of hearing range, waiting for him to tee off the tenth. He waved them on, saying he had a security matter and would catch up with them where the twelfth doubled back if he could. He searched the tiny phone book he always carried, and after twelve minutes had long distance overseas, and after twenty minutes the duty officer at MACV headquarters in Saigon. For the next five minutes he railed up and down, thundering question after question— *why* had his son-in-law been singled out for disgrace if there was no proof he had failed in his duty? No proof, no reason would be acceptable. He demanded they track this one the Christian way, the decent army way, and find some responsible position for the kid—or he would know the reason why.

The general slammed down the phone and strolled out to the twelfth tee. The autumn sky was bright blue and the Maryland meadows rolled away from the green fairways in gorgeous fall colors of yellow and orange. He was two over par, and the guys would let him play ten and eleven over after they finished up eighteen. He'd done all he could, there was no use worrying.

The murder at the Mai Loan Hotel stayed a civilian affair and never was solved. The general blew an easy approach shot on ten and a little six-footer on eleven and had to settle for four over. And two weeks after his frantic phone call, Edgar was promoted to major with responsibility for slightly more than half the MPs in Saigon.

2-4

But the depression that settled in was deep and long lasting. Edgar was a goal-oriented person, and since he'd given up doctoring, all his hopes had been rooted in the infantry, in his dreams of pegging Victor Charlies on his trophy wall. Now that was all gone, blown away by the mortars that had taken out his men. He frequented the bars and nightclubs and whorehouses, gravitating slowly to the wilder, more out-of-bounds places common GIs couldn't afford, where there was less chance of a drunken outbreak or of discovery by any of his peers. He would sit for hours in the bars, shaving paper napkins or the little cardboard coasters with one of his little surgical knives. The bottom line was, nothing he did worked. He stayed depressed, and he couldn't get it up for a lay.

A few months after his promotion, he was lying on his bed with a tumbler of scotch on his bare chest, when the general's story came back to him. He was amused at the mental picture of Garnstalt, who he'd always thought of as a sturdy puritan old fart, standing there in garters and underpants, looking down at this poor naked gook with a gaze that slowly turned to lust. He imagined himself in that situation, the men looking on, himself diving on the helpless spread and driving, driving, driving . . . and surprised himself with the first erection in months, just peeping at him over the glass rim of the tumbler.

So he ventured into an old French velvet-glove place, a conservative mansion on Pasteur Avenue so expensive it was only frequented by men in long limosines with foreign license plates, top ARVN generals, and occasional lucky Americans who came along as their guests. But his troubles hadn't ended, and his fury again erupted when he couldn't live up to his dream. The girl had been marked badly, especially for the old-customed place, where a gentleman was expected to know how to punish a lady. It took all of his savings to get out of that one, and he was no farther than before.

A few nights later the image of himself as the general came once again, in a dream. He knew he was dreaming, he felt himself dreaming, and yet he watched himself slowly sit in the chair, one by one take off his boots and line them up under the chair, then stand to take down his pants. Garnstalt/ Munson looked funny in his garters and baggy boxer shorts. He looked down at the girl. She writhed on the floor, moaning. She was indescribably beautiful as she struggled, with her slim wrists and ankles bound with knotted clothesline. His eyes followed the line of her body, taking in the full breasts with their dark brown nipples, breasts that heaved as she panted in fearful anticipation of his lust.

Mouth open in wonder, and eyes shining his lust, Garnstalt/Munson let the silly boxer shorts fall around his socks. He gazed on the smooth olive skin of her legs, feeling his own member harden to a wooden rod as his gaze wandered up the inner side of her thigh to her virginal—

Edgar sat bolt upright in his bed, ignoring the firm rod between his legs. She had been a virgin! That was the missing link! He wandered around the room until dawn, unable to get back to sleep, planning his next moves. If *that* was the problem, he knew how to handle it . . . but God, it was going to be expensive. . . .

Through the contact he had paid off at the velvet-glove mansion, he found a specialist willing to furnish what he requested. The girls, usually very young, would be brought to his room. Often as not they would be in pigtails, or with straight black hair down to their buns, flowing behind their white schoolgirl *ao dai*s. He never knew what the provider told them from behind his silver-mirror sunglasses, but they submitted without a word as Edgar undressed them and then tied their thin wrists and ankles with silk scarves to the bed. Sometimes they shuddered, from the chill air-conditioning or the thing to come he never knew, but that was good, it excited him.

He found it was better when someone watched, as the men had in Korea so many years ago, and so he hired the bar girls. If they were very good and it felt right, he allowed them to undress and help him. Practically speaking, it was better to have one of the girls up from the Bristol, too, because they could translate his desires to the little bitches, and comfort or command them when things got a little out of hand.

He didn't know why it worked so well, over and over again, the same thing, but for him it did. Usually they lay there and stared up at him with their huge round innocent eyes, looking at their bound wrists and probably wondering what was next in the strange little game the flush-faced American was paying her dad or uncle or brother or friend a week's adult wages for.

What he needed was extremely rare in a city like Saigon, and so they all tended to be slim little things he guessed were anywhere from twelve to fifteen, fresh refugees in from some blown hamlet, and that was tremendously exciting, too. He would tease them and play with them, exciting their nipples and his own with strands of the little girl's or the bar girl's hair, and all the time pausing to leaven his excitement with slow sips of scotch that warmed his very soul.

When the time of passion came, the time when he would avenge his men and his career, he put all the games aside, mounting them swiftly and thrusting savagely for long minutes while the little dark bitches often as not squealed in pain and horror and had to be gagged by the bar girl anticipating this need, to collapse finally in a spasm of pure hateful love as their bodies were joined in a hot liquid coating of blood and sweat and sperm.

There were some few wonderful times when they just lay there, even when he forced himself in them. They remained dark and passive, and he shuddered in delight as he drank the naked hate from their eyes. In those supreme moments he knew he had truly gotten back at the cruel enemy, back at Victor Charlie who thought he was so clever sneaking around in the night, back at the spirits of the land who had swarmed from their evil resting places in a vain attempt to warp his life and his ambitions.

His was an expensive vice, made even more so when a tiny little thing hadn't survived her trip up to the American's room on the fifth floor of the Caravelle—but that was (thank God) after his personal financial revolution, after he had a lot of money. For the time being, he could only afford to unleash his passions once a month. Always a Jockey briefs man, Edgar took to wearing boxers . . . and he even bought a pair or two of garters from a fancy tailor on Tu Do Street, a pompous old half Frenchman whose claim to fame was to have suited Ambassador Henry Cabot Lodge in the good old days.

2-5

Edgar sat in his favorite booth in the posh Bristol Bar, drinking the blues away and carving a stack of intricate paper doilies with a little folding surgical knife that he could make appear and disappear as if by magic. He was tall and erect, a handsome man with heavy waves of dark hair slightly graying at the temples and firm flesh that was just beginning to take on the sag of middle age. Back in Monterey, California, where he had left his perfect family (one decently well-preserved wife—Trudy—and two kids, a boy for him and a girl for her), he could have passed for a lawyer or a prosperous doctor. Tonight he was feeling trapped in his rank, impossibly far below lieutenant colonel where he felt by this time he belonged and not that far above captain, from which he knew he never would have been promoted had it not been for his father-in-law.

He raised his heavy tumbler full of rich, Johnnie Walker Red and clinked the ice cubes, a silent toast to the war. A bit slopped over the rim onto one of the cuffs of his dark cashmere jacket. He set down his drink and fine English Oval cigarette to sponge carefully at the material with a damp napkin. Edgar appreciated the fine things of life, perhaps because he had not been born into them, and they came to him later than they did to most. And equally important, he had acquired them through his own cunning and nerve. Thank you, army, but fuck off.

The girls, nearly all at the top of their profession, gave him an occasional wary glance from under their long dark eyelashes, and knew enough to leave him alone. He never bought

"Saigon whiskey" for them, feeling the old French-Chinese customs to be artificial and a waste of time. What he wanted, he came directly out and paid for. That was the American way. Once in a while, late in the evening, he might bid for one of his favorites, and they would spend the night in the air-conditioned European luxury of the room he leased at the nearby Caravelle Hotel. He was almost never turned down unless a girl had a relationship with another man, because they were afraid to say no. True, his needs were strange, even in a town where tastes commonly ran from exotic to somewhere past kinky . . . but he did pay outrageously for what he asked.

They hated him and called him names behind his back for the things he did behind locked doors in that expensive room up on the fifth floor. They hated themselves for taking the money and doing nothing to have him discovered. But, they reasoned, he would do it anyway, with or without them. And he certainly had the money to pay off any ugly rumors. And finally, to them it was a great sum of money for doing practically nothing. After all, when it is said and done, a woman's body is made for love, and whether she enjoys it with which man first is a random toss of the joss sticks of love.

Edgar had gone in some interesting directions since his assignment in the city. Stuck with the command of MPs responsible for the well-being and security of tens of thousands of GIs stationed at the north end of the city, at first he thought the dull desk job would drive him crazy. He was real army; all he wanted were his little plastic soldiers back so he could move them around the paddies and down the dusty paths from hamlet to hamlet to drive out the Cong.

When the dope problems first came to his attention—pills and LSD from the States, and hash and hard stuff from the locals—he had no set regulation to deal with the disposal of the confiscated items. It all ended up in obscene little bundles or packets of waxed paper, Saran Wrap, or the ever-present all-purpose aluminum foil, in an untidy stack on his desk.

His weekly procedure had been to call his ARVN equal, a captain who handled the QCs, the Vietnamese military police. This man would send a nattily dressed civilian lieutenant representing the local police force over to Edgar's office. The courier would nod politely, talk a bit about the coming monsoon rains or the trouble they were having with the swelling ranks of refugees from the countryside, all the time perfunctorily cataloging the junk that he dumped in a plain paper sack that he brought with him. This went on for several months while the Edgar fretted over his life, which seemed to be going nowhere. Then the ARVN captain and his well-dressed accomplices were caught under questionable circumstances, quite accidentally, by some of Edgar's own men. They had been engaged in peddling the same dope back to other Americans. A routine investigation uncovered the tip ends of a thriving business that seemed to lead everywhere. The major had no alternative but to turn the smooth-talking dinks over to the proper local channels, where they had enormous difficulties explaining how they had acquired their various bank accounts and land holdings.

In the process of his investigation, Edgar ran across an amazing piece of paper, an analytical report laying out the cold facts of the dope business in Nam, from its pervasiveness to the difficulty of catching the top dealers to the tremendous profitability of that type of work.

Visibly shaken, the major took an R and R to Hong Kong, where he contemplated his past life while he allowed perfumed young ladies to massage and manipulate his body. He had something to look forward to; one of the enterprising local merchants had managed to find a fresh young lady suitable to his tastes, to be delivered to his room that evening. Edgar found his thoughts drifting to his career. Once it had been his life. Now he found it lacking.

As the massage continued, he visualized the suburban, two-bedroom home near Seaside that he had leased (with an option to buy), and its cracked stucco walls and struggling sod front lawn displeased him in a way he had never before considered. He'd never really thought much about material possessions. His home had always been simply the place where his family lived. He'd been an army man.

As soft hands rubbed scented oil over every inch of his body, he thought of his perfect major's family dressed for Sunday morning worship, and the feel of his inexpensive Sears suit bothered him as he saw himself walking out the front door with its chipped brown paint across his imperfect lawn to the two-year-old Chevy Impala with its already rusting side panels. He was a Chevy man, he realized with disgust. What separated a Chevy man from his betters, anyway? What was there about him that couldn't slide perfectly behind the wheel of a long dark Lincoln with a burl-wood dash and stereo radio?

He looked the same when he came back from Hong Kong . . . perhaps a little red-cheeked from the freshening pleasures of the old English colony by the sea, but otherwise basically the same sound plodder the army had come to rely on. "Got a little nookie, eh, you old fart?" his acquaintances chuckled, elbowing him knowingly over drinks on the Officers' Club patio, which overlooked bustling Hai Ba Trung. Though the book was written on Edgar—he was a major for life and basically a boor to boot—it didn't hurt to kid with old Garnstalt's son-in-law, the army being what it was. Edgar smiled quietly, sipped his scotch, and kept it all inside.

Back in his office, he waited for almost a month while the strange little pile of bags and parcels accumulated in his lower desk drawer. No one ever called from the local authorities to renew their weekly pickups. And Edgar Munson quietly became a man of commerce.

He realized early on that, in spite of the ease and commonality of the transactions he could make, real profit was not to be made serving the relatively penniless grunts of Nam, particularly once he made the right contacts and raised his volume to a decent level. Choosing his partners with great care, he was able to set up a small steady traffic that flowed along with the personal effects of out-country bound GIs he never met or knew to a dockside warehouse in Oakland, and then on into the mainstream Stateside dope scene.

Behind his back, the Vietnamese called him *Cai Xau My*, "The Ugly American," because of the things it was whispered he did to little girls it was said he took behind the thick walls of his room in the otherwise quiet and stately Caravelle Hotel.

For this and other reasons, in spite of his conservative manner and appearance, he wasn't a man to be approached without a reason, as the front *ba* at the Bristol warned the surly black Frenchman who approached her.

"Monsieur Ugly-face," she said with the particular scorn Vietnamese occasionally reserve for half-breeds or for anyone unfortunate enough to have skin darker than their own, "he say he not to be disturbed!"

But the mulatto abruptly dismissed her and headed for the man pointed out by her protests. She had no alternative but to make a scene, following after him, shrieking insults and pulling fitfully on one of his arms to assure the American that this was none of her doing. "No! You not disturb him! Go away, Ugly-face!"

She made the mistake of pounding on his back and was repaid with a swift blow that bloodied her mouth, leaving her stunned and speechless. She retreated to her post by the front door, where one of the girls gave her a perfumed handkerchief for her split lip, so the blood wouldn't ruin her expensive brocaded orange silk evening dress.

The black man slid into the cushiony maroon plastic booth and spoke across the table to Edgar Munson. His voice was in soft and broken English heavily corrupted with French pronunciation. "Monsieur. You do not know me, but zees ees of not importance *pour le temps*."

The *Xau My* raised his eyebrows slightly but said nothing.

He looked like a criminal lawyer gazing down from the great height of his position on one of his pitiful clients.

The mulatto continued, "Eez matter of ze importance of a beeg deal."

"A deal?" the American said mildly, flicking a piece of lint from his jacket. "Whatever sort of a deal?"

"Ees concerns wiz zee simple flower, *aussi* zee fruit . . . ehh, zee fruit *du pavot blanc*," he said, making an effort to speak quite clearly. "Zat is, fruit of zee white poppy."

"My word, man—what do you take me for?" The *Xau My* spoke quietly, but he started back in indignation and would have risen to leave the table. However, he could not, for faster than he would have thought possible, a black hand snaked out and firmly grasped his wrist.

"Hu-*zut*, monsieur—ehh, mis-ter. Look!" And the black man dropped a freshly developed snapshot on the table between them. Grainy and out-of-focus as it was, the blowup caused the American to blanch. He took the photo in trembling hands and took a closer look. It had obviously been taken with an extremely long lens from someplace with a view in through the window of his room at the Caravelle. He glared at the man across from him with an intense, new-found interest. "What do you want?"

The black Frenchman shrugged and turned his hands up on the table. One of them contained the negative of the shot, which he tossed on the table in front of Edgar. "No harm for you," he slurred softly, "we find it—ehh, *seulement necessaire* to talk wiz you—only to talk." The American snatched the negative and the photo from the table and quickly placed them in the pocket of his soft jacket, which somehow seemed not to fit quite as well as it had a moment ago. He was as ready to listen as a man gets.

2-6

It was an old dream, one that Tuy knew well. There is a moon, full and too low, hanging pus yellow over the edge of the shoddy houses along a certain street in Da Cau. She and Larkey walk the street alone. It is just past curfew. His face looks pale and pocked in the harsh moonlight. "Dead already," Tuy's mind says to herself in her dream, and she does her first slow mind-sick turn, her body twisting and crawling to get out of the enfolding dream-sack. But the vision is relentless, she can't get out, and they continue on to the house she rents at the end of the street, which is a dead end. They argue endlessly. About nothing. An argument she has started, that she continues, that is her self-defense from her own emotions.

Angry, he sits on the single step outside while she fumbles in her purse. She finds the key, quickly steps inside. She has a last eternal look at his face. He isn't angry any more, just bewildered, a little lost kid. He starts to say something, lips forming a word he will never speak. She quickly slams the door, locking it and then dropping a heavy bar in place. The noise of the bar as it slams into place seems to drum in her mind. In her dream she cries No! but back then in the reality-time she had said, "There is nothing I can do for him. I must save myself."

There is a moment of silence. From the other side of the door he speaks. "Tuy? Tuy, this is silly. Come on, I'm sorry. I know you're tired—we're both tired. Let me in."

Her hands shake. She sinks to the floor and starts to cry, as much in terror for herself as for him. And then the gunfire begins.

But in her dream, he doesn't die. He walks through the door, his shattered body streaming blood from a dozen gaping holes. He looks at her from hollow eyes, slowly raises his smoking automatic pistol . . . and then lowers it again.

"Your punishment will be to live," he says. "To live and remember . . ."

She wakes and is in the center of her huge, four-poster bed, alone except for her memories in a tangled pile of silk sheets and pillows. "Larkey," she whispers, "kill me and get it over with. . . ." But he is gone. The big bedroom is empty except for Antoinette, her cat, who meows sadly at her from across the room. Tuy sighs and rubs her eyes with trembling fists. She turns up the reading lamp at her bedside and tries to get back into the middle of Dofillion's *Passion in Another Time*. Dofillion is one of her favorites, but now she can't concentrate, and soon the book goes flying across the room to skitter under a lacquered dresser. She lights a candle, presses a hidden spring that opens a secret drawer in a bedside table, and takes out a small silver pistol. Then she begins to pace back and forth throughout the house, a silent figure in a long silk nightgown, stalking her memories.

It was often this way for Tuy. Hers was the restless sleep of the superstitious, the fearful, the guilty. She tossed and turned the long nights through, alone except for her memories, which returned like thin-membraned, bloated monsters to haunt her.

She was too young for this, she knew, and yet she had tried everything; sleeping pills from the American PX, herb teas from a Chinese medicine witch, the finest silk and satin sheets and bedclothes, counting sheep, counting piasters, counting dollars *My Kim*—American—counting gold bars. . . . She even tried legend: A young and beautiful woman, so the story went, was married to a handsome and kind nobleman. The tale, as with most Vietnamese legends and songs, was laced with bitterness, and the nobleman for all his kindness was poor and unable to defend himself from the lances of the envious neighbors who lusted for his wife. After his murder, the virtuous wife received many offers to wed, but spurned them all in memory of the one great love of her life. She spent her nights alone in the dark of her bedroom, rolling dice on the floor and blindly groping for them until dawn. And when the woman died, very old, they found the dice worn smooth from all the years of her complicated habit. But when Tuy tried it, she found she had no patience for the ways of the legend; after several hours of fear punctuated by the sheer terror of stepping on her cat's tail, she flung the dice out the window. Finally, she tried reading books.

She had come to Saigon as a raven-haired little girl without any immediate family. Tuy was adopted by the bar girls, who saw in her some bit of that simpler and safer family life they all yearned for. She learned to speak street English working as a peanut girl, and by the time she was fourteen knew thousands of subtle variations of the man-woman relationship at its most basic levels; she had her own first relationship at that early age, and in the years since had known more men than most girls do in a lifetime. Now almost twenty, she had loved for the romance of it, for friendship, convenience, survival, and for dollars *My Kim*. She had moved through her teens like a dark-fated angel, her perfect oval face, heart-shaped lips, and great, dark, sad eyes moving through violence and hate and destruction and death. She had not escaped untouched, having been herself scarred and beaten, raped and almost throttled to death. . . . And the things Tuy had done to survive then would not let her sleep.

She resolved to read in English, a better grasp of which would help her deal with the Americans at the same time she was whiling away the slow-moving night hours. Her first book was one of a famous and popular series that she picked up in the streets, *Little Angel Go Fuck*, printed in Hong Kong by The Hong Kong Press. Armed with a red-covered copy of *Hoa's Vietnamese-English Dictionary*, and a somewhat fatter *Webster's Dictionary of the English Language*, she curled up at one edge of her immense satin sheets and with her fluffy gray blue-eyed cat looking on began haltingly to gape and wonder and occasionally relate to Little Angel's amazing exploits. The hours went by and she was able to drift off into the beginnings of sleep that nearly always lasted the night through. Once again she had found her way to survive.

In the months that followed, the physical gyrations of the cock books began to bore her, and she moved on to romance novels, which she had the girls in the bar pick up at the USIA library. At this time she was beginning her first business venture, a grubby side-street bar on the bad end of Hai Ba Trung Street. She had reason enough not to want to be seen publicly, and went to great trouble to hide herself. It was no problem at all for one or the other of her girls, who took the opportunity to walk in the sun and possibly meet a rich American, all on business hours. Since the girls read no English, they judged the paperbacks by the flowery pictures on the cover. And so it was almost accidentally that Tuy discovered the historical novels and the gothic mystery-romances that became her favorites—big thick books filled with details of strange and interesting countries, with the spice of other simpler eras, and all held together with the hot soup of human emotions and passions. She read the nights away, and one day realized she could read English better than her native tongue.

But in spite of this ploy, there were times in her sleep when the past broke through her every resistance, and she would cry out in terror, tossing and flailing her arms as her brows knotted and her closed eyes saw horrors too awful for the light of day. Then she would wake, and if she was so unlucky that the dim reading light by her bedside had gone out—this was the case often as not, for electric power in the city was unreliable at best—the room would take on the fantastic gro-tesquerie of her nightmares. Her lavishly furnished bedroom with its huge, Byzantine, wooden four-poster with its hang-ing silks had sinister overtones; the twisted posts looked like torn limbs of trees or people. Cedar chests lurked about, the carved figures on their endless, black-lacquered surfaces tak-ing on a ghostlike power. Figures moved, became three di-mensional, and the faint whiff of incense was a sure sign dragons watched with motionless, unfeeling, yellow, slit eyes. . . . In times like these, she could not bear hiding under the covers in the dark, and she would light a candle and move about until dawn.

Characteristically, she lived in a small city villa that showed almost nothing of itself to passersby in the street. She rented for a modest sum—by American standards—from an absentee landlord who preferred a small income and the relative security of Bangkok in those disturbed times. The house had a patio and very little else for grounds. With the general collapse of the rural economy throughout South Vietnam, the most expensive furniture and hangings could be had for a song if you knew where to look and had an interest; and as her first bar prospered, she began to fill the villa with heavy, Chinese-style chairs and tables of ebony, teak, rosewood, and mahogany, ornately carved and often with center slabs of cool gray or pink marble. The walls she hung with brocaded hangings, and richly ornate rugs covered the cool white and brown French tile floors. Shiny black Parsons tables held painted vases, intricately carved figurines of jade and rose quartz, and carefully sculpted ivory tusks. There were black lacquer bowls and serving trays, some inlaid with the delicate eggshell process, some depicting the ancient legends of the kingdom of Xich-Qui, Country of the Red Devils. Electric light she muted everywhere to soft golden tones with the addition of oiled paper lanterns, themselves skillfully ornamented with ink designs. She had even purchased—with some reluctance at the cost, in spite of the excellent bargain she drove—a matching pair of golden-dust wall dividers with ancient brushstroke paintings depicting country scenes of the olden times, men and women in flowing, colored robes who seemed to float on clouds—scenes with wisps of rock, craggy pine branches, waterfalls, and lakes surrounding them. The doorways from room to room she had hung with beaded chains of antique enameled wood, multicolored and mysterious; to move from room to room in her villa with the smell of incense and the soft tinkle of porcelain wind chimes was to be in another world.

Tuy had come a long way in a very short span, if you measured time in simple years. But her experience was not at all uncommon in the wild swings of fortune that accompanied the arrival of the free-spending Americans, the *Nguoi My*. There were two avenues open to the girls who worked the whiskey dens of that oriental city. The bars were not whorehouses; of those there were enough of every type in every section of town. Rather, the bars performed a function not unlike that of the Japanese geisha houses. They provided young female companionship, a soft touch, an understanding smile, teasing conversation all in return for glasses of Saigon whiskey, or cold tea, which their male guests paid for. Those who used their looks and wits and bodies might marry a well-to-do Vietnamese—or even a foreigner, who would be fantastically rich by local standards. The second path to success was the more rare, but still it happened; the money a girl could make at a decent bar like the Cherry or the New York was already a decent living. The Americans were far more generous than the French had been when it came to paying for bedtime favors; indeed in the years of transition the Europeans had complained bitterly that the newcomers were ruining the economy. This additional income could provide a girl with a sizeable fund for investment, or cushion the blow of the inevitable early retirement.

Tuy knew exactly what to do with her money, and she understood the business she selected for her financial base. She soon had bought her second bar, and then finally the Tuyet Lan, which was in the heart of the Hai Ba Trung business district, around the corner from the PX, near Cheap Charley's restaurant and the fabulous New York Bar. The Tuyet Lan wasn't old French like the classy Tu Do Street bars, but owning such a place would have caused too much notice. Tuy was satisfied, for the moment. With the three more modest bars she had, she was able to pay the police, the politicians, her own protection, and still add slowly and steadily to her bank accounts and to the little collection of heavy square chunks of pure gold she hid around the house.

Sometimes she imagined herself the heroine in one of her treasured novels, the oriental woman of mystery and intrigue facing great dangers and the unknown with inherent cunning and a sultry sensuality that drove men wild, and to their various destinies. She was to meet a man from the Western world, tall and powerful, and have her own great love. Together they would face off against powers and evils greater than the both of them, and win against heavy odds, ultimately to gain a place of quiet and love for themselves. Such daydreams helped push back the half-crazed fears of the times when she wandered the house in one of her trailing silk gowns, heart beating loudly against her chest, a candle in one hand and a long butcher knife (she had killed a man with one such, just after her fifteenth birthday; he had gone down hard and bloody, and his dying curses fed another of Tuy's recurring dreams) or her silver pistol at the ready.

And so she read and walked and waited the nights away, meeting the ghosts of Din, the madman she had stabbed to death, of dear brown-eyed Charley whom she had loved blindly without reason or pay until he had died in the rain forests of the Central Region, or of kind Larkey who had died because she would not—*could* not—had been afraid to—help. She knew in her heart that no great love would come for her. Indeed, her heart was steeled against it; she could not allow the possibility. Already there had been too much sorrow, the rivers of blood had run, she had her ghosts. She would not hope, or ever care for another, for that giving part of her was dried into something forever watchful and mistrusting.

But in spite of everything she said and did and felt, Tuy was wrong. She could love again, feel joy again, feel pain again. And although she had no idea, she had already met the man.

CHAPTER THREE

3-1

MAD DENNY STOOD ON THE FIRING LINE, SINGING LUSTILY
and blasting away with the automatic pistol Weird had handed
to him.

"Throw a silver dollar (BLAM)
Down on the ground (BLAM)
And it ro-o-o-o-o-lls
Because it's round (BLAM).
A woman never knows what (BLAM)
A good man she got (BLAM)
Until (BLAM)
He turns (BLAM)
Her down (BLAM, click)."

Smoking pistol in hand, he swung around questioningly
to the ordnance sergeant, Weird Elliott, who chuckled merrily. "Eight shots—that's all she wrote, son."

Mad Denny put down the Luger P'08. "Well, like you
say, it may be a great antique—but I don't like it. Seems
always to shoot off to the left."

"Hey, that's the shooter, son!" Weird broke out a loud
guffaw.

Denny grinned in spite of himself; you couldn't get heavy
around Weird, who refused to get serious about anything.
"Okay, then—what I really need is a firearm that shoots right

to correct the natural imbalance in my style. You got anything like that?''

"Does a duck have lips?'' Weird hopped off the rusty barrel he'd been sitting on and dug through a large orange nylon bag that bulged with an odd array of handguns and personal weapons.

"Whoo, wait a minute—let me see that!'' Denny reached for a stubby M79 grenade launcher Elliott had unearthed from the depths of his bag.

"Certified Cong-killer!'' Weird bubbled enthusiastically. "You don't want that one.''

"How come? I kind of like the idea of all that punch.''

Weird shook his head. "Naah. Where could you use it? Anyway, this model is obsolete. Single shot. We're due to get repeaters in a couple of months.''

They were interrupted by a pimply-faced private first class who came running down the line. "Uhh, sirs,'' he said nervously, looking at Weird's stripes, "uhhh, the lieutenant over there would like to know if you could make a little less of a racket. He's trying to concentrate.''

Denny said mildly, "Christ, this is a *firing range*. . . .''

Weird squinted in the direction the private pointed. "You mean that fresh young thing way down there at the other end of this range wearing those coppery things on his shoulders? We're not bothering him.'' He dismissed the situation with a shrug of his shoulders, and went back to his magic orange bag.

They were at the ARVN training range about twelve kilometers northwest of town. Their fire disappeared into a gently sloping hillside covered with tattered green shrubs and pockmarked with small, saucerlike depressions. The line of view ended about four hundred yards up-slope in a straight thick line of trees. They were in a bona fide war zone, a gray security area, and the range had none of the specialization of Stateside training ranges, being used for everything from pistols and rifles to heavy Brownings, grenades, and mortars.

Weird had brought some empty tin cans from mess, and they stuck them on sticks about fifty feet from the firing line to keep Denny's efforts from simply vanishing into the dark green hillside.

It was an early Thursday afternoon, and the range was entirely deserted except for the zip officer in charge, who was in his little shack centered well behind the line, his legs up on a makeshift desk, chain-smoking Chesterfields and idly lingering over the tattered pages of a two-year-old April *Playboy*—and the lieutenant on the other end of the range who had just been pointed out to them.

Weird handed Denny a Walther P38, and the game continued.

"So-o-o, listen to me, honey (POW!)
While I try to make yuh uh-un-derstand (POW!)
As a sil-ver dollar rolls from ha-and to hand (POW!)
So a woman goes from ma-an to man (POW, POW!)."

Not five minutes went by when the private was at their station again, this time a little red-faced, as if his superior had rubbed him in the dirt for not precisely following orders. "Hey, look, I *asked* you guys nice to hold it down over there—the lieutenant has got to get another hundred shots in."

"He ain't gonna make it, lessen if he can put 'er on automatic." Weird chuckled happily, looking up at the darkening cloud masses in the sky.

"What kind of bug's that guy got up his ass, anyhow?" Denny snarled. He was wearing a blue and yellow Hawaiian shirt and shorts. He could have been anything up to a young captain.

The private was taken aback, sure his first impression had been correct, that he was addressing an officer. He gritted his teeth, well aware that every officer in the military outranked a second lieutenant. But orders were orders, and he grimly persisted. "Lieutenant Arboy is a champion rifle shot, probably the finest in the U.S., and certainly the best in the army."

"Well he ain't *in* the U.S. right now," Denny grumbled, shading his eyes to get a better look down the line at the man who stood with folded arms, frowning back at them. "What the hell kind of popgun *is* that, anyway?" Without a moment's hesitation he strode toward the waiting officer, with Weird and the private tagging after.

"Wow, that's quite some shooter you got there, Lieutenant!" he said, as he came up to the man holding the unusual rifle. It had a radical custom stock designed to cradle the weapon into the structure of the human body and a thick barrel topped by a powerful scope. "What do you call it?"

"I don't think we're discussing what I am shooting with," the lieutenant said with a look of disdain. He took the gun and cradled it in his opposite arm so Denny couldn't look at it.

"I see," Denny replied, his own manner suddenly measured and as quiet as the lieutenant's. "Well, perhaps you wouldn't mind if we just quietly watched you plink away, maybe pick up a few pointers."

"I really would prefer—" Lieutenant Arboy bit his lip midsentence, for Denny was already seated. The tanned young shooting champion, impeccably dressed in his custom-fitted summer khakis, scuffed the ground with a shiny patent leather boot. He started to say something more, then sighed and looked at the tiny paper stapled to a wooden post over a hundred yards away. It had the black outline of a turkey printed on it.

"Go ahead, old man, just pretend that little Thanksgiving feast out there is a VC in a tree," Denny encouraged him. "Let's see some fancy Cong-dusting!"

The lieutenant, who had raised his rifle, now lowered it with some irritation. "That is absurd!"

Denny shrugged. "Can't do it?"

"That's not the point!" the man shot back, now a bit upset. "This weapon could, under favorable conditions, bring your so-called Cong down from his tree at a distance of over a mile! However, competitive shooting is a gentleman's sport and not at all involved with the killing of fellow human beings! Now would you people kindly leave me to my work?"

Weird saw the look in Denny's eye, and half dragged him back toward their own end of the line, Denny muttering all the way in an easily overheard snarl, "Fuckin' eastern college preppie dropout bastard. I *know* that son of a bitch. That's General Arboy's son. If you can't *evade*, join 'em—but on your own terms. Shit world we live in, Weird."

The ordnance sergeant's chuckle was thinner than usual, but he managed to get Denny interested in a fine Browning High-power, a GP 35 that he hadn't really planned on showing him. A few minutes later everything was back to normal.

"Now a maaaaaaaan without a woman (KAPOW!)
Is like a ship without a sail (KAPOW!)
A boat without a rudder (KAPOW!)
A shirt without a tail (KAPOW!).
A man without a wo-man (KAPOW!)
Is like a wreck upon the sand. . . . (click, re-cock)
But if there's one thing worse (jam, re-cock)
In the universe (click, re-cock)
Then it's a woman (KAPOW!)
I said a woman (KAPOW!)
A wo-oman withou-ut a man—"

The private interrupted the end of Denny's somewhat off-key but heartfelt wail. He seemed breathless and disturbed. "Sir—uhh, this isn't my own words, sir, please. But the lieutenant over there says that you sing like you have—have—"

"Yes, my boy?" Denny said, looking him over with a mild smile.

"—have Cong shit in your mouth."

"And he sent you back here to tell me that."

Elliott sighed, moving between the two of them. "Denny, did I ever tell you the one about the guy who wanted to legally change his name?"

"No, you never did."

"It's a funny story. You listen, too, Private. Ya see, this guy went before the judge, that's the way you do it when you want to change your name, and when he tells the judge what he wants, the judge says, 'All right, that doesn't seem too difficult a request; what is your present name?' And the guy replies, 'James Cocksucker, sir.' The judge gives a little knowing laugh and says, 'Well, my, I certainly see your problem. And to what do you wish to change it?' The guy thinks for a moment and replies, 'I think to George, sir.' " Denny smiled as Weird broke up over his own joke, "He says *George*!"

"I—I don't understand, sir," the private stammered.

"You don't get the joke, sonny?" Weird's brows lowered over eyes that were suddenly piercing and hard. Looking at him, Denny was struck with the thought that there were probably reasons he had never suspected why Weird got his nickname. The ordnance sergeant reached out with one hand, and it shook as if some dark force fought with his calm exterior. He managed to pat the boy's shoulder. "It's not really necessary. You run down there and tell that baby officer the word 'cocksucker.' He doesn't have to know the rest of the joke."

The private stood in his tracks, jolted that a noncom could talk that way to a commissioned officer. "Sir, I can't—I just *can't*—"

Denny interrupted with a smile. "I think I know how to settle this." He calmly reached in the orange zipper bag for the M79, not unlike a minor league ballplayer hitting .225 might reach for his mild-mannered bat. "You got any shells for this mother?"

"Yeah, I got a couple in here somewhere. . . ." Weird

handed him one and rummaged about in the bottom of the bag for more. Denny cracked the shotgunlike grenade launcher open and inserted the chubby little shell, which was about the size of a can of tomato paste.

"My god . . ." the private whispered, backing away.

Denny flipped up the range sight and took careful aim across the green hillside. The M79 fired with a fat *poomph!* sound, and a second later Lieutenant Arboy's turkey target went up in a ball of flame. "Son of a bitch," Denny said in mild irritation. "That pulled off to the left a bit, too—it *must* be me, after all."

Arboy dropped his rifle and stared unbelievingly at the thick cloud of black smoke that rose from the crater in front of him. The range officer poked his head from his shack, saw nothing extraordinary, and went back inside. Mad Denny eyed the private coldly. "Tell Asshole over there, as soon as I can load 'er up the next one's for him. He's gonna get his name in *Stars 'n' Stripes*. . . . I see it now, front page: AR-BOY'S SON GETS ASS BLOWN UP IN RANGE ACCIDENT."

The private never heard the proposed headline, for he was already running wildly back down the line to where the lieutenant, who had figured out the broad strokes of what had happened, stood gaping at them. And by the time Weird found the second shell, neither of them was anywhere to be seen.

3-2

In his own way, Toady Lorrie had been scarred by religion, much as had Simon Peter, whose tears of remorse had carved his face . . . or Job, who God saw fit to inflict with everything from piles to zits. The only child of a wild-assed drinking and gambling man who had given it all up for a woman raised in the serious ways of the Jehovah's Witnesses, Toady had both scars and zits. Pappa Lorrie had exchanged the five-card flush for a handful of pamphlets, and the church became a very big part of his life. His old friends, impatient with the long sermonizing he subjected them to, chuckled among themselves and shrugged him off.

Toady grew up under the name William Lorrie and was subject to the pressure of a higher way of life and death practically from the day he pooped his pants during a long sermon and had to wait it out for hours with a pencil between his teeth to keep him from crying. Of course, he had embarrassed his family; his father told the story many times as he was growing up, and young William bore it stoically as just another of the things he personally would do penance for before he gained his own reward.

His folks believed with an unshakable faith that the sad mudball earth was in its last few rotations, and if you needed proof, you need look no further than the Korean War then raging, the genocidic crimes of the communist Russians and Chinese, the insidious pollution that was creeping steadily over everything and would surely blink out the light of the sun before the twenty-first century if the atom bomb didn't do it first.

Life was never easy for the faithful, but those were extraordinary times. And as if growing up in full knowledge of the earth's impending doom were not enough of a burden for young William to bear, there was no church school near enough, and he was forced to attend public school with unbelievers. These kids were not baptized into the one true faith. Most of them believed (innocently or not, if they believed anything) in the Antichrist, the filthy vile devil who had come to trick and weed out the weak and the vain before the final burning. They didn't even know they were unclean.

From his earliest recollections of his family's walking door-to-door through the dusty streets of Corona, California, to pass out pamphlets and spread the faith, Toady was aware of the abuses the unclean heaped upon the people of his faith. He remembered how a violent red-faced man, cleaning his backyard on a Sunday afternoon when they came calling, had slung a shovelful of sticky dog shit on his father's black suit.

At the time, he had wanted his father, who was a big strong fellow, to climb over that fence and pound the man until he bled, and then rub the same shit in the man's face and hair. But his father was stronger than he in ways he had not yet understood, and had simply gathered his dignity and spoke compassionately to the man, trying to pull even the one who had done him that great wrong back from the brink of his own destruction. William Lorrie had learned from that. He willed God give him the strength to be strong like his father.

In the long years since he first found himself standing with the faithful on those hot breathless weekends of prayer and proselytization, he would never have admitted he was lonely, for if he did not have close friends he had a closer family. He told himself he didn't really miss any of the misguided trappings or presents of Christmas, the liars' holiday, or Easter, the hang-over pagan Greek spring bacchanal to false idols, or Halloween, the devil's own rite of the dead cleverly hidden behind little costumed children begging treats. The family had its own celebrations, tied in with cycles of the church. He also did not need the foolish sock hops and ridiculous crude football and basketball orgies his high school classmates seemed to relish, for the church had socials and gatherings, and then, too, the time for frivolity was short, and there was so much work to be done.

Time, indeed, was shorter for his tight-knit little family than even it anticipated, for on the way home from a long afternoon of pamphlet passing in August of the year after William graduated from high school, his father had a sudden, massive heart attack. He was cruising at sixty-five on the Pomona freeway, headed back to Corona after they had spent a scorching day on the sweat-sticky streets of downtown L.A. talking to the poor blacks, confused Chicanos, and hopeless drunks. His dad fell across the wheel without a sound, and their '59 Dodge did a little hop across the center divider into oncoming traffic. William, who had been sleeping in the back, looked over the seat as his mother screamed and a huge rusty blue Peterbilt with a chrome grill like sharp devil's teeth came blaring down on them . . . and woke in the hospital to learn that both his parents had been carried off to their eternal reward, to the land of milk and honey where peace and prosperity flowered among the rolling green hills of heaven.

He was not badly hurt, and once he recovered had no choice but to go live with an uncle who ran a laundry and cleaners in Woodland Hills. At first he thought it would be all right, for there was a big Jehovah's Witness hall within walking distance of his uncle's house, just down the street from the infidel St. Mel's Catholic church. His uncle actually went to St. Mel's, and there was work to be done.

But his uncle proved impossible. During a particularly distressing after-dinner discussion the man had the nerve to admonish *him* to open *his* mind. William had gotten a little sharper than he intended, reminding his uncle of the blistering rewards intended for the unclean at the just-around-the-corner Final Day. The uncle dismissed it all and then shocked William by describing his father with a hearty laugh as "an example of the lengths a man will go to get a piece of ass—no offense meant." William had left the table, shaking with frustration and fury.

His cousins, the Lorrie girls, were wild and unpredictable, even in the weeks before he started putting on weight and getting the awful scratchy deep zits that had plagued him ever since. They never had any locks on the door to the one bathroom in their beaten old house, and Kathy, who was older than he was by a few months, came bursting in when he was losing a sexual bout with the forces of evil. Rather than being shocked at her discovery, the hussy gazed fully upon him, closed the door behind her, and offered to help the devil. William had violently shoved her from the room. Luckily they were home alone at the time. He realized later she must have been spying on him and had probably been looking in through the keyhole in the old-fashioned door. He still shuddered when he thought of that, and tried to put it out of his mind. It was one more thing he had to do penance for. Kathy, on the other hand, made him pay in a hundred different ways with her mocking smiles that said nothing to anyone else and everything to him. She would burn on the final day, he was sure.

As summer dragged into autumn, his uncle became impatient with him, and Kathy's smirks and suggestive leers became intolerable. There were times the devil got the best of him and he actually saw himself rolling in heat with her. At such times he would fight the swelling erection between his legs by imagining they were rolling in awful smelling sticky dog shit, and by putting his hands inside his pockets and pinching his legs through the thin material until the skin broke and bled.

Worse than all that, his mother and father were calling him from beyond the grave, from that sweet place of clear flowing streams and gentle rolling hills where the sun always shone. He heard them clearly in his dreams. He would wake and the voices would not quite be gone, calling him with ever-dimmer voices trailing off into the distance. "William, William, we love you, we love you, we want you to be with us . . . with us . . . with us. . . ." He would never have considered himself suicidal; man's job was to work the earth like a field, gathering those souls he could like a harvest, and to be finally called, as his father had been, when the time was right.

The pistol was his father's, a little .32 automatic left over from the gambling days. William had found it in the garage, buried under a stack of poker chips, late '50s *Esquire* magazines, and even earlier amateur black-and-white photo blowups of a gathering of naked ladies at what looked like a quarry or a swimming hole. To his shame, William lost a bout with the devil over the photos before he regained his willpower and burned them in the backyard trash can, along with the gambling gear and the magazines. The pistol he kept.

It was late one October evening when he came to the cold realization that something was terribly wrong. He hadn't been able to tell anyone his parents were contacting him—who would listen, his beer-drinking unclean uncle, or his uncle's weak-willed wife who seemed to let the man get away with anything he wanted, or Trash-Can Kathy, as he came to think of her?

The air was chill, and he had risen for the hundredth time to the beckoning of the sweet voices in his head. It was his father, stern and yet kindly. "Take the pistol, son. That's what I left it for. Take it in your hand. That's right. Now put it in your mouth. *In your mouth!* That's right. Your mother will tell you what to do next."

And his mother reached out her milk white arms, imploring him. "Just end it, son. Come to us. You don't deserve to live in these corrupt times. Come to us, to your reward."

He felt the cool barrel of the pistol between his lips, ran his suddenly dry tongue over the huge round opening in front, and knew terror.

His religion saved him. Hadn't his father told him there would be false temptations, cunning masks to lead him from the path? This wasn't his father and mother, this was the work of demons! With shaking hands, he took the pistol from his mouth, afraid it might go off of its own accord. His path was to continue. When it was time, he could be called to his reward. Man's job was to wait and work and endure the slings of shit heaped on by his fellows, until that time when all would be made right.

But he had to get away. He needed a home, someone to take care of his day-to-day needs. He lay awake, plotting and planning, until the gray light of dawn, while the pistol lay forgotten at his side. That morning, after his uncle's family had all left the house, he went to the master bedroom where he found three hundred and fifty dollars behind their wedding picture.

He had spent boring weeks helping his uncle in the laundry shop, until the day some of the regulars complained he was bothering them with his pamphlets and convictions. Week after week without pay.

Then, too, he had labored long and hard to give his father's brother a chance at redemption. Three hundred and fifty dollars seemed a fair enough reward, if you added the harassment and sexual abuse he had suffered at Trash-Can Kathy's hands. William took the money with an easy conscience, packed his few belongings in an overnight bag, and took a bus a few miles down junky Ventura Boulevard to the nearest army recruiting office. Little matter that it was against the teachings to join the army. Olive drab would be his trial, his earthly work, and so his personal road to the light.

The army had not been easy, but he was convinced it was his calling, to work among the very dregs of society, the paid killers, until he was called. After basic training his body plumped and his zits swelled as never before. He was sent overseas to the Thirty-third, where he carried out his real mission in life when he wasn't called upon to peck at an old Royal typewriter. They called him Toady, but he didn't care. He had endured worse.

He looked up from the stack of new pamphlets he'd gotten from the Woodland Hills assembly hall in the previous day's mail in time to see Mad Denny signing out for the firing range. "Finally taking something serious, I see," he grunted.

"How's that, Toady?" Denny had replied. Mad Denny felt at peace with himself and the world in general, having just made three decent deals that got rid of over half of the hash he'd picked up the week before.

"You'll be ready when they come."

"Who's that, Toady?" Denny said with a resigned little sigh. He had heard the whole shot from the fat little corporal, all about the final angel blowing golden trumpets, the earth split by purifying fires that saved the innocent and scorched the guilty, sending their tortured blackened bodies to their eternal punishment. But today Toady surprised him. He gazed blandly up from his desk, his round face so pocked with old zit scars that it looked like a little moon. "The VC, of course. Why else would you take firearms practice?" Toady liked to know everything about everything, thinking of himself as the CO's "ear among the men."

Denny gave him a look of disgust. "The VC? Sure, we're gonna hold 'em off right out here on the parade grounds with a few M14s that still fire semiautomatic."

"Single shot is still a valid way to eliminate the enemy," Toady archly replied, defending the outdated weapons issued to the members of the Thirty-third.

"Sure. So are clubs and rocks."

"Why *are* you going to the rifle range anyway?" Toady leaned forward for Mad Denny's answer, scratching under one damp armpit as he did so.

"Though it's none of your business, I'm going because we're supposed to once a year, you little toad. Don't you read any of the stuff you type?" Denny's nose wrinkled. "How come a guy like you who never takes a bath doesn't just putrefy from tropic-rot or something?"

The corporal's face turned sour as he put away all pretense of being nice. He honestly didn't like the open-air showers, because you had to wash in open stalls, naked in front of all the men. He knew they laughed at the sagging pimply body God had burdened him with. But how this example of abomination, who everybody knew was one step away from a dishonorable discharge, had the nerve to talk openly to him about such personal matters was beyond him—as was Haller's own salvation. He sneered. "You can't fool me, mister. You're getting away with something. It's the only reason you do anything."

"Oh good—now you going to have a witch hunt or a book burning? It's guys like you that put Salem on the map! Wonder if the Puritans used soap. Probably not." He sniffed the air in Toady's direction, then gasped as if it were almost too much to bear.

Toady put on a silent look of superiority and went back to sorting out the pamphlets that he intended to hand out with the mail. When the Final Day came there would be a cleaving, and Specialist Haller was going to find himself the clam in the clambake. "I don't know much about the Puritans," he replied loftily, "but they were justified in everything they did, if they had to deal with people like you."

After Denny left, slamming the rotting screen door almost off its hinges, Toady thought some more about it. "Witch hunt . . . not all that bad an idea . . ." He hunched his flabby body out of the chair and wandered innocently back to Captain Anderson's office. "You know, Captain, Spec-five Haller just left for the plink range. . . ."

Captain Anderson looked up from the latest crossword puzzle that was defeating him. "Five-letter word for command?"

"Order, sir," Toady replied automatically.

"Oh yes—*order*. Thank you, Corporal. . . . So our Mad Dennis has finally decided to give a little back to the army."

"Oh, he's got his own reasons, I'm sure, sir," Toady said, his face a dark mask of anger as he remembered all the times Haller had twitted him about body odor. "I was just thinking, sir—after Corporal Stringer's allegations, this afternoon might be a really nice time to hold an inspection of the enlisted men's barracks."

Captain Anderson threw his folded newspaper down with a grin. "A sneak? Excellent suggestion, Corporal! Let's get on with it!"

In the hours that followed, stand-up lockers were opened and sifted through at random. Here and there a bunk was torn up, the sheets dumped unceremoniously back on the naked mattress. But when they came to Mad Denny's area, they had a field day. Every piece of clothing was taken off its neat hanger, carefully felt and dumped on the bed, which had already been stripped and inched over. The contents of his footlocker were also dumped on the bed and then indi-

vidually examined. Socks were unrolled, underwear gone
through, leather belts checked for secret compartments. His
toilet articles were each opened separately. His foot and
crotch powder cans were emptied in the john, on the hope
that packets were concealed within. A Visine container, a
favorite hash stash among the enlisted men, was pried open
with a tweezers. Even his toothpaste was squeezed out in the
sink.

The total inspection took three hours. Half of the time was
spent churning with ever increasing frustration through the
mess they'd made of Denny's area. When it was over, they
stormed back to the CO's office. "What a waste of a perfectly
decent afternoon!" the captain complained, forgetting that
he had been doing nothing.

Toady felt he had to justify his suggestion. "I know the
dope is there somewhere! That guy is a dealer! You should
have given me permission to cut his jackets and coats, and
to rip off the bindings of the books—he's guilty! He's the
guy!" The fat little corporal couldn't have explained just why
he felt such fury. Throughout the barracks they'd found the
usual scatter of cock-books, a few bottles of booze, and a
little tinfoil packet of marijuana hidden in one of the men's
effects—but the hash turned out to be in Stringer's locker,
and so the search could hardly be considered a success.

And Spec-five Haller's area had been a terrible failure. If
he was in the dope business, there wasn't a bit of evidence
to prove it. Additionally, his clothing had been spotlessly
clean and pressed, and his shoes had shone with a hard gleam
almost impossible to get in the sodden tropics. Back at his
desk, Toady fumed and picked furiously at his face.

On returning from the firing range, Denny's initial rage
would quickly be replaced by a grim mirth. It wasn't hard to
figure out that he personally had been the target of the entire
sneak. And they had found nothing. They never would. How
could they? . . . All his stuff was hidden in the TOP SECRET
KIMBO file over at the White Shack.

3-3

But Denny wasn't overconfident. His little operations were all too vulnerable, as the sneak had pointed out to him. If the captain had conducted his raid one day the week before, the searchers would have found his wall locker jam-packed with fifty-two cartons of cigarettes he'd collected to sell on the black market. And a week before that, he actually had his entire hash stash in his footlocker for a couple of hours before he could move it over to the White Shack.

And so Mad Denny rose early the next morning, caught a clammy shower, and got into a pair of long pants and a medium sweater. He took out his bulky rain slick and readied himself for a damp walk over to the White Shack. He wasn't going out of business, but from now on he was going to be a lot more cautious.

Melvin Brownstone poked his head from under his mosquito netting in the bunk area he occupied next to Denny. "Hey, white nigger—you headed where?"

"Downtown, Mr. Brown. Better shag your black ass if you're comin' with." Denny knew there was no chance his assistant would take him up on the offer—Melvin took ten minutes just to tie his shoelaces.

Brownstone rubbed his eyes with two curled paws like a big sleepy teddy bear and shook his head. "Naaw. I gotta teach some English at the *Hoi Viet-My* at ten-thirty."

Denny grinned. "Better get going then—you only got three hours."

"I'm lightning once I wake up."

"Yeah, Melvin, but it takes a while to connect your electrodes. . . ."

Brownstone rolled over to get out of bed, got tangled in his netting, and ended up with a thump on the floor. He sighed, pulling on his thick wire-rimmed glasses, and grinned sheepishly up at Denny. "Where you goin' anyway? You found a twenty-four-hour café where you can harass the locals around the clock with your feeble attempts at the language?"

"Naw, Brownie—I got a financial transaction to conduct."

"Fi-*nancial* trans-*action*! My, last week we just called it dumpin' our cigarette rations on the black market. . . ."

"You have a biting and sardonic tongue, Mr. Brownstone; and I, your last remaining friend on the planet, hope your penchant for using it to lick stray bar broads doesn't give you a disease which causes it to fall from your mouth."

"Thanks. I know you mean it," Brownstone said from behind a tremendous yawn. "Look, I'll meet you at the Royal Bar at eleven; if you can make it, we'll catch a cab back to the base together."

Denny agreed and stepped out into the heaviest rainstorm of the year. His pants were soaked below the knees before he had gone ten steps, but he didn't care. As he walked along the concrete runway apron the rain thundered all around him, drumming off the tin-roofed airplane hangars and rattling on his own slicker. He could barely see the outlines of the planes lined up twenty yards from him, and the downpour was so thick it gave him the claustrophobic sense that he couldn't breathe. He knew it couldn't last, and yet it did. He muttered a happy little tune as he went along. The weather was going to help him. It would divert the attention of the already bored guard at the White Shack. He needed a little edge, because this morning he was going to withdraw his money from the Kimbo file and deposit it in the Bank of Hong Kong.

"Joshua fit de battle of Jericho
Joshua fit de battle of Jericho
An de walls came tumblin' down.
Talk-a-bout-your Gid-e-on
Talk-a-bout-your Saul
Aint-none-dat-fit-like-Joshua
At-da-bat-tle-of Jericho. . . ."

The guard at the White Shack looked up to see the singing apparition of Mad Denny looming up through the wall of rain. He had commandeered a chair and sat under the White Shack's small false-front portico just out of the downpour. "Halt. Who goes there?"

"Denny Haller. You *see* it's me, asshole."

"Green badge," the guard said, not bothering to lift his feet, which were on the small sign-in desk blocking the way in. "Yeah, I see it's *you*, Denny, but I don't see the badge."

"God damn. It's *raining* out here!"

"Hadn't noticed. Better button up or you'll get wet. Green badge."

Denny swore and dug in his slicker through the head hole. As he did so, the rain dribbled down both sleeves to soak the sides of his sweater. He got his hands on the green badge, which was sweat-damp from being next to his skin. He pulled it out on its neck chain and flipped it at the guard, who heaved a sigh and moved his feet out of the way.

"Green badge! . . ." Denny grumbled as he moved in through the door. "I father three illegitimate children by the asshole's sister, girlfriend, and mother—and he doesn't recognize me. . . ."

The guard grinned after him. "Haller, if you'd of tried that tiny prick of yours on any one of 'em they'd of laughed you out of the state."

"What state was that, total confusion? . . ." Denny called back over his shoulder. And then he was inside, surrounded by the shocking cold of the air-conditioning. He hurried down the deserted hallway back to the enlisted men's workroom. Once in the room, he hastily spread his dripping poncho over a wooden hall tree and went to the Kimbo file.

The work his section did was classified "top secret code word." They had two words, *dinar* and *kimbo*. All the ordinary transmissions were stamped TOP SECRET DINAR and air shipped in the overnight pouch to the Puzzle Palace, the huge NSA building at Fort George G. Meade in Maryland where an unusual assortment of specialists spent their working lives decoding and reading covert junk mail from around the world. Kimbo stuff, on the other hand, was considered a much higher priority and was hot-wired immediately back to the Palace.

The Kimbo file was actually an ordinary-looking metal file cabinet with three drawers. The individual locks were augmented by a custom-welded steel bar that secured all three drawers by means of a big Yale padlock. Each drawer had its own incendiary grenade, with a complicated and detailed list of emergency instructions covering what to do if the ''host'' government became unfriendly or the enemy overran the base.

Since messages stamped KIMBO were only sent a few times a year, the entire file could have fit in one fat envelope. And the duty officer had the master file in his office anyhow, Denny's Kimbo file being nothing more than a duplicate reference source to keep the enlisted men from tramping in where the intelligence officers and the Thirty-third's two pilots were running the war, usually over Havana cigars and chilled tumblers of Jim Beam with yesterday's Stateside baseball game blaring on Air Force Radio Saigon.

Mad Denny, as lingie section head, had the only key to the padlock. He handled entries into the file himself and had never had a request to open it in the two years since he took over the section.

He unlocked it now. Digging under loosely stacked masses of unsorted Dinar transcripts and Louis L'Amour westerns, he pulled out six or seven fat manila envelopes and an empty brown paper grocery bag. He swiftly placed them on his desk, listening carefully for footsteps from down the hall. Graveyard shift had gone home, and it would still be twenty minutes before the morning guys started trickling in. Still, it didn't hurt to be cautious, and he decided to take his operation into the closetlike john across the room where he could lock the door.

Safely inside the tiny bathroom, he opened the manila envelopes and hurriedly stuffed rubber-banded wads of money into the grocery bag. It was all in twenties and fifties, and by the time he was finished, the bag was over half full. He saw that it was going to be a problem. Not only was it heavy, it would bulge a little even under his rain slicker.

With brows furrowed, he went back out into the staff workroom, which was still deserted. He double-checked the Kimbo file, which he had locked before going into the john, and shrugged into his poncho. Even with the bag scrunched under one arm, it was a touch obvious. He thought about it; some little piece of business was going to be necessary . . . something neat and simple.

He checked the coffeepot and found it still had a cup at the bottom. After pouring the smoking thick fluid into a white Styrofoam cup, he headed for the front door, praying the guards hadn't changed yet.

He got lucky, and the same guy looked up from the chair where he'd left him. "Short day you put in, Haller."

"It's the *quality* of the work, my boy. . . ." He handed the coffee over. "Here, asshole. Sorry it's so strong, but it's all we got. Seen the navy bus yet?" To board for the trip downtown you had to be in uniform, caucasian, or negroid. In other words, no zips allowed.

The guard gratefully accepted the coffee. "Naw. Couple minutes. You better get out there; driver doesn't stop unless he sees somebody."

"Yeah, I know." Denny moved quickly into the rain. He got about five steps from the door when the guard called after him.

"Hey! What you got under that poncho?"

Denny turned, thinking fast. Giving the guard what he hoped was a sheepish grin, he wiggled inside the loose garment and caused the end of the umbrella to poke out from under one corner of the slicker. "Umbrella. Wouldn't want to get it wet." It was weak, he knew, but he couldn't think of anything else to say.

The guard snorted in mock derision. "Makes about as much sense as the rest of this fuckin' hitch," motioning him on with a wave of his hand. "Thanks for the mud."

Denny gave him a smart little salute with the umbrella and walked off at a crisp pace, trying hard to move along in a loose and carefree way and at the same time hang on to the twenty thousand dollars under his arm.

3-4

In the long weeks of waiting that were to follow, thinking back on the fateful string of events that took place that day, he would blame much of it on his own inexperience. He was acting impulsively, on secondhand information, and without a backup plan. The previous day's sneak had been triggered by his own remarks to Toady-the-Worm. There was no well-thought-out plan to bring him down. His funds would have been safe in the Kimbo file. But all that wisdom would come a long time after the facts, as it always seemed to. For the moment he was running, and that day there would be times he wouldn't have bet he was going to be alive at the finish.

It all started with a bad feeling. Denny sensed it, a vague shivery intuition of something not right, down to the soggy soles of his tennis shoes as he rode the gray school bus ever closer to his destination. He got off downtown at the embassy. The bulk of the passengers disembarked with him, and then he took a cab a few blocks back along the way he'd come. Without any hesitation, he walked confidently in through the heavy glass front doors of the Bank of Hong Kong.

The theory on which he operated was one much discussed among the amateur economists at the Thirty-third: that the Chinese banks were eager for dollars because they had ties with the mainland chinks. The Chinese, as anyone who read

Newsweek knew, were hungry to balance their import-export payments, or something like that, and they needed hard dollars to pay for stuff like grain or Motorola hi-fi sets. But as he stood in the large bank, feeling naked and exposed in the too white fluorescent light, all that didn't seem very real. Denny had the sinking feeling that other principles might apply here, monetary or other forces the clever writers of *Newsweek* might not have considered. He remembered a long-ago in-country briefing, something about GIs not being allowed to engage in the normal monetary transactions. They had scoffed at the time, jawing back and forth that in a country as corrupt as South Vietnam you probably could do anything you wanted if you had the money. And he had another sobering thought; if this deal fell through, there was no way he could explain how he had accumulated the damp bag of *My Kim* under his arm. He could see himself trying to explain it all to the spooks. He could see himself in jail, a very clear image.

He found the neat desk rows of clerks in spotless white shirts and ties intimidating. "Out of place," Denny thought. "I'm just a petty doper. My cash belongs in a shoebox, not a safe. . . ." He made up his mind to leave, but it was too late; as he turned, he bumped into a smooth-faced oriental in a light gray suit who had apparently moved in to intercept him. Or was he just being a little too overwrought? He fought to calm himself. It *seemed* okay. The man was all business. About forty-five years old, eyes blinking behind the latest Japanese imitation-French fashion, horn-rimmed glasses. "How may I be of assistance, sir?" Denny eyed him suspiciously. He looked like an owl of commerce, but you never could tell. The guy was between him and the door, or he would have bolted.

"I—uhh—I'd like to discuss opening an account with your bank."

"Very good, sir. Savings or checking?"

"Uhh—just savings, I think."

"Ahh-hah! Very good. New account. Come with me, sir."
He took Denny by the elbow, forcing him to shift the slicker-covered grocery bag to his other arm, and led him across the room. "This is my desk. Please seat yourself." The man lowered himself into a chair behind a wide desk. They were in the center of a large open area surrounded by a desk-high railing. Denny looked around as he slowly lowered himself into the chair. They were near a window from which the steel grill had been pulled back to let more light into the room and give it less of a jailhouse effect. Not ten feet away on the other side of the plate glass, street merchants squatted beside piles of mangoes, oranges, peanuts, and pineapples. Denny saw them soundlessly hawk their wares, the noise not traveling through the thick glass. They might as well have been in another country ten thousand miles away. And the front door was light-years away.

Denny didn't want to show his money in this place that was open to anyone who came in, as well as to the rows of clerks. He didn't realize no one had entered after him. And the few customers in the bank were gradually leaving one by one as they finished their business. It just didn't feel right, he couldn't exactly say why. "Don't you have anything more—more private?"

"Private, sir?" The Chinese executive raised his eyebrows slightly, examining his smooth fingernails with studious care. Denny couldn't get a reading off his broad expressionless face. "Please. Bear with us for one moment. We are perhaps not as efficient as your banks back in America."

Denny's eyes flicked around, wondering what he meant. All he saw was the backs and averted eyes of busy typists and paper shufflers. A younger man in a brown sharkskin suit appeared, and the two men conversed in rapid-fire Cantonese. Owl Eyes smoothly introduced the sharkskin as his assistant. Denny's heart thumped as he saw that both men were between himself and the front door. "Stay calm," his mind whispered. "Calm. Calm. *Calm.*" But he silently

cursed Toady, realizing for the first time that the events of
the day before had caused him to jump out of his little box
where it was safe.

On the other side of the plate glass window to his right,
the Saigon street traffic bustled along, oblivious to his feelings. He should have brought his gun—but how could he—it
was a bank in a war zone! First sight of a snub-nose and the
air would be thick with flying lead! It's gonna be okay, okay,
okay, he tried to tell himself.

The assistant nodded to Owl Eyes, gave Denny a thin little
smile, and went away to another desk, where he quickly got
on the phone. Owl Eyes also smiled at Denny, a professional
grimace that showed the nicotine-stained bottoms of his lower
teeth. Grinning chinks, Denny thought. Take note: remind
self to never trust a grinning chink.

"So," the man said after what seemed like an eternity,
"you wish to open an account with us."

"Yes, I already said that. Is that possible?"

The man shrugged. It could have meant anything. "You
are with the American military?"

Denny hesitated a moment, could think of no way to deny
it. "Yes."

"And you brought a deposit?" The eyes behind the thick
glasses flicked to the bulging slicker in Denny's hands.

"Yes. I—I can open an account, can't I? I mean, it is my
money. . . ."

"We must wait to talk to the office head. I am just the
manager." Owl Eyes pursed his lips and tapped his fingers
together, watching Denny with a completely expressionless
face. "How much do you wish to place with us?"

Out of the corner of his eye, Denny saw the sharkskin suit
dial another number. He was speaking urgently into the
phone. And then he saw the three shady-looking zips, grown-
up Saigon cowboys in cheap polyester suits. An unsavory-
looking trio in dark sunglasses, they took up loose positions
by the door, working their teeth with toothpicks and looking

everywhere but in his direction. Clerks were starting to leave their desks, casually drifting in twos and threes to a back room. The place was definitely starting to empty out.

The manager, seeing the direction of his gaze, gestured broadly with open hands and a smile Denny read as even more menacing. "Morning coffee break. We are very good to our people here."

Denny stood up. "I don't think so. That is, I think I'll come back another time."

"I think you should not try to go," the little owllike man warned, this time with a hint of steel in his voice.

And Mad Denny went into overdrive. The simple thought, "Banks are built to keep people out, not in!" rang in his mind like a clear bell. From the corner of his eye, he saw the three thugs moving in his direction. "We're not waiting for the spooks, or the QCs, or the MPs," he said calmly. "In fact, we're through waiting."

Dropping his slicker, he placed the wrinkled grocery bag on the edge of the desk nearest him. In one motion he lifted Owl Eye's heavy electric typewriter and hurled it at the nearby window. The plate glass exploded outward in a thousand shards and a clanging alarm went off overhead.

Then the little manager surprised him by executing an amazingly nimble dive across the desk. Denny just managed to jerk the money bag away as Owl Eyes slid by. Palm half open, Denny connected with a blow to the side of the chink's head. Then the thugs were coming fast and there was nothing left for him but to lunge blindly away after the typewriter. He pulled in his chin as his shoulder smashed through the long splinters of glass still hanging in the window frame. There was pain in his left arm, and then he was rolling through the glass and scattered produce on the sidewalk outside. The street vendors howled and slapped at him, but he had no time for formalities. The overgrown cowboys were already stepping gingerly through the window frame. He jerked to his feet and ran away, dodging through the heavy pedestrian traffic.

He ran until he crossed Tu Do Street, bouncing off a slow moving Renault's fender and upsetting an empty pedicab. The three were a half block behind him as he cut around the front of the Caravelle, heading for the PX and the Brinks BOQ where he might find some GIs and a little friendly firepower. A White Mouse cop idly watched him pass, a wild-haired young GI madly pounding along for no apparent reason. It was none of his business, and he casually turned and walked away. Let the MPs handle their own. The Americans meant nothing but trouble for everybody anyway.

3-5

But the PX was closed. Mad Denny stood gasping outside, one hand through the iron grillwork drawn across the entrance. "Help! Hey—anybody in there?"

A pretty Vietnamese girl looked up from her stocking chores, "You no read sign? C-wose now. Open in one hour."

"No, you don't understand! I've got to see the boss!"

She frowned as if he didn't understand English. "Bossman in back room, not want to be bother."

"Goddamn it, you cunt—this is an emergency!" He looked over his shoulder. The three pursuers had become six and were closing fast.

The little zip girl gave him an icy pout and used her best English, the proud result of four years of painful tongue twisting at the *Hoi Viet-My*. "You no have use bad talk. You have come back in hour. I aw-ready say so."

He slammed one fist against the grillwork, which rattled but was in no danger of opening, and left the PX, darting in and out between the tight phalange of cars packed in the open square. His followers saw he was going to try for the safety of the Brinks BOQ and neatly cut him off, leaving only the relatively native environs of Hai Ba Trung Street.

Cheap Charley's was still closed, so he pounded on past,

looking for any place a couple of GIs might be gathered. There was a light mist and the bag under his arm was getting soggy. He cursed himself for turning away from the river— he might have reached the Officers' Club if he'd gone the other way. The New York Bar was closed, and as he skidded past he narrowly avoided a gray stream of water flung from the doorway by a cleaning man.

Now he was pinched off from any of the really popular GI hangouts for five or six blocks . . . except for the new one, the Tuyet Lan off on his left. "Better the dragons we know . . ." he muttered under his breath in a hoarse gasp, and darted through a break in the traffic across the busy street and on into the dark doorway.

The Tuyet Lan too was deserted, except for a group of bar girls idly playing cards and chatting at one of the tables. Knowing the men to be right behind him, Denny dashed across the room and through a curtain of beads into the back room.

The bead strings wrapped around him, and his velocity pulled the rod holding them from the wooden door frame. Someone just inside the back room tripped him and he went down, skidding across the floor. And his worst fears were realized as the paper grocery bag broke open and wads of his money went flying all over the room. He was lifted and turned around by a thick-limbed Chinamen who smashed him across the face and then held him dazed and helpless in an armlock. "Wait," Denny cried out, gesturing toward the door behind him. "Wait! I'm just trying to get away!"

There was to be no easy escape. The doorway was filled with the first of the breathless thugs, who screamed in Vietnamese, "The dirty American stole our money! We must have it back!"

Denny went berserk. "Not after three years of work!" With an almost superhuman effort he broke out of the grasp of the big Chinamen. He lunged across the room and lashed out with a spinning kick that connected to send the cowboy slamming back against the wall. The man's cracked sun-glasses seemed to flake in bits and pieces off his blood-specked face as he slowly crumpled to the floor. Denny got the next one in through the door with a chop to the ribs followed by another hard-driven kick. But the reinforcements had arrived; one of them managed to catch Denny's leg and the four remaining cowboys swarmed him. Two of them pinned his arms, and the other two swung away. They might have done more damage, but in their impatience to do him harm they kept getting in each other's way.

Tuy watched intently for a moment while Denny took their punches, his head lolling from side to side. The outcome was obvious; they could kill him by inches. She snapped her fin-gers and motioned to the black Frenchman. "George." She nodded her head at the Chinaman. "Mako." The two men shrugged to one another as if to say, Who could explain their lady's motives? Their assignment wasn't very difficult, for the cowboys had focused all their attention on the American. George laid the first two out, *whap! whap!* with a short length of taped pipe. Mako kicked one in the balls, and the fourth left before anyone could lay a hand on him.

3-6

Denny stood in the center of the suddenly quiet room while what was left of the cowboys dragged themselves out. "Uhhh . . . thanks, I guess." He dropped to his knees and began to pick up the money. A sharp crack startled him. She had struck the table in front of her with a short leather riding crop. "Stack the money over here, Dennis."

Time stopped for him as he stared up at her. He noticed she was again wearing the traditional *ao dai*, this one of pale peach, and the short leather whip seemed oddly out of place in her small hands, even with what he knew of her. He sensed behind the revealing fabric of the light garment her slim and yet voluptuous figure hovering over him, the outlined perfect breasts, the gently flaring hips—"Number one bod in Nam!" Charley had raved, and Larkey had never disagreed.

The memory of those friends steeled him, and he slowly stood to face her. "I should have killed you," he said with a slight tremor in his voice. Mako, who knew the danger in the sounds men make, grabbed him from behind and held him helpless in a crushing headlock.

Tuy's voice rose. "Mako! Let him go!" She waited while he shook the ringing from his head before she spoke. "Dennis. Why do you think to kill me? I never did any harm to you."

"You murdered Larkey! I can't prove it, but I know you did!"

"That is a lie!" she cried, cracking her whip against a hand-painted vase on a small lacquered stand on a table nearby. The vase shattered into a hundred pieces, scattering over the floor. "I could not save him!"

"So you let him die!" he shouted, somehow intuitively guessing far more than she wanted him or any other person to know.

She denied it, as if denial could make it go away. "No! I could do nothing. I was just a girl. I was afraid. . . ."

"You were afraid to help—my friend died and you saved yourself!" He might have stopped there, for she was already hurt, stunned that anyone alive knew so much about her, but the fury was on him and the words rushed out of his mouth. "You probably killed Charley too somehow!"

Her face drained white, with two livid red spots remaining, one on either cheek. The whip cut him before he could even think to raise a hand. "Never even think that!" she shouted at him.

Denny's hand went to his face where the blood flowed freely. A little higher and she'd have taken out an eye. He muttered numbly. "I should have killed you when I had the chance."

Her lip curled. "You never had the chance. We have

watched you sulking around across the street like a common thief. You find me after years—that is my bad luck. I am trying to start again here, to forget the black karma which came to my life with your silly Dimbo Patrol, with the love I had for dear Charley—yes, *love*! Are you such a shallow human that you think a young bar girl cannot honestly love such a great and high person as a spec-four GI from Bayonne? Are you so unfeeling that you can't believe I suffer with the knowledge that, yes, I might have done something to save our friend Larkey? You weren't there! You don't know what I faced! You will never know." Her voice trembled, and she felt tears tumble unchecked down her flushed face. She had not felt so vulnerable with anyone since her Charley died, had not thought she would ever cry again.

"Easy tears," he sneered, shutting his mind from the possibility that any of what she said might be true. "But they are both dead."

"You have never made such a mistake."

"And killed a friend, a loved one? Never!"

"Pray to your God," she said in a small voice, "that you are always so lucky." The fact that he didn't believe her cut as deeply as if he had wielded the whip. She turned from him a moment, rocking back and forth on her feet. "All right. Don't believe me," she said softly, closing the doors hard on all that had so recently come flooding out. "Sit over there—" She gestured to a stool across from her desk. "—in the dunce's chair." He started to flare back at her but stopped midsentence when he saw the mulatto had him covered with what looked like a White Mouse issue .38 special. He watched furiously as Mako collected his money and set it in a damp little pile in front of Tuy.

"How much is here, Monsieur Dennis?" she asked him coldly.

"Twenty thousand six hundred dollars! It took me three years to earn!"

She nodded and then carefully counted out two little stacks

of three hundred dollars each, which she handed to her men. Denny's mouth twisted, but she stopped him with a wave of her hand. "You *owe* them; did they not save your foolish life?"

Had his world not been so crazy then, he would have agreed, but he was conscious of little but his pain and dizziness, and the best he could do was bite his tongue and say nothing. The room spun about him. The person he thought he hated more than any other sat calmly in a chair in front of him, her hands on his money, her perfect red lips going in and out of focus. "You owe me, too, monsieur. But I have a somewhat higher price."

"I'll die first!"

Tuy studied the battered young man who stood before her, remembering the times the Dimbos had descended on the old Cherry Bar, ready for "wild roaring times." Denny had always been the wildest, the crazy unpredictable one. Yet there had been an honesty about him, a pleasant simplicity that struck a responsive chord in her even back then. She thought he should be out in some cornfield in New Jersey or wherever the Americans had them, tractoring by day and living it up in the local beer bar at night with his buddies. She saw the deep bloody cut that she was responsible for on one cheek below his eye, which was puffed shut and colored deep maroon. She sighed. "Don't compliment yourself so. What you think is an insult to me. I am interested in your money only, your 'twenty big ones,' as your American detective novels so colorfully describe it."

"No!" he shouted. "Nothing!" She was a living nightmare; she hovered in the center of his consciousness like a lady spider in a pastel disguise. He had to get away, away, away. . . .

She looked up from the money, and the pretty little bar girl who had been used such a short time ago by his friends was far away. "I'm not asking, Dennis," she said quietly. "We are going to make a deal. A business deal."

"You take my money—that's some deal!"

"I *would* take it . . . from anyone else." Her voice dropped until he wasn't sure he heard her correctly. "You will not understand me, but you and I are . . . tied by blood, old blood, blood other than that on your face. . . . I do not know where it will lead us, but you cannot escape it. And neither can I."

In his rage he couldn't get past the money part. "Sure, *trust* you—I'll never see you again!"

Had he been in any condition to notice, he might have seen he'd gotten to her again. There was a long silent pause. Tuy finally expelled a sharp breath and continued in a carefully controlled voice. "I wish that were true. The venture—*our* venture—has a risk, the nature of which is not your concern. Barring that difficulty, your precious *My Kim* . . . will increase."

She looked down at her hands, which were crossed over the money, her attention on the dark red ring on her finger; she finally looked up, giving him a long uncertain stare. He knew in that moment that he had said too much, and was sure she was thinking how dangerous it might be to let him live. Suddenly she nodded and gave him a little smile. To Denny it looked as if she had made up her mind as easily as deciding whether to have iced crab or hot *pho ga*, chicken noodle soup, for lunch. She motioned him to the door. "You are not welcome here for six weeks. After that . . ." Her voice trailed off and she shrugged. Mako and George rose to see him out.

He found himself back on Hai Ba Trung, under a dark sky that was beginning to dribble rain. Blood coated the left half of his face and soaked his sleeve on the same side. He couldn't see out of one eye, and his chest felt as if he had some broken ribs.

A skinny ten-year-old newsboy rushed up to him, a stack of plastic-wrapped *Viet-Viet* dailies under his arm. "Hey, GI, you beat up plenty bad! You say wrong thing to pretty *co-*

gai?'' Denny waved him off and turned away, but the kid came after him like a sticky fly. ''Hey-*hey*, GI—you no want to pull own pud, you like good girl? Go sucky-sucky fucky-fucky, plenty good all day, all night!''

''Xau nguoi nam!—ugly Vietnamese'' Denny thundered, swinging wildly with a clumsy fist. He missed by a mile, and the kid went skittering away, yelling the usual street garbage. Denny shook his head in a hopeless attempt to clear his rage and confusion, and then limped on down Hai Ba Trung toward the river, wondering exactly what had happened and what he could possibly do about it. All this had taken place . . . his money was gone and his life was changed, and he still had a half hour before the time he'd said he'd meet Brownstone at the Royal.

CHAPTER FOUR

4-1

DOOLY WAS ACTUALLY ONLY A SO-SO SPOOK, IN TERMS OF
what his agency would call success or accomplishment. His
real name was Patrick J. Dooly, but everybody just called
him Dooly. The army had been his home ever since he graduated with a liberal arts major and a C+ average from a
small Ohio college in 1955. More than a home, the one to
three year rollover existence had become his way of life; he
moved from tour to tour quietly, thankful he was without the
snarly baggage of a family to complicate his ways. He didn't
miss kids, having come from a packed Irish household of
ten, and sex was casual, easy, and dirt cheap even in a place
like Nam, where you couldn't get it free from other guy's
wives. He was an E-7, a staff sergeant, but he really didn't
have a staff. He operated, as much as possible, entirely alone.
That was the way he liked it, and that was the only way they
liked him to do it.

Dooly was tall, with a lumpy potato face, sandy hair receding over his temples, and skin that never knew a tan,
going from Idaho white to lobster red at a glance from the
torrid tropical sun. He stood six foot six in his tattered black
socks, which he patched himself when they got holes. Looming as he did over the locals, the embarrassment of his life
was the frequency with which he popped up in the background of news photos printed around the world. If one were
to take a magnifying glass to the famous photos taken by
Malcolm Browne of the Vietnamese Buddhist monk Thich

Quang Duc immolating himself in the middle of Le Van
Duyet Street, Dooly's somewhat plumpish potato face can
be seen just to the right of the traffic light in front of the Tan
Tao bike shop. He's wearing the uniform of a naval officer.
There is a shot of a jubilant crowd of Vietnamese wheeling
the statue head of Madame Nhu through the streets of Saigon
after Ngo Dinh Diem was overthrown that has a fuzzy image
of a tall caucasian who looked suspiciously like Dooly lurking in a dark doorway. There is another shot of the crowds
on Hai Ba Trung gawking at the remains of the Brinks BOQ
the morning after its infamous blast that has a clear picture
of the top third of a Mr. Potato Head intently maneuvering
behind the close-packed natives. And much to the chagrin of
the agency, he is all over press photos taken of the blood-
and-flesh-spattered street scene after an old Citroën loaded
with ep plastic went up outside the U.S. Embassy on
March 30, 1965.

Nothing seemed to help. They had him brush up on his
invisibility, threatened reassignment, begged him to slouch
and wear low-heeled shoes. Dooly remained himself
throughout and got the reputation of a dependable, straight-
minded, slow-talking, awkward gink of a fellow who was
totally unpromotable. He had studied the Vietnamese language so long ago it had then been considered a punishment,
a go-nowhere discipline leading to a backwater outpost. And
as the war flourished and bloomed, he had plugged away
while others rushed in, got the promotions and the pats on
the back, and then rushed on to other flashy assignments
around the world where peace and democracy the U.S.A.
way were in peril.

The agency-encouraged assassination of Diem, so filled
with promise at the time, had left the Saigon government
without a strong man, and the series of shake-ups that followed weakened confidence and public trust on both sides
of the ocean. Whenever the agency was looking for a fall
guy, somehow a batch of long lens shots of a Buddhist riot

or attempted internal coup would crop up with red ink circling Dooly's round potato head sticking out over the natives. Dooly worked the streets, others wrote the reports, and Dooly took the falls.

So there he was, after three tours in and out, back in Saigon, still E-7 and still on the streets. With the war now in high gear and so much going on, Dooly never allowed himself to believe the obvious, that he was batting cleanup on the second string. He got the odd little jobs, even occasionally a little spook stuff, stuff he had convinced himself was too delicate for the ordinary spooks who jetted in and out on a per-assignment basis and didn't really even know the language or the local scene.

Now he sat with his long feet up on the CO's desk, looking amiably around at the Thirty-third RRU's little staff, who had gathered to discuss their problem with him. He picked the white flaky stuff from the eyebrow over his left eye—he'd caught some kind of rot and his hair caked up with maddening regularity with something he called "superdandruff." "You guys got to get one thing straight, first off, okay?" he said, eyeing each of them with a bland friendly smile. "I ain't a spook."

"Sure, right, Dooly," Anderson quickly replied, winking at his guys.

But the man from the agency caught the gesture and was not to be a part of it. "Hey now, look, I don't want to embarrass anybody, but I'm serious. If there is any such thing as a 'spook' or a 'spook branch' of the agency, I don't know anything about it."

"Of course," the captain agreed. "Like you say, the agency is just interested in our little problem, and they sent you to give us a hand."

"I don't know what agency you are referring to," Dooly said with another small smile, inspecting an unusually large white flake of skin with a half dozen of his eyebrow hairs in it. "But it doesn't matter. When I show up here, I'll park

my Jeep about a block or so down the road outside the compound. I'll always wear civvies, casual. Just another civilian
contractor. You spread the rumor your company is in line for
new barracks, and I'm the guy who got in low bid. Got it?''

"Yeah. Neat!" Animal breathed enthusiastically, grinning
at Toady. C-I-A! This was the real stuff!

"Neat," Dooly repeated dryly, dismissing the stubby little
clerk and his zit-faced pal with a bored look. "Neat it is not.
You realize we're fighting a war, and creeps like this Insane
Denny or whatever you call him are cutting Uncle Sam off at
the knees. I'm sorry, but dopers make me real ugly. This guy
ought to have his face ripped off, he ought to have an accident
or something. . . ." He looked from face to face, and without
having to say another word, they got the idea they were guilty
of not handling their own little problem, of having to call a
professional in for a job that was hardly worth the time.

Animal's face lit up. "Hey, an *accident*! Not a bad way to
go. . . ."

Dooly silenced him with an icy stare. "No one here actually *recommended* a course of action."

"I—I just meant, if all else failed, I mean, if an accident
happened, well—that would have solved our problem. . . ."

Dooly nodded, a good idea planted. You never knew when
it might spring up and make all their lives a little simpler.
He bent over the wastebasket and gave full attention to scrubbing his hair with the nails of both hands. Anderson, who
was sitting closest to him, had a little twinge of revulsion as
a minor flurry of gray-white flakes drifted down in the general vicinity of the basket. "Goddamn stinkin' wet . . ."
Dooly muttered without real violence, as if he had said the
words a million times. "White man wasn't meant to live in
this fuckin' rat hole." He saw they were all watching him
and felt he had to explain. "Doctors tell me it ain't catching—they gave me some new stuff supposed to help." He
waved a small tube of ointment from his pocket, then
squeezed a half inch of white paste on his finger and rubbed

it in the raw area over his eye. "Okay. Now, short of some accident—which I never heard about—what's our plan of attack?"

Captain Anderson opened a thick file on his desk. "We've got nothing but hearsay to go by. We got a couple of the men drunk the night before they were shipping out. No big deal, we try to do that with everybody. They had nothing to lose by blabbing, if you know what I mean, and they claimed you could get anything from Haller."

Animal nodded. "I'm tellin' you, he's the original Ugly American, I know from my own—ahh, investigation."

Dooly, who might have gotten a hint of Animal's own weakness for hash, picked up immediately on the wrong thread. "Anybody ever call him that? 'Ugly American?' "

Toady sneered. "Only everybody who meets him."

"No, no—I mean *zips*. Any zips call him *Cai Xau My*?"

The captain shook his head. "I dunno—we don't speak good gook."

"Yeah," Animal added. "In fact, none at all."

Toady figured Mad Denny had run through any chances he had to be redeemed. The man deserved to be put away so more people wouldn't be hurt, and he didn't even have to think about it as the words popped right out of his mouth. "I heard gooks call him that—lots."

"Where? When?"

"Uhhh—you know. Downtown, around here. He pisses people off real easy. Everybody I know calls him that . . . how did you pronounce it? I can *say* it, I just can't pronounce it."

"*Cai Xau My*. Boy, I'd like to get my hands on him!"

Toady nodded. "Yep, that's what they call him all right!"

Dooly didn't really know what to think. On the one hand, the description didn't quite fit. The big dealer whose whispered name was The Ugly American had huge sums of cash at his disposal, and it was assumed he was an officer—but then again this Insane Denny was an old-timer and maybe, just maybe . . . Dooly saw visions of a giant bust, himself the guy in charge, a bit of sweetness for the years he'd spent handling the no-headline grimble. He hoped his excitement didn't show. He spread his hands wide, as if to ask what the problem was. "So—if you can get anything from the *Xau My*, how does he do it?"

Animal's hand shot up like a bright sophomore in biology class. "Network of gooks, sir—cleaning ladies, barracks boys, linen girls, soapers from mess. He's slick—you give him the money and a couple of hours later some gook drops the stuff off—"

"Dink," Dooly corrected.

"Beg pardon?" Animal said, completely bewildered.

"You keep calling them gooks. They're dinks or zips. You wouldn't call a slope-eye a dago."

"No . . . I guess not. . . ."

"Okay. It doesn't matter." Dooly looked at his watch. Three o'clock already. He was going to miss his afternoon lay if he didn't hurry. He looked at the captain. "Bring the hired help in one by one, all of them. Hit 'em hard. Threats—family, jail, anything you can think of. See if anybody cracks. Then we'll get 'em working for us, catch this guy with his pants down—in the act, you know?"

"But won't Denny get wind of it?"

"Not if somebody assigns him somewhere. Don't you have little missions or something that takes them out in the bush?" Dooly knew as well as Anderson, having read the reports on the Thirty-third, that three-man radio intercept teams routinely were trucked out from Tan Son Nhut to set up mobile listening posts anywhere from the delta to the DMZ. Although trained linguist-cryptographers rarely went along, it did happen.

Toady jumped at the thought. "I could juggle the rosters, sir—send a few too many on R and R so we come up short-handed!"

Captain Anderson nodded. It felt right to him. "Oooo-kay. And how about his work area? Can you handle that, Sergeant Dooly?"

"Yep. Leave it to me." Dooly spoke in a clipped, super-confident tone. That was intelligence, his beat. He didn't want anyone to question his clearance, which in fact was secret, a gray badge he carried in a small inside pants pocket next to his crotch, a badge mostly good in the streets to keep other operatives from popping him off. He felt he probably wouldn't have any trouble getting cooperation from the chaps in the White Shack. It was nobody's business a green badge was as far out of his reach as a pair of angel's wings. "No other questions?" he said, getting up as he spoke. "Good, well I'll be in touch."

Five minutes later he had hopped in his Jeep and was roaring back downtown, hoping he hadn't missed his appointment. About half the day shift of the Thirty-third and all the hired help had seen the puffy, red-faced guy wearing a gaudy Hawaiian shirt cinched in his white civvy pants with a brass-buckled olive green army issue belt. One of the little laundry girls staggered out the guard gate, walking bent under the too huge bag of soiled clothes on her shoulder until she saw Dooly get in his Jeep, start it up, and drive away. And so by two P.M. that afternoon, a few minutes after Ong Den-ny limped back from town, he already knew that his CO had called in the spooks. Perhaps because he had so much else on his mind at the time, he chose not to worry about it. And that was a mistake . . . for, as any Vietnamese will tell you, a hundred rats can bring down a tiger.

4-2

A few kilometers to the north of the broad fertile delta through which flows the muddy slow water of the Mekong, and so far west that it juts into Cambodia like an irritable little spike, is the southern Vietnamese province of Tay Ninh. This strategic chunk of land runs from the Mekong delta rice lands into the foothills of the Annamese mountain chain. It is a place of swamps, paddies, buffalo grass high as a man, rain forest, scrub brush hills, and war.

Tay Ninh is important because it is the end of the Ho Chi Minh Trail. Saigon is less than one hundred kilometers to the east, while to the south the flat, rich rice lands stretch on away to a hazy horizon and beyond that to the South China Sea.

Mad Denny was heading there for a week of radio research and other camping fun. It was July, approaching that time of the year known to westerners as "the heart of the wet" and a month after Denny had unwillingly become Tuy's partner. The cut on his cheek had healed to a flaming red line, and the rest of his bruises were mostly memories. The night before, his staff had done the town, a staggering merry round of their favorite bars that had ended at the old Chez Rene whorehouse in Gia Dinh.

Now it was morning, and the brilliant sun glanced down through bulging white cumulus clouds that seemed to grow larger and more menacing while they waited. He and Doober Hayes sat on gray folding chairs just inside the deep shade of a hangar, caps pulled low over their eyes, wincing as the jets lifted off from the Tan Son Nhut runway. They were in olive jungle fatigues and had their weapons and feet up on their duffel bags. Denny had an M16 that he had conned out of Weird, as well as the M79 grenade launcher and five or six rounds tucked away in his bag. Doober, who looked about as out of place as a cocker spaniel police dog, had the standard issue M14. He didn't think he'd have to use it. He studied his surroundings, as he did everything, with his serious brown eyes peering from behind thick glasses. He sniffed constantly, trying to suck enough of the heavy air in through breathing passages clogged by allergies.

The other Dimbos, Brownstone and Finegold, had dropped by in civvies to see them off, on their way up the runway to catch the navy bus. They had told a few bad jokes, patted each other nervously on the shoulders, agreed to hoist a Ba Muoi Ba together when they got back. But they had to run to catch the bus, and now there was nothing but the slow grinding hours until their helicopter jump showed up.

Someone pushed Doober roughly. "Hey geeks—you're sitting in our chairs!" He was a big-shouldered guy with wavy hair and tailored fatigues. He had a photographer in tow, a little European-looking guy dressed in tight-fitting khaki shorts and an olive-colored T-shirt that showed the scrawn in his body. The big one took a fistful of Doober's sleeve. "Had a big press briefing in here about an hour ago. Myself and Dominique here *saved* these chairs."

Denny squinted up at the two newcomers, at the same time putting a restraining hand on Doober, who had started to get up. "Fuck off, piss-pens." If there was one group of people he hated as much as lifers, it was war correspondents. The one who had Doober's shirt started to say something; but his companion, who read nothing but trouble in Denny's savage look, intervened.

"Come, come, *mon ami*—I really would like a cup of coffee anyhow."

"Fuckhead . . ." the big guy muttered over his shoulder as they moved off. He should have realized there were not that many flights going anywhere that morning; a few hours later on board the Huey he found himself shifting uncomfortably in the seat next to Denny as they waited for the pilot.

He was Phil Darby, a few years out of Yale, with press credentials from *Playboy*, for which he had done a few free-lance articles. His slender companion, Dominique Carré, was building a photo collection he hoped would one day grace modern art museums in Europe and America, as well as become an expensive coffee-table book. Dominique had unslung the cameras from around his neck, and was showing Phil a sheaf of 8×10 black and whites from his knapsack. Crammed in next to Phil, Denny looked over his arm at photos of naked corpses, of peasants with blindfolds over their eyes being dragged along by faceless soldiers, of hopeless wrinkled old women, of plump GIs in a rice paddy newly landed and suddenly wary like quail before the hunter. Phil

chatted with Dominique as if the others didn't exist. "Bitchin'
stuff, buddy—just bitchin'!''

The little Frenchman glowed. "Week last, I was with a patrol that was hit bad," Dominique said, happy with his luck in
getting such rare shots and in getting out alive. "Look at these!"
He proudly pulled another wad of 8×10s out of his pack. Action shots of the same group of plump GIs Denny saw in the
first pile. Men running, firing over waist-high grass from standing positions. The same men on their bellies as the fire is
returned. Distant smoke from a line of trees, the GIs getting
artillary support. Smoke from a close explosion. A man down,
writhing. A series of shots of this man. He is black, looks about
eighteen. Different angles. Pain. Blood spattering the black
man's pants. Blood on his hands. Blood on the grass
around him. Shock angle, close-up: He has no legs. Another angle, extra-close-up: his doomed eyes.

Denny reached over and took the last shot from Phil's
hand. "He step on a mine?"

Dominique nodded, his eyes shining. "It almost got me!
One step either way, *KAPOOM!* And such a sequence of
shots! Monsieur, for me, this is the real war, the real tragedy
of Vietnam! He will never see the VC, the ones his masters
have told him are victimizing the South Vietnamese—yet this
poor black man, a victim in his own country, becomes even
more a victim when he leaves to serve it, paying the ultimate
sacrifice in an ultimately stupid war!''

Denny looked more closely at the photograph. The
wounded man's glazed eyes stared back at him in shock and
horror, and Denny knew he realized his legs were gone. He
had a sudden thought. "You sure this man died?"

"*Mais, oui*—but of course. He bled to death in minutes. His
life came pumping out—so fast! Fffft—like that! It was almost
one half hour until the medevac chopper would come in.''

"What did you do?"

"I filmed it all! We were pinned down—I was the only
one who risked to move around. The men could not believe

it—they said after, that I actually stood up in fire to get better angles! I could not believe what they said that I was so brave, I do not accept that what I did was heroic at all . . . yet, I was not afraid in the slightest. All I knew at the time, it was of the greatest importance. I am a photographer, I have a special sense for it. At that moment, I was with a sense of lightness, of knowing the need of capturing the essence of what I saw and heard and felt on film; I do not think a true firefight has been photographed in this way before . . . if so, I have not seen it.''

"Didn't you ever hear of a tourniquet?''

Dominique's face took on a look of baffled surprise. "You mean that I—?'' He couldn't finish his own sentence.

Phil tried to snatch the picture from Denny. "I think you better give me that!''

Denny easily held it away from him and looked steadily at Dominique. "Did you even try?''

"*Mais*—it was not that way! There, it is all confusion and gun cracks! And I am not a medic! I could do nothing for *him*! I do not know those things!'' There was a long pause. Taking Denny's silent gaze for condemnation, the young Frenchman's tone became tinged with outrage. "You—you were not there! Who are you to—to look at me like that, to attempt to judge me?''

"Just one person, like you—only I don't have five million readers.'' Denny slowly crumpled the still photo into a little ball. He threw it across the aisle, where it popped against Dominique's forehead and fell to the floor. "You're the fuckhead. You and Fuckhead sitting next to me here.'' The Huey engine coughed to life, and the blade spun over their heads. In five minutes the helicopter was lifting off toward the ominous dark-bellied clouds above, carrying them away to war.

Captain Anderson watched from his office window as the helicopter came into view over the rim of the wooden fence surrounding the Thirty-third. He'd had words with Denny a week ago, when the young man learned he and Doober Hayes were being assigned to check out one of the hot new portable receivers just in from the states. Anderson wasn't in charge of the covert listening operations, so it was about the only thing he could think of.

The CO still wasn't quite sure how Denny did it, but the conversation had moved swiftly and unerringly from the assignment at hand (which Denny had shredded with a sentence: "How do you test new equipment in the wet, when the earphones just form little barrels of static around your ears?"), to possible reasons for the assignment that he saw as a punishment for petty offenses, to Anderson's own career (evaluated in not very complimentary terms). By the time Haller was ready to leave a few minutes later, Anderson was shaking with rage. In the old-time army he had joined in the '50s, a troublemaker like that would be doing time on the rockpile at Leavenworth. The way they did it in Korea was to let the guy take point until he got religion or got blown away. That would work here in Nam, too, but getting Denny out in the bush was a fluke, and they really didn't move around at all, just sat and listened at one location. . . .

Anderson thought about that for a while. In fact, he stayed up most of the night thinking, alternately cursing the rain, which was gusting in from a direction that wet his sheets, and his stomach, which was burning from the half bottle of Jim Beam he had gulped down since evening mess.

He made a few important decisions. First, he decided Spec-five Dennis Haller was a disgrace to the uniform he wore and a disruptive force to the company. Hence, he was a hindrance to the war effort. As such he was expendable. Also, anyone who associated with him was just as worthless, though Haller was obviously the ringleader. So the Dimbos were expendable, any or all of them. They would continue with Dooly-the-Spook's little plans, but war was a funny thing, an unpredictable affair where so many things could not be taken for granted . . . even the simplest things, like life and limb.

Captain Anderson had a best buddy in Nam, a good ol'
army guy. The two of them had drunk and whored on every
continent on earth except Antarctica, and they expected to
get there too if they lived long enough. They were more than
drinking buddies—for a week they had shared a winter foxhole with rotting corpses surrounded by jabbering Chinese
and North Koreans and lived to tell the tale, had been best
buddies at one another's wedding, and Anderson was in fact
godfather to the guy's oldest kid. This best buddy was a major
and had an artillery unit that covered part of Tay Ninh. For
over five years, off and on, the Thirty-third had been staking
a tent on the hilltop where Haller and Hayes would be camping out. Artillery knew where that tent would be, to within
a couple of feet. They had to; they'd been called on for support any number of times.

As soon as the departing Huey was lost to view behind the
high wooden fence, Anderson rang his old buddy on the
phone. He talked earnestly, pouring his heart out for over
twenty minutes.

4-3

These are times one remembers from the wet
in the long gray days of the city,
Haunting singsong snatches
of an almost-human alien tongue.
The beat beat beat of the raindrops
on rust-weakened sheet tin roofs.
The hiss and splash of traffic.
High-pitched call, the Old *Ba* Soup Lady,
Calling *phooooo, phoooo, phooooo*.
Thin old pedicyclist under his rain slicker
hurries along, eager for fares
and perhaps a hot cup
nuoc café, avec sucre.
The sidewalk vendors folded and gone,
wares stored in doorways

or carried under shelter somewhere.
Orphan kids in doorways
nowhere else to go.
White Mouse cops in doorways, too
trying to keep their white pants
from the splash of passing autos.

"Whatcha doin', Doober?" Denny asked. He looked up from the radio, which he had set up in his corner of the big army tent.

Doober quickly turned over the page of his notebook; he didn't want any of the guys to know he kept a journal of impressions, and wrote freestyle poetry that occasionally got published when it wasn't about the war. "Uhh—just writing a letter back home . . . how's the radio?"

Denny ripped the earphone jack from its socket and gave him a sarcastic look. "I tell ya, Doober, I'm about done for the week. Works *just great* out here in the middle of an uckin-fay yphoon-tay." He gave the receiver a ringing slap. The set, on which Anderson had put a price tag of fourteen grand, squealed in protest, letting out a long static squawk. "It speaks! Oh, Guido, what have we created here?"

"Nozzing, master. I theenk we must find different way to create life."

Denny plugged the earphones back in so they wouldn't have to listen to the endless static mixed with bits of weather-garbled transmission. "You're right, Doober," he sighed. He gazed out the open tent flap at little dribbles of rainwater spilling off the fabric, and a whole series of thoughts popped unbidden into his head. "Why did you extend, Mad Denny? You're not creating life out here. An even better question: Why did you extend the second time? Are you becoming that which you despise? Are you becoming an army lifer?" Doober, he knew, made him think like this; Doober Hayes, so serious, so methodical, wheezing his way through Nam with his head buried in the Vietnamese classic *Kim Van Kieu*, looking like a round-faced sixteen-year-old behind those huge, too-thick glasses. The Dimbos were used to Doober ducking his poetry out of sight. They had agreed among themselves that it was strictly personal. They'd also had a hot discussion about just what percentage of poets were fags; the Dimbos ended up agreeing Shelley and Keats and T. S. Eliot probably were, and Robert W. Service, Rudyard Kipling, and Doober Hayes certainly were not.

Doober looked mildly out the tent flap at the sweeping veils of gray rain that could be seen moving across the heavily overgrown green valley below them. "Well, Ong Den, such being the case, my vital mission completed here on the western tip of Nam, can I go home now?"

"Well, no, Specialist Hayes, we can't exactly do that for you. You see, your assignment is for a *one-week* camping trip. You must learn how to build the bonfire. How to identify rare birds and other incoming whistles. Never to crap uphill. How to shave with a sharp stick, also a weapon when that M14 jams, which it surely will."

"Hmmm. Sounds grim. . . . What do we do for recreation?"

"Ahh, I'm glad you got to that part! There are many diversions here in southwest South Vietnam—"

"In Southeast Asia."

"Don't interrupt while I'm lecturing."

"Sorry. It was so interesting I couldn't help myself."

"That's all right. For fun and sport, we have the buttfucking of wild gazelles, which one must first catch, leaping naked through the jungle flora."

"Hmmm . . . I've always voted *for* bugamy, but it is storming out there."

"Wellllll, we could hike on down yonder muddy road and spend the night at Anna's Bar and Roadhouse just outside Tay Ninh."

"You're serious?" Doober brightened at the prospect, but then got worried again. "What if Anderson calls us?"

"Asshole wouldn't know how. And if he did ever figure it out, we wouldn't hear it anyway—all I got the whole afternoon was snap, crackle, and pop. . . . *Believe* me, we're on our own out here."

Denny was already pulling his boots on. He had no qualms about leaving the exotic radio receiver-recorder-transmitter out in the bush. He just didn't ive-gay an uck-fay, as he would have said. He did switch on the deadfall incendiary, which would torch the set if anyone who didn't know the defuse code tried to use it. Then he stuffed an extra few grenades in his pockets, put on his slicker, slung his M16 and M79 over his shoulder, and started down the hill.

As he slogged on down the muddy path with Doober wheezing and sniffing behind him, he thought over the odd help he'd been getting from the support group in Tay Ninh. The captain of the group had insisted on sending a squad to help the two men from the Thirty-third set up camp. And the squad had insisted on setting up their tent in exactly the same location it had been before . . . in fact the old stakes were still in place, and they simply strung the loops and tightened up the wires. Denny wasn't used to all the help. He had camped out here several times in the last few years and had always been allowed to struggle the five miles from Tay Ninh up the muddy hill road by himself, to find his own impression of where his rural quarters should be placed.

On casual inquiry, Denny learned from the helpful squad leader that the Thirty-third's CO had called the day before, requesting assistance in getting his men set up on that precise location for their radio testing. It wasn't that Denny was a superstitious man, but when he heard Captain Anderson had acted in his behalf, he got shivers up and down his spine that could not be blamed on the weather.

Anna's Bar was a big smoke-filled room packed with noisy GIs. Denny had been there before, in the early sixties when a glass of Ba Muoi Ba with a lump of ice in it cost five piasters. Back then it had been a rustic watering hole plus, where the local village self-defense units and the VC could set aside the war for a couple of hours and rub shoulders over a beer, no questions asked, and where the occasional American was a center of attention. Now there was lukewarm Schlitz at a buck a can, and the girls hustling a brisk trade for the little rooms in back cost a small fortune. The locals, who couldn't afford the good times, had probably taken their trade elsewhere, if beer trucks still braved the journey out from the capital. Denny toyed with the idea of hiking around a bit and seeing if they could find a place that wasn't so much like the ordinary Stateside off-base beer hall, but the weather was stiffening, and he didn't really feel like heading out into it again.

Money, of course, was no problem for Mad Denny. Resolving once and for all not to be nostalgic for the good old days, he sat back and tried to enjoy a few beers while a portable radio carrying Air Force Saigon blared "Wooly Bully" and "Mister Tambourine Man." Doober became somewhat of a minor personality when it became known that he spoke Vietnamese, and he cheerfully acted as go-between for a rowdy crowd of Seabees who wanted to teach the girls their high school football cheers. But Denny drank alone, isolated within the shouting and beery laughter and the Turtles singing "Happy Together" and the Rolling Stones doing a rowdy version of "Let's Spend the Night Together."

He found himself thinking about Tuy. He had been one hundred percent about her, so sure she'd been responsible for Larkey's death—Christ, the poor slob had been found dead on the front steps of the little house she'd rented in Gia Dinh! But when he accused her, her reaction wasn't a simple one that he could read and say, "Aha, I'm right, she did it!" He had accused her of murder; she had admitted cowardice. And that fear, her fear for her own life, had contributed to Larkey's death . . . she had as much as admitted that, too. But that wasn't the same thing as killing the guy. Was Dominique the photographer responsible for the black with the blown-off legs? He could have tried to help, but maybe the guy would have died anyway.

What was it that Tuy had said to him? "Pray to your God you are always so lucky, to never, never make such a mistake." So she thought about it then, she realized what she had done. Whether she loved Larkey or not, his death wasn't a little thing with her.

Denny could follow all that. What had started him thinking this way wasn't the fact that she had his money—it was the way she'd cut him when he'd mentioned Charley. He shook his head, remembering how he'd behaved. It wasn't enough he accused her of Larkey, he'd actually blamed her for Charley's death. Charley'd had the ill fortune to come to the attention of a VC squad while he was radio researching the bush, just as he and Doober were supposed to be. Tuy had been hundreds of clicks away at the time.

Denny now believed Tuy had loved Charley; nobody could fake that instant reaction. He smiled, fingering the scar on his cheek and remembering how lovable all the girls had found his friend. They all teased Charley, they said they wanted to give him a little *em* with big brown eyes and dark curly hair like he had . . . and they meant it, too. He *wanted* to believe Tuy had loved the guy, for Charley and he had always been very close. Thinking back, he remembered resenting the way Larkey moved in on her. Sure, she was a common bar girl back then, but the whole thing felt cheap, and he had held Larkey responsible. Larkey, on the other hand, had shrugged the whole thing off. "For Christ's sake, Ong Den, she's available and she accepts me—what are you asking me to do?" Denny had been close to popping him in the face with a fast left. And he *had* gotten into a full-blown punch-out with Larkey about a week after that . . . a fight over Tuy. Were his emotions really so pure back then? He saw an image of himself raring back to let go with the wild one that was to bloody Larkey's nose before the rest of the old Dimbos could move in to pull them off one another. No, he was jealous of Larkey, he could see it now. Jealous the pudgy Texas loudmouth had that sweet round face, those perfect tulip lips, those delicate full breasts and sweet thighs all to himself.

Nobody realized at that time what bad news she really was. Then Larkey had learned; it had cost his life. And now he, Spec-five Mad Dennis Haller too had learned; but the lesson had only cost his bankroll. He ordered another warm Schlitz and wondered if he would ever see that money again. If I don't, he thought in a dreamy beery way, I'll off her. But he didn't believe it. He didn't kill for money, not even for his own.

The hour grew late and the crowds thinned, and he managed to negotiate a decent deal for the rest of the night for a couple of rooms and two of the girls who didn't look like Saigon retreads. But once in the little room, sleep wouldn't come, and he couldn't get interested in the girl. She carried on that she wasn't doing her job and so wouldn't get paid, until he had to get up and fish around by the light of a flashlight for ten dollars *My Kim.* "It's the war," he said, by way of explanation. "I am sad and I just can't." He lay next to her on the damp mattress so close their arms touched, sharing a joint he'd brought along. The rain beat on the tiles of the roof overhead and bodies and occasional snatches of conversation could be heard through the thin partition walls separating the rooms. The smoke was powerful stuff, but it wasn't able to penetrate all the beers he'd downed, and so he found no enlightenment or instant insights. The long night wore on, and he thought more of Tuy.

And that is how it came to pass that Denny Haller and Doober Hayes were warm and dry—and six miles away— when three stray rounds of incoming obliterated the space where they were supposed to be on that windblown rainy night in the summer of 1967.

4-4

It was to be a day built out of three or four different jigsaw puzzles, an impossible sort of day when everything looked great, but nothing really could be relied on to fit. It started out well enough; the sun came up in the heart of the wet, shining down on the unbelieving damp vegetation with a hot yellow glare that had steam rising from fields and hillsides, moisture that didn't know where to go and so hung in the air as visible wisps. The huge clouds towered all about, sure this was some momentary joke to be played on the waterlogged mortals below, a cruel game masterminded by the gods of wind and thunder to give the little earthlings a peep at a blue sky before they would be forced to endure more endless days of gray. But the hours went by and it was nearly noon, and still they waited, huge glowering thunderheads over the hills to the north of Tay Ninh and a high wall with puffy ramparts to the southwest out over the Gulf of Siam.

Doober Hayes reached for his glasses at about eleven. With all the beers he'd had, his head should have been splitting—but he felt great. The girl he'd spent the night with had been young and silly and very good. She had fit his mood, and they had giggled and whispered the night away. Mad Denny yelling at them to ''For od-Gay's ake-say shut the uck-fay up!'' had sent them into spasms of laughter and Denny had been forced to give up with a long grumble that just caused another round of giggles.

The girl was on her feet and around hours before Doober woke, and by the time he finally did get to a sitting position to try and clear his nose with a few sniffs of Vicks spray, she came back for another round of lovemaking, just to show him he really was appreciated. So it was close to noon when he wandered out to the big front room of Anna's, all mellowed out and looking forward to a great day.

The chairs were up on the tables, and an old man swabbed the splintery wood floor with a mop while two of the girls rinsed glasses behind the bar. The place smelled a bit of stale beer, but all the windows were tilted open to let in some air, and Doober couldn't have cared anyway; he was on top of the world.

Denny was sitting over a hot cup of strong black *nuoc café*, a cigarette hanging limply from one of his hands, which seemed to be shaking. Doober gave him a little frown. ''Thought you gave up smoking—regular tobacco, that is. . . .''

Denny looked up at him with a pained expression that told everything. ''Oh my God, if it isn't the all-night giggler! A guy like you would drive a person to alcohol—however, as I'm already well on my way to life as a drunk, I thought I'd take up a different vice.''

''Death warmed over, that's what you look like.''

''My, yes. That's the way it feels.''

Doober's girl brought two steaming bowls of *pho tom*, the tasty noodles floating around dozens of pink river shrimp. For a moment Denny thought he was going to get some, but the girl took Doober's arm and they went off to a corner together where they soon were chopsticking and chattering away with the bowls held under their chins in the slurping style that is particularly Vietnamese.

Yet it was mellowed-out Doober who got them on the road. Denny would have been willing to spend the whole week at Anna's, but his conscientious young assistant was worried about the radio, and about the possibility that someone might be trying to call them now that the weather had cleared. Denny's point of view was that they had already done their best to fulfill an impossible mission. But Doober insisted, and so he reluctantly agreed to a compromise; they would spend the night on the hilltop and then come back to the bar the next day. The pair finally got away after Denny got his own soup, but even then he was reluctant to go back into the bush and insisted on walking two clicks the other way into town to the market square. He dickered around, buying a fifteen-by-twenty-foot square of heavy plastic to hang over the tent and then some oranges and a couple pounds of green-husked *chom-chom*, a spiny plumlike fruit just then coming into season.

Doober shook his head. "Those aren't ripe. They gotta have a red tinge."

"Doober, you don't know anything. These are *green* choms."

"I don't think so. You're gonna have the runs all night. . . . Come on, let's go, you're just stalling and we gotta get back."

Denny squinted at him in the bright sunlight. "You're right, old oober-Day—I am. I don't want to go back. I got a bad feeling about it."

Doober made a funny sound in his nasal passages, trying to clear them and get a decent breath. He was very serious. "We *gotta* go back. We gotta." He turned and started down the road out of town.

Denny, who was looking over some pineapples, shrugged at the old *ba* hovering nearby. "Sorry, but we gotta." He shifted his weapons over his other shoulder, took the plastic roll and his bag of fruit, and followed Doober.

As they hiked back along the road he grumbled it was about to rain and he wanted his dry bed at Anna's. Doober led the way, cheerfully assuring Denny he would trade girls the next night so he could have a laugh or two. He chatted on about furthering relations between the two great nations, the U.S. and the zips, by peace, fellowship, and lots of good healthy fucking. He kept up both ends of the conversation all the way to the top of the hill. And the strange pattern of the day changed again for them.

Denny, who had stopped to take a piss, was lagging about fifty yards behind. When all he heard from Doober was the sound of silence, his brow furrowed. "Doober? It's unlike you to give me thirty seconds of peace and quiet. . . ." But Doober still didn't answer. "Doober? Hey, buddy, what's going on—?" By this time he had rushed to Doober's side and could see for himself the cratered devastation that had been their camp. His mouth flopped open stupidly. "Where the hell's the tent?"

"Oh Christ," Doober whispered in awe, "fourteen thousand dollars worth of radio . . . on my salary I'll be paying for it till the day I die."

"That's bullshit," Denny snapped. "We'll say the incendiary grenade went off by accident, bad fuse or something. . . ."

"But how would we explain the tent, our gear? . . ."

Denny walked over to one of the craters, which was about four feet deep, and saw the fused metal frame of the receiver at the bottom. "Easy. Went up in the fire. Almost got us, too. You can see the VC didn't get our precious radio—there it is." He pointed to the twisted blackened mess lying in several inches of water.

Doober's courage crumbled. His jaw quivered and his glasses slipped a bit down his nose. "Dennis . . . I thought this was a secure area. . . ."

"It *is*, Doober—at least as safe as anywhere else in this fuckin' country. At least that's what they told us. . . . "

"Well, the VC had to get close enough to lob a few mortars in here."

Denny shook his head. "Nope. Wasn't VC."

Doober didn't believe him. "Come on, Denny—who else could have done it?"

"Big holes like this? . . ."

Doober was on the verge of panic. "*Our* guys? How could they make a mistake like that?"

Denny eyed the craters, and his eyes were cold as marbles. "Sure does make you wonder, doesn't it. . . ."

Now that they had no tent, the weather decided to shift, and the clouds that had held off all day began to squeeze in on the shrinking spot of blue overhead. A stiff breeze came up. The hilltop where they stood was fairly flat. The spot where the tents had been had been bulldozed clear when the dirt road was put in, but the other end of the hilltop was boulder strewn. Denny wandered around until he found two fairly large shrubs he could tie a line to and managed to get the plastic he'd brought over it. He stretched out the sides and pinned them down with two lines of heavy rocks. One open end of the shelter was against a boulder, and he had arranged it so the other side was downwind. As he finished, the sun ducked behind the first line of swiftly advancing clouds, and the first drops of cold rain spattered loud against the plastic.

Doober, who seemed to be having a fit of paranoia, was no help at all. He had taken a little fist-sized pair of binoculars from one of his pockets and was running from point to point on the hilltop, studying the foliage-covered landscape in all directions. Several times he interrupted Denny's work on the makeshift tent to point out suspicious-looking things that turned out to be oddly shaped tree trunks or simply patterns of green-on-green leaves. Denny shrugged into his poncho, slung his weapons upside down over one shoulder, picked up Doober's slick, and went looking for him. "Doober!" he called, "where the hell are you?"

"Shhhhhh!" Doober whispered in a hoarse call. "Over here! Be quiet, *for God's sake*!"

"What is it, Oobs—another sinister tree limb?" He shuffled over to Doober, who was standing on a waist-high rock. His friend had taken his thick glasses off and had hung them on a tree limb over head. He was sitting, elbows on his knees to steady the binoculars to his eyes.

"Dennis," Doober whispered in a voice coated with fear, "*shut up. I* see a *tank*!"

"Well, ullshit-bay, Doober—we got tanks and half-tracks all over Tay Ninh. That's why it's *secure*. Let me see." He took the binocs, and several things happened at once. He couldn't see at all through the focus set for Doober's myopic eyes, and had to curse and struggle with two knurled dials to clear the picture. There *was* some sort of vehicle across the valley, but it was going behind a hill by the time he got the focus straightened out. He saw a black-suited peasant carrying a stick—or was it a rifle?—and then he too was gone. "I donno, Doo—coulda been a truck. That's a long way away—must be a couple of miles. Anyway, it's gone behind a hill now. Probably nothing . . ."

But the possibilities disturbed him, and he continued to sweep the area with the binoculars. All the way back up the hill they had heard an occasional distant crackle of weaponfire. It was an everyday sound in Nam, where GIs and ARVNs alike walked with hair triggers any time they got out from behind their normal defensive positions. Now, with the light failing and both night and the rain setting back in, Denny wished more than ever he had followed his instincts and hung around Anna's for the rest of the week.

"I *saw* it," Doober repeated stubbornly. "And it wasn't one of ours."

"Oh, now you're a heavy armor expert."

"Damn it, Haller—it had no markings. It was tall and funny looking—like the World War II jobbies you see in the movies. And these guys with black pajamas were around it."

"Probably just an ARVN tank. There's no other explanation."

"Unless they brought it down the trail!"

"Impossible."

Doober took a long sniff to clear his nose. "You sound just like a lifer. Nothing's impossible. Ho's men dragged cannons through swamps for hundreds of miles to surround the French at Dien Bien Phu. I read about it."

Much later, when he had time to think about it, Denny would realize he shouldn't have been arguing with Doober about the Ho Chi Minh Trail, about whose tank it was, or about anything at all. He should have been ordering his young assistant to huck his ass down off the rock where he was standing exposed to the entire valley. The rain was coming down harder now, and the wind whistled through the bushes.

Doober rubbed both eyes and then stood on the rock and reached up to the branch where he'd hung his glasses. "*Uck!*" he gurgled.

"No, the word is uck-fay," Denny replied, still pissed that Doober had called him a lifer. Although he didn't know it at the time, and never thought consciously about it again, it was the last time Denny would ever think in pig latin. He scanned the valley, puzzled at the sudden puff of smoke he thought he saw in a clump of rocks almost a mile away. But Doober didn't say any more. He'd said the last word. His feet slid out from under him and he sat down with a thump, back against the rock, eyes staring blankly at everything and nothing. A thin line of blood ran down one side of his nose from the pencil-size hole just to the left of center in his forehead.

4-5

Denny Haller, sobbing as he knelt between several dark boulders, smashed Doober's M14 against a rock until the barrel was bent and useless. He threw the ammo into the dense undergrowth. It was nearly dark, and he did not intend to spend the night on the hilltop.

They had been pinned on the rear side of the hill, away from the path and the road back to Tay Ninh. Denny was sure he wouldn't last until dawn on the hilltop alone. The bad guys would be coming up after him just like in the war movies, drifting up the slope like deadly armed spirits in the starless black night. His only chance was to try to get away in the next half hour or so.

By staying low, he could work his way through the boulder-strewn area. He moved carefully around the perimeter of the hilltop, scanning with the binoculars in all directions in the failing light, much as his friend had done such a short time before.

Then he crawled back to the limp body, sprawled where he had left it. He wrapped the eyes with a long plastic strip, securing the makeshift bandage with Doober's army belt, as much to hold the head together as to keep him from looking at the kid's face. All he could see was Doober's nose and the cake of dark red blood around his open mouth. "Okay, Doobs, gotta lighten you up." He took Doober's boots off and tried to hoist him.

Simply slung over his shoulder, the body was heavy and awkward, so he set it down again. It got away from him and slipped down a small incline, landing with a thump against a pile of rocks. Breathing heavily, expecting a bullet between his shoulder blades with every movement, he clambered ten feet down after it. He dragged it back up and then tied the hands to the feet with shoelaces, wincing as he pulled the string tight around Doober's wrists. He also strapped the M79 around Doober's shoulders. That would make his load awkward, too, and he knew he wouldn't be able to get to the stubby little launcher easily, but he didn't want to leave that much firepower behind. He felt there was every chance in the world he was going to need it.

"I know, Doobs—we can't be impatient. Just a few minutes and we'll start out of here," he said softly. He had been talking to Doober for over an hour now, ever since his friend took the bullet. It was his way of controlling the rage and terror that swarmed through his mind.

"*FUCKIN' AAAARRRRRRMMMMMYYYYYY!*" he had screamed, seeing Doober's lifeless stare for the first time. The response had been another bullet from the distant marksman, this one striking the rock near him and whining futilely away at a sharp angle. Mad Denny dove for the ground. Getting Doober's body off the rock drew another near miss. Then he had worked his way out of the line of fire, crawling and dragging Doober back over the slippery rough ground away from the lip of the hilltop.

When he finally felt ready to go, there was only the last failing flicker of twilight to guide him. He shouldered Doober's body, slipped and almost fell as he bent for his M16, and then started down the muddy trail. By the time he had gone a half mile, he realized it was impossible. He had slipped and fallen heavily several times. The trail, plain as it was in the day, was simply not there in the dark. His plan would never work. He was making noise. He couldn't see where he was going. They would get him.

Even though they had to be moving around the hill at that moment, he fought his fears and set down Doober's body. He sat in the brush by the side of the trail, head low against the back of a rock so he made no outline. He could go no further.

Fifteen minutes went by while he tried to collect his thoughts. The hillside was rough with slabs and chunks of rotten old granite, all heavily overgrown with vegetation. The VC were able to see in the dark. They could move through barbed wire, over punji stakes, over ten-foot-high bamboo walls. He remembered all the stories he'd heard over the last three years. Couldn't be true . . . couldn't physically be true. But it was their land. They had farmed it and made war in it for centuries. They were used to traveling it by night. A blind man doesn't have to see to move—he uses his other senses.

If it had been a moonlit night, Denny would have picked up Doober and slowly made his way down the path. And they would have ambushed him, easily cutting him down with a U.S. claymore they had rigged a few yards before the footpath met the paved road to Tay Ninh.

But it was dark, so dark Denny couldn't make out his hand in front of his face. The rain whispered as it fell on leaves and rock, and the wind sighed over the brow of the hill. Feeling he was too close to the trail, Denny shouldered Doober again and crawled on his hands and knees around behind the boulders away from the muddy path. There was a feeling of false security in the little pocket he found in the rocks. It was barely two feet wide, simply a space between two irregular Jeep-sized boulders, but it extended back about six feet and was surrounded by brush. He managed to get Doober's body into the crevice and then leaned against one of the rocks to wait out the night.

Maybe the VC knew the land, but they couldn't cover every inch of it. And he had the element of surprise in his favor—he hadn't really thought out his position, simply stopping when he realized it would be dangerous to continue. There were probably ten or twenty more secure little natural shelters on the hillside; he figured they would search them all before daylight.

He dared not put the slicker over his head, because the rain striking it would drown out the sounds of the night. His ears and nose and lips were numb from the chill, and water dribbled down inside the poncho until he was soaked and shivering. And he thought again of Tuy. In the blackness of that hope-forsaken time, her words took the shape and form of a dark curse. "Have you never been responsible for the death of a friend? How lucky . . . pray to your God it never happens!" His head came down between his hands and he cried softly, blaming Tuy, blaming Asshole Anderson, blaming himself.

After a few hours he drifted off into a light, fitful sleep. Once he dreamed or imagined he saw all the dead and gone Dimbos—Charley, Larkey, Beale, and Doober—lined up, looking at him with pale bloody faces. Funny, he thought of Beale as dead, probably because the guy had wanted it so badly. They were in mess hall and they carried empty aluminum trays in one hand and chunky army-issue knives, forks, and spoons in the others. "Sure the dead-and-gone eat," Larkey intoned, his dark eyes just dark holes in a pale, expressionless face. "What did you think, fuckhead?" Denny couldn't stand to look on Doober, who stared reproachfully at him with the same blank look he wore the last time he'd seen him, the thin line of blood from the little round hole in his forehead running down into the red river that had burst from his nose.

Denny woke with a little animal cry of terror. His teeth chattered and his body shook from the cold and the fright. He shifted his stiff legs. His back ached and he felt feverish and chilled by turns. And after a long time he drifted off again.

Sometime later during that endless night he woke again to hear a piece of wood scrape on a rock. Nothing more or less. No voices, no other sound. He couldn't tell if it was near or far. He held his breath, fought to relax the iron bands that were his fingers around the M16. But he made no sound, the dark held around him, and seconds, minutes, and hours passed. And finally he could see an outline, the five fingers of his left hand, against the deep gray of the sky to the east.

He remembered there was a steep and rocky brush-covered dry wash to the left of the muddy path, a gully that angled down in the general direction of the main road. It was less direct, but would keep him off the skyline while he could still gain some distance, so he slowly started down that way. The wash was better than he thought; it would take him right up to the road. Halfway down the hill it turned into a rock-clogged little stream that ran in the right direction. He stayed as low as possible, wading at times through water up to his thighs. The way was hard, and he fell several times, once twisting an ankle and striking his head against a jagged rock as Doober went tumbling on ahead. Denny got him over his shoulders again and limped on, crawling over dead logs and through heavy brush that tore his fatigues and scratched his skin. He had no choice. He was making too much noise, and anyone still in the area would be after him. No time to rest; he had to go on.

It was nearly noon and still raining when he finally staggered up out of the rocky wash and stood on shaky legs by the gravel roadside. His hands and knees were torn and bloody, and his tattered uniform was dark with Doober's blood as well. But he had made it to the road.

Later in the afternoon, the lead vehicle of a resupply convoy headed for Nui Ba Den pulled over when the driver spotted him sitting by the roadside. Denny was cradling Doober's body as he had his kid brother in the almost-forgotten time . . . ten years before, before all the trouble, back in Wisconsin when his mom was out and somebody had to put the twirp to bed. He rocked back and forth, softly singing over and over the simple Vietnamese lullaby:

"Bay la la bay la la bay la
Bay la la bay la la bay la . . ."

He knew Doober would like that.

4-6

Phil Darby had three strong convictions about the war: We didn't belong in Nam. We didn't know what we were fighting for. And we were getting our butts kicked.

His historical perspective extended back to a fuzzy image of Dien Bien Phu and the '50s when the colonial French had gotten *their* butts kicked. He'd even skimmed through *Street Without Joy* as an optional in modern lit class. And he had a vague notion that the Chinese had sat on the place for thousands of years before that. It wasn't necessary to know anything more about the locals; after all, it wasn't their war any more.

He also didn't speak Vietnamese and wasn't interested in learning. Language didn't come easy, particularly not this high-pitched whiny one that sounded like everybody was talking with empty piss-pots on their heads. What was the sense? Just about the time he might get semifluent there would be a terrorist bombing, a coup, a revolution, a kidnapping or a little war in Europe or the Middle East or South America to capture the fancy and swing the social consciousness of his readership somewhere else around the globe. Try talking a little dink to the mayor of Tel Aviv or to a revolutionary in Chile, see how far *that* gets you. . . . bottom-line, it didn't seem to matter; none of the correspondents in his acquaintance knew more than which way to the bathroom? and *co muon di-ly*—young lady, would you like to fuck?

Casual as he may have been on old dead history, he was firm when it came to discounting the official U.S. version of the way things worked (whatever it was this week). The entire military effort was personified in his mind as a blowsy drunk—boastful and arrogant, puffed with lies and rosy schemes, lacking art, lacking manners, lacking common sense, lacking introspection. From what he'd seen and heard, not one of them had any real solid idea why they were there, not from the lowliest E-1 grunt to Westmoreland himself. For most it didn't matter; they just followed orders, did their best to hang on to their balls for twelve months until they could jet the magic carpet back to real life. Phil's home base was a shabby little apartment in downtown Saigon, and from there he hopped around the war, *gracias* to the omnipresent helicopters, like a flea on a cricket's back.

He figured his readership back in the States didn't give a shit for vague philosophic reasoning either. Listening to a gum-chewing sergeant or pimple-faced kid blather on sophomorically about democracy and self-determination for the peoples of the world was enough to make him sick. How like army green parakeets they seemed, pea-brained little birds mimicking their master's voices! Once, at a big army press-mess in Ving Long, a Spec-four riverboat gunner held him up with a five-minute monologue on what it all meant, a meandering speech spliced full of half quotes from the Declaration of Independence. Sixth-grade history at its worst. And the young pimple-brain kept interrupting himself with a big self-deprecatory grin and the hope his captive listener didn't think the line of reasoning was too mushy, too shirt-sleeve patriotic. The next minute the kid had changed the subject to his job, started in bragging his duty was to spray hot death on practically anybody he could see running up and down the riverbanks, presumably to make the way clear for truth, justice, and democracy.

"You always sure that's Charlie in your sights?"

"Well," the kid admitted with a shy grin, "you have to fire on anybody suspicious."

"How do you know—suspicious?"

"Well, if they're running away, wearing black pajamas, maybe lugging a rifle . . ."

"I always thought black pajamas were all the delta fashion rage."

"Well, I guess you have to be there. Here's a for-instance, typical way it happens: we catch some sniper fire, maybe a mortar round. I open up, start to spray the ground cover. We power around the bend. I see a guy with maybe an old M1 running like hell. I gotta dust that guy!"

"Suppose he's a hundred yards off? Suppose that old M1 is really a fishing pole?"

"I could tell the difference. . . ."

But the writer-as-observer could see the doubts well up in the kid's eyes. He'd be willing to bet it happened *a lot*. He pushed a little more. "Is it always that clear-cut?"

The eyes look away, evading. "Well, most of the time." But the kid was able to shrug it off, trying to change the subject to something about a cache of grenades they had blown in a little fishing skiff. An obvious attempt to justify himself in his own mind, to paste over all the images he must have of jerking limbs and blasted bodies in black pajamas who incidentally just might have been Victor Charlies. Phil had walked away, feeling a jolt of revulsion and clarity. We hold these truths to be self-evident, indeed!

The war was shit. Little else about it mattered, with the bottom line for the whole U.S. so easy to read: Vietnam was halfway around the world, and an entire province with a tongue-twisting name like Quang Tri or Kien Giang wasn't worth the life of one kid from Mississippi or Illinois. Who were we defending it from, anyway—other Vietnamese? The war was being run by the Pentagon, with stubborn, dim-witted, trigger-happy LBJ's consent, against the will of the majority. It was morally wrong. It was unethical. It was a shit war.

What was left for him to record was the madness. There certainly was an abundance of that. Insane juxtapositions were his stock-in-trade: air-conditioning and the icy draft of fear as your Huey plunged hundreds of feet into a hot LZ; thick juicy steaks and dead-hamburger GIs, muggy hot Saigon bars all steamy with sex and the verdant, rotting jungle with its silent tripwires and punji stakes . . . or, John Wayne somehow covered with bravery and clean dirt charging up the hill at Iwo Jima played against your own gut-wrenching fear as you leap fifteen feet down into a slime green, stinking paddy while the gunners hammer out a death-rock beat overhead; dripping poncho over your smelly, sweaty body against cool, white sheets and the smell of Old Spice in the Hotel Caravelle or the Rex or the Catinat; foot patrol along the coast in Quang Ngai against prowling for a decent lay on R and R in Hong Kong; hootch against villa; wine against blood; dink hooker's olive skin passive after fierce climax against black GI skin after stepping on a Russian antipersonnel mine . . . he sat before his little portable typewriter and the images came pouring out, all of them, in howling clots of angry protest.

Not that the process was ever easy; going out in the choppers made his head ache and his stomach burn. He worried constantly about being caught in a real firefight, dumped in a real situation with no flight out. He had a vision of incredible irony: it was of him, the innocent bystander, catching a real round in the guts. That was the problem; lead was blind and the faint hard whisper of death all too present in his ear. He visualized that dream a thousand thousand times, in every conceivable situation.

Still, he fought his fears with a gritty élan he hoped lived up to his profession. And he went on, chopper-hopping from delta to coast to highlands, living the war through the stories the grunts told him, listening to hundreds of GIs, to anyone who would talk, and then mustering the stamina for that one last bone-tired hop back to Tan-Son-Nhut or Bien-hoa. Totally exhausted, he would sleep the impossibly short taxi ride back to his grubby little apartment.

But after all that, what he had absorbed wouldn't let him rest. He would pace in front of his rusty Royal, and the torrent of words would start. After an hour or so, when the first flush wore off, he had to pop an upper or two to stay at it. But that was just to keep the body up while the ideas whirled endlessly in his brain and came spinning off the tip ends of his fingers.

His war was colorful, apple-pie American (lightly dink-spiced for authenticity), full of shock value, dramatic, incredibly wasteful, deadly, going badly, and wrong. He didn't need any more than that. The ideas flickered and flashed like hot incendiaries; he dumped it all out on paper and sent an intermittent stream of fictional and semifictional stories back to New York. It was contemporary literature, real stuff full of absurdity and hard edges. His editors loved it, sandwiched it in between the sweet thighs of the girls and the latest trends in herringbone or seersucker. His readers loved it, too; it confirmed everything they already knew in their hearts about the Washington baby-killers, fueled their courage to burn their draft cards and get out in the streets to chant ''Hell no, we won't go!''

He would finish late in the night or even after dawn the next morning, totally drained and yet unable to sleep. Then sometimes when he could get it, he'd take in a slow pipe of bubbling opium, just lying there in his three-weeks-mussed-up bed until the clouds came to dope over the raw spots and let him forget for ten or twelve hours . . . until the next day or the day after that, when he'd mail his stuff and start to get interested in a taxi out to Tan-Son-Nhut and the next chopper back into the war. He could feel the candle burning on both ends, he was giving so much of himself. . . . Where was the little boy he'd been a few weeks before, the high school dreamer of yesterday, the promising and idealistic English major graduated less than an hour ago? He gave his youth, he gave his life, he gave everything. From time to time he would play with the idea of long-form; there had to be a book in this somewhere.

The last three days had been a nightmare. Dominique and he had left for the airport together, timing their entrance to come in on the military briefing after the long-winded statistics and justifications and before the coffee and fresh donuts were all gone. Old pros at the waiting game, they had commandeered chairs for themselves and then wandered after the briefing officer, intent on the Xeroxed handouts that would sum it all up in a speed-read glance.

The officer had proved to be more of a pompous ass than the usual sort, and when they finally got back to the chairs, which they had folded and hidden behind a stack of fifty-five-gallon drums, they were occupied by a couple of enterprising grunts. Phil's head ached and he wanted nothing more than to sit with his hands holding on to it—but one of the two soldiers was hostile. Phil was over six foot three, and a force to contend with, even though he was down about thirty pounds from his burly college days. At Yale he'd been an Ivy League champion at the arts of boxing and wrestling. He would have made an example of the two, but gentle Dominique, who didn't even like to raise his voice, pulled him away. They still didn't have their coffee, and Phil reluctantly agreed.

The jump west to Tay Ninh was bothersome as well, for they were joined by the two surly GIs, one of whom insulted Dominique and trashed some of his photos. But that was all just absurd and a bother; after Tay Ninh, it got frightening— dangerous, actually. They had choppered out to some little hilltop LZ called Maryann, and he and Dominique were committed, on the ground staring at the receding dragonfly, before anyone bothered to tell them Maryann was hot and they could expect mortars before dawn.

Phil spent the night with the cold fear gnawing his guts

and was out at the pad before full light, praying for the hop that didn't come for another day—only to take them on to Lucille Jane, which was hotter than Maryann. He spent very little time listening to stories and most of his moments as deep in a foxhole as he could get, up against a silent dirty marine rifleman who farted a lot from the C rations and smelled like the rotten war itself.

After a day and a half of that they felt supremely lucky to dash out and find space aboard a Huey headed back for Tay Ninh. Totally exhausted and emotionally drained, they hung around the cement LZ all afternoon waiting for a ride back to Saigon. Just when it looked as if nothing was going to turn up, they got a chance on a Chinook. The big, noisy machine was filled with a ring of living grunts slumped around a pile of body bags stacked three high, but beggars couldn't be choosers, and they scrambled in. It was like falling into a little modern chunk of Dante's Inferno. Filthy and exhausted as he and Dominique felt, they looked clean next to the tattered GIs, most of whom fidgeted with their M16s and looked at them from hollow, sunken eyes, or stared at the floor, seeing nothing, feeling nothing, thinking nothing. "God damn Nam," Phil thought sympathetically. He could relate to their sense of loss, to their helplessness in the face of the monster that was the war and the army that brought them to it. He gave out a big sigh as he stretched his way over the pile of body bags to an empty seat on the far wall, thinking, "Nam the oriental siren with cruel claws, dragon claws. Nam, sucking away at our blood and our youth . . . you didn't have to look any further to see hell, just take a look in their eyes." He flopped on the metal bench seat, leaning back and yawning as he rubbed his temples.

"Get your feet off that body bag," a quiet voice from across the compartment said.

"Beg your pardon?" Phil looked around with arched eyebrows, surprised that anyone had spoken. The military was acutely aware of the bad ink running wild back home, and as a general rule grunts were briefed to be supernice to the press.

"Your feet. Off the bags."

He saw a spec-five, grimy and bloodstained in tattered fatigues. It was a moment before Phil recognized him—the same surly noncom he'd hopped out with a few days before! What incredible shit luck! Well, that was the way the week was going, and it was up to him to face into it. He turned his palms up, fingers spread. "Come on now, fellow—be reasonable."

"It's a reasonable request."

Phil couldn't believe it. The bloody ass was serious! He saw with a flash of empathy the grim face, the almost blue-white lips pulled in a thin line, the empty eyes. The poor grunt was like all the rest of them, a paid killer just beginning to try to work off the horrible memories that would last a lifetime. He shook his head, honestly feeling sorry for the guy. "Soldier, come off it, will you? I can see you've had a bad time, but why me? You know, you've been picking on me since we shipped out."

"*Off!*"

Phil sighed and took his feet off the bags. "Look, be reasonable—they're gone! They've bit it, wasted, offed! Offed is offed, as they say. And like I say, you're picking on me! Look around you—these men all have their feet anywhere they want." He waved his hand angrily around the compartment.

"These are all *men*, the living and the dead. You are not. It's a sort of club."

Phil felt he wasn't going to be able to take the shit. He could hear his voice rising. He felt the blood pumping in his temples. All this was going to lead to a black monster of a headache, fitting end to a nothing trip. Dominique was trying to get him to sit down, but he was tired and he just didn't care. His lips twisted. "Oh sure, that's just about the last of it! And you *are*, you're what it takes to be a man? Johnny got his gun all right! Well, you didn't use it on any Victor Charlies from the look of it . . . so what are you going to do now, take your own frustration out on me, you poor silly bastard?''

''Not a bad idea, fuckhead,'' the grunt said evenly, slamming home a clip in his M16. It came over Phil suddenly, like a cold dose of water, that he was trying to reason with someone over the edge. He took a slow, deep breath. They gave these kids guns and lots of incidents happened, crazy things you'd get put in jail for back in the States, things nobody had the time or interest to sort out. Phil didn't want to be an incident. He grabbed his rucksack and dove over the stack of body bags, rolling and skidding until he fell out the back door.

He sat on a waist-high pallet of burlap-bagged rice, watching the Chinook rise and churn away to the east. Then he sighed and reached in his shirt pocket for a crumpled aluminum envelope that contained his last fat little half joint. That was one of the things about the war, he mused, one of the funny inconsistencies—an uneducated asshole like that could get away with outrage, might have actually blown him away and written it off as a stray round, a burst accidentally left in his M16. He leaned back on the rice bags, feeling the burlap scratchy like a hair shirt on his neck and thinking how good a hot shower would feel. The heavy gray clouds moved from right to left over his head, low enough practically to rub against his nose. He took a deep drag on the little toke. It was powerful stuff, enough to get him over the top for sure.

The burlap against his skin didn't really bother him, nor did missing the Chinook, although he'd been plenty hot at the time. He'd get another ride to Saigon. A couple of months ago when he was new meat, he would have felt differently; but now he saw it as just another step in the growing process, in learning to be as objective as possible. . . . How could he take a thing like that personally? It had happened. It was a part of the war. Now it was up to him to find a way to give it meaning, to work it into a story.

CHAPTER FIVE

5-1

THE THIRTY-THIRD'S EM CLUB HAD BEEN CLOSED FOR OVER
an hour, it being past the forbidden hour of midnight when
all good enlisted men were to be in bed with the lights out.
The chairs were stacked and the cheap imitation stained glass
overheads all dimmed. The army regulation random pattern
brown-and-lighter-brown floor tiles were coated with little
scummy pools left by the casual mopping at the hands of the
hired help. However, one booth was still occupied in the
back. The table at that booth was awash with empty beer
bottles and ashtrays with a variety of butts in them, everything from filter tips to the chewed-up ends of rum-flavored
cigars to the tiny black ends of wasted joints. The sergeant
in charge of the EM Club, seeing who it was, tossed them
the key on his way out with a vague threat to lock up or else.
It was the CO's bunch, and he knew a war party when he
saw one.

"How *could* they let him get off the hook like that?" Animal said for the tenth time.

Stringer, who was intently rolling a new whammie, shook
his head. "That Dooly-the-Spook ain't as smart as we
thought—he never even got in the White Shack to check Denny's stuff! 'I'm gonna get to that right quick,' he says. Shore
he is! Now that the cat's out of the bag, there ain't gonna be
nothing to find; Denny's gonna clean it out slick as a whistle!"

Toady, the third man in their little group, came back from

the bar with three sweaty-cold Buds. "I don't get it either. If you had seen the way Anderson let Dooly sit in his chair, and put his feet on his desk! He'd of killed anybody else tried that!"

Animal shrugged. "I don't think he had any choice on that one. That Dooly's got the white rot. You don't want to be anywhere near him. Guy like that walks in my place, he sits any place he wants!"

"Leprosy—" Toady nodded seriously, handing the Buds around. "—some shit like that, and he doesn't know it—or won't admit it. The day will come, his head's just gonna putrefy. He probably done some shit and it's God's way of getting even."

"We're gettin' away from the point," Stringer said, licking the fat, rolled Zig Zag paper. "The *point* is, Dooly was gonna *handle* it, and he *didn't*—"

"Well, we didn't do so good either!" Toady shot back at him. "We had four witnesses—those gooks swore in writing they took packages from Haller and left them in bunk areas of guys in the company, as directed by him. We didn't even have to threaten them . . . too much."

Animal took a big swig of beer and let out a tremendous belch. "Well, you was there, how'd he get out of that one?"

Toady's lips twisted in an angry sneer. "I couldn't believe it. Listens to the charges and the evidence and calls it 'inadmissable in a military court.' I coulda dropped my drawers, and believe me, old Dooly had his mouth open so far the flakes from his hair was fallin' in it! I guess he was countin' on Denny cracking. We all were, come to think about it."

Stringer puffed on his new smoke, getting it going. "What'd he do?"

"Denny? He started talking about you, you asshole."

"Me? Shit, I ain't involved . . . he can't pin that opium on me! I'm clean!"

"No, no, dink-brain. That Hoa business. Remember how

he tried to frame you for raping that little cunt with the nice
ass who worked—''

''Yeah, yeah, I remember,'' Stringer cut in quickly. ''What
about it?''

''Denny claimed the CO set a precedent when he wouldn't
listen to native testimony. And that he could get just as many
GIs to swear he was innocent.''

''Yeah, *sure* he could—all Dimbos. . . .''

''Yeah, I know. Anyway, that's when the whole meeting
started to go crazy, everybody yelling at everybody else. The
captain was furious, of course, 'cause he thought he had him
dead to rights this time, and here he sees Denny slipping off
the noose again.''

Animal grinned, in spite of himself. ''Wish I'd been there!
What did Dooly say—I'll bet he stayed cool!''

Toady reached for Stringer's roach. ''I'll tell you, right
now that man is convinced our Mad Denny is the *Xau My*,
which was about the only good that came out of the meeting—but he did not stay cool. In fact, he was the worst.
Denny got to him slicker than pig grease, called him a spook
to his face. 'I'm not a spook,' Dooly replies in that quiet,
watching way of his, but you could see he was a little unset-
tled. He'd just got a new crew cut, real short, see, and his
face started getting a little red, and when that happened that
rot stood out like white crud. I was glad I was sitting on the
other side of the room, let me tell you! Anyway, Denny looks
him right back and says, 'If you're not a spook, how come
you don't throw no shadow?' That's a crazy thing to say,
right? You know and I know, Denny's dinky dow anyway,
but Dooly don't know it. He can't figure it out, he thinks that
Denny is onto some CIA code word or something, and he
ought to be able to get it but he doesn't, so he starts yelling,
too—and, boy, what a scene!''

''Lovely, lovely.'' Animal reached across the table for the
toke. ''So the good guys are all yelling and asshole Haller
keeps his cool, acing everybody again.''

"Well, no—then *Denny* started screaming about the bull-shit mission Anderson sent him on; you know he suspects it was all a setup."

"Shit, he's lucky to be alive. . . ."

"He was upset because his little four-eyes flunky caught the big one."

Stringer's lean elbows pushed beer bottles out of the way, making room for him to lean forward on the table. His eyes gleamed. "He *better* be upset . . . 'cause he's gonna be the next one home in a box!"

"Goddamn right!" Animal seconded him. Toady nodded furiously, taking a last drag before passing the roach reluctantly back to Stringer.

"Here's how I see it," Stringer continued. "Dooly's out; he's just a lot of spook bullshit talk, right? And the CO's taken his best shot and come up a zero . . . right again? Now we gotta do something, it's up to us! We can't let that shithead get away with what he's doing!"

Mutters of "Right on!" and "You said it, man!" went around the table. Emboldened by their reactions, Stringer took three little folded wads of paper from his pocket. "Thanks, guys! I really was counting on you being with me!" They all eyed him, saying nothing, suddenly serious. He pushed the litter aside on the table and played with the three wads, first stacking them on top of each other and then setting them in a little row.

"What have you got here, Stringer?" Toady's voice was strange, a little thin, as if a cold dry hand had him by the throat. The sudden shift of emphasis bothered him, he couldn't exactly say why. Things were going good for him, he had built a life that was working about the way he wanted it. He didn't like things out of the ordinary, things that might menace the smooth flow of what he had.

"Oh, that's nothing," Stringer countered. "It's what I've got *here* that counts!" He reached in his army jacket pocket and produced a smooth, olive-colored grenade. He set it gingerly in the center of the table next to the three wads of paper. ''An L2A1,'' he said proudly, ''A limey grenade. Absolutely untraceable. I won it in a poker game from a guy from Sydney.''

Animal was so drunk, he would have cheered if Stringer had revealed a pack of Trojans. ''Hey, man, that's number one!''

But the party was starting to sour for Toady. ''What—? I mean, you're not really suggesting—?''

Stringer sneered at him. ''Goddamn it man, what are we going to do, just *talk* about it? What, are you chicken-shit?''

''Chicken-shit, chicken-shit,'' Animal mocked him. ''Naaaaw, not the bawk-bawk-bawk. Toady is *Toady*-shit.''

Stringer got mean. He knew it was now or never. ''Look, Toady, it's one for all around here—if you guys want out, git out of here! I'll handle this myself!''

''Naaaa, shit, you old hillbilly,'' Animal sang out, ''Toady's with us, ain't you, Mis-ter Toad?''

''Well, I guess—''

Stringer picked up the grenade and flipped it from hand to hand. ''Shoore . . . lookit, son: there's only one chance in three any of us is gonna git to huck this here pineapple, anyhow. . . .'' He reached his big lean hand across the table to grab Toady's shoulder. To Toady, it felt like a claw. ''So, you with us, good buddy?''

''Yeah, I guess so. . . .''

''Look at it this way—it's the Lord's work, man,'' Animal chimed in, ''to rid the earth of the vermin and the scum.''

''Okay, okay, *okay*. I'm in. What do we do?''

Stringer's eyes glittered like hard little chunks of glass. ''Right! Now here's how she goes down: three folded sheets of paper, all identical, all taped shut. Two of 'em is blank. The other one is tied to this sweet little limey lime here.''

''Who goes first?'' Today asked, doubtfully eyeing the three deadly squares of paper.

"Why, *you* do, shithead!" Stringer retorted gleefully, pushing in just the right way.

"Oh no, not me! That's not fair!"

"He's right," Animal agreed. "You thought it up, Stringer—you should pick first."

Stringer sighed heavily, hoping it masked his elation, and selected the little folded paper on his far right, the one with the tiniest tip edge of tape ripped off. He slowly opened it, then dropped it to the table. "Hmmmm, blank . . ." He leaned back with another sigh and took a long pull on his Bud, eyeing the other two. "Who goes next?" It wasn't that he wasn't ready to do the dirty deed, he told himself. In fact, had it fallen differently, he had steeled himself to allow the other two to pick first. But his daddy had taught him to be a good poker player, and like his daddy always said, "No sense takin' foolish risks."

"It don't matter," Animal said. "Fifty-fifty either way. Let's each take one and open them at the same time." The olive-colored grenade sat ready between them, its matte-finish surface seeming to suck up all the light in the room. Toady nodded and reached for the one closest to him.

Animal's paper, like Stringer's, was blank. The one Toady held like white-hot steel between his trembling fingers contained only four big block letters scrawled in pencil. They spelled the word FRAG.

5-2

The weeks after Tuy sent Mad Denny away were very busy ones for nervous Phong, the fat White Mouse cop who worked for her. Tuy could not risk direct contact with any government officials, so she used her policeman to reach the proper bureaucrats. He also acted as money drop and picked up the paperwork from the various offices downtown.

Phong knew he was both the best and worst man for the job. Tuy was paying him a ten percent commission, a sum of money that could represent over a year's salary. He wouldn't think of cheating her, and he really wanted that money. But now, as he stood outside the Immigration Documentation Office, his heart fluttered in his chest, and sweat formed big rings under his arms and made the front of his cotton shirt stick to his soft tummy. He took a deep breath and pushed the door open.

He had the boy's real ID. The kid had just turned seventeen, so he was draft age, ready for the automatic three plus three plus three that would spit him out nine years later . . . maimed, drunk, a dopehead, or psychotic—if he lived. Tuy, who had more than a passing interest in the process of identification (she had lived under a fake ID for several years now, since Larkey's death), realized that a false ID would not work for the boy. They could change his name, but he would still be draft age. They could falsify his birth date, too, but that was a questionable route, considering he was big for his age and robust to boot. So more was needed; they had to manufacture a reason to get a healthy, draft-age youth out of the country with iron-clad laws passed to prevent just such flight. It couldn't be done . . . which, in a country like South Vietnam, simply meant it was going to take patience, the right contacts, and a lot of money.

After three days, Phong was finally led to the office of the director of Immigration Services. So far, he hadn't spent a dime of Mad Denny's twenty thousand *My Kim*. The director eyed him over his paper-cluttered desk, then sent his assistant away with a wave of one fat hand. Phong caught a glitter of opal and sapphire, and observed the clean cut of the dark silk suit the director wore. He smelled the scent of English Leather, a men's fragrance obscenely expensive as it could only be purchased at the end of a black market trail that led back to the American PX. He knew he was in the right office.

The flutter in his chest increased tenfold as he was bade sit down, and his teeth actually chattered as he began to speak. "I-I-I-I n-n-need to dis-dis-discuss some p-p-paperwork. . . ." Words failed him. He could go no further. He reached for his handkerchief, rubbed his damp forehead and cheeks.

The director made a bridge of his fingers, put his elbows on the desk before him, and set his chin on the little bridge. "Amusing. And ironic."

"W-what is?" Phong, frightened as a plump white rabbit, didn't know whether to stay or run.

"Sit—*sit!*" the director assured him with a wave of his hand. "I find amusement in the study of all types of humanity. It is nothing personal. I see you here before me in the uniform of a Saigon policeman, the very embodiment of the word *bribe*. You are here to talk with me about . . . something . . . complicated. . . . You should be cool, detached, at ease. I would have anticipated that. So what have we here? Either a person impersonating a policeman—an offense, I can assure you, calling for capital punishment—or, that rarest of all creatures, an honest White Mouse."

Phong was able to examine the director for the first time during his long speech, which had a calming effect on him. He noticed with a small flash of pride that the man was actually much fatter than he was. "I am a policeman." Phong straightened a little. He was going to get through with this. "In this case, I am operating as a private citizen, in behalf of a friend of the family." Phong went on to explain, as Tuy had briefed him over and over, that they needed to get a draftage youth with medical problems out of the country.

"Hmmmmm . . ." The director looked grave. "What sort of medical problems?"

"Chest—uhh, heart. He has a very bad heart."

"Stomach, too, no doubt . . ."

"Beg pardon? What do you say?"

"The youth undoubtedly has a bad stomach, too—for the war. . . ."

"Undoubtedly . . ." Phong looked down at his hands, which had mindlessly twisted his gray handkerchief into a knotted little ball.

"And you will have unimpeachable medical opinions, recommendations, diagnoses sending him to this as-yet-unnamed foreign country for what will be most necessary and urgent treatments?"

"We—uhhh, I—had hoped for a recommendation. . . ."

The director leaned back in his chair with a heavy sigh. "In other words, we start at the beginning here."

"Well, yes—I came to you first. I did not want to make a mistake."

After a long moment, the man behind the desk nodded, tapping his smooth fingers together. "You did correctly. But all this is words. Medical opinions of the type you require are very expensive. As are the many signatures required to obtain the passport." He began to shuffle through the paperwork on his desk. "No. No, it is impossible. It cannot be done." He selected one paper and studied it a long time, then finally looked up as if surprised that the White Mouse, who he had dismissed, was still in the room.

On seeing this ploy, Phong felt at ease. Relief blew through him like a chill wind. This superfat little paper-pusher wasn't going to throw him out. It was an act, a game, a show. The next question was simply, How much? He allowed himself a mild little smile and reached in his pants pocket. "I am not permitted to accept 'no' for an answer. If I might be so . . . forward . . . as to suggest a way: these admittedly very difficult procedures perhaps *might* be accomplished with the proper legal fees paid in *My Kim*. . . ."

He dropped a sweat-dampened roll of ten U.S. one-hundred-dollar bills on the man's desk.

The director blinked, caught off guard. "I misunderstood. I thought you came to me with a piasters deal. This is good, however, very good." He covered himself as smoothly as possible. "Of course, it would take a great deal more than this. . . ." He waved the money away as if it were insignificant, and then did a trick with his hands, causing it to disappear into his silk vest.

As if by magic, Phong thought, a trick of greed. He nodded his own agreement, and stood to leave. "Of course. I am prepared to pay considerably more to save the life of this . . . critically ill child. I am relieved to have your assistance in this . . . humanitarian gesture." He had a momentary flash of concern, afraid he was pouring it on too thick, but the porky director just gazed down at the rings on one hand and nodded, accepting his rhetoric as fact.

Getting the paperwork in order proved to be more expensive than even Tuy anticipated. The open-ended passport to Thailand with its critical signatures cost over eight thousand *My Kim*. There was an additional forty-five hundred for the medical papers directing the boy to specialists in Bangkok for the delicate and dangerous surgery to repair the defective valves in his heart.

But even with such careful and costly measures, Tuy realized the boy's chances were not all that good. Fraudulent paperwork was commonplace, and getting past the skeptical airport security would be a nasty business. To make matters worse, the boy was such a ruddy, strong-looking specimen, it was difficult for anyone to entertain the notion he was the victim of a failing heart.

Worse, he proved to be lazy. Tuy assigned Mako to train him to hunch his shoulders instinctively and to drag one foot slightly as he walked. The boy couldn't have been less interested. He didn't see the need. He wanted to spend his last days in Saigon out front in the Tuyet Lan, flirting with the girls. Tuy threatened the old man, but the graybeard merely shrugged his shoulders. Their deal was that she was to deliver the boy to the distant kingdom of the Thais, no matter how.

Worse yet, when pushed the boy showed flashes of the legendary obstinance in his rural bloodlines, that peculiar combination of temper and stubbornness that historians have noted makes the Vietnamese fierce enemies as well as unstable friends or allies. There was no time for niceties; the kid had a plane to catch, and Tuy was to get him there no matter how.

The corrective technique was a simple one: Mako threw him stomach-down on the floor and sat on him while he yelled and squirmed. George grabbed the boy's left leg and viciously hammered it with the hard cutting edge of his palm until the hamstring gave. After that, their young apprentice could only move about with the aid of a crutch, and applied himself fearfully, if sullenly, to the practice of his hunched-over look, lest they decide to operate on his back as well.

The morning of his departure, Tuy herself gave his face a light coating of makeup with a touch of dark olive under the eyes to give him a pale, sickly look. But the boy was hopeless. At the airport, he disobeyed Phong's instructions to remain quietly seated in a far corner of the prestressed concrete terminal and instead wandered away to engage in what he thought was sophisticated conversation with three lovely *co-gai* who worked as hostesses for Air Vietnam. Phong, discreetly dressed in his new tailor-made civilian suit, paid one hundred dollars apiece to assure they wouldn't pass on the remark that his eye makeup was smudged. By the time Phong brought him back from hasty repairs in the washroom, the *co-gai*'s boss was there with his hand out, and that cost another five hundred *My Kim* and a carton of Marlboro flip-tops, which he produced from the dark green plastic Air Vietnam flight bag he carried. Getting the boy's passport stamped took two payments of two hundred fifty and one of five hundred *My Kim*. Phong began to sweat it; he had bought his expensive suit on credit—if the American money didn't hold out, he wouldn't get his ten percent commission. He could see himself trying to tell the tailor he was going to have to wait three years while he paid it off bit by bit on his regular salary. He was down to two bottles of Jim Beam and one more carton of Marlboro, this one the soft-packs not used by the rough-and-ready American cowboys, and hence less desirable to their Saigon counterparts.

The boy had several thousand-piaster notes with him, as well as one thousand dollars *My Kim* well hidden in the lining of his suitcases. He would never use his own money, stubbornly refusing even at Phong's urging, and so it cost the policeman a bottle of whiskey and the cigarettes to get the baggage through the inspectors without its being ripped apart.

After hours that seemed endless, Phong stood in the muggy heat of late afternoon on the tarmac outside the airport restaurant. He rubbed his forehead with his frayed handkerchief and watched the boy painfully drag his leg across the apron to the waiting Air Vietnam DC-3, hitch himself up the portable aluminum stairway, and disappear into the dark interior of the plane.

There were no further delays. The passenger plane taxied out onto the runway after a long string of F-105s and gently rocked into the air on the tepid, tropical afterwash of the departed jets. The chubby White Mouse continued to wipe the sweat from his forehead and neck, trying to keep his suit as fresh as possible. He breathed a long sigh of relief as the sturdy old plane with the green dragon painted on its side grew tiny in the distance, lumbering west toward towering piles of snowy white cumulus clouds and the Cambodian overflight.

That evening, the old man waited patiently in a corner of the railway station near a particular phone booth. Tuy had supplied him with a cheap outfit—secondhand, ill-fitting clothes more suited to a poor old city chap. He drank tea, squatting with the peasants, passing time. He read the papers, his lips slowly forming the words. No one even gave him a second look, except when he went out to the street corner and lowered his pants, exposing his thin haunches to passing traffic, and relieved his bowels. He was lucky no police were nearby, for such behavior, common in the countryside, would have cost him a fine. A passing taxi driver yelled, "Go fuck a buffalo!" a reference to his rural origins, and gave him a violent hand gesture, but street passersby just looked the other way and stepped quickly to avoid him. Unperturbed, the old man finished his business, pulled up his baggy pants, and retied the twine that acted as a belt.

Sometime late that evening the phone rang. He moved swiftly for an old man then, slipping into the little booth before the first ring had even finished. Holding the frayed and chipped black plastic receiver to his ear, he heard the cryptic message, spoken in his native tongue over the crackle of a long-distance line. "The last seed is safely planted."

He stared unseeingly across the busy train station for a long time after hanging up the phone, a vague smile playing on his lips. Tuy had fulfilled her part of the bargain. Now it was up to him, even though keeping his word would be as dangerous as anything he had ever done.

5-3

Tuy had not been in the countryside since her flight to Saigon over a decade ago. In addition to her girlish dislike of all things insect, she found herself afraid, filled with a raw, throat-stopping fear that someone would materialize out of the trees or from around the corner, sneak up behind her, and have her mercilessly garroted and left for the bugs and the rats, her punishment for having escaped the death sentence passed on her family ten years ago. The Vietcong kept long lists, she knew. They never forgave, never forgot. What was she doing there anyway? She was glad she had changed her *ao dai* for jeans and the good imitation leather jacket Larkey had bought her from the PX. She hugged her arms together as if she were cold, and stayed close behind George and the tottering old man.

Early that morning they had left the city, traveling west in a 1940s vintage black Citroën. The auto, which George had rented, sported huge rounded fenders and a big hood out front over the engine, and so impressed Tuy as being a "gangster car" like those in the old-time movies. It was actually a common enough car in any of the old French territories, and that pleased her, too, because it would not attract attention. Her excellent fake ID passed the test at every checkpoint, where they were waved through the barricades by olive-uniformed QCs. With George behind the wheel and the old man in the passenger's seat, and her and Mako in back, they soon found themselves speeding westward over the two-lane blacktop. The sky was unrelentingly gray, and paddies and low hills swept away in morose shades of green, interrupted only by the occasional beige dots of an isolated hamlet.

Their destination was the town of Ben Suc, capital of Binh Duong province. The distance was not great, Binh Duong being northwest of Saigon and approximately equidistant between the capital city and the Cambodian border, just east of Tay Ninh province. The roads were clear, and they were there before noon.

They felt it important to be as inconspicuous as possible, and so took muddy and rutted back streets. The old Citroën suffered no more than a few splattered vegetables thrown by the local urchins before they came to an isolated and run-down villa at the far edge of Ben Suc, away from the highway.

"Not much now," the old man muttered, indicating with a wave of his hand that they were to take the weed-overgrown gravel drive to the structures set back in the trees on the little estate, "but once it was pretty nice." He cackled, looking back over his seat at Tuy. "My family used to have money, you know. A great considerable deal of money. We got it in . . . transportation. We lost it in the war."

Tuy said nothing. She didn't know what to think of the old man. He wasn't afraid of them, that was for sure. And he insisted he would live up to his end of the bargain, that there was a fabulous pot of treasure at the end of this unlikely rainbow, and that it was hers for the taking.

"Old man, I am reminded of a book I once read of the Spanish explorers. It was a juicy one, with many a lingering between lusty men in armor and pure redskin girls, 'nature's innocents,' I think the author called them."

Mako snickered and she struck him on the back. "Shut up, illiterate!"

By this time the old man had motioned them to stop in a broad turn-around area before the ruined garage. He managed a small bow back at her from his seat. "Even the old can learn. What is the point of your story?"

"These poor Europeans, weakened by disease, lack of food, and their commitment to experience all the natural innocence they could, let themselves be led halfway across North America by an ancient, half-mad Indian who claimed to have seen fabulous cities of gold."

The old man nodded. His wrinkled face bore no expression, at least none she could read. His blank white eye seemed to stare at her, causing her mind to wander from the story. "And? . . ." he said.

"And when the silly Spaniards finally got there, all they found were a few crude mud huts by a dirty stream."

"A good story," the old man said. "I like a good story. It makes one wonder what the Europeans did to their crazy old guide, does it not? In spite of what you may have heard of their sophistication, they have been known on occasion to be a cruel and savage people." He patted George's arm where the pistol he carried just made a small bulge under the arm, and gave out his high-pitched cackle again. "Come. We do not have mountains to cross. In fact, we are here."

Tuy grimly followed the ancient as he led them from their parked car through wet, waist-high weeds to the garage with its mossy walls, knowing all the while he was laughing at her. He cracked the weather-beaten wooden door and disappeared inside. The three remaining looked uncertainly at each other for a moment. Tuy motioned them in. Last of all and with her hand deep in her jacket on a little silver pistol, she slipped through the opening.

It was not pleasant. Things rustled about overhead, probably bats, while other large creatures scurried about on the floor. It took several moments for her eyes to adjust to the light, and then she saw the only object in the garage—a battered truck.

"This is my city of treasure, old man?" Tuy said, gazing dumbfounded at the rusty Mercedes-Benz delivery van. He nodded happily, indicating she should inspect it more closely. She walked completely around it, making sure George went before her to brush away the cobwebs and scare off anything that might be lurking in the shadows. On the broad side of the van, printed in faded red letters, was the name Larouse. In the good times, before the Japanese and World War II, and for a bit in the late '40s and throughout the '50s, Larouse had been a French-run delivery service and warehouser in Vietnam, Laos, and Cambodia. The van was up on wheel blocks, and in its battered state looked as if it had given the last mile. Not worth dragging away, or surely someone would have done so already. The interior of the building itself did not inspire confidence, with its sagging roof and dark inner space infested with rats—and with spiders that looked healthy enough to take on the rodents in hand-to-hand combat.

Tuy took the ancient by the shoulder, surprised at how slight he was, and turned him to her. "Old man, please stop joking. Honestly, I do not find anything about the country or being here now pleasant. If there is no treasure, say so. You are too old to beat or kill." George muttered dangerously, but Tuy put her hand on his arm. "No, George, there is too much at stake here."

"Like what? If this old fool—!"

"Like our lives." She flashed him a warning look. "I said no."

With shaking fingers, the old man pulled a key from his pocket, and with a small bow, placed it in her hand. "The key to your golden city. You will notice the van has a lock, and it has not been tampered with. . . ."

The padlock was rusty, but after ten minutes of wrestling, Mako managed to get it to turn. The heavy rear door on the van swung up to reveal it was loaded to the top with cartons.

Mako lifted one to the ground. The cartons were carefully packed with ten-kilo boxes of Tuyet Lan brand cane sugar.

The old man carefully opened one of the boxes and held it out for her inspection. The brown grains had solidified into a semicrystalline mass. She gingerly tapped at it with one long fingernail. "Raw sugar . . ."

"No," he replied, "although it is raw. This is unprocessed; it was simply dried and ground into crystals, some time ago . . . but sugar, no. . . ." He thrust the box at her, inviting a closer inspection, and the triumphant gleam in his good eye was unmistakable. "The fruit of the white poppy, as I promised. . . ." He took in her surprise with a distant little smile and placed the box in her hands as if it were a rare and precious gift. "Yes, young explorer, here is your treasure—raw opium!"

5-4

The old man was full of surprises. He sat across from Tuy at a small table in the Hai Cua Restaurant in Cho Lon, the Chinese section of Saigon. They were sipping the excellent steaming-hot crab soup and discussing the illegal drug trade of the '50s. Tuy had a way of drawing out a man, the benefit of her years of training as a bar girl, and she listened well. The old man, on the other hand, seemed to want to talk. "We were very helpful to the Larouse family. We did everything, from cutting and scraping the flower pods to transportation to refining—"

"You had a factory?"

"Of course! One cannot get rich shipping raw sap as you are doing. Others take the big end. And rightly so—there is too much bulk. You give them problems."

Tuy heard herself sputtering, "But you never said—but this must be difficult—but this is impossible. . . ."

He made a deprecating sound with his lips, as if the young knew nothing at all. "Any second-year chemistry student with some five-liter flasks, a source of heat, a little tubing, a few chemicals, a touch of specific knowledge . . ." He shrugged his shoulders, his one blank eye gleaming in the candlelight. Tuy again had the odd impression he saw out of that eye, but of course that was impossible. The old man continued, "It depends on you . . . perhaps, for you, the money you gain is enough. I must ask, how much is rich?"

"You are suggesting I might increase my profits—?"

"By a factor of ten, on a continuing basis." He nodded, going back to slurping his soup. ". . . just a little factory. There are two steps. With the first, you extract the morphine. This is the heart of the opium, with only ten percent of the bulk. Next, you may reduce the opium to heroin—'white death,' as the moralists call it. Much easier to ship—and ready to sell. Wealth so concentrated that it staggers the imagination."

"Why did you not tell me this a month ago before I sold half of my treasure to *Xau My* Munson?"

The ancient cackled merrily. "How soon you forget; just that short time ago you were so without funds you took on this crazy American, *'Dien Cai Dao* Den-ny,' as your banker . . . now you have over one hundred thousand *My Kim*—but would you have listened to this a month ago?"

"Perhaps not . . ."

"And then, all of what I am saying goes beyond our original agreement. . . ."

Tuy eyed him carefully, more and more aware that it was she being led by this feeble old fellow, rather than the other way around. "Old man, it sounds like you have come up with a new deal. . . ."

He nodded, looking down at the noodles floating in his almost empty bowl. Tuy indicated the waiter was to take it away and bring the second course, crisp little egg rolls and a dish of chicken and bean sprouts in lemon sauce.

He reached for a piece of lettuce, rolled some chicken and sprouts in that, and dipped it in a bowl of *nuoc mam*. "You see, my dear young dragon lady, when I originally bargained for the last seed, I was desperate, I had to have that one thing, I was willing to give up even my life. I am not sorry for the bargain we made. But now I find there is life after the bargain.'' He bit off half the roll of lettuce and wiped with the back of his hand a thin dribble of sauce that ran down his chin. "I find myself alive, comfortable, eating good food here . . . and it has occurred to me there are perhaps yet some few years left to me, and also that I have some few chips left to bargain.''

"They are?"

The small cup of tea shook in the old man's hands. He sighed and set it down. "My knowledge. My contacts. This difficult business of the *pavot* is one I know well. I have, in a sense, given my life to it.''

"You propose that we become partners?"

The old man laughed until his wheezing sounds became a panting cough and she had to gently pat his back to bring him around. "Thank you, miss. . . . No, no, no, not partners. Were I a younger man, I would have that, and more, too . . . but you already have Crazyhead Den-ny, and I am much too old. But I have a little store of memories that can be useful.'' He tapped his head with a long bony finger. "Very useful to you . . . a disillusioned pharmacist who would jump at the chance to develop a distilling process. A small band of wealthy pirate-farmers in the highlands wringing their hands over what to do with last year's crops. Drivers who are willing to drive, who know the way, and who will say nothing. . . . You, of course, must be willing to pay generously for all, including the heavy Vietcong taxes on your vehicles, tolls to get across each province. You will need every penny you can get to begin.''

"The Vietcong," she whispered. "Deal with them?"

"You will find they are not so different from the officials in Saigon.'' He chuckled. "If you understood politics, I might describe them as the party out of office. . . .''

"The VC are baby-killers and rapists! I know from first hand—!"

The old man silenced her with a simple gesture. "How is our beloved Army of the Republic of Vietnam better? A shell from a rifle or cannon is blind as this eye, once it leaves the mouth of a gun. How do you think my family was reduced to the last seed? And the napalm of our allies is as blind as our own shells. It is the war that kills babies."

"They will kill me."

"You are babbling, child. This is not the young dragon lady I wish to see. The Vietcong are realists. They will not be very difficult once they realize your operation weakens America. I can assure you of this. They cooperated fully with us all those years against the French."

She was interested, in spite of herself. "Well . . . are the growers of *pavot* so eager to sell to anyone? After all, they do not know me."

"Things are very bad. The war has interrupted commerce; they sell to the devil himself if he brings *My Kim*. In some places opium is almost as cheap as the raw sugar you first thought was in the boxes. They store it in cans, in drums, in deserted houses and churches and schools. Like the pictures of America one sees, with the crops of grain piled wherever they can put it. They wait for the few with courage to come and get it."

"In Laos?"

"In Laos."

"And what do you want?"

The old man rolled and ate more of the chicken in lettuce. He licked his fingers and studied her carefully. "A place by the fire."

She refilled his teacup. "What? I don't understand. . . ."

He looked down at his thin, wrinkled hands, cupping the tea for warmth. "I think you do. I cannot have the strain of partnership, and my needs are small. I will give you my experience, my advice, and my contacts . . . you will provide me a place of quiet and peace and anonymity—as your housekeeper.''

''What?'' Tuy had been pouring her own tea, and it spilled over the white linen tablecloth in a light green stain. A black-coated waiter came and politely pressed a hand cloth to damp up the moisture. Tuy impatiently took the cloth and waved him out of hearing range.

Her behavior seemed to amuse the old man. ''Don't look so startled. I will ask a few hundred piasters a week as a living wage, and a little bed in back somewhere by the kitchen. And I do not work on Sundays and the days of the saints—I am a good practicing Catholic, you see. . . .''

''Housekeeper?'' she echoed dumbly.

''I can sweep the entranceway and the floor, and order the cook around and occasionally accompany her to market to make sure she isn't bleeding off too much of our household money. You can't ask much more than that of me . . . I am very old . . . and slowly going blind as well.''

Tuy somehow got through the rest of the meal. She knew she was going to agree to the deal; the clear vision of millions in *My Kim* just lying there like heaps of rice, waiting for a person of enterprise, was too much to pass by. But she was shaken by the old man's request. She had preferred to live alone, except for an occasional lover, because it was less conspicuous. Now she was to have a housekeeper, and he took it for granted there would be a cook. The thin ghosts of the terrorists who had killed her family must have been laughing. She would be obvious. If they didn't get her now, the local police would.

The paranoia mounted in her like a little flood of panic, and she was forced to shake her head, as if trying to throw off rats clinging to her hair. It was a long time ago. There were no terrorists. They were perhaps all dead. Yes—war must be very dangerous to terrorists as well as to the people they victimized. She sipped her tea and felt a little better. Finally composed, she placed her cool hand in his frail old

one. "All right, old man. We have a deal. Now advise me
what to say to the *Xau My*. . . ."

The old man breathed his own little sigh of relief. It was
true that his needs were small, and the arrangement with Tuy
could possibly provide for him for the rest of his life. But he
also had his own reasons for wanting to stay far in the background. That last Larouse truck had been a gift from the
departing French, to be shared with the entire pipeline that
had toiled over the years to create the Larouse family's huge
Swiss bank accounts. But the driver had died under questionable circumstances, and the truck had ended up on cement
blocks in his abandoned garage.

The old man wondered how many people in the business
still bore that grudge, or even suspected he was alive after
all those years. He shrugged his shoulders. One did one's
best, and left the rest in the hands of Jesus. He turned his
mind to the question of the *Xau My*. "Huh. I think he should
be delighted with your enterprise. I think he shall be the
happiest of men." He had no way of knowing the next time
Edgar greeted them it would be with a U.S. army issue .45
automatic in his hand and rage in his cold, blue eyes.

5-5

Major Edgar Munson brought along his own firepower:
six beefy MPs, guys from his own inner circle that he could
trust. Muscle was no problem. He could have had sixty if he
wanted, but that would have been too conspicuous. What
was needed here, he thought, was something precise and
surgical.

Two he stationed outside the heavy wooden front doors of
the Tuyet Lan Bar. It was one o'clock on a Tuesday afternoon, and as he expected, the bar had no customers. The
second two MPs neutralized Tuy's two thugs, George and
Mako. The third pair watched the girls so nobody ran for
reinforcements, and kept an eye on the door to the back room.

Edgar was wearing a dark business suit of gray herringbone and dark sunglasses, even though the rain-spattered day showed no hope for sunlight. He drew his own .45 from the soft leather Bianchi shoulder holster he had special ordered from Stateside, and stepped into the little back room. It was the way he liked to enter a place, the master of the situation, with no question about it. Tuy was there, behind her desk, her delicate hands on the table. The only wild card in the deck was the person she was talking to . . . a very sour-faced Denny Haller. Denny had just found out some good news and some bad news. His money had tripled. But Tuy needed capital, and was "reinvesting" it for him.

Munson leaned against the door frame, waving the nose of the .45 at Denny. "Who is this sad sack?"

Tuy remained totally unruffled. She could see through the doorway the MPs covering her men, yet she kept her composure, giving the *Xau My* a little smile. "I did not know this is what you meant when you shook hands to the start of a 'long and beautiful relationship.' That was only a few weeks ago, I recall."

Edgar angrily brushed that aside. He had come to confront Tuy. Another American, even one of her young lovers, complicated matters considerably. "None of your garbage. I said, Who is this dork-brain?"

Denny, already furious at the loss of his money, almost choked. He slowly stood, with his hands stretched out in the open to show he carried no weapons. Tuy smiled innocently, and told the obvious lie. "He is . . . my lover."

"Well, I want him out of here. Git, dork-brain!" He pointed the big automatic at Denny, who slowly walked to the door. "One grunt coming through!" he yelled to his men outside. "Let him out. See he keeps going!"

Two of the MPs roughly took Denny by the arms and half carried him across the barroom. "You're lucky, grunt-brains. You could be implicated in this mess." Denny didn't say anything. He caught George's eye on the way past and then was turned over to the MPs outside the front door.

"Move on down the street, punk. Don't look back."

If Denny had had time to think at all, he would have said he was acting to protect his interests, not to save Tuy. But he had no time . . . and the real truth was he hated Munson from the first moment he saw him. He shook his head at the big MPs. "No. You guys don't understand. The guy inside's in big trouble."

The larger of the MPs, a kid who could have been a tackle for the Nebraska Cornhuskers, took a piece of Denny's collar. "What do you mean?"

"There's a back way! Did you guys cover the back way? They got a whole gang out there! They're slime, man! They're gonna blow out the dude in the suit!" The two MPs eyed one another uncertainly. Denny knew he had won. "Come *on*! One of you. You only need one guy here. I'll lead the way. Hurry, before they blow him away!"

Denny turned and ran down the side alley that led to the deserted, garbage-cluttered back lane where he had first been beaten by George and Mako. After a moment's hesitation, the Nebraska tackle lumbered after him. The big MP rounded a corner to catch Denny's high-thrown kick in his throat. He went down, gurgling and grabbing at his neck with both hands. Denny kicked the wind out of him, then swiftly tied his hands with his regular belt and his feet with his white web belt. He stuffed a rotting piece of banana in his mouth and ran back around to the front of the building.

"Quick! I was right! There's four of them! Your buddy's holding them off!"

The second MP was bent over the first, starting to untie his arms, when Denny slammed the hard edge of his palm on the back of his neck. He too slumped to the ground and in a few minutes was trussed up securely. Denny pulled out his shirt and stuffed both their .45s in his pants.

Meanwhile, inside the back room, Edgar calmly seated himself in the chair vacated by Denny and poured a cup of tea from the pot in front of him. "Allow me to explain the reason for my present mood. Until I met you, I ran a modest little operation. Low profile, low risk. You and I go into business, become associates of a sort. The only reason I bother with such an amateur operation as yours is that you promise a volume business.'' He tapped the antique china teapot as he spoke, barely conscious of the ancient figures painted on the sides. ''Yet I do give you a chance—and yesterday, a one-in-a-billion risk becomes a reality. One of my shipments is opened, uncovering eighty thousand dollars worth of my investment.'' Edgar's face was suddenly a mask of fury, and he crushed the teapot with a glancing blow from the automatic. Tuy winced; she often smashed things, but it was all for show, and she was careful never to break anything of value.

''Describe what happened.''

''Why? I know what happened—you found a way to double-cross me!''

''That is not true, Mr. Munson. Please describe what happened.''

He blew out a sharp breath of air. ''Very well. I had a shipment in somebody's refrigerator. Standard procedure, the guy's an officer, shipping household goods back to the states. At the last minute he opens it up, he claims he was going to fill it with Ba Muoi Ba, nostalgic for the goddamn formaldehyde local brew. . . .''

Edgar set down his pistol and took a mango from the tray in front of him. He pulled out one of his small surgical knives and petulantly began carving a grim jack-o'-lantern face in the skin. The blade cut through the fruit effortlessly.

His behavior made Tuy a little nervous. There was something very wrong about Major Edgar Munson, something deeply malevolent that even his cruel behavior with little girls only hinted at. Tuy realized that before her was a man capable of any evil. Still, there was nothing to do but continue. He was her only client. ''And you think we had something to do with it? I can see you do. Well, nothing would be more foolish. I need you to ship our product—on a continuing basis." She leaned forward and smiled.

He picked up his revolver again. "You don't understand. One more loss like the one I suffered, and I'm ruined. I'm ruined anyway. The only way I can think of to ship bulk out of Saigon is in GI personal effects, and they are going to be inspecting that stuff from now on with a fine-tooth comb!"

She smiled again. "What can I do to win back your trust? A gift perhaps? . . ." She opened a small black lacquer box on the top of her desk.

"What is this?"

Tuy laughed confidently, the sound a low throaty chuckle. "The answer to some of your problems. You don't want to ship bulk, so we refine for you."

"Heroin?" His eyes bugged at the thought. He had occasionally run across small amounts of the drug, never more than a thimbleful, and it had always proven tremendously profitable. In fact, word from Stateside was that anyone trustworthy with factory capabilities in Southeast Asia could wear the king's crown. And here this insignificant little dealer bar girl was handing it to him on a silver platter!

"The white death itself." She nodded briefly. "This is about eighty-five percent pure. My chemist assures me he can do better." She saw the way he looked at the lacquer container as she carefully replaced the lid. Her red fingernails were a bright contrast to the deep black lacquer, which had an eggshell art drawing on the surface depicting a Vietnamese knight on a white horse, charging through fire with his lance at the ready. But, she noticed with a flash of alarm, her ruby ring had no color at all. It was as dark and unreadable as the rich black lacquer itself. That was an omen, she was sure. This alliance with the *Xau My* would lead to great evil, and to death. She tried to shrug it off, but a feeling of thin dread remained. Still, she had to go forward. They were talking about riches here, not silly girl feelings.

She tapped the top of the box with one of her bright red

fingernails. "There is enough here to at least soften your losses. Take it as a gift of faith."

"But . . . I told you, my pipeline is broken." Still, he could not keep his attention off that little lacquer box and the riches it represented.

"A man like you will mend the old pipeline—or find a new one." If Tuy, with her own ghosts to haunt her, had at that time even the smallest inkling of the horror this simple alliance with the *Xau My* would bring, she would have turned and fled in terror. Instead, she held the box out to him, and he accepted it eagerly. "The next time we meet, it will be under happier circumstances, to discuss the shipments, and, of course, your payments to us. . . ."

Edgar shook her hand, and tucked his .45 under his arm and the precious little box in a pocket. Then he stepped out into the next room where Mad Denny brutally knocked the wind out of him with a kick to the stomach. For Denny had managed to get the drop on the rest of the MPs, who were dividing their attention between George and Mako and the flirting *co-gai*s of the Tuyet Lan. Things look differently when seen through the dark wide barrels of twin .45s pointed at you, and Tuy's two men were able to silently disarm all of them. They finished just in time, too, for not ten seconds later the *Xau My* made his unfortunate appearance in the doorway.

Denny was in midswing, ready to give him another punch, when Tuy grabbed his arm. "No, *no*, my dear Mad Denny!"

"But this guy—?" Denny spun around, bewildered.

Tuy stood between him and the *Xau My*, who was groggily getting to his feet. Edgar triggered the wrist holster on one of the surgical knives, which he cradled, hidden in his left hand. As he got to his feet, he gradually inched to his left. Another foot, he calculated, and he could take the grunt's carotid artery. No hope, just one quick slash to the neck and he'd be thirty seconds dead. In his heightened state, he could see the blood pulsing, just the right place—

"I could blow a hole in you, monsieur, big enough to stick

a bamboo pole through,'' George said quietly. ''It could be helpful, for your men to carry you away.'' He levered a round into the chamber of one of the .45s liberated from the MPs.

The metallic snick served to bring everyone back to their senses. ''It is a mistake,'' Tuy repeated, still holding on to Denny's arm. ''The *My* and I have arrived at an understanding.'' She took Edgar's arm with her other hand. ''You must understand, my lover is very jealous. That is all. . . .''

Edgar looked at Denny from under lowered eyebrows. He brushed himself off, managing to slip the knife back in its sheath at the same time. He had underestimated the grunt. He raised a shaking finger. ''You're dinky dow, messing with me, boy! You understand 'dinky dow'?''

''That's my name,'' Denny said steadily, keeping his eyes on Edgar's hands. ''That's where the word comes from.'' He had seen the knife and was ready for anything. ''You're a weird cat yourself. We've not met before, but from the description, I'd say I'm looking at His Ugliness, the *Xau My* himself.''

Edgar flushed a deep red and clenched his fists. ''Nobody calls me that—''

''Not to your face. But, behind your back . . .''

''You *are* crazy.''

''That's a fact, Jack. Now why don't you pick up your little gang of white-belted fairies and hustle your butt out of here. You'll find the other two in an alley in back.''

''Mister, this is my town. I'll have you picked up on sight—''

''Somebody'll die first,'' Denny said simply. ''Out.''

And Edgar Munson, under the trailing observation of a half-dozen army automatics lifted off his own men, had no choice but to obey.

CHAPTER SIX

6-1

IT WAS ENTIRELY LOGICAL TO DENNY THAT HE FOLLOW HER.
After all, she had his money, and one way or the other he
was going to get it back. He had to find out everything about
her: where she lived, who her contacts were, what she did
besides the Tuyet Lan. He didn't think twice about it, although it changed the pattern of his days.

First, he had to get around the army bullshit, the rule that
E-5s and lower had to sleep in their sagging bunks back at
the Thirty-third. Since there was a lockout at Tan-Son-Nhut
after midnight and Tuy didn't leave her bar until it closed at
one (the Saigon curfews of earlier military regimes having
been lifted at that time), he would have to bend a technicality
or two. He still worked the night shift at the White Shack,
even though transmissions were down so low the Dimbos
often finished before nine.

It was the long-standing policy at the Thirty-third that
shacking up was good for the men; it relieved their tensions.
There was an ammo box full of cheap prophylactics next to
the sign-out book by the front gate. And if you signed out
for downtown in the evening, and then signed back in before
eight the next morning, the duty officer looked the other way.
That meant he could get away with his plan, if he could find
a decent place to spend the nights.

One night he finished at the White Shack and took a little
white scooter-bus to the main gate. There he switched to a
taxi, and rocketed away through the rain squalls and water-

filled potholes to the west end of Truong Minh Giang Street. Truong Minh Giang ran fairly close to the base, had many places for rent or lease, and was not packed with Americans. The prices were decent because most of the GIs preferred hotel rooms downtown. He was interested in one specific villa, a place first leased by Ranley, the sergeant who headed the Dimbos when Denny had first landed in Nam.

After Ranley rotated back Stateside, three or four of the NCOs took over his lease, turning it into a beery sort of frat house. The usual tour was twelve months, and whoever was left holding the lease was usually looking for new blood to share it. Denny didn't know who was in there at the moment—he just hoped there would be a vacancy.

He tipped the cabbie twenty P extra for luck, and stood in the mist in front of the villa, thinking back a few years. Ranley had been of that long-since-discredited train of thinking that had deeply believed in American involvement in Southeast Asia. He had believed in Dulles's domino theory, believed Ngo Dinh Diem's nationwide elections were the best they could do at the time, believed that without our help the Communists would swallow South Vietnam, Laos, and Cambodia, and that a bloodbath would follow. He was a John F. Kennedy man, inspired to work with the local natives to ensure democracy and raise their standard of living, while his brothers in the Peace Corps strove for the same ends.

Ranley's was an idealistic time, and it had ended badly. Diem and Kennedy were both assassinated, and somewhere in those heart-rending months the focus of the war was lost. The next time anybody looked, impatient, arrogant Johnson was there scratching its ears, and the war rolled over to show its huge, ugly underbelly. As U.S. involvement escalated, the percentage of grunts who were trained to know or understand—and hence could relate to the Vietnamese people—shrunk until it was tiny. Of course, it was logistics that made that happen, you don't teach hordes of high school–grad grunts oriental language and culture, not when you've got a war to knock over before the back-home folks get too irritated. No one else seemed to think it was that important, but to Ranley we had made a critical mistake. He felt breaking through the barriers of language and custom was a major key to winning the war. Once we gave up on that, we were doomed to Americanization, to the mad attempt to bull our way to victory on our own. Ranley had read the history books, and felt the stupidity of what was happening . . . and when his long slow disillusionment finally crystallized, he had divorced the war, the army, and the Vietnamese people in one bold stroke.

Although they shared little of Ranley's idealism, the Dimbos had all worshipped him. He spoke Zip like a native. He found out-of-the-way hamlets where they could still see the centuries-old rituals of birth and marriage and death, customs still untrammeled by the war. He was a martial arts expert, and enough of a regular guy to help them bypass most of the army bullshit. The Dimbos had been his friends, his gang . . . and when they one by one had lost their lives, Ranley had given up on the war.

"Hey, Denny! Madness himself!"

Denny looked up, startled out of his reverie, to see Weird Elliott standing in the doorway with an open can of Schlitz. "Weird! You live here?"

Elliott's grin was enormous, "Does the moose crap in the woods? Come on in, my boy, don't stand out there in that drizzle-shit!"

Inside, there was an NCO party going on. Five or six sergeants sat around an iced tub of beers, eating cold hamburgers from a crumpled box that had survived the long taxi ride from the downtown Enlisted Men's Club. There were two or three Vietnamese girls in various stages of undress wandering around, chatting with the men in their simple bar girl's English. A few of the sergeants grunted acknowledgment as Elliott plunked a cold beer in Denny's hand. He had made no effort to win the affection of the lifers, and they had always repaid his feelings in spades.

Elliott had always been an exception, but Elliott could do anything—everyone knew he wasn't quite right in the head. Now he waved his hand at the activity around them. "It's pretty quiet yet. Wait till the bars start to close—we'll have a gang bang yet tonight!"

Denny launched his case. "Look, Weird . . . I need a place to hang out nights. I mean, I'll pay, I've got plenty of money." As he spoke, a stern, leather-faced E-7 moved closer to them, a man Denny only knew as Roller-coaster.

Weird laughed his high cackle. "Why not? Why not! I think we could fix you up, and I just love the sound of your greenbacks! There's just me and old Rollie here right now."

The leather-face frowned. "Uhh, Elliott, I don't think we should. . . ."

Weird chuckled again, his mad little laugh riding over the hi-fi blaring Johnny Mathis's "Chances Are." "Why not, Rollie—there's just you and me paying right now. Rest of these freeloading bums will be out of here by midnight."

Roller-coaster sucked his teeth, eyeing Denny through narrow eyes. "He's just a E-5, and besides, he says stuff against lifers."

Elliott put one arm around Roller-coaster and the other around Denny. "Awww, come on, Rollie . . . nothing any of us hasn't said. And His Madness here should have been an E-6 years ago. Asshole Anderson hates his guts, is all. . . ."

Roller-coaster gave a sigh and walked away. "Whatever you say, Weird. . . ."

"Come on, ol' Denny—have I got the room for you!"

"What about the third bedroom? I thought this was a three-bedroom bordello?"

Weird gave him a wink and his high laugh. "Aww, you can't have that. That's the arms room—come on, I'll show you."

When he unlocked the door, Denny had to gasp, for it

contained enough automatic weapons and explosives and ammo to keep a company happy for a week. "*Je*-sus, Weird . . . where'd you get all this shit?"

"My private collection," the sergeant said proudly. "As you know, my friend, I buy and sell. Look. AK-47. I got a dozen of 'em. Some day I'm gonna make a fortune . . . if I can figure out how to get it all home."

"Aren't you afraid Victor Charlie's gonna move in here and wipe you out?"

"Oh, it's all booby-trapped," Weird said with a smile of boyish pride. "And I got it on a timer, too . . . I can set it so the whole thing blows if I don't come back in up to seventy-two hours. Come on, I'll show you to your room. . . ."

It turned out to be Ranley's old den. It was a large room with two walls floor-to-ceiling with bookshelves. One corner had a small fireplace stacked with magazines and obviously now not in use. Denny went over to the shelves with a feeling of mounting excitment, "Ranley's library!" Ranley had left his collection of books, books in French and English and Vietnamese, books on war and the ancient kingdoms of the Annamese cordillera and Chinese history and dozens of other subjects that had caught his interest.

Elliott shrugged. "Yeah. You know how hard it is to get firewood during the wet. We tried to burn them, but they just smoldered. Kinda nice anyway, don't you think, the way they add a spot of color on the shelves?"

"You were gonna burn his books?"

"Yeah. Nobody reads 'em. I sure thought they would light up, but they didn't."

Denny looked around. There was a small cot in one corner, sufficient for his needs. Since taking up gung fu, he would only lie on a straight, rock-hard bed, and the thin mattress on its heavy wooden planks would work perfectly. "Weird, I'll take it, but I gotta have the books in the deal, okay?"

Weird shrugged again and gave his strange laugh. "You don't even want to know how much?"

Denny wandered over to the bookshelves, again lost in thought. "Naaa . . . deal's a deal. You'll be fair. . . ." Mad Denny knew he didn't *believe* in the war, and that his thinking was light-years away from Ranley's. What he didn't realize was that their conclusions were strikingly similar. Ranley didn't think the war could or would be won, either; you didn't have to be a real historian to see MACV was committing the old mistakes of the French, running a defensive war from the cities, darting out in brave little sweeps to "clear" areas that wouldn't stay sanitized for a day once they left. The difference was that Denny had no patience for any excuses about how we had gotten into it in the first place, or why we stayed.

"You know, Weird—if they hadn't force-fed me Zip back at the language school, I'd be just like all the other grunts around here."

"Kind of a white elephant, ain't you?" Weird responded in a not entirely unfriendly voice. "Not much difference to my mind. We see 'em as dinks or gooks, and you call 'em zips. Big deal."

"No. I see them as poor human slobs, like you and me."

"Oh, yeah?" Weird gave a derisive hoot. "And what do you think of their lofty aims and aspirations?"

"Not very much . . ." he was forced to admit. "But I don't think any more of our own." Not having any ideals about the war, he was free to speculate, as they all did, about the real reasons they were there. "Du Pont must be heavy into napalm . . . it's the only reason I can think of."

"Naaw, my boy, you're losing sight of the historical perspect-ive." Weird grinned at him over the grimy bottom halves of reading spectacles. "It's the culmination of the great American western movement!"

"Shit, Elliott, what are you talking about?"

Elliott took him by the shoulder and steered him back to

the party. "Come, my boy, sip another beer and it will all become transparent to you as Father Weird opens your eyes. It's all about offshore oil rights and *Dac Biet* Fried Chicken franchises and all those beautiful white tropical beaches from here to Hue. We got a job to do, real American work—we got to clean up the natives, put 'em on reservations, get 'em eating the Colonel's original recipe, get a *Hoi Viet-My* in every village so they learn to talk like white folks and niggers, punch in the freeways, get those condos up, get ready for statehood—boy, we're gonna call it New Florida! Am I right?" After a few more beers it all seemed perfectly clear to Mad Denny.

6-2

Actually following someone when you don't want to be seen is more difficult than the detective stories make it out to be; at least it was so for Denny. One night he waited for two hours in a cab across the street from the Tuyet Lan, and finally she didn't come out at all. Or maybe he missed her, for after a while the steady light rain drumming on the rooftop made him sleepy, and he dozed off. The cabbie didn't mind . . . the meter was running, and he wasn't burning gas.

The second night, after long hours of waiting, Denny was again half sleeping in a rusty old blue-and-cream. The driver at least had kept him awake; a thin, surly man, he wasn't content to sit and be paid—and feeling there was something wrong about it, he said so, continuously, for the entire time, while rain thudded on the roof and Denny's temper went up and up.

Finally Tuy did come out, rushing through the downpour for a cab. *"Di, di, mao len!"* he shouted at his driver. But the man was slower than a slug. She was gone so fast the red of her cab's taillights was swallowed up in the traffic flow while the surly fellow fished in his jacket pockets for the keys, which he had taken out of the ignition.

The third night, a nervous old cabbie was able to follow her three blocks before losing her. And after six days of the routine, no one had been able to stay behind her for more than seven or eight blocks, even though she usually headed in the same approximate direction.

What was needed was a driver in the spirit of *True Detective Magazine*, and so Denny took a few days off just to cruise around town in taxis, looking for natural daredevils behind the wheel. Finally he found him, a happy-go-lucky young Chinaman with one hand who drove like the wild wind. His name was Han, and he'd donated his upper body part to the war. He held the steering wheel with his stump while shifting with his good hand. After a hair-raising ride from downtown to the airport in what must have been a record time, Denny nicknamed him Han-from-Hell and signed him on.

Han-from-Hell was one of those cabbies who loved to talk while driving, and he couldn't talk without looking into the backseat at you. Denny thought he probably did it for effect, because he usually thought of something while rocketing along between two deuce-and-a-half army trucks or negotiating a treacherous potholed curve or threading a rapid path through an intersection full of heavily-loaded-down pedestrians.

He had the additional problem that his stump occasionally slipped on the wheel in the damp weather, causing him to interrupt his shifting to correct the cab from speeding into a lamppost or jumping a wide boulevard into the oncoming lane of traffic.

Han-from-Hell eagerly accepted the challenge. He kept the engine of his little Renault running, the wipers beating a little rhythm on the windshields. "They come out soon, Mister Den-ny?"

"I don't know, Han. . . ." Denny mumbled out of his slouch in the backseat for the hundredth time. And just then she did come. She stood on the corner for a moment, looking mysterious under her rain cloak, half hidden by the purple umbrella she carried. "That's her!"

"Ahhh, a lady!" Han chuckled. "We go pick her up, boss?"

"Nooo!" Denny yelled, for Han was already sliding out in traffic and down the block toward her. "No! Pull to the side here! We do as I said—just follow her!"

"Ok-ay dok-ay, boss!"

A cosmopolitan Vietnamese woman on a street corner in the rain will outmaneuver her New York counterpart nine times out of ten. They may be petite, but they know how to call over a cab. Fortunately another blue-and-cream cut in front of them almost immediately. Denny felt sure she still hadn't seen him. Her taxi drove off, and the chase was on.

Much of what took place in the next twenty minutes was a blur to Mad Denny. He had the image of native faces close up yelling through the glass at him as they wound their way through the city, clinging to the tail of Tuy's cab. Han-from-Hell took the corner off a pile of stacked pineapples when he went up on the sidewalk to get around a parked truck. He nearly took out a White Mouse directing traffic at an intersection.

Han saw it as great fun, even if he didn't quite get the distinction between trailing someone and racing them. At one point, with a huge grin on his face, he pulled neck and neck with the other cab. Denny had to yell at him from the floor where he crouched down out of sight. "Noooo, Han— just *follow* them!"

But in the end, he got the job done. Tuy's cab pulled over in front of a villa in a residential section outside the downtown area—on Truong Minh Giang, not a half kilometer from Ranley's old place. Denny instructed Han to drive slowly on past. He saw Tuy pay her cabbie and walk quickly toward the villa. Then he had Han drop him off a block from Ranley's place. The young amputee was delighted with the one-thousand P tip he received. "Boss do funny things all for a piece of ass!" he shouted out the open window as his taxi rocketed away.

In true detective fashion, Denny decided to stake out her house, to watch who came and went. He found a humble

little native restaurant kitty-corner across Truong Minh Giang
from her house. It was a shabby, one-room affair with a lean-
to kitchen in back. It had a board-plank patio covered with
stiff corrugated plastic sheets of Jell-O green. There were
actually more tables outside than in, and the patio had a
decent view over a thick wall of shrubs. At night two bare
electric bulbs overhead augmented the flickering light from
the fat candles placed in empty jelly jars on the occupied
tables.

Again, the waiting proved far more difficult than you read
about in the detective mysteries or see in the cop shows on
TV, particularly for someone as impatient as Mad Denny. If
it weren't for his money, he told himself over and over, he
would dump the whole crazy scheme. And here is where
Ranley's library came to his aid.

When he'd found that library, it was a stroke of fortune, a
good thing, not unlike running across a treasured old rabbit's
foot or a lucky walnut. It was a link to happier, more innocent times, and it pleased him more than he knew. But now,
with all the time on his hands, he began to read Ranley's
books—using the reference sources to track words he didn't
know, or to find the western names for roots or herbs or fruit
he found in the market place. He ran across a worn English
language version of Camus's *La Peste*, and that interested
him, the pervasive rot and death of the plague reminding him
of where he was.

He took a half dozen or so books along and spent all his
time on the patio, when he wasn't working or caught up in
the army bullshit. Often it was foggy, and he would sit alone
outside in the chill with the dribble of water in old rain gutters
in his ears. He wore a heavy old sweater of Ranley's that he
found, and heavy sweat socks that he got from the PX. He
whiled the long slow hours away, eating steaming bowls of
pho and sipping hot tea, with stacks of Ranley's books to
occupy his time.

They sold no beer, and so Americans never came there,

but they served him without comment. He said he was a student, and after a time he and the little lame woman who waited on him became friendly, joking about the weather that never seemed to stop dumping rain on them.

This new phase of his detective work proved less rewarding than he would have imagined. After a week, he had established the presence of a half-blind old housekeeper and a middle-aged *ba* who was probably the cook. He would have thought Tuy kept her two thugs about, always lurking in the shadows, but he never saw them. And no one else showed up. She apparently did all her business at the Tuyet Lan or elsewhere, and kept her private life to herself. If this continued, he would have no choice but to try and track her from the Tuyet Lan Bar again and see if she went anywhere else during the day . . . a course of action he didn't want to take because of the danger of being spotted. He even was beginning to think of giving up entirely.

It had been one of those rain-drenched weeks in the Mekong delta after which the water doesn't know where to go any more so it dampens boots until the leather goes to mush and thin tendrils of fungus grow inside, and the skin also becomes pale and weak and susceptible to rots too various and unappealing to think about. It was getting to the end of a Saturday afternoon when a cab unexpectedly showed up outside Tuy's villa. The door opened and a purple umbrella appeared, followed by Tuy herself, carrying a bunch of packages as she ran for the door.

There had been more than the usual activity earlier that day, with both the old housekeeper and the cook going out twice for market stuff—greens and fruit that they carried in string-loop baskets, and freshly plucked chickens. Nothing earthshaking; Mad Denny was bored and ready to give up his vigil. Doober had always ranted on about the glories of Vietnamese poetry, but Denny found he just couldn't get into it. In his state of mind, counting the line of ants parading across the patio to an abandoned scrap of fish on the floor was the most interesting thing he could think of.

And then George showed up, driving an old black Citroën. He got out from behind the wheel, his black skin shining in the rain, and put on an appropriately sinister hat. Then he opened the trunk and took out what looked like a carton with fresh bread loaves and a few bottles of red wine. He was met at the door by the old caretaker, and he returned to the car and drove away.

That was only the beginning of it. About an hour later, the half-blind old man left the house yet again. This time, instead of heading on down the street he bowed his head under a wind-spavined and tattered black umbrella and crossed the street, walking directly toward the restaurant.

For a moment, Denny thought of slipping out the back way. Then he remembered he didn't know if they *had* a back way. And then it was too late to do anything but remain where he was and fudge it through.

Heavy evening had descended on the city; headlights pushed away tendrils of fog as they cut through the dark, and wheels sent out side currents of spray followed by little water rooster tails. The old man stood for a moment in the soft candlelight of the patio, blinking as if he were lost. He leaned his umbrella to drip in a corner by the entrance and picked his way hesitantly through the irregular sprawl of tables and chairs. Everything was vacant, so he had his pick of the place, and Denny had a good chance to study the man. He was very ancient, probably ninety or more. He approached steadily, and was practically up to Denny's table before the dumbstruck American realized he meant to join him.

He stood at the table, so small and hunched over that Denny didn't have to look upward very much to see his face. ''Good evening, young sir,'' the quavering old voice said in Vietnamese.

Denny half stood and gave him a small hesitant bow.

"Chao, thua ong . . . please be seated. Can I get you some *pho*—or tea, perhaps?"

The old man nodded, pulling his frayed black trench coat tighter around him and taking the seat across from Denny. "Some tea would be nice." He pointed to the stack of books on the table and laughed a little soundless laugh that showed his black teeth, testimony that old *ba*s weren't the only ones addicted to chewing the betel nut. "I see you are a scholar of Vietnam. Interesting. *Kim Van Kieu,* our greatest classic."

The old man spoke with the ambiguity that comes so easily with the language, and Denny didn't know if he or the classic or both of them were interesting. He decided that it didn't really matter. "I'm not much into it, *thua ong.* Too poetic for me. I mean, it's got the real dirt of life in there somewhere, but I don't have the patience for all that flowery language."

The old man showed his teeth again. "It is probably not meant for you. Our women like it, though—Kieu is their heroine."

"I thought the *Su Tu Ha Dong* was their heroine." Denny poured the old man a cup of tea from his pot, which was on a old iron trivet over a warming candle.

"So you know some of our ways . . . that is good. You may have a chance."

"What do you mean, a chance?"

"To survive, always to survive." The old man wrapped his fingers around the warmth of the cup and studied Denny through his one good eye. "Who can read the complexity of the female dragon's mind? One moment soft and sweet, the couple to the body, and the next beat of time lashing out like steel to strike sparks on the poor devil who happens to be closest. . . ." He shrugged, as if to say it was part of the eternal mysteries.

Denny set the teapot back without filling his own cup. After a day of waiting, he was ready to float away. "You didn't come here to talk about the female dragon's mind."

"Yes and no," the old man said. As he held his cup to his

mouth, his hands shook so violently that a thin dribble of tea ran down his wrinkled face, through his wispy white beard, finally to drip on the tablecloth. He didn't seem to notice, carefully replacing the cup on the table and wrapping his old hands around it again for the warmth. "The mind of the dragon lady . . ."

Denny sighed, realizing he was a total failure at the detective business. "I see. Then you know I have been watching you."

The old man nodded thanks as Denny refilled his cup. "She is, I think, most annoyed that you are so obvious."

"Tucked away in the back of this restaurant?" he protested, waving his hands around to emphasize the emptiness of the place.

"Like a pink flower in a snowdrift . . . it is an old Hanoi saying. Did you know it snows in the north? On the mountaintops to the north and west, and sometimes even in the capital itself. I came from the north myself . . . my whole family did . . . so long ago it seems impossible. . . ."

The old man lapsed into silence. Denny didn't know what to say next. He sputtered, "Well, I *didn't* know that, and about this following business, your mistress is unjustly holding on to a great deal of my money, and I'm angry, too. . . ."

The old man's shrug indicated the unimportance of all that, at least to him. The white film crusted over his blank eye like an irregular translucent scum, and Denny could see the faint outline of the pupil behind it. There was a long pause, and finally his doddering guest spoke again. "The young mistress invites you to dine with her tonight."

"What?" Denny was rattled again. In a fight or a battle he could be cold as ice, but he had to admit Tuy was always outguessing him. He shook his head no and started to gather his books to beat a hasty retreat. "Look, *thua ong*, I'm afraid—I mean, it's really out of the question."

"Out of the question . . ." the old man repeated after him, as if he didn't understand the meaning of the words. "But it wasn't a question . . . it was a very firm invitation." And with that he took a .45 automatic from the pocket of his trench coat and pointed it across the table.

"Oh," Denny gulped, "a *Vietnamese* invitation . . ." It was army issue, probably one of those lifted from the *Xau My*'s MPs, Denny thought. He marveled how huge it looked in the frail hand. He noticed the old fellow dribbled again as he took a last swallow of tea . . . but he held the weapon steady as a rock.

Denny gave up any thoughts of taking him out and slowly got to his feet. He held his arms wide to show he meant no harm. Being careful to explain what he was about to do, he reached slowly in his shirt pocket and dropped a two-hundred-piaster note on the table. Then he carefully gathered his books and started across the street.

"Fifty would have been much more than enough," the old man commented with a belittling air. "The French were right, I think—they always said you free-spending *Nguoi My* would ruin the economy for the rest of us."

"Yeah, sure. I wasn't thinking about exact change with that .45 in my face. Did you know the MPs like to file those actions down to a hair trigger?"

But the old fellow got in the last word. "Of course, young sir. This one must be one of those; it fired by accident in the living room when I was testing it. I'm glad to hear it wasn't my fault." For all his doddering, he was a careful old man. He stayed five feet behind Denny, with both hands jammed in the wide pockets of his trench coat as they moved away from the restaurant. Although the rain was cold on his thin white hair, he didn't bother with his umbrella, which he could pick up any time later in the evening. The gun didn't go off, and in less than a minute they were safely inside the house across the street.

6-3

An antique French cut-glass chandelier hung from the center of the ceiling. It had managed to survive its transition to electricity with some grace and now poured a soft red-orange glow on the table beneath it. This was set with silver, fine china, and linens, the best Tuy could find of what the colonials had left behind. A coal-burning Franklin stove gave off a cheery blaze from a corner of the room, and there was a vase of colorful fresh flowers on a side table. Somewhere hidden in an armoire a hi-fi softly played cuts from Pete Fountain's LP *The Blues*.

The old man ushered Denny into this room and told him to make himself comfortable by the fire. He returned in a minute, bundled in a huge fisherman's sweater. "The mistress bought it for me," he said self-consciously, as if he realized how unusual his combination of peasant's robes and the ornate wool sweater was.

"Needed something big to hide the gun, I suppose," Denny grumbled.

The old man frowned but said nothing. He moved closer to the fire and held his hands next to the hot metal surface as if nothing could drive the chill from them. Finally, he gave Denny a sideways look from his good eye. "The mistress does not do much work here, only when she is forced to. I did not respect that at first, but I do now."

"Meaning?"

"You should truly attempt the role of guest."

"Oh sure—that's too much! You drag me over here at gunpoint, and I'm supposed to mind my manners!"

"Life is strange," the old man admitted, "but you have been a serious embarrassment to the mistress. We have all felt the effects of the discomfort you caused one of her clients—"

"The *Xau My*? I thought he was going to kill her!"

"Yet it was not so. She had resources you did not expect,

and was in no jeopardy. Your rashness was the real danger. She has been advised not to deal with you."

Denny frowned, "Advised? By who?"

"By her advisors," the old man replied calmly, seeming to look at Denny with his blank white eye. He waved a hand at the room around him. "You can see she chose to ignore the advice."

Tuy entered through a heavy beaded curtain across the room. The sight of her took Denny's breath away. She was not only gorgeous, she was wrapped in a glittering surprise, a low cut flapper dress of clinging silk and silver sequins. Her hair was cut short and bobbed, and she wore long pearl strands around her neck. Her outfit was perfect even to a small bead purse, which had the inlaid outline of a faded dragon. She stood in the soft light of the room and seemed to glow in her own loveliness.

Denny, caught completely off guard again, stumbled through his feelings. "Tuy—you look like you stepped out of a fashion magazine—you look—truly—wonderful!"

She came across the room in a shower of little glimmers, the dress clinging to her lithe form as she walked, and held her hand out to him. Caught up in the moment, he hesitantly took it. Her hand was soft and warm and trusting in his, and he had already brushed the skin on the back of it with his lips before the realization of who he was and who she was returned. He stiffened imperceptibly, dropping her hand, as the memory of Charley and Larkey welled up to warn him.

Tuy seemed not to notice, favoring him with a bright smile and a courteous little curtsy, and then turning to the old man to give him a mysterious, triumphant look. The ancient returned her look with his baleful, half-blind stare and hobbled from the room. "I'll get the wine, mistress."

"That damn old guy brought me here at gunpoint," Denny growled.

A momentary cloud passed over Tuy's mood. She shook it off. "Let's not talk about it right now, Denny. Do you like my dress?'' She spun in front of him and the short skirt flared in a revealing blaze of sequined tassels.

He had to admit he did. ''You really—I am surprised. I never saw you in anything but an *ao dai*, and this is so different. Where—? How—?''

''Come Mad Denny—we will sit in chairs by the fire. The old man will bring us wine, and I will tell all. . . .'' She laughed gaily. ''Well, *almost* all.''

The old man came from behind the bead curtain, where he had been waiting her command, with a pair of crystal tulip glasses and a newly opened bottle of French champagne. He poured and, setting the bottle on a black lacquer Parsons table nearby, discreetly left.

Tuy's eyes sparkled as she watched Denny over the rim of her bubbling wine. ''So, where to begin—you may ask me . . . almost anything!''

''I know I'm sounding like an idiot, but I'm just surprised. I know I'm gaping. You don't look—you're not dressed—this place isn't anything like I would have expected.''

Tuy inspected her patent leather high-heeled flapper shoes. ''And what did you expect? The little bar girl that once you knew is gone a long time now.''

''I know, but . . .'' He couldn't take his eyes from her. The hi-fi set slipped down the next record and Benny Goodman started in on ''Stompin' at the Savoy.''

She jumped up, pulling on his arm. ''Come on! Teach me to jitterbug! You Americans all know how to dance!''

''Well, actually, I *do* know how to dance, but this is a swing—''

''*Le swing* then. Teach me *le swing*!'' Her eyes shone with her eagerness, and the whole evening began to strike a responsive chord with Denny. He actually was a very good dancer, back before all the trouble started. Dancing had been his mother's passion, and she had taught him everything she knew. He had a natural flare for it; he could do all sorts of steps—the hop and the cha-cha and the samba—and many more exotic and almost forgotten moves from the heyday of the grand ballrooms. For him, dancing had led to a cappella choir and to the drama club, areas where he had natural talent and would have been rewarded, had he not also stood aside, apart from the crowd, rebellious and moody. That had been the fifties. Ike was king, and fitting into the peace and prosperity was everything. So much for rewards.

She kicked off her shoes and stood eagerly before him, a slim girl with a wide grin on her pretty face. In a few moments, he had outlined the basics of the swing, and he led her through the happy rocking motions of the dance. The music went on and on, the champagne had its effect, and he got into it. It was a good feeling, the first time he had really let go since the army, and he even showed off a little with the silly Bees Knees, ending in the Shuffle-off-to-Buffalo.

She was a fast learner and kept after him, wanting more steps, more dancing tips, more of his skills. There was something pathetic, almost a touch of frantic, about her desire to learn. For his part, Denny had forgotten what it was to shine, it had been so long since he had used his talents. He was soon lost in the fun of it, rocking and swaying as he taught his young partner. And all the while they laughed and danced, the old man stood motionless on the other side of the bead curtain, not really a presence except for the hint of his one white eyeball.

Finally Denny collapsed back in the chair and grabbed for his wineglass. "Stop! Stop. I've got to rest. Got to get my breath back!"

She sat beside him, breathing hard, her happy glow enveloping both of them. "That was great, Ong Denny! You are a master of the dance! What other hidden talents might you have?"

"Oh, I don't know," he replied without thinking, "I can fire an M16 pretty good."

He was unconsciously sardonic, but his words had the

effect of sending a little chill through her. "I meant—like dancing. . . ."

"Ohh, I'm sorry. . . ." He was sincere, but the mood had changed and he knew he had done it. He no longer was the exciting paramour who had swept her off her feet, and she no longer was the wild and mysterious rage of the Roaring '20s.

She got to her feet with a little sigh. "No matter. It was fun. Great fun! That is how to live!" She reached for his hand. "Come, we will have dinner."

Tuy's cook had been selected by the half-blind old man. For over twenty years she had been responsible for the table set for a branch of the Larouse family. The meal she prepared for them that night would have fared well on any colonialist's table in the good old days. There was a platter of the delicate Vietnamese egg rolls, and chicken in lemon sauce, and shrimp in lobster sauce with just the right hint of garlic. All was served with rice, done just a touch sticky, the Vietnamese way. There was an unobtrusive bottle of the best grade *nuoc mam* sitting side by side with a bottle of A-1 sauce.

The old man returned to pour the wine, a fine French red from the '50s. They ate in silence. Denny finally picked up the bottle of A-1, searching for some way to straighten out the mood of the evening. "Now this seems a little out of place!"

Tuy rewarded him with a smile. "It was obtained with great enterprise from one of the Officers' Clubs, specially for you."

"Then you knew I was coming. . . ." He saw her mood get serious again. "Damn it, I'm sorry. I *am* trying. It's just that there's so much . . . so much *history* between us." He paused and saw that he had her full attention. She watched him, fork poised in midair, waiting for him to go on. "To tell the truth, I was so sure you were responsible for Larkey's death for so long—and then when I finally saw you on the street—I'm not sure what I was going to do to you, but it was going to be violent."

She sipped the wine from her glass slowly, unconsciously holding it delicately with two fingers, as she knew it was right to do from all she had read. "And now? How do you feel about me now?"

He sighed and reached for his own wineglass. It never occurred to him to tell her anything but the truth. "Mostly angry, I guess. Distrustful."

"Why? I have never lied to you."

The old man returned and filled their glasses. Denny looked down into the circle of glowing red wine, which was reflecting the light of the chandelier. Then something caught his attention across the table. He thought it was her wine glass, but when he looked closer it proved to be the rich ruby color of the stone on her ring, which made the wine look dull by comparison. She followed his gaze and had a sharp intake of breath when she saw the intensity of its color. In that moment Tuy had an almost superstitious feeling there was something special to what was about to happen, indeed what was already happening. There was a magic, an unknown quantity, in the ring the old man had given her; she had known that from the moment she tried it on her finger. Yet it was a force she felt without understanding. Why was the gem so bright, so almost unnaturally glowing now? She felt motionless, trapped outside time. While the ring flared, her pulse beat faster and wild thoughts raced through her head. . . . Was it romance with this unlikely, rash American? Or his blood, the blood of yet another unlucky Dimbo, that would be on her hands? She couldn't decide and came out of her shocked reverie to see him staring at her. "You look at my ring. . . ." she said, her eyes wide, her mouth slightly open.

"Yes. It looks like it's on fire." Still she stared at him, and he wanted to continue. He meant to say he thought it was important, because it obviously meant something to her, but all that came out was, "I think it's important."

"You do?" She looked up at him, now truly shaken. "Important how? To whom?"

He stared back at her, trapped in a conversation he didn't really understand. "Important . . . for us. Yes." He gave her a firm little nod, as if that were that, and managed another sip of his wine, hoping he had said the right thing. After all, he told himself, he didn't want to offend her. She still had his twenty thou *My Kim*.

"To us . . . to our ventures, perhaps . . ." She let it trail off, uncertain, watching him for another sign.

He didn't like being on ground he knew so little about, and so took the easy way out. "By the way, how are our ventures coming? I mean, it's obvious I'm worried about my money, tracking you down like this . . . making an obvious fool of myself, as your old housekeeper and part-time gunman has assured me."

"It means so much to you, that money?"

Denny had to admit it. "Yeah. It does. You don't know much about me. To you, I'm just a crazy guy who yells and kicks around too much at the wrong time. But I got worked over a couple of years ago—I mean framed, you know 'framed'? I—I guess I don't expect much of anybody . . . which means I don't much trust anybody either. . . ."

Tuy leaned forward, with a faint mysterious smile playing on her perfect tulip mouth. "Tell me about this 'frame.' I want to know."

"They said I raped this girl—back home."

"Did you?"

"No!" He almost shouted. He could feel the old rage shuddering through him. "I was the guy who *found* her, after she'd been had by a bunch of the senior class. But somebody had called the cops, and the police chief found me untying her."

"So you took the fall. . . ."

He looked at her, surprised she had used that expression. She smiled. "Don't look so startled. I read a lot. English is not an *impossible* language, even for an ex-bar girl. But your story—''

"Well, that's about all there was to it, except she was the class whore and the kid who let things get a little out of hand in the first place was the chief's own son, and it was his word against mine. I was lucky, I guess. She was the minister's daughter, and they didn't want the mess of a trial, so I got a one-way ticket to the army. . . .''

"So the money represents your victory over them."

"Yeah, in a way. It's like a big 'Fuck You!' I don't do anything everybody else doesn't—I just do it more and better.''

She stood and gazed across the table at him. "I cannot do any more than promise you. Your money has been vital to me, so important that you are a full partner.''

"Great. So is the *Xau My*. I don't like that guy. . . .''

"The *Xau My* is not a partner. He is a client, and I do not trust him.''

"And you trust me?'' he said skeptically.

"Yes.'' She gave him the slightest hint of a nod. "But tell me more of your life before the army.''

"Do you really want to know?''

"Yes, I want to know everything about your life in America,'' she said, teasing him, "because as you know it is the true aim of every bar girl to marry a rich American.''

"You're not a bar girl any longer—you said so yourself.''

"Ahhh,'' she said, only half mocking now, "but how do you see me?''

"Not.'' He replied simply. "Whatever you are, you're not that any more.''

That seemed to please her more than anything else he could have said. She rose and took his arm. "Let us sit by the fire and drink wine and talk of your young days in America.'' She skillfully drew him out, and he told her of used Dodges and Pontiacs, of school and dating and homework, of his first .22 rifle and deer hunting and fishing for pike in the northern Wisconsin woods, of his slightly zany mom who loved to dance, of the high school plays he'd been in and the time he caught the winning touchdown and lost his virginity both on the same Friday evening.

The hours passed, and the old man replaced their wineglasses with brandy snifters. Denny was talking on and on, he couldn't even remember much what about, when he looked up to see a tear start in the corner of one of her soft dark eyes, which looked huge and magnificent in the firelight glow. "What—did I do something wrong? Was it something I said?"

"No. Thank you, Denny. You started me thinking of my own times, when I was a little girl. . . ."

He gently touched her hand. "Tell me."

She gave him a shy smile. "It's nothing. I mean, not really big things."

"Tell me," he insisted.

And so she talked of the good times in her hamlet. She told him how excited she had been at the autumn Tiger Festivals, how much fun it was to put on the mask of the tiger and go around begging sweets from the elders. The great days of Tet, the new year, when they all got presents and had the traditional feast of *Thit Bo Bay Mon*. She confessed that she'd had a favorite doll. "Back then, all I ever dreamed of was growing up to be a fat peasant *ba* with a pear shape, a happy man, and five or six kids running around. . . ."

"What happened?"

"My father was very outspoken against the Vietcong. They had to make an example of him. They do what you call 'scorched earth' plan against their examples—nothing left alive in the house. I was away overnight. I returned to a silent house . . . bloody . . . throats all cut . . . *all*! The VC truly are baby-killers, it is not just a propaganda word."

He took her hand as the tears flowed freely down her cheeks. "I guess it is better to try to forget the past."

She shook her head. "No, I do not think so anymore. I have not thought of those wonderful girl times in years, since coming to Saigon. To block out the bad, you have to block out the good as well. . . . This is such a wonderful time. Thank you, my friend Denny.'' She held his hand for a brief moment, looking into his eyes, and then left the room.

It all ended so abruptly that five minutes passed before he realized the evening was over. He could have grabbed his sweater and darted out the door; instead, he decanted himself a small last hit of brandy and sat in front of the dying fire. The hi-fi had gone through its full round of platters and was starting in on Pete Fountain's *The Blues* again, and as the plaintive clarinet filled the room with old sadness, he stared into the glow from the stove and tried to sort out what was happening to him.

He didn't make much headway with his thoughts, and after a long time the old man came back. ''You will not be able to get a cab easily at this late hour. The young mistress has invited you to stay the evening.''

''Another firm invitation?'' Denny said sarcastically.

''No.'' The old man watched him, his face a blank shell. Denny had no way of knowing, but he was the object of the other's thoughts. Compared to the *Nguoi Phap*—the French— he had dealt with over the many years, this young *Nguoi My* was terribly abrasive. Yet, it could not be denied he honestly said his mind, and there was value in that. After a time, the ancient spoke again. ''I use my own tongue because you understand it well. Were I to attempt *English*, my thoughts would resemble those of a child. You acted well, young man. You surprised everyone here tonight. You will be safe here . . . for now.'' He gently took Denny by the arm. ''Come, let me show you to the guest room.''

6-4

When Tuy had been a very small girl, she had wandered away from the fields where the entire village was busy with the spring planting. She had gone to the nearby river, a slow curling offshoot of the Mekong. She threw pebbles at the lotus blossoms on the pollen-glazed surface of the water and then wandered deeper into mangrove forest. Here the trail became faint, and the exposed many-legged roots of the trees seemed enormous.

Tuy wandered along happily enough for a time, picking flowers that she waved at the big blue dragonflies hovering in the sunlight-golden air around her . . . until she noticed how quiet it was. She had never before been on this particular path, which seemed to have given out almost entirely. The ground was marshy, the cool wet grass sucking a bit at the bottoms of her feet as she gave an anxious glance at the roots, which now definitely looked a little like grotesque human arms and legs and torsos. She picked up her pace a bit, but was no longer really sure of the path . . . and then she was running, a panicked little girl with mud spattering the bottom of her white *ao dai* and her long black hair flowing behind.

There was a fallen branch in her way, just a small one, and she easily jumped it—only to sink to her knees in cool gray muck. She struggled, felt herself slowly slipping deeper. Her mouth opened in a desperate cry for help.

Back then, a boy who had been fishing the close-by waters heard her screams and came running to pull her out with his bamboo pole before the mud was up to her thighs. But when the boy did not come and the water passed her hips, Tuy knew it was a dream.

But knowing you are dreaming and being able to wake up are two entirely different things, as anyone who suffers true nightmares will tell you. Tuy moaned and twisted in the silk sheets of her huge four-poster bed, and the sucking horror of the hungry mud was real as any there ever was. And worse yet, the trees began to shape-change, to writhe, to realize their potential as the *ma*—spirit—within took control of their external form.

The roots of the mangrove trees assumed the forms of her slain brothers and sisters, and then her father and mother. Blood oozed from the crusted slashes on their throats, from the deep wounds cruelly stabbed in her naked mother's lower belly, the Cong's way of saying, No more childbearing here! The unspeakable raw stump where her father's organ had been! Her attention jerked to their faces, to the dark burning lights pouring from their eye sockets. She knew they had come for her, only she couldn't run, the foul muck was over her belly, she felt slime touching her breasts . . . and then horror compounded horror as new uglier *ma* shouldered their way through and the twisted bleeding roots shape-changed again and it was dear Charley and poor sweet Larkey. Dear and sweet no more, they towered over her in grim determination as she slipped in deeper up to her throbbing, white neck—and then the boy with the bamboo pole *was* there finally, but he wasn't a boy, it was poor rash Mad Denny, and the two great bloody *ma* pushed him away with a coarse laugh and a casual backhand swipe, and they returned their attention to Tuy and reached for her neck with hands hooked like talons, and her last scream was a thundering echo. . . .

Mad Denny woke with a start. For a moment he was totally disoriented. He was in the woods, listening to the cry of a wildcat. The hair on his body stood on end, electrified by the almost human quality of that lost-soul wail. And then he realized where he was and that the cry had been real. And his naked body was taken with a second violent rush of chills.

He quickly sat up in bed and pulled his pants on. The room he was in was almost pitch dark. From the moaning sounds of the wind, he guessed the rain continued. He fished the wristwatch from his pocket, and the thin glowing green hands said five o'clock. He numbly wondered how that could be until he realized it was upside down. He groped around and found his shirt, but before he could pull it on a slight, flickery, indirect glow passed by outside the open crack of his doorway. Denny froze. There was no sound, and the glow passed on, the room returning to its former blackness.

He gritted his teeth to keep them from chattering, and

stood. He was going to open that door, he told himself, and quietly confront whatever ghost or bizarre nonsense the night had cooked up for him. But the old tile floor was icy cold on his feet and he had to tell his legs three times before they actually did his bidding. Trailing his almost-forgotten shirt in one hand, he slipped out the door and silently stole down the hallway, going back toward the large room where he had dined earlier that evening.

The light was coming from that room. Perhaps, he thought, the fire was still going. Perhaps the coals had flared briefly, startling him before. Perhaps. He breathed out a slow breath and went around the corner silent and fast the way Ranley had taught him . . . and practically ran over Tuy!

She whirled about to face him with a tiny cry of terror. The silver pistol in her hand was a blur as it came up to shoot him.

As if in slow motion, he saw it all: Tuy like a deadly angel in her white silk nightgown, her lips forming a perfect round *o*, the candle she held tilted, wax spilling to the floor, the deadly weapon in her other hand coming up, pointing to his heart. . . .

For a flash-frame he was frozen; he would never know why. Denny lived by his instincts, and freezing up just didn't happen to him. But in that moment, he was *afraid*. Not frightened of what might happen to him physically—but rather frightened for what might become of the two of them together. In that split second of paralysis, he almost died.

The gun came up centered. The flashing red flare of her ring caught his attention, bit through his frozen mind, and even as he was thinking it would be the last thing he would ever see, his muscles relaxed and he lashed out with a savage parry. The pistol went flying across the room, sliding under the chairs by the Franklin stove where they had sat.

Tuy gaped at him, her eyes like huge saucers, "I—I would have killed you. . . ."

He stared back at her, not knowing how to say anything without shattering the tenuous bridge of friendship they had started earlier that evening. ''Why? . . .'' he croaked hoarsely.

''The *ma*. In my dream. They came for me again. My brother Hong . . . my father. Larkey. Charles of Bayonne. All of them.'' Her speech faltered, and she nearly fell. ''So I couldn't go back to sleep. When this . . . happens, I walk here until dawn, I walk and when I see them in the shadows, I walk toward them and they retreat. It is a slim margin, my victory; but still, I stalk them instead of the other way around. . . .''

''You didn't mean to shoot me?''

It was as if he had physically slapped her, so dismayed was the look on her face. ''Noooooo! Oh, no, my dear Mad Denny . . . but I almost did. You were too close—all I saw was a quick shadow. I knew it was a *ma*, come to do evil. . . .'' She touched his arm, needing his trust. ''You do believe me?''

''Yes. I do.'' Denny spoke with a rush of relief. She looked so frail in that moment, like a pale lotus in the soft candle-light. He took the candle from her hand. ''Come on. I'll stir up the fire.'' He found a few coals and soon had it blazing again. Then he sat beside her and put his arm around her.

She huddled next to him until she finally stopped shaking. ''I feel better now,'' she said with a weak little smile.

''You should,'' he said, half-teasing, ''because this makes us even. . . .''

''How so, Mad Denny?''

He gave her a crooked grin. ''Remember how I dashed across the street when I first saw you? Now we each tried to kill the other once. . . .''

''Huh.'' She smiled. ''We've come a way since then. . . .''

''You think so?'' he said, pulling her a little closer to him.

''I do. You know—I'll tell you something. Earlier tonight,

when we parted, I didn't want to go, but somehow I felt . . . afraid for us.''

"I know what you mean," Denny replied grimly. "I've had similar feelings myself. . . .''

She stood to warm her hands against the light streaming from the glass squares in the stove door. He looked with admiration at the outlines of her body backlit by the fire. Suddenly she turned to him and, bending down, softly kissed him on the lips. Seen so close, she was incredibly lovely to him. He felt the light brush of her lips on his own, the gentle trailing brush of her fingertips on his cheek.

"What do you think now, Mad Denny . . . about our ventures?''

He stood and held her hands, looking down at her. Again he noticed the way the red stone on her finger pulsed, almost as if it had a *ma* of its own, a dancing spirit that would not be quenched. Denny had the crazy thought that the *ma* was thirsty for human emotion, for love. "I think . . .'' he said, groping for words, "that we have to accept the ghosts of the past . . . but we cannot let them rule our lives.'' He took her in his arms, and his mouth found hers, and they held one another in a long tender embrace.

After a time she pulled away from him. Her breath came a little faster, and she had to swallow before she spoke. "I think you are right, my dear Mad Denny. I feel much better now. I am going back to my bedroom.'' Her fingers trailed on his cheek again, her soft eyes locked to his.

She turned and left him then. His mind was a jumbled tangle of emotions, of old anger and new desire, mingled with a strange twinge of fear—or was it anticipation?—of the unknown. He watched her full hips under the revealing gown as she picked up the candle and moved away from him.

He stood alone in the room by the fire for a moment that seemed like hours, then picked up his shirt, which had fallen by the chairs. "Christ help me,'' he muttered to himself with a sigh. And then he followed after her.

CHAPTER SEVEN

7-1

EDGAR MUNSON HAD SOME OF HIS BEST IDEAS WHILE FEED-
ing his white rats. Although they would eat practically anything, he preferred to give them raw meat. He would bring
the "big fellows," as he liked to think of them, a slab of
steak or a couple of chops from one of his MP mess halls.
There was something comforting about watching the inevi-
tability of nature at work. Seeing the husky little pink-eyed
carnivores tear away at their bloody nourishment also rein-
forced his already strong notions about the weakness of the
twentieth-century American patsy, that common goody-
goody herd of sheep that made up ninety-nine percent of his
countrymen. Men were, after all, only animals. "Ashes to
ashes and dust to dust" . . . and after that—nothing. That
was the true meaning of the scriptures; after all, the steak
wasn't going to come back to haunt his little white pets.

He inherited the rats from the man he replaced in his present job over the MPs. That officer had been a collector of
bric-a-brac, of the flotsam of strange articles that drifted
through his office as a law enforcement head in a war zone.
These things all were kept in the interrogation room, a large,
windowless room near the rows of barred temp-cells in back
of MP headquarters. The collection of drug-user artifacts
housed in a glass-faced cabinet included everything from
dirty needles and syringes to ornate, yellow-stained ivory
opium pipes. There was a grouping of homemade weapons
displayed on one wall of the office, everything from wooden

stakes to brass knuckles to the widest assortment of ingenious clubs. The previous major had typed each weapon's
mean history on a three-by-five card that he had tacked next
to it. And then there were the two cages.

The tiger cage was made of bamboo lashed together with
heavy baling wire. It was a simple cube, four feet a side. Its
beauty lay in the fact that a prisoner tucked inside could never
stretch out. Edgar Munson had seen former VC prisoners
hunched over for life after a few months' "reeducation" in
a tiger cage. That was not to say that the Republic of Vietnam
didn't use them too—of course it did, and with equal success.
The one in Edgar's office had, according to the little card
taped nearby, been liberated from an ARVN special security
headquarters. Forgotten, it had been lying in back of the
compound with the skeleton of a wispy-bearded old dissenter
moldering in it.

The other was the rat cage. More ingenious in concept, it
was somewhat smaller than the tiger cage. It had a sliding panel
on one side that could be removed to allow a man's body to be
lashed to the cage with bars under his armpits—so his head and
neck were exposed to the sharp teeth of the rats, while his arms
were bound helplessly to his sides.

The *Xau My* himself had put the rat cage back in working
order. He had gotten the idea while rummaging through the
boxes of stuff his predecessor had left behind. Out of nowhere,
he remembered a friend from his premed days, a balding jovial
fellow who also was getting borderline grades. The poor asshole had become discouraged, knocked some bitch up, and so
was forced to quit school and become a salesman for a science
lab supply house. Edgar wrote him a letter. The friend, bored
with his own life, had been glad to ship a dozen of their
grade-A white rats air freight special handling to Saigon. In
fact, he had insisted on sending them free of charge.

Edgar had never put a human in his rat cage. He never had
to. The few Vietnamese nationals brought to him for interrogation had turned to Jell-O at the mere sight of the cage. He

never even had to threaten to place them in it. And that just made him all the more curious.

One afternoon, while conducting an experiment with his "big fellows," his mind wandered to Tuy, and from her to the young American who had humiliated him in her bar. He had starved the rats for the better part of a week, and now was teasing them with strips of raw bacon, which was driving them into an eating frenzy. The day after that incident at the Tuyet Lan, he had begun a dossier on Mad Denny, and now knew a great deal about him. But in working up a file on Tuy, he had come up blank. All anyone knew was that she was a smart businessperson who kept her nose clean. So she knew who to pay off, and how much. But her past was filled with vague nothings: She came from the "country." She had "worked her way up" as a bar girl. Where, who, how, what, and when . . . the five friends of the investigator all were missing.

While teasing his sleek little friends, two of whom had almost killed one another over a scrap of bacon, Edgar came to the conclusion that it wasn't simple police incompetence in the face of all the population upheavals—if that were the case, something would exist on her. Tuy did not want her past to be known. So, he figured, she must have done something very wrong, something that she had gone to great lengths to cover up.

And that idea had led to his partners in law enforcement, the QCs, and then on to the downtown files of the White Mice themselves. At first he didn't know what he was looking for. He tried missing persons, which was an unbelievable mess . . . probably intentionally, for civilian enemies of the Diem regime and those that followed had an uncomfortable habit of simply disappearing. But gradually, as he worked the problem through, he concentrated more and more on unsolved crimes.

They just gave him boxes and boxes of files on loan, and he went through them with his feet up on the rat cage, occasionally stopping for a sip of coffee or to toss another strip to the hungry pack inside. The hours ticked by as he went through file after file, amazed at the seeming lack of law and order in the capital. And finally late that night, just as he was running out of both bacon and coffee, he was rewarded with his answer. And what an answer it was!

An American linguist from Mad Denny's Thirty-third RRU (it didn't explain what that was, and Edgar made a mental note to find out), one Specialist Larkspun, had been assassinated by a squad of Victor Charlie irregulars late one night in a Da Cau back-alley street. The MPs' report was very straightforward and told him nothing, just that the specialist had had a .45 and used it rather effectively before dying from a hail of bullets from the death squad. There was a statement from a wounded terrorist that Edgar found much more interesting. It was taken before the man died, by the White Mice, and probably by torture. This statement implicated with some detail a young bar girl as having set up Larkspun.

There were two snapshots in the file as well, taken from the dead GI's wallet, of this bar girl. Edgar examined the first carefully. It was a black-and-white studio portrait. He placed his fingers in a halo over her head, cropping her hair short, and mentally added some years to her age. Although all Vietnamese girls tended to look alike to him, still Edgar was sure the beautiful round-faced little girl with the perfect tulip lips staring back at him from the photograph was Tuy.

Having solved to his satisfaction that question, he turned to the second picture, which provided a revelation of another sort. It too was a black-and-white print, but entirely different from the first. It was one of those shots infatuated young men take of their only partially willing girlfriends. In it, an uncomfortable and shy-looking Tuy stood at the foot of a bed, cupping one hand over her left breast and the other over her pubic hairs. The pose was far more innocently seductive than if she had made no attempt to cover herself. In fact, Edgar was just able to make out the shape of her erect nipple peeping through her fingers, and even imagined he could see some of the fine hairs behind a corner of her other hand. He stared at the picture, finding it hard to believe she was implicated in a murder.

And then he became aware, to his amazement, that he was getting it on. It was a new experience for him. Since his sexual enlightenment, he had tried to get a spark out of kiddie porn, of which there had been a large portfolio left by the last major, as well as a continuing stream through his department in the conducting of their day-to-day affairs. But the snapshots, black-and-white or color, glossy or matte finish, portrait quality or done hastily with a cheap Kodak, all had done nothing for him.

He realized that the fifteen-year-old bitch in the picture was more real to him because he knew her, and that excited him even more. It was late, and he was alone in the station except for the duty sergeant at the front desk and a few of the guys who would be in the front office. He locked the door from the inside and took down his pants.

It was a wonderful experience; he tugged at his organ, which felt hard as a rock, and his breath came in gasps as he glared at the pensive soulful eyes staring back from the picture. "I'll—get—every one—of you—bitches—Nam!—Every one!" And then he was faced with the eternal masturbator's problem, at the moment of climax . . . what to do with the evidence. The answer came easily to him, and as his ecstasy flooded him with shuddering delight he shot the milky white ejaculation into the rat cage. The rats didn't seem to mind at all. That's real life, Edgar thought with a sigh of pleasure as he sank back into his chair. None of this crippling morality, this placing humanity on some special pedestal. We're all just rats . . . and the strong eat the weak. After a time he pulled up his pants and then carefully replaced her photos in the file. He returned to his chair to sit back, arms behind his head and feet up on the cage, an absolute picture of contentment as he watched the rats climb up the sides to eagerly lap at the last remaining drops of his come.

This whole Tuy business was going to be a very valuable

weapon to him. Not that he would turn her in—right now she was too valuable. But he needed something to hold over her, and he was sure he had it. The best partners were those you could trust. And the best way to trust partners was to have them firmly under your thumb.

There were all sorts of possibilities. For instance, did her impetuous American friend Mad Denny know she had killed his comrade? If he didn't, Edgar had a great wedge to annihilate their alliance. Whether she actually pulled the trigger or not, the White Mouse report was deadly in its implications. He thought more about it, rolling it over in his mind—perhaps this Mad Denny also was implicated in the old assassination, a love triangle or something of that sort. Either way, the *Xau My* knew he had a new sword with many cutting edges . . . and he could be trusted to find which cut deepest.

Still, as good a day as this one had been, it was nothing compared to the day that followed. For up until then, Edgar was stumped by a problem central to his fortunes, indeed to the continuance of his role as a supplier, and ultimately to the expensive lifestyle that he had chosen. It was imperative that he find a way to ship bulk dope back to his customers in the States. Tuy had gone some distance in solving his problems when she had somehow come up with the means to refine the stuff. (Try as he had, he'd drawn a blank on that one. How she set that up would remain a mystery through all their dealings.) Still, shipping heroin in the quantities he looked forward to involved a creative breakthrough.

And once again, the solution came to him while he was feeding his plump little pets. The day had started badly for him. He had felt guilty about his starvation experiments, and so had brought two pounds of raw hamburger for his rats. But when he got to the office, the two who had fought the day before were dead anyway.

Edgar unceremoniously dumped them into the garbage can, gingerly hoisting them out of the cage by their long pink tails while the rest backed into the far corners, hissing and showing their teeth at him. That little chore completed, he began rolling the ground meat into little balls and dropping it in through the bars.

He was interrupted by a knock on the door. A couple of MPs dragged in a blank-eyed doper, an E-6 air force mortician with h-tracks running up and down both arms. They went on and on, detailing the evidence they had against the poor guy, who was shaking from withdrawal, but Edgar stopped listening after the first few sentences. He didn't need to hear any more. It was the million-dollar idea he'd been looking for, and the *Xau My* recognized it immediately.

7-2

"Why is it, Captain Anderson," Mad Denny asked his CO, "every time I ask you for a private talk, you bring in a bigger audience than the pope gets?"

Anderson nervously shuffled the papers on his desk. "That's nonsense. Toady has a right to be here—he works here. As for Mr. Dooly—"

"*Sergeant* Dooly," Denny interjected. "Dooly-the-Spook."

Dooly raised his hand for quiet. "I don't know why they let one smart-mouth like you get away with the things you do."

"Great. Let the inquisition begin."

"I believe you requested the meeting, Specialist Fifth Class Haller," Anderson replied coldly. "What is the subject of our little gathering to be?" Without waiting for an answer, the captain went into one of his long tirades about enlisted men's responsibilities.

Toady grinned over the top of his yellow legal pad. While he was supposed to be taking notes, he knew that was just his excuse to be there, so he had been doodling. He drew a crude F-101, and then a few cyclones and a lop-tipped star or two, and then concentrated on a larger drawing of a naked woman. He drew in big tits and an even bigger belly. When he was satisfied that it would convey the idea, he wrote "Hoa" in big block letters. He folded the paper carefully and passed it quietly to Denny.

When Denny opened the paper, his face turned red with anger. Toady had seen Denny in action and was sure that with his violent temper he would crack and dive at him to create a scene; in fact he counted on it. He held a heavy lead Buddha paperweight hidden in the palm of one hand, ready to do some serious damage before they pulled the raging madman off him.

But Toady hadn't counted on Denny's unpredictability. Instead of launching an attack and making a scene, he quietly leaned over and took the pencil from Toady. He wrote, "I may have to cut your balls off, you silly fanatic. I understand in your church that's considered one of the highest honors." Toady could see from the grim expression on his face that he meant it. His own face went a little gray when he considered what he had done. He was definitely going to have to strike first, to put an end to this follower of the Antichrist. Dooly had watched the interchange with a strange puzzled expression on his face, but the captain raged on in his own little world.

Dooly, who was going to miss his nookie-nooner if he didn't get back downtown, finally interrupted. "Uhhh, right, we all get the idea, Captain—but let's see what it is Specialist Haller has on his mind."

The CO blinked, coming back to the immediate reality. "Um. Right. Of course." He leaned his chin on his knuckles. "What is it, Dennis?"

"This, sir!" Denny said, flinging a batch of papers on the desk. In his anger he threw them a little harder than he had intended, with the unfortunate result that they caught the captain full in the face before falling to the desk in front of him.

Toady could hardly restrain his glee, but the captain was furious. "What is the meaning of this?"

Denny refused to back off, much less apologize. "It's my report of the incident that ended in Doober's death, that's what it is! I find it in the dead-end file over at the White Shack! You don't even care enough to pass on the little scraps of enemy information that made up his last contribution to this fuckin' mess!''

"What information? That silly business about the Victor Charlies having a tank?''

Denny went livid. "It was there! I saw it, too!''

The captain spoke quietly, as if talking to a little child. "It was probably one of ours. There is just no other answer. Now, if there's nothing else . . .'' He made a motion as if to dismiss the meeting.

Dooly, who had been making a few hasty mental notes, now spoke up. "Wait, Captain. This is new stuff to me. I'd like to hear more.'' He had originally shown up at the meeting because they all had suspected Mad Denny was going to counterattack with some cock-and-bull story to prove his innocence in the drug dealing charges they had laid on him. While they couldn't prove any of those charges, he had to be sweating it plenty. Dooly had found out in the course of his long career that a guilty man often needlessly implicates himself. But this talk about the enemy tank took him by surprise.

"Okay! I'll go over it—again! It was late afternoon, rain starting to gust in. The night before our position had been shelled to shit, probably by our own guys. . . .''

"By your own guys? How could you know that?''

"By the size of the fuckin' craters, for Christ's sake—you could put three Charlie mortars in one and have room left over for GI hamburger!''

Dooly nodded, his interest suddenly up. He didn't know what it was, but there were a few threads of something here. "Okay. So your position was shelled the night before. What's the point?''

The lines on Denny's forehead creased as he remembered it. "So Doober—Spec-four Doober, that's the guy that died—he was nervous, scanning everywhere in the hills around with an old pair of binocs he had. I was digging like crazy, trying to get a foxhole with a real deep bottom in it. He calls me, he's seen an enemy tank. I say impossible and we start to argue about it. Finally he gets pissed and gives me the binocs, and he was right, it was a tank all right, a Soviet T-55!''

The captain sat bolt upright in his chair. "*WHAAAT?* Now, weeks later, you're going around saying you've identified that little ass-end scrap of a vehicle you say you saw as a Russian tank?''

Denny lost control and started screaming. "Goddamn it, that's right!''

Dooly once again raised his hands for calm. "Gentlemen, please. Wait a minute. I know the Spec-five here is badly out of order, but just let me get up to speed on all this.'' He paused a moment and scratched his hair with both hands, letting loose a shower of white flakes between his legs. The room got quiet, and he looked up to see he had everyone's attention. "Okay. Haller. You're running around claiming you saw a T-55 out in Tay Ninh, is that right?'' Denny nodded, and Dooly's Mr. Potato Head mouth opened and closed. "Now that's a cleared area, definitely not even a contested zone. Christ, look at your own maps!'' He waved his hand at the map on Anderson's wall that clearly showed that area of War Zone C above the Iron Triangle to be in friendly hands.

"No,'' Denny shook his head impatiently. "I mean yes, that's the way the maps show it, but no, that's not the way it really is, not much of anywhere in Nam. That area's all un-inhabited hill country—scrub brush and tangled forests. We get covert transmissions from places you wouldn't believe, from friendly mountain villages to peaceful secure areas in the heart of the delta.''

The captain cleared his throat. "Ahhh-hem, I don't be-lieve Mr. Dooly has been cleared for—''

"Neither have you, for that matter, Captain. But what I'm saying is no big secret; it's common mess-hall chatter around here. It just happens to be true, that's all!''

Dooly sighed. He really *had* to get this thing rolling if he was going to make his appointment. "Okay, o-*kay*! You see a tank. You think it's a VC tank. What's the point?"

"I didn't say a VC tank. And the point is, you could hide whole battalions in there—NVA battalions supported by tanks!"

Toady threw his pad and pencil in the air and talked to the ceiling. "Oh wow, what has this guy been smoking?"

Anderson stood and waved his hands at Denny. "This has really gone too far!"

The whole scene was finally too much for Mad Denny. In a flash he also was on his feet, screaming at his CO. "Why too far? Why are you covering this up? Somebody doesn't want to hear it, that's right, isn't it?"

"Oh, bullshit," Anderson growled angrily. He had his own reasons for not wanting that report to go past the Thirty-third, to make sure that what those three strays had landed on never got back to his friend in artillery. They were close friends, but you never knew in the army. "You're talking through your hat, Haller!"

"Bullshit, yourself!" Denny cried, now completely worked up. "Doober died to get you this and it doesn't count anyway because somebody way up there doesn't want to hear it—maybe *none* of you do—"

"You're talking nonsense, boy!"

"Am I? You get your war after all these years. So it ain't going exactly one hundred percent? What do you care? War means promotions! Another two years, you're gonna make major. War lasts long enough, you'll be a fuckin' general! Am I right?"

The captain sat back in his chair with a heavy thud, his fists clenched, his face twisted in what he hoped was a mask of fury. He had to get this over with. "You are so out of order . . . just get out of here. I'll deal with you later."

There was a long silence after Denny stormed out. Finally

Toady spoke hesitantly. "Somebody's gonna get that guy *good* . . ."

The captain gave him a bleak stare. "Well, somebody better get it done, before I have to handle it myself. . . ."

Dooly didn't know what to say. His CIA-trained sixth sense was telling him something, but he couldn't figure out quite what it was. Anderson had tried to bury the report, which didn't make sense, considering it was just a sketchy tale of enemy strength that would probably be discounted by any expert at a glance. Dooly was a tenacious thinker with a strong belief in the basic amorality of man, and would probably have come to some interesting conclusions had he given it a half hour or so. But he was once again late for his noontime freshener, and he had to break away from this petty stuff at the Thirty-third or he'd be doing without again. He excused himself and legged it for the Jeep, which he still parked a half block outside the compound.

That night, Mad Denny slept in his bunk at the Thirty-third for the first time in almost a month. Most of the bunks sagged with rump-sprung springs, but since he'd been active with his gung fu, Denny's back wouldn't allow him to sleep like that. He had shored his mattress level with two pieces of cut-perfect plywood he'd traded for a lid of so-so grass. The plywood rested between the mattress and the springs and had the added benefit of giving his blankets a little extra tightness when they bounced the quarter.

There was some action south of the airport, and the glare of the distant falling flares drew a barred design slowly across his face. Annoyed by the distant sawing of a Browning and the pop of the M1s, he pulled his second pillow over his head and went back to sleep.

The pillow saved his hearing, and the plywood board his life, for in the next minute someone softly opened the screen door next to his living area. An arm reached in and rolled a grenade gently under his bunk. There was a short silence punctuated by swiftly receding footsteps, and then his bunk was lifted halfway to the ceiling in a ball of flame.

Knocked unconscious by the blast, Mad Denny would spend the next few days in a coma in Saigon General. Aside from that, and an unconscious, deep-rooted paranoia that would be with him the rest of his days, he got away scot-free . . . except for the fingers on his right hand, which had been hanging over the side of the bunk at the time of the explosion. On this hand, the little finger was untouched. But he lost the other three fingers; the first finger gone down to the knuckle and the other two at the joint above. And the top joint of his thumb had disappeared, sliced off clean as if by black magic.

7-3

"Fools, fools, *fools!*" Dooly shouted, raging around the CO's office like a caged lion. "I work for *months* on this Mad Denny caper, digging for background, trailing the little scumbag through every bar on Hai Ba Trung, all the time getting closer and closer to the big breakthrough—and what do you silly assholes do? You frag my key and one and only goddamn suspect! You knew he could be the *Xau My*—I told you that!"

Captain Anderson and Toady sat stiffly at opposite ends of the office while Dooly paced impatiently back and forth between them, showering little sprinkles of his scalp crud whenever he tossed his head. It was impossible to know whether the two seated men were more uncomfortable about the topic of discussion or the question of just how contagious that crap in the spook's hairline was; but it was safe to say both men would have rather been almost anywhere else in the world.

"We didn't frag him," Anderson protested. "At least, I didn't. . . ." He gave a long sideways glance to Toady, who had a big clumsy bandage around his head and was looking down at the floor. His fat little clerk was sweating, and every pimple on his face seemed to have popped up and grown a white head overnight.

"Well, what happened to little Toad-shit here, then?"
Dooly strode across the room and ripped the bandage off.

"Oww! You can't do that—" Toady started to reach for it,
but the spook was already fingering the large wet bloody spot
on the bandage, and there was no way the corpulent clerk
was going to risk some leperlike disease by putting it back
in contact with his open wound. He knew all about lepers.
Once he had been intercepted by a group of living corpses
outside one of the shrines. A group of lingies had taken him
along on one of their "educational" little trips to town, just
another reason why Toady hated them. They all had run off
laughing, leaving him cornered, to face the rotting mob. All
the lepers wanted was a few coins, but he didn't know that.
He had bolted away, running until he couldn't run any more,
and then stopping on a bridge over a canal to retch until his
empty stomach was twisted in pain.

Dooly brought him back to the present, tossing the blood-
soaked strip of gauze at his feet. "You want to explain how
you got what looks like a pretty serious wound on the back
of your head?"

"It's not serious," Toady protested. "I had an accident.
Got hit with a board."

"Yeah, I'll bet," Dooly said skeptically. "Last night, just
about the time of the fragging."

"Nobody can prove that! And it's not serious. We've got
medical stuff here, I just taped it up myself. . . ."

". . . rather than going to the medics, where they'd have
to fill out a report." Dooly pulled a chair up backward and
threw his leg over it, uncomfortably close to Toady. "Have
you *seen* yourself in a mirror? Your damn scalp's hanging
down—you could use about forty stitches . . . or you're gonna
have a big cunt-shaped bald spot back there . . . if it don't
get infected!"

Toady retreated to the medical chest behind his desk and
rummaged until he found a can of antiseptic spray and another fat roll of gauze, grateful to get some distance between

himself and the sergeant. He carefully sprayed the back of his head until the hair was dripping and the liquid antiseptic mixed with the thick blood still oozing from his wound began to run down his back. He started to wind a new piece of gauze around his head, tucking the loose flap of scalp back as best he could by feel.

Dooly watched him awhile and then shook his head. "You're gonna have to get some professional help for that. But that ain't your real problem."

Toady's eyes blinked fearfully in the spook's direction. "What is?" He could barely get the word out. "You?"

"No, not me," the big red-faced sergeant said, "Mad Denny."

"But—he's down at Saigon General! He's still in a coma. He'd not gonna know anything about this."

"Sure, right. Everybody in the company's seen you with that stupid bloody white flag around your brains at mess this morning—am I right?"

"That doesn't prove anything!" Toady shot back hotly.

Dooly pressed after him, pouring out his anger and frustration. "You fucked up his right hand pretty bad. Did you know he's a gung-fu killer? That man will do things to your head that will have your scalp looking for a new home to attach itself to. He could do it with his other hand. Or with either foot. Let me give you a tip, Toad-shit, straight from the spook—you don't maim a guy like that, you waste him or you let him alone."

Toady's fingers trembled so violently he was making a mess of his bandage. No one moved to help him. He looked wildly around the room. His breath came in gasps, as if he were about to hyperventilate. "Well, we planned—I mean, it's standard operating procedure, he'll be out of here as soon as we can move him to Clark in the Philippines."

The captain, who also had every reason to be rid of Denny, agreed. "You ship a man out for wounds a lot less than what he got. I mean, he's lost fingers. We don't really have any choice. . . .''

Dooly angrily turned on him. ''SOP be fucked! Now I've worked too hard on this! I want that dope-dealing scumbag down in Leavenworth, working a rockpile for life. And it's gonna be your choice—you let him go back to the States, he's gonna live the life of a wounded war vet, lappin' up all that sweet Stateside pussy. You want that? Or you can make him stick around until I can nail his ass to the Leavenworth chain gang.''

Anderson went over to his desk and sat down heavily. He began to review the thick file that was out on the pad before him. ''He doesn't reup, just extends for twelve-month tours. Been doing it for years. Gets away with that shit because he's snowed those assholes over at the White Shack.''

Dooly went over it in his mind. ''How much to go on the current extension?''

''Under ninety days. He always waits until the last minute to extend.''

''Good. All I really need is two months, top end.''

Toady didn't like the way the meeting was going. ''Maybe we could have the MPs detain him. . . .''

''Sure, just lock him up so he doesn't do anything for the next ninety days,'' Dooly said sarcastically. ''Did all your brains seep out of that hole in your head?'' He pointed a firm finger at the captain's chest, ''You know what I need, don't you?''

Anderson leaned back in his swivel chair and put his feet on the desk. So what if Toady would be in a little danger, it couldn't do the fat little toadstool any harm. If they really could rip Mad Denny's ass for life, it was an opportunity that they shouldn't let pass. If all they had to do was cooperate with the spooks, he had the beginnings of a great idea. ''Well, we could promote him. . . . ''

''Pro-*mote* him?'' Toady cried in protest.

''Sure. Make him E-6. Give him hard stripes. What do you think?''

Dooly nodded, "Not bad . . . throw him off, get him thinking the heat's off."

The captain smiled. "We'll give him his Purple Heart, of course . . . but I'll put him up for a big medal for whatever the hell he did in that Tay Ninh fiasco."

"Okay. But give me a chance—you make sure he has lots of free time. Put him on half days, get him in some bullshit rehab program for his hand, give him lots of three-day weekends—no R and R so he can leave town, just plenty of time to do his scumbag dealing!"

"You got it! Toady, see to the details . . . and, oh yeah, get over to the medics and get that thing sewn up; you're bleeding all over our paperwork."

The scalp took fifty-two stitches. Instead of taking the evening off, Toady came back to the office to handle the details that would shape Denny's life for the next few months. He was too frightened to be bitter about anything.

He knew he had to have a plan. It was all very fine for Asshole Anderson to go around making orders to help out the spook-leper, but his life wasn't at stake. Toady realized he would have to take matters into his own hands. He wasn't going to get any help from Animal or Stringer. He'd done it once before, and while he may have bungled it a bit, he'd had some results—Mad Denny was never going to write or shoot or throw baseballs with that hand . . . or give anybody the finger, Toady thought with a little wicked grin.

Maybe there could be a second time. Denny was lying helpless down at Saigon General. The place was a madhouse, but if he pulled strings, maybe he could get him a private little room . . . for some reason his mind drifted to the syringes of atropine in the medical chest. He saw them in his mind's eye, lined up like ready soldiers in their little plastic case. Atropine was the standard issue antidote for nerve gas, and every company had boxes of the stuff. It came in one-time-use individual little squeeze tubes, with warnings printed all over to be used only when sure one had been subjected to chem war. Denny would already be on sedation. Heaven only knew what two or three or four shots of atropine would do to his system.

Now that he had a rough plan, his hands stopped shaking. He rang Saigon General and arranged to get Denny moved. They were more than happy to help him when he mentioned MACV and the press and the fact that the guy was a war hero. They were a little hesitant about a rehabilitation program, but when Toady insisted the wish came from the highest authority, they agreed to come up with at least some counseling.

Working on the request for a medal, he fabricated an entire story about Denny's heroics on the Tay Ninh mountaintop, having him wounded in battle while fighting off squads of Victor Charlies. He even typed up some firsthand witness reports, signing them with a flourish with the names of two grunts he dug up who had died since the incident. It was easy, so easy that he had a brilliant little idea and went back to the typewriter. It took another ten minutes, but he typed himself up an application for his own Purple Heart and rubber-stamped it with Anderson's signature. Why the heck not, he thought to himself. War is a serious business, and he was serving in Nam, right where all the action was . . . and after all, it was fifty-two stitches he got trying to squash out a heretic scumbag—he deserved a medal!

7-4

On his third day after the fragging, Mad Denny drifted up out of a dreamless sleep to have a conversation with Jack Beale, one of the old-time Dimbos, seated comfortably in the chair at his bedside. They talked about the rainy season, which it seemed would never end, and about the war, which was going badly as usual. Beale went and got him some coffee, and they talked about all the bars they had dicked around in. Beale even apologized with that self-depreciating laugh that had always pissed Denny off a little as being an affectation, saying he was sorry for getting Denny into this mess in the first place. Denny tried to wave it off with a little wave of his hand, but the damn thing felt odd, as if it was cased in cement and wouldn't move.

He was puzzling over this when he remembered Beale had been gone from Nam for years, was back Stateside after his section-eight, working on the beginnings of a career in (of all the bullshit cop-out things!) advertising. That was too much for Denny's system, so he blanked out again.

The next time he woke, Doober was sitting there, fresh as the morning after they had taken on the girls at Anna's Bar. Denny groaned and closed his eyes, rolling over before Doober could say anything.

When he finally drifted up into the real world, it wasn't anything like the other times. It wasn't bright and cheery; the light was absolutely dingy, with a depressing silence dripping over everything like a virus. Hospital, he thought, turning the world slowly over and over in his mind. Hospital. He must be hurt. He wiggled all his limbs, first his legs and then his arms. All he could find out was that his right hand was heavily bandaged. He knew it was all right, he could feel all the fingers, was actually able to move them a little bit inside the tight bandage, but his entire arm ached, a huge dull heavy ache like maybe he'd had a heart attack. The room swam around in his bleary vision.

"I think he's coming out of it!" somebody said.

He swiveled his head to see Finegold and Brownstone hovering over him. "Course I am," he slurred. "What's th' matter with you guys?"

"Denny, you been out almost a week. Me and Brownstone been coming to see you."

"Oh. It's me then. Something's wrong with me. . . ." He paused a long time while that sank in. "What's—am I . . . okay?"

Brownstone gave Finegold a quick warning look, his grave

dark eyes looming behind his thick wire-rims. "You just got it in the hand."

Denny tried to focus on his assistant. "I saw that look, Brownie. Now you tell me, how bad is it?" He awkwardly held up the bandaged arm, which seemed a little funny to him, like it was shorter and lumped in the wrong places.

"Well, you lost some fingers . . . and part of your thumb. . . ."

"Bullshit. I can feel them. All of them."

Brownstone sighed and put his hand on Denny's shoulder. "I don't know about that, man. But they're gone."

Denny felt his world slipping as he started to lapse back into unconsciousness. He fought it off as hard as he could. "How—did . . . it happen?"

"Toady, man." Denny could not remember ever seeing his assistant's eyes show other than friendship and humor. Now they were hard and rimmed with hate. "That little bastard rolled an egg on you."

"Toady got me. . . ." Denny repeated mechanically, accepting the fact. "Who would have thought . . ." He jerked up a little as he thought of Tuy. "Get a message . . . Tuyet Lan Bar . . . tell what happened. . . ."

Finegold leaned closer to Denny, whose voice was down to a whisper. "Who shall we tell, Denny, who? . . ." But Denny, in spite of his present condition, showed the first sign of the almost paranoid secrecy and discretion that would be a characteristic of his personality for the rest of his life. He hesitated a moment, then spoke so softly they almost couldn't hear. "You don't really want to know, guys . . . just tell anybody there. . . ." He started to drift away again, and then was gone. And he didn't come back out again until late the next day.

Saigon General worked under the crush of an endless schedule of repairs on broken and maimed bodies. Their chief allies were morphine and the flight out to Clark Air

Force Base, which took as many of their patients as possible as soon as they were stable enough to chance the trip.

The next few days passed in a fog for Denny, heavily sedated as he was. Brownstone and Finegold snuck him in a cold six-pack of Ba Muoi Bas and some greasy buffalo burgers, but he was sleeping at the time, and so they had to split the picnic between themselves. He didn't expect Tuy would risk dropping by to visit him, in spite of the unexpected closeness that had developed between them. Part of him longed for her, ached just to look at her, to touch her, to hold her. But the other part, the nascent Mad Denny emerging from this crucible of physical shock, understood the reasons she stayed away, and was glad.

He didn't know why, but the sedation bothered him. They were still giving him morphine every night and horse pills of codeine at several-hour intervals throughout the day. Denny started palming the codeine, slipping it into a plastic bag that he hid under his pillow. He got the Dimbos to bring him a gym bag with some civvies; he managed to slip the pills into his personal clothing on one of the staggering trips to the bathroom. If Tuy's promises went up in poppy smoke, he'd have to get his modest empire going by himself . . . lots of guys had started with less than a handful of pills.

The loss of his fingers he accepted with a pragmatic attitude that bordered on fatalism. The first time they took the bandages off so that he saw his maimed hand was difficult for him. But once he got over the shock, he gingerly reached for the plastic straw from his ice water. After several fumbling attempts, he was able to pluck the straw from the glass using the stump of his thumb and his little finger, and he was able to see that the hand would be of some limited usefulness.

He'd always peck-typed out his reports, and so still could use a typewriter. He would have to learn to sign his name with his other hand; but he had never been one for long letter writing, so that wasn't much of a problem. It was only later, after he had gone back to gung fu with a vengeance that slowly turned him into a truly dangerous hand-to-hand combatant, that he realized the hand had lost very little of its potential as a killing weapon.

The days passed unmarked by trouble and soon merged into a blur of bland food and polite, stiff-collared nurses. The doctors had skillfully trimmed the stumps of his fingers and pulled the skin up over most of them, and even taken some of the stitching out. In a day or two he would be totally off the morphine, and they'd told him once he was free of infection, he would be released. That day, Captain Anderson paid him a puzzling little visit.

The CO brought him a hip flask of Jim Beam. "Just thought I'd do something. . . . I know we haven't seen eye-to-eye on *anything*, but this is a goddamn shame to happen to one of my men." He saw Denny's skeptical stare. "Believe me, Dennis, we are doing everything possible to apprehend the guilty party who did this."

"Any leads so far?"

"Well, no . . . you've got to admit people were standing in line."

Denny found he could smile at that. "Not the most lovable guy, huh . . ."

The captain breathed an inward sigh of relief. "We've got too many clues. Everywhere we look somebody else is not exactly upset at your accident."

"Is that what we're calling it?"

"Nooo, not exactly . . . which is why we are putting you in for a Purple Heart—and the Congressional Medal of Honor. . . ."

"Whoopie," Denny said calmly. "What else?"

"You *knew*, didn't you!" Anderson said heartily, trying to be his best jovial self. "E-6 hard stripes! You're a buck sergeant, son!"

"Geezus . . ." Denny muttered under his breath, suddenly as suspicious as he'd ever been in his life. He decided to test the water further. "And you're shipping me out, right?"

"Only if you want to go!" The captain's smile could have graced a toothpaste ad. "You're going to get sixty, maybe eighty percent usage out of your hand. It won't conflict with your job at the White Shack . . . which you don't have to go back to until you feel top-notch."

"Of course, I'd like to stay," Denny said softly, trying hard to mask his mixed feelings of joy and surprise.

"Then you've got a deal!" The captain stuck his hand out, then had a flustered moment when he realized what he'd done. He recovered as best he could, and lamely reached over the bed rail to shake Denny's left hand. And then he backed out of the room, smiling and reassuring Denny he would do his best to make things work out, if his new buck sergeant could only come halfway and do the same.

Denny puzzled over it all afternoon, but couldn't figure the captain. Giving him hard stripes, the sign of a true enlisted lifer, would have been a clever insult, but he didn't think Anderson was bright enough to work that one out for himself. And the last time the CO had been nice, three shells had fallen out of the sky on his tent. He left his evening meal untouched, a Swanson' deep-dish meat pie that he couldn't get excited about. The sandman came in the form of a lean male nurse he suspected was gay. The guy was pleasant enough; Denny remembered him inserting the needle, and then he counted to fifteen before he lost interest in numbers and drifted away.

It was a puzzling dream, because then the nurse was back again, holding firmly onto his arm. "Naaaaw," he said fuzzily, "I already had my shot. . . ." But the hand just held him tighter while the other jabbed him hard with the needle. He felt the cold shock as the stuff started oozing out, spreading from his triceps into his system.

He started to drift off, but the nurse grabbed his arm again.

"Hey, wait . . . ." Denny protested feebly, brushing at the needle that wavered yet again over his arm.

"Now come on, fellah, don't give us any trouble. Just a few more shots," the male nurse said. "No trouble now, or I'll have to call the doctor." Only it wasn't the slim gay's fruity voice, it was more of a growl. Alarm bells were ringing deep in Denny's mind, and he managed to pull himself back from the billowy sleep that enfolded him long enough to focus on the dark body looming over him. His worst fears were realized—it was Toady, the fat poison toadstool personified, arrived to finish off his work!

"Come on now, fellah, come on. . . ." Toady crooned tunelessly as he tried to zero in on Denny's arm.

"Toady—you!" Denny gasped helplessly.

"Now, now, here we go down to dreamland, you little scumbag, you . . . send back word if you can—tell me how it feels in hell." He got the needle in Denny's arm, in spite of the fact that his victim was trying hard with all his failing strength to squirm out of his grasp. And he actually had over half the second tube of atropine squeezed into the arm before Denny managed a desperate lunge that snapped the needle off in his arm. Toady leapt back warily. He eyed the slumped-over form on the bed, but Denny seemed to be really out of it now. His head lolled back and his eyes rolled helplessly, showing the whites as they struggled aimlessly to focus on something, on anything, before fluttering closed.

Toady smiled and reached in his pocket for another atropine. He swiftly stripped the cellophane wrapper off. One more shot—or what the hell, why not two or three—and no more worry about good old Mad Denny. Denny sagged back on the pillow. "Out like a light!" Toady quoted smugly, reaching for the limp bare arm before him.

And that was when the spark left in Denny's mind gathered all that remained of his dwindling strength, and he lashed out from the fetal position to connect with the heel of one foot against the bridge of Toady's nose. There was a spray of blood from Toady's face, which seemed to explode in a white ball of agony.

If the Thirty-third's unwashed, moon-faced clerk had stayed to see what happened next, it could still have been his evening, for Denny tumbled over the stainless steel rail out of bed to slump helplessly on the floor. But all Toady knew was pain and fear—the fear that somehow the atropine was having no effect. He turned and fled the room in a panic, scattering syringes down the hall as he ran for the nearest exit.

Denny managed to crawl to the door, and get one hand out into the hallway before he went totally unconscious. The night duty nurse, alerted by Toady's noisy exit, followed the trail of atropine back to Denny's room. They had him in the critical ward in minutes. Even at that, his heart stopped twice in the next hour; it was that close.

But when gray dawn brought its familiar ragged clouds low over the delta, Mad Denny was able to open his eyes and see them. It was just one incident in the mad scramble that was Saigon General in those days, and they sent out one more little form to add to the bulky army file that told his life story. This one attested that he had attempted to commit suicide by injecting himself with a whole boxful of drugs one of his buddies had slipped him. They couldn't really go into it too deeply; it wasn't their job, and anyway all the evidence pointed that way.

They did a double-check on his room and took away the horse pills without comment, surprised that little was all they found. Everyone on his floor was warned to be extra careful with the key to the drug room. And in a week and a half he had recovered enough from his various setbacks to be released into the outstretched arms of his commanding officer.

CHAPTER EIGHT

8-1

A MONTH WENT BY, AND AUTUMN CAME TO PILE U.S. AND
ARVN dead and wounded like red painted leaves against the
wicker baskets of the medevac helicopters. It was a presi-
dential palace sweep for the Nguyen family, as General
Nguyen Van Thieu was elected president of the Republic of
South Vietnam, with the popular and dashing ex-commander
of the air force, Nguyen Cao Ky, as his vice president. If
there was much opposition it wasn't picked up by the local
press. The weather showed encouraging signs, as the sky
now cleared for several hours a day, usually in the late night
and early morning hours. September in Saigon, in spite of
mixed entrails, augured in a new season of hope.

Mad Denny wandered apparently aimlessly down Nguyen
Huy Street, the wide boulevard known locally as "the Street of
Flowers" for its gaily painted kiosks featuring blooms of every
type and description. He shuffled along, hands in his pockets,
stopping to talk to a street merchant or to give a few piasters
to a grubby beggar and then moving on. His morning gung fu
session was over, the surly Koreans having given him a grudg-
ing nod for the ferocity of his attack, and he was on only the
first day of a three-day leave. The sky was uncharacteristically
blue above him, with just a few puffy hints of the clouds that
would build up a few hours later. He was in a good mood; he
even caught himself whistling the tenor part from Victor Her-
bert's *Naughty Marietta*, a strangely out-of-date tune he re-

membered from his a cappella choir days, and a song he now associated with his memories of a certain girl.

The old black car pulled out from between parked cars and cut in front of him at a cross street. A girl leaned out the backseat window. "Denny. It's Tuy."

He hadn't seen her since the frag. He didn't want to see her now. He didn't know why. "Tuy. We can't talk. I'm being followed."

He saw her eyes widen. "You're not lying to me?"

"Big guy. Crew cut. A half a block back, looking through Minh's stack of fuck books. He hasn't seen you yet. Better drive on."

What she did next surprised him. "I will not," she said firmly. "You meet me somewhere—anywhere you say—or I'm going to walk with you, to talk to you right now. We have things to talk about."

He felt the gaze from her soft dark eyes boring right through him. "I had an accident," he said simply.

"I know."

"I got hurt."

"I know. And you're afraid I cannot . . . like you any more. . . ."

"That's not true!" he shot back, afraid to admit his weakness. But he left his hands in his pockets. He didn't have to show anybody anything, he thought to himself.

"Yes it is," she said, arching her slim neck to have a better look at him. "You are an inconsiderate, bullheaded, stupid, foolish, macho pig, and the only thing that keeps me from driving off is . . . you are my business partner and I have to have a word with you. Will it be now or later?"

He gave her a long look, drinking in the face he had ached for weeks to see. There was no other way, he told himself; he had to see her one last time. "Later. Your house tonight. I can't say when for sure." He shrugged one shoulder, indicating wordlessly he would have to give the man behind him the slip.

She motioned for George to go on. Denny took a quick glance backward over his shoulder, then said, "Wait! One second!" Dooly still had his face in the cock-books, so Denny went swiftly to the nearest flower stand, which was no more than a few steps away, and grabbed a long-stemmed white rose with his good hand. Putting it under his other arm, he fished in his pocket for a one-hundred-P note, which he tossed into the outstretched *ba*'s palm. Quickly returning with the flower, he passed it in through the window, pausing a moment to look deeply into her eyes. He seemed about to say something, but he caught himself with a little shake of the head. "Go now. Quickly."

As George drove her away, she studied the beautiful white bud. It was perfect, just halfway opened. Her heart did a little song as she realized Denny was really a romantic, in spite of himself. She held it next to the bloodred ring on her finger, and perhaps it was the reflected light from some passing car window or strip of chrome, but just then the ruby flared so brilliantly that she had to gasp. "What does it mean?" she whispered softly to herself. "What does it *mean*?"

Denny spent the rest of the afternoon at the Enlisted Men's Club, slouched in a soft chair drinking milk chocolate shakes and reading Durrell's *Justine*, which he had found in Ranley's library. He found himself absorbed in the portrait of the sultry and mysterious Egyptian lady, and soon was drawing all sorts of dreamy parallels between Tuy and Justine, and between himself and the hero in the tale. He almost forgot the supposedly invisible presence of the spook, who hovered over the Sheena, Queen of the Jungle pinball machine all afternoon, lightly dusting the glass top with stuff that floated from his scalp as he expertly whacked the side near the flippers to get his better bounce.

Four-thirty was closing time, and Denny ambled a couple of blocks over to Chez Brodard. The café used to be solid

French, but lately the record player had offered the Beatles and the Rolling Stones instead of Piaf and Aznavour, and the owners had even added a "Hamburger Américain" to the menu. Denny munched a ham-and-egg sandwich, absent-mindedly putting it down to lift his glass of cheap Algerian red to his lips with the same hand. He pretended not to notice as the tall, potato-faced fellow with the stuff in his hair squeezed into a stool at the counter to his left.

He waited until Dooly's order came. It looked like he'd asked for the steak sandwich au jus. Too bad, Denny thought, if he'd only ordered the burger "Américain" he could have taken it with him. As his spook-tail reached for the knife and fork and was sawing off the first bite, Denny scooped up his own check and made his way toward the cash register. Out of the corner of his eye, he saw Dooly fumbling for his wallet and trying to stuff a piece of steak down his face at the same time. The big sergeant realized he didn't have his check yet, and was frantically trying to get the waiter's attention as Denny left. He walked the length of the plate glass window, turning the corner and heading down a side street, still in plain view of the frantic spook, who now was yelling at the waiter.

Once out of sight, Denny moved quickly without galloping. The trick, he knew, was to go fast without attracting undue attention. There was always a White Mouse around smart enough to plug a running pedestrian. He crossed the street and reversed his direction, hoping Dooly wouldn't be able to spot him in the twilight from inside the brightly lit café. Just to make sure, he walked another block and then ducked into a dark doorway. It was a thing Americans just didn't do, and he was sure Dooly wouldn't think he was there.

It was thirty seconds before he realized he wasn't alone. "Who's there?" he whispered in Vietnamese. Somebody giggled, and then somebody else. His eyes began to adjust to the light, and he realized he was in the middle of a bunch of street kids. This long drafty hall was probably their den, their only shelter from the rain in one season and the choking dusty heat in the other. And then he saw Dooly approaching down the street, somehow still gamely on his trail. It was a lesson he wouldn't forget; the guy assumed he would double back! *"Zut!"* he whispered. "It's a game. Twenty piasters for everybody who doesn't say a word!"

Dooly actually poked his head in. "Hey—anybody in here?" But he didn't have a flashlight, and he didn't think to light a match. Rule one in the manual, take it from the spook, you don't crawl around dark holes in Nam. He wrinkled his nose, not liking the smell of it, then backed out and hurried on down the street. Denny paid his bill all around, and after waiting five minutes caught a cab for Hai Ba Trung. He bailed out of the ride halfway there, pushing money in the cabbie's hands, the man protesting that they weren't there yet. Denny panicked, hiring a pedicab and pointing it in the general direction of Da Cau; then when he was as sure as he could be that no one was following, he paid off the peddler and took another blue-and-cream to Tuy's place.

The old man answered his knock at the door and let him in without a word. He found Tuy waiting by the Franklin stove. She was wearing tight jeans, riding boots, and a soft Pendleton wool shirt open at the neck.

"Where's your riding crop?" he said with a little smile. "Just trying for a little humor," he added. "Guess I shouldn't have said that. . . ."

She replied with a gaze that was both direct and bold. "Denny, Denny, Denny. What am I going to do with you?"

"What—do?" he said, trying to avoid the subject. "There's nothing to do."

"Nothing? And there was nothing between us the last time you were here? Perhaps it was the wine, the mood of the evening, we were swept away like two lovers in one of my novels? In another minute you are going to have the most angry woman you have ever seen standing right here in front of you, and by God, Mad Dennis, I don't know what I'm going to do—"

He couldn't think of anything better, so he swept her to him with his good arm and stopped her yammering with a kiss. She struggled, but only for a moment, and then gave in to him as their lips melted together in a deep passionate kiss. When he pulled away, she looked at him with her large, luminous eyes, her lips parted, her breath soft against his cheek. "Carry me away, Denny! Now, to my bedroom. Surely you know the way! . . ."

She threw her arms around his neck. He swelled with desire as he felt her pert breasts against his body. "I thought you wanted to talk business."

"Business. Yes. I have a good report for you. We are making money." She moved gently, teasingly against him. "Now let's get down to the real business."

That night she was insatiable, and again and again she found him ready, eager for her touch, eager to thrust deep into her until her blood thundered in her ears and she was lifted again to the distant, unreachable stars. It was a night to be dreamed about, a night around which authors wove the long romances she knew so well, the characters dancing their slow waltz through the chapters of their lives to climax in the unfolding wonders of those few magical hours.

Finally in the early hours of morning they lay exhausted, entwined together, and Tuy reached tenderly for him. "Now. Show me."

He had a momentary twinge of fear, then held what was left of his maimed hand out to her. She took it, caressing it gently, and turning it over to examine it carefully. Her fingertips trailed over each stump where his fingers had been, as if to memorize them, and he was almost ready to pull back, to say with typical bravado that it "wasn't much." But she said another thing then, and their relationship took a new turn, deepening in a way he found as unexpected as anything that had happened between them.

"Soul mates," she whispered in what sounded like awe to him.

"What?"

She held her own right hand up to the dim candlelight. "You mean you never noticed my right hand?"

"No. I mean, I never did . . . what is it?"

"Can't you see? I can't bend it any more than this." She held her hand so he could see it was half-closed, like a bird's claw.

He rolled on his stomach and examined more closely the hand she held out to him. He could see that what she said was true. The inside of her palm was heavily ridged with old scars, deep burns that must have seared her flesh down to the bone. He remembered she had worn gloves the night she had been the flapper, and he'd just thought of it as part of her costume. "I never noticed, Tuy. Honest. How did you get such horrible scars?"

"Burns," she said simply. "My cousin Din held it to red-hot coils to torture me, the night—the night that Larkey died."

"Ohh . . ." he said, not knowing if she wanted to go on.

"He wanted to kill me, and he nearly did. He was crazy and jealous, and he did this with the hot plate that I used for tea. I blacked out, and when I came to he was choking me. . . ." She shuddered, remembering how her weird demented cousin had wanted her to die while he was raping her. "Hold me, Denny. I don't want to think about it any more."

He held her with his good arm, and she snuggled close to him, cupping her scarred right hand inside his maimed right hand and covering them both with her good one. She was afraid to look, but she was sure as she was a woman that there would be a glow from her ring even in this almost absolute darkness. They lay happily together for minutes or hours, they didn't know, and the time made no difference anyhow. . . . The wind and the war howled outside, but for those moments to these two people it didn't and it couldn't matter. "Soul mates," she whispered once again, as she drifted off into deep dreamless sleep.

Denny wasn't yet halfway into a three-day leave; he had nowhere better to go, so the next morning it was almost noon before he crawled out from between her silk sheets. Tuy was gone. Since there was no hurry about anything, he found the shower, and after a brisk few minutes that convinced him no hot water was to be had anywhere in Saigon short of the Caravelle, he rubbed himself down and pulled his civvies back on.

Tuy was nowhere to be found, so he headed for the front door, still yawning as he tried to shake the cobwebs from his brains.

The half-blind old man was sweeping the hallway near the door. He paused and silently gestured to Denny, fumbling in his pocket as he did so. He handed over a folded scrap of paper.

Denny saw it had scrawled in Tuy's tight script an address in Switzerland that he had never heard of, followed by a long string of numbers. "What's this," he asked sleepily, "code? . . ."

"No, young sir," the old man replied. "Your bank account. We recognized the difficulties you may encounter in trying to deal with sums of money . . . in these times . . . in your present position. We took the liberty of calling on old acquaintances to set this up for you in Europe. . . ." The conversation was closed, and the old man went back to sweeping, as if it was the most important thing in his day.

Denny left Tuy's villa and walked slowly and thoughtfully along Truong Minh Giang toward Ranley's place, wondering at a world where nothing was ever exactly what it seemed.

"I'm so short I got to piss up to hit the urinal!" Weird chortled gleefully. "I got to use a ladder in a dink whorehouse!"

He was disassembling his collection of weaponry and tossing it in footlockers while all around him and through the other rooms of Ranley's villa his fare-thee-well party had taken over. This was a lifer's farewell, and so instead of the upstart Beatles thrashing out their "Love Me Do," Tony Bennett sang of losing his heart high on a hill in San Francisco, and Frank Sinatra recounted the very good years of his life by recalling a string of broads he'd laid. Later there would be the mandatory hard drinking. One or two fistfights would break out. And the party would finally dissolve in a rush as almost everybody headed for their favorite bar girl or house of ill repute.

But for now, the rooms drifted with blue-gray smoke, and the men swigged beers, passed around joints, and talked about hitches in faraway places like Okinawa and Addis Ababa. The record player did a hiccup and started on a platter of Johnny Mathis Christmas songs. Johnny sang about sleigh bells in the snow, and to a man they remembered the eternal vague promises that they would all be out by the time the snow flew. It was a bittersweet joke; the only white stuff that floated down south of the DMZ was snaky phosphorus . . . or maybe white ash from the burning hootches.

Weird Elliott was going home for a month, mostly to pack his collection in grease in a barn with a good roof out behind the three acres his family owned off the Interstate near Rensselaer, Indiana. Then he would be flying on to his new assignment with a unit stationed near Berlin that was doing radio research work next to the Iron Curtain. He wasn't particularly relieved to be leaving Nam, as he had never really been worried about his personal safety. Weird always had an automatic weapon or a grenade within easy reach, and he left the rest in God's hands. For weeks after his out-country flight, Denny kept finding handguns stashed around the villa—behind books in the bookshelves, taped behind pictures on the wall, and sitting on out-of-the-way wood beams overhead. He even found a grenade in a tightly sealed jelly jar in the tank over the toilet bowl. It wasn't all that bad an idea, and Denny left everything where it was.

Mad Denny sat on a sofa, arms around his legs, drinking a Ba Muoi Ba and looking on as Weird packed his war machinery. "Guess we're gonna get that third bedroom back now. . . ."

"Yup." Weird chuckled. He burped and staggered over to the booby-trap bomb he'd shown Denny when he'd first rented in the villa. "This is a goddamn shame!"

"What is?"

Elliott lifted a shopping bag by its handles. It was white and black with big letters running across the outside that said SAKS FIFTH AVENUE. "It's my seventy-two-hour *designer bomb*!" The sergeant cackled, his high laugh finally squeaking out into a little gasp. "My fashion-designer bomb! Something for the little ladies, fourth floor, lorgnettes and other intimate apparel. . . ."

"Weird, you are drunk as a skunk!"

"No, I ain't, Denny!" He paused for effect, wrinkling his nose and crossing his eyes. "I'm *drunker* than a skunk!" And he broke up again in his strange laugh. "But look here, podner, this is serious. This is the best bomb I ever made. Look, new dry cell and everything!"

"Just dismantle it and ship it home with the rest."

"Yeah, I guess I could. . . ." Weird sighed his disappointment. "It's just such a *perfect* bomb."

Denny burped, his third straight Ba Muoi Ba getting to him. You didn't turn down beers at a lifer's party. "Balls, there's no such thing as a *perfect* bomb."

"Yeah, well look at this timer—whoops! Other way! Almost bought the farm that time, Your Royal Madness!"

Denny bent over to look in the bag. "Great, Weird, how precise is it, to the half-hour?"

"You shittin' me, Den-Den? To the half-second!" the ordnance sergeant replied proudly. "I hooked this baby to a double
timer—the seventy-two-hour number . . . that's over here . . .
and to this little guy here, see? A little racetrack stopwatch."

Denny had an inspiration. You didn't throw back a gift
from the gods. "Give it to me."

Weird blinked at him, his mind trying to float its way up
out of all those beers. "What for?"

"For old times' sake."

"You won't let it go to waste?" Weird burped politely into
his hand. "I mean, this is my best bomb ever. . . ."

"Solemn scouts'-honor promise. I won't let it go to
waste. . . ." Denny gave him the Boy Scouts' sign and
crossed his heart with it.

"All right . . ." Weird said. He gave Denny an embarrassing hug and a sloppy kiss on the cheek.

About a week later a war party gathered late one night in
the EMC at the Thirty-third. As usual, the chairs were all up
on the tables, and the worn-out club sarge had tossed Toady
the lock-up key hours before and gone to bed. Stringer was
bent over a piece of paper on which he was printing in huge
block letters, THAT WAS NOTHING, TURKEY—NEXT TIME
WE'RE GONNA BLOW YOUR DICK OFF!

Animal hunched over in his seat. "I don't get it—you think
you're gonna scare Denny off? He's a crazy man!"

Stringer passed the paper over to Toady. "Put the thumbprint on it, just like in *Treasure Island*."

Animal wouldn't stop complaining. "Didn't they use a
page from the Bible or something?"

Stringer expelled a breath sharply. "Man, I am losing patience with you! You don't go maiming a Bible! This here
note is gonna be all *The Word* he needs. He's gonna get
rattled and do something stupid. An' we're gonna get him!"

Toady, who had used a black ink stamp pad he brought

from the CO's office to apply carefully his thumbprint, passed it across to Animal. "How are we gonna get him?"

Stringer gently lifted a rumpled paper bag onto the table. "Look at this, man," he said, carefully taking items from the bag. "Bouncing Bettys, three balls of plastic, bamboo splinter grenade . . . I traded booze with a lurp buddy of mine for this stuff . . . I went lurpin' a time or two myself, ya know . . . and I got more back in my locker!" He took the ink pad from Animal to apply his own print. He noticed the first two prints were a little inky, but otherwise clear as those on an FBI wanted poster. Saying nothing, he took even more ink than they had used, and carefully smudged his print so there would be no chance to trace it.

A calm voice spoke out of the darkness next to the doorway. "Hi fellows . . . is that for me?" Denny walked over to the booth. He was wearing black pants and a black turtleneck sweater.

"Hey—nobody's allowed. . . ." Toady had barked, before he saw who it was. His voice trailed off into silence.

Denny grabbed an upside-down chair from one of the tables with his right hand, managing to hold it between the stub of his thumb and his little finger, and flipped it in front of the booth. It landed backward, but he threw a leg over and sat with his arms on the bentwood chair back. "Look—a note for me!" Before they could do anything, he snatched it from the table. "Hmmmm, somebody here knows how to print—I wouldn't have imagined it. . . . "

Stringer knew they had nothing to worry about; after all they had three to one. "It's your warning, Haller," he sneered. "It's the only one you get. We're gonna take you out. You can spend your time worryin' about it, but you'll never know when or where it's gonna hit you."

"Kind of like syphilis, isn't it. . . ." Denny replied softly. "I like to use comparisons all of you can relate to. . . ."

"Sure—insult us!" Toady glared. "It ain't gonna work!

You're not gonna pick a fight here. You're gonna wait and wait and wait for it. And when it comes, you're gonna get yours!''

"Of course, you sweet little pus-bag. But let's be friends in the meantime. How about a game of cards? Five-card poker. You're good at cards from what I hear, Stringer. . . .'' Denny pulled a deck from his pocket. "I'll deal them all face up; that way there'll be no surprises." He wasn't sure he could pull it off with his fingers missing, but he had once been very good. And he'd practiced this one little trick constantly for the last three days. He shuffled the cards, shuffled them again, and then deftly slipped the deck between his legs, replacing it with the one held with a rubber band on his wrist. He dealt, and the cards flew down on the table one by one. Denny intoned as they hit in front of each person, "Ace of spades, ace of spades, ace of spades, ace of diamonds . . . ace of spades, ace of spades, ace of spades, ace of diamonds . . . hmmmmm, lots of aces of spades, wouldn't you say?'' He continued dealing until five black aces were in front of each of the three, while he held five red ones.

Toady and Animal were uneasy, wondering how Denny had done it. Stringer, who had tapped his fingers impatiently throughout the deal, gave him an impatient grimace. "Very funny, Haller—how many decks did you have to waste to set up your little card trick?''

"No joke, fellows," Denny said, waving their warning paper with the thumbprints on it. He folded it and carefully stuck it in his pocket. "Just a friendly warning in return. You guys split up right now, this very second. Don't you ever get together in one room to plot how you're going to get me— not ever again, do you hear me?''

"Yeah, we hear you, Haller . . .'' Stringer replied in his best bored know-it-all voice.

"Fine." Denny stood and held both hands out chest high, showing that he had no weapons. He sprayed the rest of the cards at them. All aces of spades, they fluttered down on the table. And then he backed away from them across the room and was gone.

It was very quiet. "We should have jumped him. . . ." Toady said lamely, breaking the silence.

"Yeah, sure—'*we*'!" Stringer snarled at him. "Me and you pussies! I can see me hangin' on to him while you two wonder what to do next! Assholes! Look, he's got the warning, that's fine. Scared shitless or not, he's gonna die, man!"

"He's a faggot . . ." Animal said, taking another swig of beer. "Mad Denny's a faggot."

"Lord, give me a little help here!" Stringer looked at him like he was a disgusting piece of snot. "Animal, what the fuck are you talking about?"

Animal didn't let it bother him. Stringer was too smart for his own britches. He knew he was onto something. He had their attention, so he let them both wait while he let out a big fart, sighing with pleasure, and repeated with drunken insistence, "Mad Denny's a queer, you fuckhead, don't you have ears? He shops at ladies' stores. Look—he left his shopping bag!"

The realization came instantly, like a cold bucket of fear. They all had been in Nam for months, eating and drinking and whoring in places where innocent packages, battered suitcases, and even rusty bicycles exploded without warning. The three locked eyes for one wild awful moment, then upset the heavy table as they dove for the door. But it was too late.

Denny had worked his way out under a loose board in the rotten wooden fence, at a place he had marked earlier. He was a block away from the Thirty-third, headed for the main gate, when the roof of the EMC was lifted up in a thousand splinters by a fiery, orange-red ball. Sirens wailed and fire trucks rumbled by as he caught a white cyclobus. Extra guards were pulling up as he showed his ID at the gate. The harassed MP gave him a perfunctory glance and waved him through. "What the hell's going on back there?"

"I don't know, guy," Denny answered over his shoulder as

he made for the nearest waiting blue-and-cream. "Victor Charlie's got all the dynamite in the world, seems like. . . . "

8-3

Money, whether it be French or Swiss francs, dollars *My Kim*, or Vietnamese dongs, can be enjoyed on several levels. Obviously, it buys things and so is to be desired. But beyond this, it can be collected, and the gathering of large sums of wealth has historically been one of the great passions, if not joys, of the human race.

This is not all good. Anything so desirable has to be subject to excess and abuse. It is news to no one that gathering wealth can be a vice every bit as consuming as gambling or physical lust. It can even be argued that one of the great contributions of the capitalist and communist systems alike to the morality of our modern society is that they both have done such a great deal to take these temptations from the hands of the common worker. But that is not the main point. The key issue is that real money has many levels, and you have to set your own goals or the end is never in sight.

Edgar Munson, no longer a simple worker ant, was experiencing some of this. He was collecting real money in huge irregular sums. It came in carefully wrapped shoeboxes in the normal armed services mail delivery. It came in rumpled packs of old twenty, fifty, and one hundred dollar bills. It came, on the average, every third day.

Tuy, after helping him get his operation rolling with a first load on credit, demanded her money on delivery. That cost to Edgar, his major expense in hard dollars, was just over sixty percent of his operation. The guys in his shipping system (there were only three, one in Saigon and two in the States) he paid in high-grade; and so, in a sense, he was bartering for their services, which ultimately cost him next to nothing.

Behind the locked doors of his interrogation room, Edgar Munson ignored his sleek "big fellows" more and more as he took up a new hobby—counting his money, and dreaming of what it could buy him. When he opened the first shoebox from the States, his fingers trembled and he'd had trouble with the strap tape. He finally remembered one of his surgical knives, and then he gleefully slashed through the irksome tape. The lid came off, and it was a moment before he realized what he was staring at—the edges of a box full of tightly packed bills. He shook the paperbound packets of green money out on the table in front of him, and a feeling of sweet comfort overcame him.

He started his tally on a legal notebook, adding up each bill. The numbers mounted, and so did his excitement. When he finished, it was as good as the bank, his total coming to exactly the same as the number scribbled on a plain scrap of notebook paper enclosed in the box: $167,550. He would find that it represented a light load, but at that time it was more money than he had seen in one place, and he couldn't contain his emotion.

His profit from the shipment represented by that one shoebox was roughly $67,000, or forty percent. He thoughtfully separated out that amount, careful to take only the hundreds. His pile came out to three little stacks of bills, just over four inches high. What could he do with $67,000? He could own his house in Seaside, pay cash for that little crackerbox and have money left over for a new Cadillac Fleetwood, the big gray one with plush black leather seats. He could get the windows tinted gray, for privacy, just like the Hollywood movie stars. He laughed a little embarrassed laugh at that last thought, that was just a bit crazy, going too far . . . you didn't want to attract that kind of attention. . . . But the money looked back at him from the table, and he knew the Seaside house and the Cadillac, with or without the tinted windows, were right there in front of him, and he would even have—my God, he calculated swiftly—he would still have just over half the money left! Edgar spent the rest of the evening in a euphoria of imagined spending sprees. He bought his wife a puffy white fur coat with tassels, insisting she model it naked in their bedroom, while he lay there on his bed like a tycoon in his new silk robe, thinking of success rather than sex as he sipped twenty-year-old un-blended Scotch and puffed a Cuban cigar. He bought his son a snowmobile and an English two-seater convertible, and his daughter the white Boss Mustang with the clean, creamy leatherette interior she had always wanted. His son told him he wanted to go to Yale to try premed, and he felt his chest swell with pride as he imagined himself saying coolly he thought that would be all right. They rented—no, they "leased with option to buy"—a cabin in the mountains near Tahoe. It was great, sliding around the mountains, but after a few days it started to snow and the family had all left for Seaside and Edgar was alone building a fire in the fireplace when the neighbor's daughter, a willowy, blond-haired slip of a thing about fourteen years old, skied up to his cabin door and said her parents had gone back to San Francisco, leaving her for the week. . . . The *Xau My* zipped down his pants and thought some more about it. The rats eyed him hungrily.

As time passed, the shipments went out by the dozens, always without a hitch. There was a tremendous backup of raw materials in the dreamy Lao highlands, and a real demand on the streets of major U.S. cities. Tuy was forced to set up a second factory, and even then was hard-pressed to keep up with the demand. The little shoeboxes appeared in his mail with increasing frequency. "Magazines and cook-ies," he joked to the mail clerk. The clerk, who sensed Major Edgar Munson wasn't one to fun around with, never asked to share an Oreo.

The *Xau My* found himself busier and happier than he had ever been. In addition to his bullshit army job, to which he paid less and less attention, he personally packed every shipment. He had a natural talent for it and got to where he could do one in just under a half hour. Still, the half hours added up, until he was skipping his fun sessions in his room at the Caravelle just to keep up with his work flow. It was ironic, he thought, not to have the time now to enjoy himself when he had all the financial resources he needed.

The operation progressed smoothly, and less than a month after his first shipment Edgar was staring in dumbfounded amazement at another pile of money on his desk. This one was just over a foot high. Made up entirely of one-hundred-dollar bills, it contained exactly one million dollars. And it was all his!

What in God's name could he do with a million dollars? He could buy a big house—not in Seaside where all the lifers lived, but over in Monterey where you could get a view of the bay or Pacific Grove by the little cove where the sea lions barked and the blond surfers maneuvered around the nasty rock outcrops while their neat little trickster-cunts waited on blankets spread on the warm sand, or even in tony Carmel-by-the-Sea. He could outright *buy* that little ski condo—no, he could even buy a two-story chalet with a Swiss-looking log front and a steep shingled roof! And fuck the house by the beach, he could get acreage, by God, he could buy a ranch up in the hills over Carmel, and have a view of the rolling hills and the ocean for miles in every direction! And cars—why, he could have a Jag—fuck the Caddie—a big gray Jag sitting in the long curved driveway in front of the ultra-modern low stone ranch house! Edgar saw himself sunbathing back by the pool. He wore silver sunglasses, and a plush towel of royal blue was draped over his loins. His family was all on a trip over in Europe, and he was attended by three—no, six!—dark-eyed little girls his supplier had shipped up from Mexico.

He leaned back in his chair and began to paint in the detail, the finer brushstrokes on his dream. He felt the first stirrings of desire as he imagined the little bitches one by one and began to think what he might do to them. The rats, by this time almost totally neglected, stirred fretfully in their cage.

But if the money was incredible, so were the risks he was taking. The idea of what might happen if he was caught was sobering. This wasn't the kind of thing one did for a living; you got in, made your killing, and got out a rich man. Even as he industriously worked on his second million, Edgar Munson was already thinking about an early retirement.

The problem was, you could buy more with two million than you could with one . . . and still more with three. He was no fool; he realized that the expenses didn't just stop when you bought something like a ski place in the mountains or a gentleman's ranch. There were bills and taxes to pay. His twin-engined prop plane had to suck gas like a mother, and there was the pilot's salary, and the stream of fresh maidens he was going to need, and the list went on and on.

Although the money was great, he wasn't really satisfied anymore. Here he was taking all these risks, and he had to share his profits with Tuy. He pursed his lips, thinking about it. If he hadn't agreed to the original cut . . . but he was new to the game then and didn't know any better. Maybe he could still convince her to accept less—if he could get her take down to around forty or fifty percent, he could pocket the rest. He knew she had just gotten into the business when he did. She would have no choice, because he was her only customer! And if she proved unwilling, he might play that interesting little card, the file on the unsolved Larkspun murder. Who knew? Maybe . . . just maybe, she was in worse trouble than he knew, and he could take over her end of the operation as well. . . .

He went to pay her a surprise visit the next day. He went alone, and as it was early afternoon, found himself chatting in street English with a little doe-eyed peanut girl in the deserted Tuyet Lan. Tuy arrived an hour later and proved to be monumentally uncooperative.

"You want a new split? Fine, go find a new partner!" Tuy literally screamed at him as she stalked around her small back room. "I am handling my end with no trouble. You said you needed more volume, I increased our production.

You grumbled about ninety-two percent pure, and we got it up to between ninety-five and -six!''

"Yes," Edgar lied, "but we're flooding the market, and the price is coming down."

"I could believe that one, if I didn't have my own sources who tell me exactly the opposite! Major Edgar Munson, U.S. Army—you are already shading the percentages to your advantage from our original deal! Don't try to deny it!''

"That's pure bull . . .'' Edgar grumbled, but he couldn't look directly at her. She was such a bitch! He thought to himself—what to do, what to do?

She sat in her ornate wooden chair, resting her hands on the dark dragon's heads carved on each side. "I should not tell you this, but I have the extremely good possibility of clients in Europe. . . .''

"You don't know anybody but me!" he flared angrily, wondering if she had read his mind.

She calmly studied her long red fingernails, noticing that her ruby had again gone dead black in the presence of the *Xau My*. "They are old contacts, difficult to touch as old money . . . but they understand this business, as you do not!''

"What do you mean? I created this whole thing, with one— I must say 'brilliant'—idea! You couldn't ship without me! The stuff would just pile up . . . wherever you make it!'' He studied her slyly, hoping for some clue that might lead him or his men to her factory.

Her face was totally calm, the bland face of the Orient that he hated so much. She even had the nerve to smile an infuriating little smile, "You'd give a lot to know where that is, wouldn't you.'' It wasn't a question, and the way she said the words just made him angrier.

"You don't have any reason to be so smug!" he railed at her. "You think you're so damn smart! Well, let me tell you, sister, everybody's got a past, and yours is closer than you think to catching up with you!''

"What do you mean?''

"I think I'll let you worry about that!" Edgar spun around to make his exit and bumped into Mad Denny, who had just come in. Edgar shoved him violently. "Out of my way, you dumb grunt! The grunt and the cunt, what a pair. . . ."

"Edgar . . ." Denny said softly, his voice cutting across the room like a whip. "Edgar, you're gonna die." A month ago he would have screamed it. But the frag had scrambled him inside, and when things settled, there was a new Mad Denny left to face the world. Any man used to serious one-on-one confrontations would far rather have faced the old one.

Edgar was beyond reason. "Oh fuck you, asshole—we're all gonna die, someday. *You* are the one, you're the innocent here! Smart young GI, off on a roll. You don't know what you're playing with!"

Denny took an innocent step toward him, now definitely in range, and again spoke calmly. "Edgar . . . what are you talking about?"

Tuy tried to change the conversation. "Denny. It's just a business argument—"

But Edgar sensed his advantage and pushed in the wedge as hard as he could. "It's this bitch, man! She killed a GI in cold blood—and I got the evidence! What do you think of that, grunt-brains?" And the *Xau My* got out, moving swiftly in that one moment of outrage before the stunned younger man could decide whether or not to tear his head off. Denny looked uncertainly at Tuy.

"Nooo . . ." she pleaded, "he doesn't know that, it's not true . . . it's not true. . . ." She was startled out of her former composure and stood there looking suddenly older than her years, wringing her hands and caught up in the old grief that had come back to overwhelm her. "Please, Denny . . . please! . . ."

He managed to shake his head. "I don't know . . . I'm not accusing you. . . ."

"You *are*!" she cried as the tears began streaming down

her face. "You don't believe me! You think I'm guilty; I see it in your eyes!"

He shook his head again, upset and starting to get angry, more as a response to her quick judgment of him than anything else. "No, Tuy—you can't just go saying that about me. I don't know what to say. I've got to think. . . ."

"Oh sure, go ahead and do your big man-thing, think everything out," she shouted sarcastically through her tears. "And when you do, come back and tell me what you've decided!"

"Okay, I will!" he roared, now really angry. He turned on his heel and stalked out of the room, through the bar past the table of idle bar girls who turned curious faces up to him, and on out into the street.

"Can't you see I need you now? . . ." Tuy said in a choked little voice to the empty bead curtains swaying in the doorway. She looked at the ring on her finger and involuntarily let out a gasp as she saw it gave off not even a flicker of light. She rubbed it fearfully, now terrified for her future, the long endless days to come when she would never again hold Denny in her arms. . . . But the stone remained black, black as the doorway she imagined led to hell.

8-4

The Tour d'Argent was an elegant French restaurant located on Ben Chuong Duong, by the river near the Club Nautique de Saigon and right next door to the My Canh floating restaurant. Denny had convinced Tuy to join him for dinner, in spite of the old man, Mako, and George, who had each come separately to advise her against it. Denny had won the day, arguing they couldn't let old ghosts come between them. He declared he loved her and trusted her, and that he was sure the *Xau My* was lying for some devious reasons of his own. Tuy came reluctantly, for once breaking her old rule—never to put herself in a position to draw unwanted attention.

Denny wore a dashing new Thai silk dinner jacket, a dark fabric showing hints of deep purple that the little man in the Oxford tailors had assured him was all the rage, and a black string tie. Tuy thought he looked wonderful and was proud of the way he stood out in the room full of polyester-suited middle-aged military men.

Tuy, who loved to wear costumes, thought long and hard before deciding on a sexy low-cut orange dress of filmy silk. She wore an expensive wig of long shiny black hair and made up her face a touch on the heavy side. She ended up looking extremely sexy and very expensive; but the real plus was she also looked just a touch cheap, and therefore not that much different from every other high-class hooker and officer's girl in the place.

Denny was bubbling over with good humor, and he treated her like a real lady. "My dear woman, may I ply you with another glass of champagne?" She said he could, in spite of the fact that it was frightfully expensive, and he called the waiter over. The endless courses of French food began. The meal passed uneventfully enough, and she felt attracted to the strength and calm joy that seemed to be pouring out of Denny. He apparently was going to be able to make good his word to put the past behind him. She actually began to enjoy herself.

They were giggling over another glass of wine when an older man nearby put his fingers to his lips and said, "Shhhhh!"

"What is it, old fellow?" Denny asked with a tipsy grin.

"I'm nobody's 'old fellow,' young man . . . I happen to be a general in the United States Army—and this is the most expensive restaurant in Saigon."

"Oh, I'm sorry, sir. You see, I was just promoted, and this dear lady and I were celebrating—"

"To what rank?" the officer asked stiffly.

"E-six," Denny said with a grin. "Un-fuckin'-believable, ain't it?"

"I find your humor un-funny and your vulgarity out of order. . . . You might take your appetite and your manners down to the nearest buffalo-burger stand."

"Wheeeeuuuu . . ." Denny whistled, thinking it over. He didn't want to continue what he thought was a silly argument with a surly old man, but he didn't want to be put down in front of Tuy either. But what really bothered him was that he felt he had caught a whiff of the stench at the top—the army rot went deep, all the way to the core. They looked down on the rank below them, passing preconceived notions on everything from information about Victor Charlie to a lousy E-6 sipping French wine. "Frankly . . . may I speak off the record, sir?"

"You may. But be brief."

"I believe your attitude stinks, sir. You seem to be saying this is one of those spoils of war off limits to enlisted men."

"It would be if I had my say! On your pay, you shouldn't be able to afford it anyway!"

"Still off the record, they print your salary on the back of the pink, right next to mine, and neither should you, sir. . . ."

"That's quite enough!" the general ordered, slamming his linen napkin down across a half-eaten strawberry tart on the plate in front of him. In his anger, he jostled his coffee cup and a little spurt splashed up to splatter the front of his light jacket. "God-*damn* it!" He stood and grabbed the napkin and angrily rubbed at the stain, just making it worse as he rubbed it in.

The girl across the table from the general, a slim young thing about forty-five years his junior, reached out a concerned hand, "That's o-kay, Ho-ney. Leave for now. All o-kay, o-kay. Ju-dy fix for you."

Denny smiled at the man, who was glaring daggers at him. "Is this Ju-dy your wife, sir—the one I've heard so much about? Gosh, she's young, sir, I had no idea. . . ."

The general muttered under his breath, "You shithead . . .

I'll get you. . . .'' He grabbed Ju-dy's hand and pushed his way through the crooked aisle among the little tables, heading for the door like a juggernaut.

"So long, Ho-ney! . . ." Denny called after him.

Tuy just shook her head at him like he was a bad little boy. She wanted to crawl under the table to get out of the spotlight, but there was nothing she could do about it. It was over anyway, and in another minute everyone went back to their own table conversation. She let the wine bubbles tickle her nose as she flirted over the rim of the glass at Denny. She was listening to the violin music and dreaming they were soon-to-be lovers trapped in Vienna by Nazi spies like the wonderful couple she had read about in *And Once Again, My Love* . . . when she spotted the tall, crew-cut man Denny had pointed out to her on the Street of Flowers. "Denny—don't look now, but that spook-man you pointed out to me is sitting at a table across the room behind you."

"I know. I've been meaning to go over to talk to him."

"No!" she protested, sure he'd had too much wine to know what was good for him. "He might hurt you!"

"Nonsense, my dear," Denny replied with a cavalier gesture. "I'll buy him a drink. Please excuse me for the briefest of moments." His attitude changed and she saw he was not as affected by the wine as she had thought. "Honest. I'll be all right." She watched him stop the waiter on his way to the other man and wondered how often she had underestimated her lover. He *was* rash; they never should have come there. But he held his liquor well and in a crisis seemed able to think quickly and clearly.

Dooly put his hand over his face and turned his head a bit to the wall as Denny approached. It was no use; Denny simply walked up to his table and sat in the unoccupied chair across from him. "Dining alone, sailor?"

"Shit, Haller—can't you play the game? You're not *supposed* to come over here. . . .''

The waiter came and started to pour the wine. "No,"

Dooly protested, seeing the expensive French label on the bottle, "I ordered Algerian—*Al-ger-i-an.*"

"Yes, monsieur," the waiter said with a little sniff, "the wine was ordered by your companion here."

"I know," Denny said, spreading his hands, "I shouldn't have. . . ."

Dooly took a sip of the wine and nodded his appreciation. "Look, kid—you're gettin' your jollies off, out here havin' fun in fancy restaurants and runnin' around with two-hundred-dollar hookers—but it ain't gonna last! You're in plenty of hot water already—where you get the dough to frequent this kind of joint?"

"I just made E-6, didn't you hear? Everybody's got a right to blow a wad once in a while."

"Yeah, I heard. Everybody in the place heard. . . . What did *you* hear about that explosion back at the Thirty-third?"

"Yeah, big mess, wasn't it . . . what about it?"

"You tell me—it took out the three guys in the world you got the most reason to hate." He nodded at Denny's mutilated hand. "That makes you the prime suspect."

"I don't think so," Denny said. He pulled a sheet of folded paper from his jacket pocket and carefully unwrapped the cellophane from around it. Dooly reached over, but Denny moved it out of his reach, opening it himself and holding it up for Dooly to read. "Somebody was going to blow my dick off. In other circumstances, that might be an interesting proposal, but I hardly think that's what they had in mind."

"Who wrote that?"

"Can I trust you to find out?" Denny carefully rewrapped the paper, which he had handled only by the edges. "It's got three thumbprints in ink, and my guess is that even those incompetents at Spook City could come up with a dozen more prints with a little dusting. . . ."

"What are you suggesting?"

"That this little piece of paper not only proves who fragged me in the first place . . . but suggests they blew themselves to eternity setting up a second shot.'' He tossed the paper in Dooly's lap. ''Here. Check it out yourself. I trust you.''

''Sure. Of course. I'll check out your goddamn alibi. But we're gonna get you on something, sometime, sooner or later. . . .''

''You wish. Unfortunately, later you don't have. You've wasted months on me already. Better hurry up . . . couple weeks, my extension's run out, and it's adios army!''

''Not thinking of extending again? . . .''

''Sure, let 'em get my other hand. What an inspired idea.'' Denny gave him a half wave, half salute as he made his way back to his own table.

Tuy looked at her watch. ''We'd better go—George will be double-parked waiting for us!''

They came out the door, talking and laughing. Someone yelled, ''That's him!'' and three MPs stepped up to grab him. It was Denny they wanted. One cut between him and Tuy, and the other two grabbed his arms. She was able to melt into the darkness. As the MPs roughly dragged him away, he saw her hurry to her car and jump in the open door. The old black Citroën spun around in the center of Ben Chuong Duong and swiftly drove off into the darkness.

''Hey, man! You can't do this to me! How did I know he was a general? He was wearing civvies—*cheap* threads at that, lousy styling, bad cut and all!'' He argued about it as they threw him in the Jeep, and all the way down to MP headquarters. They didn't say a word, and he still thought it was about the fuss he'd caused in the Tour d'Argent—until he was dragged inside and pushed through an office door to confront the distinguished-looking officer in charge, one Major Edgar Munson.

''You may go, men,'' the *Xau My* said. ''Thank you for a job well done.'' The three MPs saluted, turned smartly, and stalked out of the room.

''Gee—surprised I didn't hear their heels click,'' Denny muttered sarcastically.

"Not really a bad image. I've thought of that myself."

Denny glared at the man. "Look, major, we've had our misunderstandings, but you've got no right—!"

Munson curtly held up his hand for silence. Denny's eyes flicked, wondering what was up. He noticed nothing but the retreating footsteps of the major's men, walking down the hall. When those had died out, the major sat behind his desk. "Pull up a chair. No, *do* it, I'm not going to bite you. . . ." He waited until Denny did as he said before continuing. "I'm sorry for the way I got you here, but I had to talk to you. . . . and you wouldn't have come if I had simply asked, would you?"

"No. I guess not."

"Fine. Here. Read this." He tossed a fat file across his desk.

"I can't leave here until I do, right?"

"Smart boy."

Denny took the folder in his lap and opened it. The first thing that caught his eye was the black and white of the naked Tuy. The *Xau My*, watching far more closely than his casual attitude would indicate, saw his fingers tremble as he picked up the well-worn old photograph of the young, naked bar girl. "So?" Denny said, trying his best to keep the tremor out of his voice.

"Read on," the *Xau My* said calmly. "We've got all night."

Denny's face was chalky as he read the old report, slowly reliving his friend Larkey's last days, hours, and then minutes. His breath caught as he read of Tuy's implication. "She *lured* him!" he whispered, "And then *locked him out*!"

"Of course she did," the *Xau My* agreed. "She's just a bitch—a worthless dink bitch! They all are, son!" He took two tumblers and a bottle from his desk drawer and poured a couple of scotches. "I don't know what you expected, son . . ." he said in his best fatherly tone. "I've seen this over and over, in this job . . ."

"But he might not have died—she—she might have saved him! . . ."

"I know, son . . . nobody can prove it, but I guess you could say she murdered him!"

Denny sat stunned in his chair, the scotch untouched in front of him. The *Xau My* gently put it in his hand. "Bottoms up, son. . . ."

Denny stared blankly at the photo of Tuy. "It all comes back to this, doesn't it? . . ."

"She probably did that for under five bucks," Munson sneered. "You know—'Buy me perfume from PX, GI, I take dirty picture for you. . . .' "

"Unbelievable," Denny said, shaking his head. He was in his own world of memories. "Tuy looks like she should be in grade school."

"There's something damn seductive about the bitches at that age—and they know it! By the way, you sound like you might have known the dead man? . . ."

"Larkey? We were buddies!" Perhaps it was the flash of triumph that suddenly glinted through Edgar's lawyerlike continence, but Denny was suddenly wary. He set the glass untouched on the edge of Munson's desk. "Why did you tell me all this? What do you want, anyway?"

"All right. I have nothing to hide. I have two reasons. First, you are a fellow American, and you deserve to know what kind of a girl you're running around with. I didn't even know at the time the poor bastard that got shot to pieces was your buddy. But I do have another reason; I'll be honest with you. Tuy and I have come to the end of the road. I can't take it with her anymore . . . and I intend to move on her end of the business. . . ."

Denny reached for the tumbler and took a small sip of the scotch. It wasn't a big gamble, he figured, because he had seen the *Xau My* drink from the same bottle. "Why do you want to do that?" he asked.

"Because that dink cunt isn't satisfied with her fair share, that's why! She's trying to squeeze me, to cut me out!"

Denny took another sip of the scotch. It was smooth old stuff, and in his present state of mind he needed it. "Well . . . what do you want from me?"

The *Xau My* gave him a hurt "after all I've done for you" look. "You don't trust me, do you?"

"You got that right! . . . I don't think I trust anybody right now."

"Okay, I understand how you feel. But maybe you ought to think twice before kissing off what I might offer you. . . ."

"What have you got?" Denny asked skeptically.

The *Xau My* nodded inwardly. A tough case, but finally he comes down to the old bottom line—what's in it for me. . . . "You're Tuy's partner, right?—her full partner?"

"That's right."

"That means you know her end of the business."

"Of course," Denny lied. "I helped her set it up."

"I thought as much. Okay. Here's the deal. A smart guy like you ought to be able to run it all without splitting with a dink cunt. You play ball with me and it's all yours. You'll find I can be generous as all getout to the guys on my team."

"What do I have to do?" Denny said, slurring the words a little as he spoke. That really bothered him; he was sure he hadn't had that much champagne.

"We'll be full partners—you show me your end of the game, and I'll show you mine. No more of this bullshit, 'The drop-off is in some dark alley at midnight.' I can't run a business like that. . . ."

"Oh sure," Denny complained, now definitely having trouble with his words. "I tell you all an'—an' you go an' bump me off!"

"I just said I can't run it all! I need you! Now you show me what you do, and I'll do the same!"

"You furst! . . ." Denny said, struggling to get the words out around a tongue stiff as a board.

"All right, me first. Come along and I'll show you."

Denny stood and found he needed the edge of the desk to hold himself up. "Howd' ja do that?"

"It was on the glass," the major said, smiling all the while. "Put in a few drops and the stuff just dries in a film on the bottom. Don't worry, you're not going to die—just yet, anyway. I needed an edge, that's all . . . you can't blame me, now can you—with the unpredictable way you have of lashing out at people? Hmmm, can't answer, huh? That's one of the effects. Just shake your head yes or no. You'll be able to walk, in a woozy sort of way, and see all sorts of eye-opening things. . . . Come along, this way now. . . ." The major took him under the arm and ushered him off to have a first-hand look at his million-dollar idea.

8-5

Half-dragging Denny, the *Xau My* lied glibly to his motor pool sergeant, decrying the injustice in a world where some people could hold a great deal of alcohol and others very little. They bundled Denny in on the passenger's side, and the major drove off in a plain brown Plymouth with the small words U.S. ARMY stenciled on the doors. As he drove carefully past row after row of MP Jeeps and out of the motor pool compound, the sergeant looked dubiously after them, wondering what the kid had on the old man, who he had never seen make a kindly gesture to anyone before. He shrugged and shot a long brown stream of tobacco juice out into a muddy puddle at his feet. It didn't pay to think too much in this man's army.

They drove in silence while the Plymouth's headlamps bored through the rain-slick streets, heading for the docks by the Saigon River. Denny tried to speak, but all that came out was a garbled sound.

"Please don't try," the *Xau My* said. "It looks awful." He took a paper tissue from a box on the dashboard and wiped at Denny's sleeve. "And you're slobbering on your silk jacket . . . that leaves a permanent stain, you know."

Denny felt stranger than he ever had in his life. He wasn't afraid; if the major were going to kill him, he would have done it already. The *Xau My* needed him for a while. But he felt loose and floaty. The street lights were hard pinpoints, difficult to look at and surrounded by beautiful halos. There was a low hum—no, a roar in his ears. He could think, after a fashion, but any kind of action was out of the question. He just had to play it his captor's way, learn as much as he could, and be ready for anything.

The major finally pulled up to a windowless gate-guarded warehouse. Denny, used to security, noticed it wasn't very tight around this place. The cigar-chomping MP out front simply waved them through with a casual glance at Munson. Edgar drove around to a side entrance. Through the small window in a metal door Denny could see a dim light.

"We're here," Edgar said, hauling Denny out of the car by one arm. He leaned him up against the side of the Plymouth. "Come on now, let's see if you can stand. You didn't have that much stuff. I assure you, it would be better, for appearances' sake . . . although my assistant isn't all that observant, I must confess. . . ."

Denny found that by concentrating all his efforts, he could balance on his legs. It was a bit like walking on a high wire. He took a few steps and giggled.

"Put a lid on it," the *Xau My* warned. "I know the stuff makes you off balance, but you can handle it. This is serious business." He waved a hand around him. "We're at the morgue—the auxiliary morgue, there being a real bumper crop of bodies these days, the war going badly and all, or hadn't you heard. . . . Oh, sorry, I forgot you're having trouble with your consonants . . . and your vowels. . . ."

He fished for a set of keys and steered Denny in through the heavy metal door. Their footsteps echoed on the wooden floor. Denny looked at the ribbed ceiling high overhead, which was separated by at least twenty feet from the hallway partitions that ended like a rat's maze four feet over their heads. It was cold, so cold their breath puffed out of their lungs in little clouds. "Interesting place, huh," the *Xau My* said, making conversation. "Used to be a slaughterhouse . . . still is, in a way. . . ."

They walked through a varnished wooden door with a frosted glass window, entering a huge, high-ceilinged room harshly lit with skirted bulbs hanging overhead on long cords. "Welcome to my chamber of horrors," the *Xau My* said with his kindest smile.

Denny wasn't sure what he was talking about. At first glance, it didn't look so bad. When you are a kid, one place that perhaps haunts your dreams as much as any other is the mortuary. When you die you have to go there, and men do strange things to your body, sucking out the blood and pumping in chemicals . . . and of course, there's always the fear you may be *not quite* dead, just unable to move, and here comes a sucker with a wild grin on his face and strange tools in his hand. . . . But Denny was a long way from the fears of his childhood. He had looked on the dead and the dying, and had long ago accepted the simple fact of it all.

It was easy to see the place had once been a cold meat-cutting room; it was icy, and the metal hooks still hung overhead on their pulley system, though now rusty and ignored. The huge area was over half-filled with plain silver coffins. Even in his drugged state, Denny could make out the simple assembly line. The empty coffins were stacked five and six high against a wall on the far left. There were four stainless steel tables, each with a brilliant operating lamp overhead. Near these tables was room for eight or twelve coffins. And the sliding door for pickup and delivery was at their back.

Only one of the tables was occupied, and a white-coated man bent over this one, his gloved hands flickering in the backlit scene. The man looked up, startled on seeing them.

Then he recognized the *Xau My*, and with a little wave of his hand, went back to work.

"Puzzled?" the major asked. "Come along, and daddy will explain it all. . . ."

"You—put—in—*cof*-fin!" Denny managed to blurt out.

"You *can* talk a little! See, that stuff is wearing off, just like I promised. . . ." The major took Denny by the arm and pulled him forward. "No, not exactly in coffins. You see, that would be far too dangerous; all they would need is one bullshit inspection, just open one lid anywhere along the way for whatever reason, and bingo, the game's up. I have taken my thinking a revolutionary step further to discover the perfect container, a place where nobody will ever think to look—the body cavity itself!" And he proudly wheeled Denny into the light in front of the shiny table.

Denny gaped in horror and disbelief. There was a dead GI on the silver slab in front of him, a big six-footer with burly muscles and reddish blond hair.

"See *here*," the major pointed out. "Thread's the code. Sew 'em up with dark green—so my guys on the other end know which ones to open." Munson's white-coated assistant was carefully and professionally sewing up a huge flap of skin on the dead man's abdominal cavity with the telltale thread. Denny could see not one, but several plastic packets of white powder inside. The breath caught in his chest, he felt his heart was burning, he was on fire. He didn't know what to do. From somewhere far away he hard the *Xau My*'s voice. "I developed the technique myself. It's only just recently I've allowed Leonard here to handle a few operations on his own. . . . It was all highly experimental." He shook his head, chuckling at his own ineptitude. "At first we operated on dozens, you know, just slipping a half kilo or so in each one. Now we just use one or two—get, oh, forty or fifty pounds in each." The *Xau My* read his expression as confusion. "Still don't get it, huh? Didn't think you were that slow. You ever gut a deer?"

Denny had, and the images it brought to mind were not pleasant in any context, much less this one. Some things a man just did because it was man's work. He nodded dumbly.

"Good. Well, then you understand how easy it is. One or two snips and you just scoop everything out! I've got a feeling we're going to be great partners after all! I just have to get you involved, get you with me on this team!"

Denny stared at him, feeling his eyes were popping out of his head.

"Oh, I get your question," the *Xau My* said. "It's no problem. We get lots of light bags—you ever see a guy who's danced with a mortar round? You're lucky you find an arm and a leg. We just put our extra in with that guy."

The work Leonard was doing caught his attention. "Now, Specialist, watch how big you make those stitches. Nice tight little thread-work, like I taught you." He took the needle from his assistant and did a few stitches, talking to Denny as he worked. "We can't get sloppy. A big loop might pierce a bag. Leonard ruined one when he first tried, and we had to take it out of his pay, didn't we, Leonard?" The pale assistant nodded nervously. He had the jitters, and looked at the *Xau My* the way a much-beaten dog eyes its master. Edgar didn't even notice. The needle went swiftly in his hands; he really would have made a first-class surgeon, he thought to himself. He suddenly turned to Denny, took his arm, and pulled him right up to the table. "Here," he said, thrusting the thick silvery needle in his hands, "you try a couple. . . ." Denny stood rooted to the spot, unable to move. "*Do* it," the *Xau My* ordered quietly, "or I'll kill you here and now—and stuff *your* guts." Denny looked down at the pale, silent body before him. He held the slightly curved needle that was attached to the greenish black thread already coiled through the dead man's waxy skin. His hand reached forward and he felt the skin's resistance as he pushed the needle in.

"Push! Push harder! You can't hurt him anymore!" the major ordered. "That's it!"

As the sharp point pierced the skin and the stitching needle looped through the flesh, Denny went totally mad; he knew it wasn't Doober, his buddy didn't look anything like this poor sap. And yet, it was Doober because they all were Doobers, they all were his buddies. . . . He saw the needle in his hand and was physically and mentally sick. If he'd had a knife, he would have killed himself, cleanly and instantly, at that moment. A feeling of revulsion swept through him, and he felt his gorge rise. Mercifully, he passed out, slumping to the floor.

It was daylight before he came to. He was in a bed, between clean sheets. He groaned, holding his head between his hands, and pulled himself to a sitting position on the edge of the bed.

"Feels like death warmed over, doesn't it?" the conversational voice behind him said. He turned to see the *Xau My* sitting over coffee and Danish at a small Louis XIV desk. "Everyone says you shouldn't mix alcohol and drugs, and now you see why. . . ."

"Yeah, right . . . where am I?"

"In my room, at the Caravelle. What a fuss we had getting you here last night. Leonard was convinced you were dead, you know. I, of course, recognizing your usefulness to the organization, had to give you every opportunity to prove him wrong. . . ."

"Of course," Denny said. The memory of that night in the morgue and what they did came shuddering back into his mind. He put his hands over his face. He remembered the tug of the skin as he had pushed in his stitch. His threading that one stitch was symbolic—his money had started the whole thing, and he was responsible for every one of those mutilated corpses, just as if he had sewn them all up with his own hand. Guilty! Doober's pale ghost had said. Guilty! Beale's voice agreed behind him. Fucking prissy Beale, always so concerned with right and wrong, now had laid The Big One on him. Guilty! Charley said with a little chuckle . . . Charley, who would forgive a guy almost anything. Guilty! Larkey added in a thundering vengeful voice . . . Larkey, who had moved in on Charley's girl . . . the same girl, the same girl, the same girl. . . . His head spun, and he found himself on the floor again.

The *Xau My* bent over him, and this time his concern was real. "Look, kid—snap out of it! You and I have a long road to travel . . . come on." Supporting Denny, he helped him to the shower. Denny knew what was troubling him wouldn't wash off, but the shower did help clear his head.

The *Xau My* laid out a pair of trousers and a shirt for him. The trousers were about four sizes too big, but Denny belted them tight and pulled on his shoes. He had to get out, to get away, to be alone by himself and try to figure out what to do next. As if reading his thoughts, the major spoke. "I've been very fair with you. I've made you a generous offer and shown you my end of the business. That is real trust. You could ruin me with a word. Now it's your turn."

Denny looked up from tying his shoes. "What do you want?"

"Do we have to go over all that again? Look, you're a smart boy. When do I meet your contacts?"

"Ahhh, it might take a few days to set up."

"I doubt it. I'm beginning to question your enthusiasm for the team, boy. . . ." He eyed Denny keenly from under his distinguished-looking brows.

Denny didn't say anything for over twenty seconds. Finally he sighed, "Okay. I have to trust you, too. Our contacts are old French. They ran the trade in the fifties. . . ." Denny had guessed as much from the fleeting glimpses of people he had seen Tuy with over the last two weeks.

"I suspected that . . ." the major said, remembering the half-French mulatto who had first threatened him in the Bristol bar. "Go on."

"Well—there isn't much to it. Tuy—we were able to make the contacts, and it was easy."

"Okay." The *Xau My* nodded gravely. "Then this is going to be easy, too. You bring them to me, tonight, at my office."

"Tonight? That's not much time. . . ."

"Tonight . . . or you're a dead grunt. . . ."

"All right . . . I don't have any choice." He stood, testing how he was on his feet, wondering if he should try to take out the major. He was wobbly, but something other than that held him back. The *Xau My* was a man of dark secrets . . . it would be foolish to underestimate how dangerous he really might be. Denny swayed a bit as he stood in front of the man. "May I go now?"

The *Xau My* stepped aside. "Of course. Remember, 2100 hours tonight. And don't try to do anything foolish, like leaving town. You'll find MPs in all the wrong places—like up your asshole—if you do." He watched as Denny left, then carefully replaced the little surgical steel knife that he had palmed in its trigger-holster up his sleeve.

Denny leaned against the side of the elevator, grateful for the rush of air-conditioning that whistled from a vent over his head. He hurried across the red-carpeted lobby and out through the glass doors. He found himself running down the street, actually free from the deadly spider up there on the fifth floor. His mission was clear. The old Dimbos had assigned him; it was the only way he could wash his hands. He had to bring the *Xau My* down, even though it would tumble the whole operation around their heads. He had a lot of work to do before nine P.M.

old Lehman—he's long years ago. I might have saved him.
I knew they would come for him—yet I locked him in. He
cried out for me . . . even after he was shot . . . calling . . . .

CHAPTER NINE

9-1

HE MET HER IN THE PARK BY THE RIVER. THE CURVED PATH-
ways were deserted, for a chill fog hung over the ground,
and the somber skies threatened more rain. Far across the
flat slow Saigon River, he could see the faint outline of the
dark green mangroves. A few sampans plied the waters, along
with a hustling river patrol boat that seemed out of place on
a day dominated by the dampness, the tenebrous fingers of
the drifting fog, and the plaintive call of the seagulls.

She moved along the path like a dream-woman out of one
of her own beloved romance novels. Her pale *ao dai* of cream
was covered with a long-cowled cape that trailed behind as
she walked. The old black Citroën that had brought her
waited discreetly in the distance. She stopped ten yards from
him, searching his face. "You saw the *Xau My*."

"Yes."

"And he told you—everything."

"Yes."

"And so now you hate me." Her dark, sad eyes held on him
as she came slowly closer. She saw him stern, tall, and dour
as she had never seen him before. Mad Denny the happy one,
the crazy one, the impetuous one who had loved her . . . was
gone. He had been wrong; you never lose the *ma* that haunt
the past trails of your life. They become a part of you.

"Tell me why I should hate you," he said.

His level voice whipped her; it was more than she could
stand, and a slow tear trickled down her cheek. "Because I

did kill him, those long years ago. I might have saved him. I knew they would come for him—yet I locked him out. He cried out for me . . . even after he was shot . . . calling . . . then whispering . . . my name. . . .''

''You were afraid.'' His voice seemed so cold, so empty of emotion. It would be better, she thought, if he shouted, if he lashed out at her with his fists and feet. But there was to be no such relief for her. That would have been the easy way, and nothing was easy.

She bowed her head, and the bitter tears came yet again. ''Yes. I was afraid.''

He was talking again, even though she was barely conscious of it; she had room for nothing other than her overwhelming sense of grief and despair. ''You were young. You were alone. You were frightened. There are greater sins. . . .'' And then, impossible though it was, he took her in his arms. He gently held her against his side and brushed her hair with awkward and yet tender strokes with the hand that was so badly maimed. After a long time he spoke again. ''At first, when I read the report, I was upset—angry and confused all over again. . . . I hadn't realized it happened that way. I know you tried to tell me once before, but I just wasn't able to accept how a thing like that could happen.''

She looked into his eyes, unable to believe he was forgiving her. ''What made you change your mind?''

''An old snapshot of you.'' A ghost of a grin the old Mad Denny might have given her flickered across his face. ''You were naked. Probably a snapshot Larkey took.''

She grimaced and shook her head, remembering the circumstances of that amateur photo session. ''That photograph caused you to change your mind about me?''

''Yes, it did. I saw a frightened, lonely little girl, barely in her teens. Whatever the girl did, the woman she became has sorrowed a thousand times over for it.''

She threw her arms around him, crying and trying to smile at the same time. ''Ohh, Denny, Denny . . . my dear Mad

Denny . . . I care for you more than I have ever loved any man!''

He looked deeply into her eyes and smiled. ''I love you, Tuy. I can say that now.'' There was iron in his voice, and the way he studied her gave her a thrill of pleasure. ''The ghosts that were between us are almost all gone now. . . .''

''Almost? . . .'' she said hesitantly.

''Dear Charley, good old Larkey, Doober—all the Dimbos . . . almost laid to rest.''

She took a step back from him, worried about the things she didn't know. The happiness that a moment before had seemed so secure wavered and took on the shimmery glaze of cruel illusion. ''Denny. Denny, if you love me, tell me what you've promised. . . .''

''We've got to take the *Xau My* down.''

''But—but he has a thousand men. Those troops you see all over town with the arm bands are his!''

His eyes burned with a fierce light. ''Tuy—he has to go down! Do you know how he ships our stuff?''

She shook her head, wondering what that had to do with anything.

''In dead GI's—in their bodies!''

She made a small, gasping sound of disgust. ''No—it is too ugly, even for him. . . .''

''Make no mistake, that's what he does! Are you with me? . . .''

She nodded. ''Yes.'' She held up a warning hand. ''But before you go cheering my bravery, remember the *Xau My* wants me dead, too. Oh yes, I know it. He is a greedy man who won't stop until he has it all.'' She gave him a bitter little smile. ''So you see, our ghosts won't let me off so easily on this one . . . they know I really haven't any choice.''

She took his hand. ''Walk with me a way and let's talk about it. I will need a week to close down my end. Dismantle the factories, stop the shipments, get everyone we can underground.''

"You've got half a day. I have to move tonight, or it's all over."

"There is no other way?"

"He's shipping it in bodies, Tuy!"

She accepted his word. They walked on in silence, but now her mind started working. With only a few hours there would be losses—unless somehow they could divert the shipments. Their trucks would never stand a concerted search. They shipped in bulk, relying on an extensive string of bribes that went to the highest levels, rather than using any creative methods of concealment. But bribery would be denied once the lid blew off; after that, everything would be searched zealously. The idea of drugs moving in large scale from Vietnam to the streets of American cities, and being transported as they were, in the bodies of GI casualties, was enough to shake the foundations of U.S. support for the war effort. The Saigon government would do everything in its power to make sure this scandal didn't touch them, and to reassure its allies they had acted forcefully to bring it to an end. Some— perhaps most—of Tuy's shipments could be diverted to the old man's place in Ben Suc.

Of course, she had her own personal escape plans . . . she'd had them ever since she could remember. They had been good enough to slip the police after Larkey's death. And the passports and fake IDs she had now were much more sophisticated. Her personal horde of little gold bars hidden around her villa had grown to such proportions that it would be almost impossible to transport quickly. However, she had almost ten thousand dollars in American money and about a hundred thousand piasters. Her Swiss bank account . . . she smiled, thinking about the almost impossible sum she had amassed in so short a time—money enough to live like a princess . . . on the interest alone! The trick was, getting to a position where she could enjoy the money.

What were her chances? Unless she had underestimated the *Xau My*, he didn't have her fingerprints. She had her wigs, and her short hair would now work to her advantage. She had also invested several thousand dollars in a discreet plastic surgeon who had provided her with certain tight-fitting inserts and attachments that changed her from a very lovely person with a round face to somewhat of a buck-toothed mistake with a distinctly horsey look. Though uncomfortable, her appearance with these additions matched the pictures on one of her passports and might serve to get her out of the country. She would have to find a place, perhaps with one of the larger Vietnamese colonies in Thailand or even Paris, and go into quiet hiding. She had done it before. It could be done. She looked up at Denny, suddenly realizing that he fit nowhere in those plans.

"What's wrong, Tuy? You look pale."

"Nothing, soul mate," she lied, fighting back the sadness that tore at her heart. She had to think of something to take her mind off her sorrow. "What—what can I do for you?"

Denny handed her a copy of *Playboy*. He turned to the page listing the contents, and pointed to an author's name. "Phil Darby. See the name here? He's a free-lance writer. Stays over at the Rex Hotel. He won't give me the time of day, but I'll bet you could get his attention. . . ." He pulled a thick envelope from his pocket. "Give him this. I wrote down everything I could think about Edgar's 'million-dollar idea.' Even drew a map how to get into his shipping department. Oddly enough, the security's pretty lax there . . . Munson probably doesn't want to draw attention to the place. Phil's a fuckhead, but I think he's got enough sheer ambition to go anywhere for a story. Tell him it's the biggest scoop of his life. . . ."

"Okay. Easy." She smiled up at him. "I have something for you." She took the back of an old postcard and drew a little map of her villa. She carefully put *x* marks and made notations in several rooms.

"What is this?"

"Treasure map," she confided with a smile. "Just like in

my favorite spy novel. I have managed to put a few things away—gold bars, ivory trinkets, things like that. If I have to move so quickly, I may not be able to take things with me. You trusted me once with your life's savings. So this is only fair.''

"But we're going to see each other again," he protested. "Our life together is just beginning, if you want me. . . ."

"I want you always, and of course it is. . . ." She stood on tiptoe and kissed his nose. "I just want you to know where these things are. You always say money is very important to you; well, we are not so far apart—you are looking at a girl attached to gold and diamonds.''

"Diamonds, too!" he said, trying to keep it light.

"Just a few," she replied with a fetching smile. "I'll try to get them to a safe place, but you save them for me, in case I am . . . detained." Tuy took the envelope from his hand and replaced it with her postcard map.

The old black Citroën beeped insistently. She waved at the people in the car, then turned back to Denny. "George and Mako held another little meeting with some of the rest of our crew, and they all decided you were no good for me. I can hardly wait to hear what they have to say about all this!''

"I don't give a damn what they think—what do *you* say?''

She gave him a long, slow kiss, a kiss that lingered as if it might have to last a lifetime. And then she straightened her back and marched away with a determined step. She couldn't look back. She didn't want him to see her tears.

9-2

Patrick J. Dooly slowly worked his way through his thirty mandatory laps. He did the ten breaststrokes first, then the backstrokes and the freestyle. As an afterthought, he did ten extra, using the crab-crawl that a man could employ to slip silently up to some beach. He felt so good he did ten side-stroke laps, the stroke that a man could do all day without tiring. And that felt so good, he went on to do the dolphin, the body stroke that would enable a man to swim even with his arms and legs bound. You never knew when you were going to need that stuff—Nam was a wet place.

He crawled out of the pool, moderately winded, and began to dry himself off by the side of the pool with one of the big white towels provided by the Cercle Sportif Saigonnais. A man was lying in a lounge chair nearby. He was apparently sleeping, with a paper folded over his head. The man spoiled his day by sitting up and pointing a .45 at him.

Dooly was dumbfounded. "Haller!" he cried. "You're not a member here. . . ."

"No, but you are—it was easy to convince them I am your guest. Help just isn't what it used to be, in these trying times. . . ."

"That's a fact." Dooly warily eyed the gun, reviewing his chances. He'd had every course known to man in hand-to-hand. He also knew it wasn't one of his great strengths. "What do you want?"

"To talk. Asshole Anderson tells me you think I'm the *Xau My*."

The idea of it really made Dooly furious. "I just hate working with fuckin' nonagency types. When did the loud-mouth son of a bitch bring that up?"

"We were discussing an explosion. He was asking a lot of questions, and when he didn't get the answers he expected— or wanted—his questions became more like threats. Your name was mentioned. The CO says you call me scumbag."

"So? That enough to make you come after me with a gun?" As a professional, Dooly had to admire the way Mad Denny deftly folded his newspaper to hide the pistol. Definitely a potential for recruitment, if the kid wasn't so heavy into dope dealing.

"That's just to get your attention. I really want you to sign this."

Dooly took the typed letter Denny thrust in his hand and read swiftly. "Why should I? You're not helping me—you're the fuckin' key suspect!"

"Two reasons: First, I could blow a hole in you. And second, I am not the *Xau My*—but I can help you get him."

Dooly's whole attitude changed, like a big hollow wind swinging 180 degrees. He grinned, showing teeth roots coated with plaque. "Tell me more. And put that gun away. Come on, I'll buy you a continental breakfast."

They sat at a small, poolside table, munching croissants and sipping hot café au lait, while Denny held the gun on him under the table.

"You handle yourself pretty good for a one-hand gimp."

"The very heart of compassion, aren't you. This thing is one of those filed ones, hair trigger, you know. In other words sign the paper, so we can get on with this." Dooly signed it. He figured, what the hell, he could always deny it as a forgery. Kid dealing dope would be desperate enough to try that. He scrawled it awkwardly, just badly enough to look like an amateur forgery. He put down the pen and rubbed his head with the towel, grimacing when he saw the amount of pasty white gunk that came away. The doctors had promised him, and yet it wasn't getting any better. . . .

Denny talked for a half hour. The spook was, if nothing else, a good listener, and he only interrupted once or twice to clarify specific points. He was impressed with the story, and after Denny left could think of little else. He showered and shaved, and threw on his clothes. By this time it was almost noon; he shook his head in wry dismay—this case at the Thirty-third was always making him late for his regular appointments! But he wasn't really upset. At long last they were making major progress.

He pondered it all through his steam bath, while the girls rubbed the tension from his back and leg muscles, and while Hoa—his favorite—massaged his stomach and belly and then touched and kissed and licked and gently blew on him until he climaxed in a pulsing golden glow. The decision came to him after they had oiled his body. He was lying there under the heat lamps, totally relaxed, the perfect picture of one of Uncle Sam's fighting men at rest.

He had to admit he had never heard such a cock-and-bull story in his life. In his line of work, he often needed MP cooperation, and Edgar Munson had never failed him, had always supplied what backup he needed with that quiet professional smile of his that said "no questions asked." The *Xau My* indeed! Dooly hopped off the couch and dressed swiftly, eager to call and share the joke with the major.

9-3

How quickly things change! Dooly grinned to himself as he stepped through the door of the major's back room to see a somewhat tousled Mad Denny tied hands and feet to a chair. What an ending to a three-month caper, to have the *Xau My* tied up helplessly in front of him! "Hi, kid!" he said happily. "Got any more stories for me?"

"Boy, are you dumb . . ." Denny gritted through his bruised and puffy lips.

The major, sitting nearby, casually slapped him across the face. "The party's over, Dinky Den! We caught you with the goods!" He motioned Dooly over to a table. "Now here's the two little bags we took off him after the Tour d'Argent arrest." He opened the twist-tie on the bag and poured a little of the white powder on the table. He wet his little finger and touched it to the powder, then licked it. "Try it."

"Liar!" Denny shouted.

"Please don't interrupt, Sergeant Haller. Now Dooly, here's the lab report my men worked up. Over ninety percent pure heroin! He's got enough here to buy a new Falcon convert! And look at this!" Edgar picked up a wad of twenty-dollar bills and waved it back and forth. "He had this in his pocket. Must be almost seven, eight hundred dollars here. . . ."

Denny angrily shook his head, but the other two men shrugged and smiled. "Tsk, tsk, tsk," Dooly clucked his tongue. "The *Xau My* at last . . ." He took Denny by the shirt front, shaking him until the chair rattled. "You know how much suffering this stuff causes among the street people back home, among your own people, you little scumbag?"

"We only let him back on the streets today hoping he would lead to his accomplices," Edgar said, smoothly buttering the cracks of his version of what had happened. He leaned back in his chair. "We'll see he gets his due process from here, Dooly. *And* that you get the commendation that's coming to you." He rose then and patted the tall sergeant on the back, steering him at the same time toward the door. "If you can just wait in the lobby for me. I'd like a word without bigmouth friend here. Then we can head out and share a bite . . . perhaps a bit of a victory celebration?"

Dooly, who was basking in the rare praise, gave the major a sly agency-to-agency wink and flipped his thumb back at the bound man. "Soften him up a little before you send him away, if you can find it in your heart, Major. You know, give him his just rewards."

Denny protested, "You're not going to leave me alone with him? He'll kill me!"

"This slimy creep had the nerve to pull a gun on me! Can you imagine that, Major?" He gave Denny a little finger wave. "See you in Leavenworth, scumbag."

Dooly left, happily scratching his head as he walked down the long hallway to the lobby. It was nine, but he bet the major could still pop up a few great steaks for them over at the Brinks. What a world, what a world! He drew in a deep breath, sniffing at the possibilities of making E-8 on this one.

Alone in the room with Mad Denny, the *Xau My* walked over to what looked like a large box on the floor covered by a grimy olive blanket. "You heard what the sergeant ordered—some sort of 'just deserts' . . . and looky, looky, looky—what we have here!" He whisked the blanket off, revealing his favorite toy, his rat cage. The huge white rats blinked in the light, chattering and running blindly around the cage.

Denny didn't know what to think. At first he didn't get it, and then his mind wouldn't accept it. He gaped, fighting down the raw terror that flooded through him. The *Xau My* caught his hair from behind, and yanking his head back, swiftly wrapped a roll of heavy silver tape around his mouth, passing it four or five times behind his head. "Good old army duct tape . . . has so many uses, my dear Dinky Dennis. We wouldn't want you to go biting back just when our little friends start dining, would we?"

He kicked the chair forward, and Denny's head slammed into the floor. He looked up dizzily to see himself head high with the rat cage. The *Xau My* slid up a heavy wooden partition on the side closest to him. "Isn't this cleverly fashioned? My, my, my, you should just about fit in there." Denny saw a shoulder-sized hole had been fashioned in his side of the cage. Edgar teasingly rocked the chair back and forth, inching Denny's head closer and closer, and finally into the cage. "Say hello to my little pets, Dinky. I would introduce them individually, but I think they'd each rather make your acquaintance personally—you know, get a taste for you."

As Denny was thrust into the cage and his arms bound to the sides, the rats backed into the farthest corners of their small confinement, hissing and chattering their warnings. Munson tied his wrists and then looped the rope around the bars of the cage. Once he was sure his captive was so securely bound that he would not be able to pull away from the cage, the major cut the ropes from the chair to which Denny had been tied and carefully replaced it around the table. "Don't want to make too much of a mess, you know," he said, making conversation as he tidied up the room. "Did you notice how I always seem to be carrying on the entire conversation with you? Oh well, rank has its privileges. You might also have noticed I have placed plastic garbage bags and newspapers under the cage? We both are such fastidious people, liking things neat, I thought you might appreciate that. Do you want to talk about it a little? I'm sure you do. Let me tell you what's in store for you, sort of a preview of the wonders to come. If what my Vietnamese intelligence friends tell me is true, they'll go for the eyes and ears first, and probably take off your nose. The blood will drive them crazy, and they'll just stuff themselves, they won't stop, not for anything. Probably what is called a 'feeding frenzy,' if I remember correctly from my old biology courses. You, of course, will last a long time, actually a lot longer than you would care to—probably until they eat their way in through your eyes to your brains, if you will pardon my graphic description; there just isn't any other way to say these things.''

He took a last look around the room and moved to the door. His hand reached for the light switch. ''I'd like to stay and see this whole thing, I really would, but as you know, I've a social obligation. And you will pardon me if I turn out the light—I think you'll find it much more fun.''

The overheads went out, and even the dim light from the hallway was extinguished as Munson closed and locked the door. His footsteps faded down the long hallway. Denny lay in a near panic, sprawled on the floor and desperately working his arms, trying to reach the knots binding him to the cage. In the blackness so pitch it seemed to ooze evil, he heard the tentative squeaks and chatter as the rats warily voiced their preliminary challenges. Then in the total darkness he felt furry things brush his face. He shook his head violently, but they were all around him. One clung to his hair, and then he felt sharp teeth tugging his ear, ripping and drawing blood. He let out a long muffled scream, but no one was there to hear him.

The evening dragged by for Edgar Munson. Dooly had thrown out some broad hints that he was a steak-and-potatoes man, so they sat through one of those long meals when people find out they really don't have much to say to one another.

Dooly didn't seem to notice; Edgar realized he was a basic bore who probably never had anything to say to anybody—he couldn't talk about the one thing of interest in his life, the agency, and that left . . . nothing.

They went on after dinner, again at Dooly's insistence, to a place he swore had the best entertainment in town. It turned out to be the Bamboo Lounge, where two Japanese go-go dancers flipped their skinny, bikini-clad butts to the thumping fuzzy strings of Johnny's Filipino Band.

He managed to avoid a nightcap, which he suspected was Dooly's excuse to do a round of the downtown bars, by claiming a monster headache. That, at least, was true, thanks to Johnny's musical attacks on everything from "You Ain't Nothing But a Hound Dog" to "Old Cape Cod." Once he had left Dooly, Edgar could barely hold back his excitement, urging the cabbie on to faster speeds as his old Renault darted in and out of traffic on the way back to his office. He hastily saluted the sergeant-at-arms and rushed back to his interrogation room. The long hallway was quiet and empty, as it should be at that late hour of the night. But when he got to the door at the end, it was ajar. That wasn't right; he remembered locking it when he left. Then he realized it had a simple twist latch that could be opened from the inside.

He threw open the door and snapped on the lights. He had made several mistakes in preparing Mad Denny's final ending. He hadn't realized that a man driven by terror can call on almost supernatural feats of strength. The original owners of the cage had never used it without bolting it to several heavy logs, which had raised it to waist height. This took any leverage away from the captive and anchored him firmly to one spot. And then, Edgar had bound his victim with the idea of keeping his head and shoulders in the cage, never dreaming Denny might try to crawl inside. This he was able to do, as well as roll over again and again to crush the rats. He had somehow managed to untie himself, and was gone. All that remained were the rats, which he had lined up in a little bloody row in front of the splintered cage. Before blind fury overtook him, the *Xau My* recognized the gesture as Denny's way of saying "fuck you."

He ran wild-eyed down the hallway, sounding a general alert. His boys were all over the compound in under a minute, and it was a lucky thing, too, because one of the dogs caught Denny just as he was trying to climb over the chain link fence. It took two MPs to subdue him and drag him struggling and kicking back to the major's office. "This is just another example of what happens to smart-mouths," the major said when they were once again alone. "You might have made it if you hadn't stopped to line up the rats." He fisted Denny to the side of the head, and his battered captive slumped to the ground. In minutes he had him bundled in the prim army Plymouth and was driving over to the auxiliary morgue.

9-4

Mad Denny would always swear that the ghosts of the dead and gone Dimbos woke him from unconsciousness that night. A more clinical person might remark it was simply the pain in his arms and rib cage, for indeed, after hanging with hands tied overhead to a meat hook for longer than a few minutes, the pain becomes intense. A more rational person would simply say it was a night to settle scores, and so of course he had come out of his blessed sleep. But Denny, made so aware of the *ma* of this old accursed land by his several brushes with death, saw shadows and heard whisperings on that night, and for him, they always would be real.

"He's such an asshole," Charley whispered. "He's always been a loudmouth asshole."

"Get up, get up, you sleepyhead," Beale chanted softly in his ear.

"What goes around, comes around, old buddy," Larkey whispered.

"You like to hear my latest poem, Den-Den? It's an epi-
taph. . . ."

Here lies ol' Denny Haller
Who 'twas thought was a pretty tough faller.
All did agree
Till he met the *Xau My* . . .
He died with courage and valor. . . ."

Denny woke with a start. Agonizing pain shot down his
arms and ribs. It was almost impossible to breathe. His
head throbbed from where the major had slugged him. He
was in the half shadows outside the bright pools of light
marking the surgical tables, hanging by his hands. The *Xau
My* and Leonard were each bent over a table, intent on their
work.

"Not at them," Charley whispered. "Look down—at your
feet." Mad Denny craned his neck and saw his toes just
barely dragged on the iron grate on the floor below him.
"That's right, asshole, you're on a bleeding rack," Charley
continued with a soft little laugh. "Just like the rest of Nam,
I might add. But you *can* get out."

"How?" he actually heard himself whispering in the icy
chill of the morgue.

"Ahhhh, awake I see. . . ." The *Xau My* looked up from
his work and turned to Denny. He left his table and walked
over to stand in front of his captive, who was strung like a
carcass on the meat hook. He wore a white smock and long
rubber gloves, both of which were smeared with gore.
"Leonard and I have been very busy while you've been sleep-
a-bye. By morning, we're not going to have a bit of evidence
lying around here. Of course, we're going to need your help."

"My—help? . . ." It was painful just to get out that much.

"Why yes, let me made all that clearer, so you can think
about it." The *Xau My* came closer, until he stood directly
in front of Denny. "Your little dink cunt girlfriend has really

come through over the last few weeks. I had no idea we had that kind of volume lying around our warehouse here. It's getting down to the short strokes, and we're actually running out of volunteers.'' He raised his index finger and drew a line from Denny's rib cage to his lower belly. ''I'm going to be forced to make an incision here—a rather deep one, I'm afraid. Then two much smaller ones, but just as deep, creating sort of a sideways *H*, if you still follow me. Do you follow me, Dinky?'' he said with a ringing slap to the side of Denny's head.

''Yes,'' Denny managed to grit out.

''Good. Get this next part—I think you'll really appreciate it. If I'm really careful—and you can count on it—I'll tie you off and all so you don't lose too much blood, and you can actually *live*, who knows, maybe a few hours, maybe more!'' He tapped Denny's upper abdomen. ''You see, all this stuff in here is really unnecessary to a short-timer like you. We're gonna replace it with some little white bags, sew you back up, and put a coffin lid over you—and you get to experience all that firsthand! I'd call that the grand prize, mister, for trying to double-cross the so-called *Xau My*. However, I can't waste all night in idle conversation. Work, work, work, the opiate of the working class!''

He returned to his table, and Denny to his ghosts.

''Why didn't he kick him?'' Beale argued. ''He's always bragging how good he is with his feet.''

''Fuck, he can hardly breathe, Ong Be,'' Charley said. ''We use my plan or he's never gonna get off the hook. Look, asshole, ya gotta throw your thumb out of joint and slip out of that rope, at least far enough to touch the ground—then you can jump up and loop the rope off the hook.''

Denny tried. For a half-hour he tried, while the major whistled merrily as he sawed and sewed across the way. Every now and again the *Xau My* interrupted his dull whistling to wonder out loud in a quiet voice about the horrors Denny might experience in the coffin while wishing he were already dead. Denny's arms were numb, and so he couldn't be sure, but the rope may have moved a half inch up his one wrist. It was bound so tightly that he felt the skin giving as he struggled. His efforts were not going to be enough, not nearly enough. And he was out of time.

The major had returned and stood in front of him. A long knife gleamed dully in one hand. In the other he held a service .45, taking no chances even though his victim was hanging helpless before him. "Welcome to the living dead, Haller." He turned back to his assistant. "Leonard, bring the syringe. I want you to see this, anyway. Doctor Edgar Munson!" The *Xau My* set down his butcher knife and accepted the syringe. He expertly squirted the air out of it. "I know you're wondering—same stuff I used on you the other night. See, you'll be able to experience these wonders without making a big noisy fuss. Come close now, Leonard, I'll show you how to administer a shot."

His leering face was close to Denny's. "Forgive me if we don't bother with any alcohol for the skin. Even you would have to admit it's a superfluous routine, under the circumstances." Leonard stared, his vacant, buggy eyes on the needle. The *Xau My* smiled and nodded his satisfaction, and then shot Leonard in the center of his chest with the .45.

Leonard's body jerked around like it was pulled on a rope and fell face-forward on the grillwork, shuddering even as it spilled his lifeblood into the drain. Denny looked on in disbelief. The *Xau My* caught his eyes. "The world is full of Leonards." He bent over the body, turning one arm so Denny could see the ugly purple puncture marks tracking the veins. "Oh, don't think you're getting off—but when they find you, they'll also find this poor . . . suicide, who finally couldn't stand the realization of what he was doing. Two 'scumbag narco-peddlers,' as our spook friend would say, both dead. A ton of evidence—somebody will eventually figure out that they should open you up; they're just about that bright. And bingo, case closed!"

The major turned back to the tables. "Just a few more stitches here, and I'll be right back to you."

"Now, turkey," Charley whispered in his ear. "*Now!* Disjoint your fuckin' thumb—what's left of it!" Denny pushed his tortured muscles past their limits until he finally felt something pop in his hand. The pain was overwhelming, and he gasped out loud.

"It is a lot to think about," the major said sympathetically, not bothering to turn around. "I guess even a callous young man like you has his breaking point. . . ." Had he taken a moment for even a casual glance in that direction, he would have seen Denny standing with both feet on the ground, the rope completely off one of his bloody wrists, a vengeful light glowing in his eyes.

Animals with glass souls—and this includes renegade tigers, bears that have turned killer, and men without a glimmer of a scruple—are said to have eyes in the back of their heads. Whether this is true or not, Edgar Munson turned to see Denny and easily moved between him and the .45 lying next to the sprawled-out body that was still leaking red fluid into the drain. "So, you still want to have a say in your own destiny! Very well, perhaps it will be more fun!" He moved in on Mad Denny, the gleam in his eyes matched by the silvery glint from the tip of the knife in his hand.

Denny circled warily, but the *Xau My* stayed between him and the automatic. Edgar forced him backward, a step at a time, slashing out with the big knife. Denny saw with a glance that he was being backed up against the stacked coffins. He realized he would soon be cornered; he was going to have to take some risks. He shook his arms, fighting to get back some feeling, some strength, so he would have a chance against his opponent.

Mad Denny feinted an arm blow, but the *Xau My* didn't back off, slashing instead with the knife and drawing blood with a deep slash near his elbow. The major grinned. "Gosh, we almost got the artery there, didn't we? . . . A couple of deep veins for sure, anyway.''

Denny came at him again, and again suffered a deep slash, this time in the other arm. ''You'd better see somebody about that, fellah,'' the major said. ''You might bleed to death. Maybe that's what you want anyway—it was suicide to cross me in the first place!''

Denny lunged forward in a forward flip, praying his arms would support him. He spun onto the floor on his hands, lashing up toward the major with one of his feet. The savage blow caught the *Xau My* on the jaw, staggering him backward and sending the knife flying. He stood there, speechless, holding his jaw.

Denny moved in for the kill. But in his battered state he underestimated the major, who slashed in a wide arc with the hidden surgical knife he had sprung out of his wrist-holster. Blood spurted from Denny's left wrist, and he grabbed it desperately. He couldn't get enough leverage with the stumps of his fingers, and blood splattered over his hands.

''Bingo!'' The major forced the word of triumph through his tortured jaw. ''Oh, yes!''

Denny let go of his wrist and drop-kicked him again, breaking the jaw from the other side. The major staggered, weaving, his small deadly knife making menacing circles in the air. Now his mouth was open, his jaw hanging loose from both sides. Denny kicked him again, this time flush in the face. The force of his blow drove the major backward. His head slammed into one of the coffins, and he silently slid to the floor.

Denny watched him carefully for as long as he dared, then took one of his shoelaces and tied his wrist. It wasn't as bad as he thought at first—big veins, but the arteries seemed intact. He found gauze and a big roll of tape, and managed an awkward bandage that stopped most of the blood. It would have to do until he could get to a hospital . . . which he planned to do quickly. . . .

"Not so fast, asshole," the voice of Charley whispered in his ear. Denny sat in the center of the room, surrounded by the old and new dead. He breathed in gasps, the blood rushed in his ears, but he knew it was Charley, he could tell the ghostly echoes of that robust laugh anywhere. "Look-it, Larkey, our chum here steals our girl and thinks he can just walk away without doing us a favor or two. . . ."

"What do you want?" Denny whispered into the gloom around him, now truly mad and believing without question.

"What do we want, Doober?" Charley whispered.

"Him," Doober whispered. Denny knew without having to see that the ghostly apparition that was the memory of his dead buddy was pointing to the body of the *Xau My*.

"Him." "Him." "Him." "Him." A chorus of faint voices rustled through the cold empty room, and Denny imagined the presence of all the maimed and mutilated GIs whose bodies had been violated by the *Xau My*. He glanced around the room, then looked at the major, who lay with his eyes closed, exactly where Denny had left him. Dead for sure, Denny thought. That last kick had been a killing blow. "It's not enough . . ." the faint voices echoed in the room around him. "Not enough . . ."

Denny staggered to his feet and untied the bloodstained rope still around his one wrist. He put on a white smock and pulled on a clean pair of gloves. Next, he bound the major's arms tightly and hoisted him onto the meat hook. Then he walked around the floor until he found the big butcher knife.

He had killed his deer each autumn in those faraway bright days in the green woods of Wisconsin. He had hoisted the deer over a tree limb, then performed the procedures quickly as possible. The *Xau My*, who had gone over this procedure with him in a general way, was absolutely right. A few incisions, a few snips, it all came right out; it wasn't difficult at all. Then he had the body up on one of the tables and was inserting the flat plastic bags of white dope. He knew he was irregular on the stitching, but he did his best. The major's

clothing went back on awkwardly, but Denny got him looking fairly presentable. He managed to lift the heavy body and
place it in the waiting coffin.

Perhaps he should have left then, but he remembered the
major's passion for neatness and wandered around the room.
He thought carefully about the *Xau My*'s plan—one murder
and one suicide, and a perfect out for the third man. That
plan might work as well for himself as the *Xau My*. . . . He
carefully picked up the .45 and placed it in Leonard's hand.
Finally, he took off his now-bloody smock, and was about
to take off the gloves, when the ghost voices whispered one
last time. "The coffin, dear Ong Den . . . close the coffin."

He went over to close the lid, and he would not forget
what he saw for a lifetime. Living or dead, he had no way of
knowing—the major was quiet as a wax figure . . . but his
eyes had opened wide and were staring up in horror at the
ceiling, at nothing, at everything. Denny quietly closed the
lid, leaving him that way. He didn't deserve any better.

And that's the way, one day later, Phil Darby and Dominique Carré found him, when they got the scoop on the vilest
dope bust ever in Southeast Asia. Dominique had a field day,
picking the widest variety of artistic angles and moods, "from
the tomb of Monsieur Dracula," as he referred to it. Phil
knew his career was solid gold—his every instinct told him
they had a big one on the war, and there would be a book
for sure in this, one of those overnight exposés that made
hundreds of thousands of dollars. Their euphoria lasted less
than an hour, until the spooks moved in.

Dooly, finding himself deserted by the major in the Bamboo Bar, had had time to think as he sipped a final stiff
boilermaker. He had come up with a few questions he wanted
to ask Denny, maybe to get some leads on the rest of the
gang, and incidentally, just to rub it in one last time. Wandering on back to the MP headquarters, he had no trouble
getting past the guards with his ID. The major and Denny
were gone, and a quick search of the major's office turned

up nothing suspicious. But the interrogation room still held the bloodstained rat cage, and the dozen-odd dead rats lined up in a furry little row. Dooly, an old Southeast Asian hand, had seen more than one doomed man in that box. His curiosity aroused, he poked around in the boxes of artifacts and criminal junk lining one wall of the room . . . and came up with shoeboxes of hundred-dollar bills. "Holy shit," he whistled softly to himself. He looked around the room, careful to observe if anybody was coming down the hall, and quickly stuffed a few wads in his pockets. He was a pro; he knew you never took enough to call attention to it, never more than ten percent.

Suspicions now fully aroused, the spook decided to call in all the chips. But Denny's other contact, the bar girl Tuy, was gone as if she had never been there. Dooly checked the Tuyet Lan as his fogged, boozy state slowly settled into a hangover, and then her villa; but both places were deserted, and there were no leads.

He finally remembered Denny babbling about the morgue in that wild story he had told when he accused the major of being the *Xau My* . . . a story Dooly was coming more and more to believe as true. He checked out the air force morgue, which was in a big, heavily air-conditioned hangar in Tan Son Nhut. There was nothing. Nobody had even heard of Edgar Munson or Mad Denny, and Dooly didn't help matters much with his indirect methods of interrogation. It was midmorning before one of the guys in the office, still puzzled by his vague questions, let slip that there was an overflow holding-place by the river.

He arrived just as Phil Darby and Dominique were walking out, flushed with victory. A quick look at the two dead bodies the reporters had uncovered, and he took them all down to his local headquarters. His chief recognized immediately that the letter Denny had written to Phil exposing the scheme would have to be confiscated. Phil, who had gotten the letter from one of the prettiest and most flirtatious dink girls he'd ever met, was furious. Dominique was not allowed to keep his photos. The two protested violently about their rights under the First Amendment while Dooly stripped the film, exposing roll after roll of evidence to the harsh light pouring in the windows. As the chief explained sympathetically, there was no way they could let such an ugly story out—no question but that it would weaken the war effort by crippling what little back-home support they had. Of course, the agency sent in their own photographers. Their shots perhaps would lack Dominique's moody intensity, but would be filed away where they might serve the agency's purposes equally as well if ever there came a time of need. . . .

9-5

Denny wandered alone through the streets of Saigon, unmindful of the light rain that fell on his woolen sweater and dampened his hair. In a week he would be out of the army. He should have a decent amount of money in his European bank account—although at the time he had no idea how much, and didn't intend to find out for some months or even years, until he was convinced the spooks had tossed him in the "inert" file. But his last days in the city known as the tattered pearl of the Orient would be lonely ones . . . for Tuy was gone, and he missed her more than he ever would have believed possible.

He had looked for her everywhere. The Tuyet Lan was being repainted, and a new sign above its doors proudly proclaimed it as the Boston Bar. Her villa was deserted. Searching desperately for some sign left to him, he carefully traced the map she had left on the back of the postcard. All the gold bars were gone but one. Near this one, which was tucked far behind a loose wall baseboard in her bedroom, he found a note and a large diamond. The note explained that she had more friends than she knew, and she was able to get her possessions out intact. It was hard to read, and he realized it must have been scribbled in great haste. Still, she had not taken the time to say anything personal, or even to sign the note.

He passed the USO club, heading down Nguyen Hue toward the river. The flower stalls were all closed, their multicolored canvases rolled down and dark in the shadowy light. The street shops themselves were all shuttered for the night, and the mood of the city was one of isolation as each Saigon native crawled into his nightly robes of fear and uncertainty, wondering when and where Victor Charlie would strike, concerned for loved ones fighting in the ARVN or the VC irregular forces, worrying how long the thin filaments of compromise would hold between the Catholics and the Buddhists, fearful for the longevity of the new parliament and the new president, fretting about how long the patience of their allies from America—an immature and notoriously impatient nation—would last in the face of a long and costly war with no end in sight.

Mad Denny looked up, and the old black Citroën cut in front of him just as it had that day several weeks before when the street was alive with daylight and flowers and people. It was Tuy.

"We brought it all down, didn't we? . . ." she said with a sad smile.

"Tuy! I've been looking everywhere for you! At last, it's you! Tuy, walk with me!"

"No, Denny. I cannot risk it. This is a terrible chance just to see you this last time—"

"Last—?"

"I promised my—my organization. I cannot come looking for you again. But they had to give me these few minutes in return."

"But I—!"

"Please, Denny. We have only moments." She smiled again, and her bittersweet look cut him like a knife stroke, reducing him to silence. "We took losses—five people at one of the factories. The government machine-gunned them without a thought. And we lost a shipment; we couldn't stop it before it got to the checkpoint. I learned a lesson, Denny . . . when you set up a company, in a strange way, you don't own your people, they own you. I let them down once . . . no matter what my reasons. The good news is that our operations, brief as they were, have come to the attention of new clients in Europe . . ." She saw his look of concern. "Don't worry, my poor Mad Denny—your money is safe. Our partnership was dissolved when all this came crashing down."

He shook his head violently. "Damn the money! You'll be caught; you were going into hiding. . . ."

She nodded, "They may catch me. I'll be trying to leave soon, for somewhere else in the world."

His mind raced, rushing to catch up, to find a way to divert what was happening way out in front of him, to change events now totally beyond his control. "You can't just leave me— can't just say what we have between us never happened!"

"No, I could never say that. But I promised, Denny."

"I can't let it end like this! I won't let go! Never!"

She put her fingers to her lips. "Shhhh, my sweet, rash Mad Denny. You'll never see me again, but know this—there will be nights I will ache for you, long, endless, and lonely nights. I too cannot . . . I will never forget you." She reached out through the window, and they embraced, her cheek soft against his, her lips brushing against his own.

He remembered last her eyes, brimming with tears as the driver took her away. He shouted after her, "I love you! I found you once before, and I can do it again! I'll search the whole world from end to end! I'll never stop looking for you! . . . Never!"

But the car did not hesitate as it drew away from him, and he stood locked to the spot by his own twisted emotions as the red taillights grew small and finally disappeared in the gloom of that late and rainy evening.

EPILOGUE

ALMOST A YEAR LATER, IN LATE AUGUST OF 1968, AN
American college student stepped off the train in Zurich. He
was working his way through school on the GI Bill, and so
traveled economy fare on one of those "bum your way across
Europe" college summer courses. It professed five credits
toward his major, which was in history; and after fruitlessly
following it through various dry lectures in England and
Scotland, Belgium and Germany, he was left alone to criss-
cross his harmless way through the rest of Europe.

He notified his bank that he was coming, calling from a
nearby pay phone where he could see the bank down the
street. He waited for hours, and when nothing out of the
ordinary could be detected, went back to his cheap hotel
room and pulled the lightweight summer suit from the bottom of his knapsack. He had the suit pressed by the old lady
at the desk, joking that he wanted to dine at a better restaurant than he had in the last several weeks. He donned a sky-
blue shirt and a tie, and dusted off the lightweight walking
shoes that would have to pass for dress-up.

He walked in through the glass doors of the bank in the
early afternoon, one half hour before closing time. He kept
remembering another bank in Saigon, just over a year before,
and the much younger man he was then, carrying his damp
sack of *My Kim* under his arm to meet Mr. Owl Eyes.

The officials were surprised; they had been alerted he was
a friend of the powerful Larouse family, but had not been

expecting someone so young. His identification was in order, and he wore a light leather glove on the one hand they knew was maimed, so they sat down in conference and gave him his options. They were surprised a second time, and this time pleasantly, for instead of choosing lifetime interest amounting to about one hundred thousand a year in American dollars, he selected a growth fund that would net him a third that for the next twenty years, but would in the long run, to use his own words, "move him up from the ranks of the wealthy to the filthy rich."

"That's all there is to it, then," Denny said, patting the portfolio and looking around the table at the four dark-suited vice presidents.

"Almost, but not quite, monsieur," the man at the other side of the table said. "I have been instructed to give you this." He passed across a light blue envelope. Denny casually slipped it into his pocket, shook hands all around, and made his exit.

He walked the cobblestone streets, looking back every now and then to make sure he wasn't being followed, and took several cabs to places he didn't want to go. The fun was out of it, he realized he wasn't in the game any more . . . he was just stalling, afraid to open that letter. He had seen the handwriting, his name across the front of the blue envelope, and he knew who it came from.

A wind came up, and clouds scudded in front of the sun. It was going to rain. That pleased him, for although the day had turned to chill, the inrushing clouds reminded him of the way it was a year ago, when he was in love. He found himself sitting on an iron bench overlooking a gray lake as the cloudburst came. The rain came in torrents, and he was drenched until his light suit clung to him like a second skin.

It was a brief shower, and when the rain slowed to a slight drizzle he took out the letter. He was shivering and uncertain, and suffered a brief moment of panic when he saw the ink on the outside had washed away. What if the note inside were no longer readable? He ripped it open with trembling fingers.

It would be idyllic to report that the sun came out and a rainbow hung in the sky over the lake and the rest of his days . . . however, in cold hard fact, the clouds bunched again and the cold rain came pelting down harder than ever. But Denny didn't care. He ran laughing and splashing through the streets like the madman everyone always said he was. For the small card inside the envelope had said it all, had capsulized his life's new beginning in three words. It read,

SINGAPORE, SOUL MATE.

ABOUT THE AUTHOR

During Vietnam, JOHN KLAWITTER left a graduate fellowship in English at UCLA and enlisted in the army to discover what all the anger and shouting was really about. He studied the Vietnamese language at the Defense Language Institute and the Monterey Institute of Foreign Studies, and was stationed as an intelligence cryptographer and linguist in Washington, D.C., and then Saigon. In the years since, he has become a successful Hollywood writer, producer, and director, working for Disney Studios, Warner Brothers, NBC, Hanna-Barbera, and many other companies. His writing credits include the screenplay adaptations of the novels *Styx* and *Hobberdy Dick*. *Crazyhead* is his first novel.